Stanley Young is Planning a Murder

in a very precise and intricate manner

———————————

Gavin Milnthorpe is a commercial lawyer who finds time to write in between working, exercising and spending time with his wife and two small children. This is his first novel. Many of Gavin's friends say that Stanley Young is very much like Gavin Milnthorpe, without the suppressed rage and homicidal tendencies of course.

Stanley Young is Planning a Murder

in a very precise and intricate manner

G.A. Milnthorpe

Arena Books

The right of G.A. Milnthorpe to be identified as the editor and copyright owner of this book has been asserted in accordance with the Copyright, Designs and Patents Act 1988.

First published in 2013 by Arena Books

Arena Books
6 Southgate Green
Bury St. Edmunds
IP33 2BL

www.arenabooks.co.uk

Distributed in America by Ingram International, One Ingram Blvd., PO Box 3006, La Vergne, TN 37086-1985, USA.

G.A. Milnthorpe
Stanley Young is Planning a Murder *in a very precise and intricate manner*

British Library cataloguing in Publication Data. A Catalogue record for this book is available from the British Library.

ISBN-13   978-1-909421-23-3

BIC classifications:- FA, FF.

Printed and bound by Lightning Source UK

Cover design
By Jason Anscomb

Typeset in
Times New Roman

CHAPTER 1

"Stanley, try to stay with me as I speak cryptically. I know you're not good at these things. Last night a girl that you know very well was, let's say damaged, in such a way that I was very nearly sick when I saw her. I haven't seen its like in twenty years. This ridiculous place has thrown up any number of suspects but chief among them is you. Do you realise how serious this is?

"Now are you going to tell me what you did yesterday or am I going to have to arrest you?

"Start talking Stanley."

07.26. The alarm went off. My eyes fluttered open only long enough to press the snooze button. The banal words emanating from the sub-standard intelligentsia that dominate local radio were cut off before they could penetrate my brain.

07.35. The alarm rang out again and I sat up, fighting the almost irresistible urge to be overwhelmed once again by sleep. Good Vibrations by the Beach Boys reverberated around the room. The volume was high, deafening, to mask any incriminating words that may have slipped out of my relaxed consciousness; translated from unrestrained dreams. I was out of bed before the neon number melted into 07.36.

It was cold. Here at Pottergate the radiators stand dormant between March and the start of November; November being still over a week away. It is the policy of the building. Some people have complained about it before - when the cold sets in, often in late October, but I can see the sense of it. It saves money. It also protects the environment, not that Newcombe cares about that – it's not in the Revelation to St John.

The cold air attacked my warm skin, only my goose bumps defended me as I stood dozily, in nothing but a pair of clean white boxer shorts. A rare moment of indecision. The fog cleared and I padded quickly across the room to swing open a small pine wardrobe. I think it's pine, I cannot say with any real certainty. I am not an expert in wood. The first shirt on the left was hastily thrown onto my back and done up in an effort to deflect the cold October morning. To deflect. I am quite the Literate. Cream with barely noticeable squares across it. The ridges of the squares gently chafed my nipples, erect due to the cold air. I added the matching light blue tie, purchased as a set by my "mother" last Christmas, before pulling on some thin black socks and black trousers which I took from a chest of drawers. The socks have to be thin: they stop my feet getting too hot and sweaty. It's hard to concentrate in such circumstances.

My "mother" once bought me some thick black socks for use during the winter. They are still in the packet. I am not an outdoor type. Next on was a thin black V-neck jumper, quickly followed by my watch and spectacles.

The room ripped into sharp focus around me as I watched the clock tick over to 07.40.

My room is small. It contains all the necessary: bed, bedside table, chest of drawers, dressing table, wardrobe and a wicker chair. Again, I am not certain the chair is made of wicker but that it the common name for that style of chair. The furniture is well made but unadorned. The walls are smooth and white, entirely clear except for a single mirror which I rarely use. I used to have a poster on one of the walls, but my father ripped it down a few years before and I haven't put it back up. The pieces are under my bed. The blu-tack marks are still visible on the wall. The room was neat and clean, as it still is, despite being searched by the police yesterday. Pigs. The Fuzz. Coppers. The Sweeney. The Filth. Word Association. On the bedside table stands a lamp and a single book entitled "How to Play Golf." Yesterday morning, the book was positioned neatly beneath the lamp, its edges exactly matching those of the bedside table. It isn't like that today. Did they think I wouldn't notice? A small bookmark entitled *What is a Friend?*" marks my current page, or what they think is my current page. I move it along one page every night so as to not arouse suspicion. Anyone who checks will see that I am learning the fine art of pitching out of the rough, using the club with a "P" marked on it.

Abdul gave me the bookmark. Maybe he was being ironic.

My room is en-suite. I did the necessary.

I sat at my tidy dressing table, which I seldom use for dressing, and prepared for the day ahead. Between 07.45 and 08.00 it is my custom to try to gather my thoughts for the coming day. Yesterday was no different. The radio was still blurting out at 07.44, but as the time ticked over to 07.45, the music was instantly cut off and the room was silent. "Everybody Hurts" by R.E.M still rang faintly in my ears. I took a moment to attune my ears to the new found silence, listening out for any suspicious noises or telltale signs of observation from beyond my door. After a moment I was satisfied that there were none and I proceeded with my morning routine.

I pulled my diary towards me and considered what I had to do for the day; the most important part of my day, frankly. Yesterday was Friday, the end of the working week. I don't usually look forward to Friday in the same way that most people do – that Friday feeling I think it's called. I enjoy my job. I enjoyed my job. I don't know if they will ever let me go back to it after what has happened. This Friday was different though, and I don't know why. I found I was looking forward to the weekend. It had been a hard week, full of nervous machinations and anxious planning, as always. I don't know why I was looking forward to the weekend so much. I hadn't planned it that way.

In the orderly diary I saw a solitary word written in my small neat writing, inscribed there over a month ago. The word was "Documentary." The day before it had been "Newspaper", and the day before that it had been "Film." Today it is "Sport," not that I am likely to be able to fit any in due to the presence of the police. The Pigs. The Filth. I try not to let it bother me, I will just have to carry it over using my Special Circumstances Exemption. Thanks goodness I have some reserved from earlier in the year. Daniels thinks the use of Special Circumstances Exemptions is unnecessarily complicated and that the System should be simplified to reduce the amount of stress I often find myself under. I disagree. I have used the System for many years; tried and tested. It serves many functions – social, educational, intellectual, physical. On a basic level it is designed to ensure that I have a varied and active lifestyle. On a "Documentary" day for example, after the rigours of a full day's work I would head to the television room, find a documentary and watch it. Any documentary will do, as long as it lasts an hour or more. Variation. A change is as good as a rest as they say. On a slightly deeper level the system allows me to better myself – to ensure that I do not give in to the weaknesses so common to humanity and rife here at Pottergate – laziness, indiscipline and complacency. I make time for the things that benefit me, and restrict those things that don't. Even Daniels can see the sense in that.

There was nothing else written in the large blank space of my diary. Work and documentaries. The simplicity of my day helps me to focus. Having a designated Documentary day forces me to watch something that perhaps I wouldn't ordinarily. Daniels often asks why I don't just watch a documentary when I feel like it. I never feel like it. I would never watch a documentary out of choice and if I did, I would only watch documentaries about certain subjects – tigers, sharks, disease; anything deadly. Perhaps programmes about Vietnam, so I could better understand what Thomas went through. But maybe not; he doesn't like to speak about it and I respect his wishes. Crime documentaries are always interesting, although I do try to ration those for fear of drawing suspicion to myself. Having a designated Documentary day forces me to consider different things – like technology, science or literature - and my mind will be expanded, my horizons broadened just by being disciplined.

As yesterday was a Friday I knew that getting to watch a documentary would be virtually impossible. Palmer always wants to watch those infernal, intellectually deficient comedy programmes – the

Friday evening televisual staple. I would have to make sure that I blocked the time out before lunchtime, otherwise he would beat me to it. Shaw always helps him.

I enjoy my system. Daniels is always going on about it. So are the others. Newcombe less so. I suppose it defines me, it sets me aside from the others and I am glad for it. I laugh sometimes about how obsessive everyone in this place is with my supposed obsession. Especially as they don't realise that it is only a cover. How stupid they all are. The diary read only "Documentary" but I knew there was something else, something hidden, a dominant purpose to my life that I dare not write down. The Plan.

I found I was becoming anxious, fretful, and I tried to calm my mind. The Plan. Excited, anxious, frustrated – my breath started to come quicker. Daniels always talks about taking deep breaths and focussing on nice things, pleasant places, happy situations - it never works. In the silence of my quiet room, I found myself thinking about *her* and I became even worse, to the point where my heart was beating faster than normal and my breath was shallow and quick, on the verge of angry, frustrated, venomous panic. *I cannot wait.*

Newcombe says I should read the Bible to calm myself down, draw on its wisdom. He claims a sense of peace will infuse my soul if I let it. I try it every morning but it never works. I try it so I can prove Newcombe wrong.

The gospel of Luke, chapter 6, verse 46: *"Why do you call me, 'Lord, Lord,' and do not do what I say?"*

Newcombe tells me to read it over a few times and then meditate on it, like a cow chewing on the cud, regurgitating and considering. He says cows have four stomachs and they process the food through each so it is properly digested. I believe that to be factually incorrect. Nonetheless, he says it is the best technique for studying the Bible, bringing contemplative peace into my mind. *"Why do you call me, 'Lord, Lord,' and do not do what I say?"* I don't know what it means. I do not call Jesus "Lord, Lord." I don't call Jesus anything. He can have no argument with me when I finally meet him. If...

I couldn't make sense of it, but I respected Newcombe's wishes and spent five minutes rolling the words around my mind. Jesus always spoke in riddles. How is anyone supposed to know what he was talking about? I have been trying to make sense of the Bible ever since I arrived at Pottergate. A verse a day, one extra on "Bible" days. I am nearly the whole way through and then I'll go back to the beginning. It never helps, except sometimes to make me angry. Not angry with the Bible or God or those Christian people, but angry with Newcombe. I can imagine him reading it and closing his eyes as he gently repeats the words to himself, perhaps strolling around his garden and enjoying the wonders of creation, searching and finding the impotent peace that is his trademark.

My duties done I sat quietly and waited for 08.00, trying to keep the teasing wanderings of my mind away from *the bitch*. It was difficult though, and without meaning to, my mind kept slipping back to the Plan. *When would it be ready?* That question was often prompted by my impatience. Eventually, I could sit at my desk no longer. I tidied my room in an effort to take my mind off it, despite the fact that I usually clean on a Saturday morning, not a Friday. She does that kind of thing to me.

08.00 finally arrived and I left the room, carefully locking the door.

I live at the very top of this residential apartment block, some three floors up. There is only one other room on my floor and it is empty. That is the main reason I like the third floor, it is so quiet. It is like living in a penthouse but without the exorbitant prices that I understand some people pay in the cities. Abdul used to live in the room opposite. He doesn't anymore. Both rooms are served by the same corridor, the doors facing each other. In the middle, the stairs. The gateway to insanity and irritation. At the top of the stairs there is a window that shows delightful panoramic views of the grounds. Pottergate, to most people, is a rural idyll, divorced from the noise and worry and aggravation of the world. My "mother" said something very similar when she was here last, marvelling as she did at the history of the place. I think it has some ruin of an archway somewhere in the grounds, not that I pay much attention to it. It annoyed me, what she said. My father said it was a beautiful place and that I was very lucky – tranquil he said. He said you couldn't help but feel calm and peaceful when you were here, although I don't think he meant it as he was constantly looking at his watch. Tranquillity? I don't agree. The grounds are well tended and landscaped, but there is nothing tranquil about this place. Not inside its walls anyway. I didn't tell him that.

As it was a Friday yesterday, I took the stairs and was in the dining room before the clock in the hall reached 08.03. There is a small lift which I occasionally use to save my joints – Tuesdays, Thursday and Saturdays. I take cod liver oil on the other days of the week to compensate.

The dining room is small and practical. The tables and chairs are made of metal and are evenly spaced so as to allow those who wish to enjoy breakfast in quiet solitude to do so. They are screwed into the ground like in some cheap, greasy café. Simile. People often find it strange to marry the outside of this place with the inside. The outside is like a postcard, the inside is like a run-down office block. I understand the Trustees picked this place up cheap. I think the previous owners may have had money troubles. Newcombe is too "economical" to refurbish. I think he's creaming money off the top – is that the right expression? Creaming. If he wasn't, perhaps we could eat in a dining room, rather than a canteen.

Breakfast is almost my favourite time of the day. I sit alone usually, unless Barnes comes down and starts prattling. That's the main problem with this place: too many wittering, inconsequential idiots.

As usual, the dining room was empty. It doesn't start to fill up until 08.30 at least - even though work starts at 09.00 and that is clearly not enough time for breakfast to be consumed. I strongly suspect that people are not chewing their food enough. Failure to masticate properly can lead to indigestion and it is not uncommon for people to confuse indigestion for heart attacks and vice versa. Either way, it will be Pottergate that has to foot the bill for the lost man-hours. I did raise this in a letter to the Trustees but I didn't receive a satisfactory response. Abdul never chewed properly and look what happened to him. Some people just do not think. Most of those people who saunter into breakfast at half past eight will be late for work, a source of constant annoyance to me, although it is just as constantly ignored by the powers that be, despite my reports.

I headed towards the serving area, following the heat of the kitchen that quivered even in the relative warmth of the dining room. Canteen.

I recognised the face of the serving lady and groaned despite myself. Yvonne Nash. Fridays. She is always on the counter on Fridays. They change them around here every day so that no-one does the same job twice in one week. Sometimes they prepare, sometimes they clean, sometimes they serve, except for Naylor, who is always on preparation. I could not see Naylor yesterday morning, but I knew she would be in the back somewhere, dicing fruit probably for those who prefer the healthy option. She refuses to man the service area – haughty bitch. It makes sense, this rotation, although it has its irritations. On Fridays, Nash is supposed to serve my food, by order of the rotation. Instead, she talks.

"Good morning Stanley," she chirped as I picked up a chipped, brown tray. Her voice is high, with the common twang of the uneducated. She is a tall woman, with a superior tilt to her head that makes her seem taller. She is approaching retirement age, but is hardly the frail grandmother type. She is a sturdy woman who wears garish make up, some of which runs in the summer months, melted by the unseasonable summer heat and the perennial warmth of the kitchen and its lamps.

"Good morning Mrs Nash."

"What will it be today? Let me guess. Cornflakes to start with. Unopened carton of milk to the side. One slice of toast, buttered right into the corners. A bacon sandwich with no ketchup. A small glass of orange juice and a coffee. Am I right?"

"Yes, you are," I said through gritted teeth. I was lying, but Newcombe said once that sometimes we should "keep our peace" and he referred to Nash especially when he said it. I am not sure what "keep our peace" really means. I think it means lying, although Newcombe says it doesn't. I think Newcombe uses the phrase when he needs to lie, but doesn't want to admit it to himself, in case he upsets God. I know lying is against the rules in the Bible – it's in the Ten Commandments although there it is referred to as "false witness". I don't feel any guilt though – I don't call Jesus "Lord, Lord" and therefore I can lie whenever I like. In fact, I have my bacon sandwich first, before it gets cold, followed by the toast for the same reason and then the cornflakes, but I "kept my peace" and didn't mention it to Nash.

She laughed as she started to prepare my tray and mumbled something about being a "creature of habit." I watched her as she prepared the tray with painstaking slowness, all the time talking and prattling. The unnecessary lack of speed irritated me. The heat of the kitchen irritated me. She irritated me. She irritates me. She asks questions and then doesn't wait for the answer. She tells stories that have no relevance. She tells jokes with no wit, nor intellectual invention and very often, not even a punchline. I just wanted to get out of the kitchen, my patience having already run thin. I closed my eyes and tried to remain calm.

"There you are. Voila."

I opened my eyes to the lady that Palmer calls "Rubber Face." She was beaming at me with a self satisfied smugness, as if she thought that knowing what I have for breakfast is to know me. Her red lipstick was smudged just above the right corner. I wanted to point out that she has just repeated herself, albeit by using two phrases from different languages, but I knew it would amuse her and I didn't want to indulge her. Here you are. Here you are. The fat, stupid, callous, painted bitch. I wanted to scream that at her.

False witness.

"Thank you."

CHAPTER 2

"**A**re you saying she's dead?"

"Answer the question Stanley. What did you do yesterday?"

The little detective stares at me, his sunken eyes concentrated and intense. I answer reluctantly.

"I did many things. A multitude of events and occurrences. It was a normal day. Like all the rest in this place. I got up around the usual time and went for my breakfast. I can't particularly remember it all that well."

I am sitting in an oak panelled room, surrounded by well constructed, deep brown furnishings. The furnishings are a step up in quality from the various items I have in my room. That very fact irritates me. I know I shouldn't be thinking about it now, but it invades my brain. I should be thinking about what has happened. I know that my full attention should be on ensuring that my story is consistent and plausible. Credible evidence is the key. But still, it's just so wrong. Newcombe is always talking about the equality of the workplace, but that is easy to say whilst you are sitting in the most luxurious room in the building. Very Animal Farm. I have always maintained that he is a hypocrite. I hate him. I am not even certain that the room is oak panelled. It could be teak.

Concentrate.

I sit uncomfortably on the edge of a deep leather seat, the metal rivets digging into my bottom as I try to concentrate. I know from the Plan that I should sit back in the chair and try to look relaxed but my body won't let me. I suppose I am coiled like a tightly compressed spring. But I won't explode, I am ready for this, I am ready for anything. My mind works overtime, as they say, despite my tiredness. The events of the night before are starting to blur already. The lack of sleep appears to be catching up on me.

"Well, that seems strange to me Stanley because it was only yesterday and everyone I have spoken to here tells me that you have a wonderful memory. I heard you don't deal in approximations or generalisations."

I refuse to respond. Opinion. Conjecture. Hearsay.

"When was the first time you saw her? Surely you remember that?"

Even the simplest of questions inspires a moment of panic within me. I try to remember my training and to breathe deeply but calmness does not come as easily as I hoped it would. This is more difficult than I imagined it would be.

I found my usual seat and waited for a moment as I cooled down. I could feel a moist heat in my armpits – a sensation which I detest. I congratulated myself however on being civil to the prattling, nonsensical woman. She is enough to get anyone angry. Some people don't listen. You tell them exactly what you want and they try to second guess you. They try to tell you what you want – which is what *they* really want. People always try to convince me that I want jam on my toast. I ask for butter, and only butter, but they won't accept it. Because they like something, they think that you should like it as well. They insist that you do like jam after all. Nash is one of those women. I pity her husband and her children. I could feel the sweat starting to seep into my shirt, brought on by the stress. My feet were starting to get hot.

It was 08.13 before I took my first sip of coffee. It tanged my mouth with that sharp nip of caffeine. I could feel my brain waking up, being cajoled into full speed. It is important to stay alert and coffee helps. It gets me through the day and ensures none of the reprobates – Newcombe says I shouldn't use that word but I am delighted by its lack of precision and its total accuracy – here at Pottergate manage to "get one over on me." I was tempted to gulp it down and ask Nash to fill me up again, but I don't usually do that. Besides, I was still hot and Nash had been a bitch. I didn't want to see her again. The thought of throwing scalding hot liquid into her face flashed into my mind and cheered me momentarily.

The dining room was deserted. That is the main reason I go down there so early. I enjoy my breakfast in peace. Only the clanging of the kitchen behind the serving area disturbed the tranquillity of the room.

I found myself watching the door as I started to break my fast.

08.15, *she* would arrive soon. She always comes down to breakfast between 08.06 and 08.27, if she comes at all. 08.18 is average. Sometimes she doesn't come, claiming she is sick. Not that she's been sick for the last ninety-three working days. In fact she has been entirely punctual and reliable for the last ninety-three working days. I believe she had menstrual difficulties before that. A difficult one to disprove.

I found I was grinding my teeth at the very thought of her. I could already feel the beginnings of the jaw ache that has become so familiar to me. I tried to eat my bacon sandwich, to work my jaw and take away the pressure, but I did not remove my eyes from the door.

I know I should try to amuse myself over breakfast, to make sure that I don't think about her. I should bring a book, or read the newspaper, or anything, but it's not that easy. I know I could fill the time, but I don't want to. I have to watch her eat breakfast. It's the only way I can make it through the day. I am like a modern day Edward Jenner. Watching her eat breakfast is like a small dose of the pox in order to ward off the more deadly stuff. That irresponsible bitch is like poison.

"Good morning, how are you? You look well. Do you mind if I sit here? I shan't stay long. I've got lots to do but it's always nice to have some company isn't it? I find it is anyway, especially first thing in the morning. I always used to say that to Sandra. It's nice to have company. We all know that. I suppose you're not too keen on company really. You don't say you are, but I'm sure you are deep down. What have you got today? No jam, you can't survive without jam. It's what all the top hotels have you know, jam, in little pots. Little glass pots, not the little plastic ones. They're fine for smaller hotels but not if you're going to spend £195 a night on a room. You expect something better than plastic in those circumstances. Do you want some of mine?"

Daryl Barnes. I didn't even see him come in. I turned my eyes outward and took him in. He is a small man, completely grey in hair and face and somewhere around sixty years of age. His face is relatively wrinkle free considering his age, but his full cheeks have the limp droop of sadness and time. His face flaps as he talks. And he talks a lot – at speed. Although at that moment he was thrusting a small plastic carton of strawberry jam at me, waiting for some sort of response, soft wet eyes waiting patiently.

"No thank you Barnes."

"Oh yes, I forgot. You don't have jam unless you're on the Continent. It's good for you, you know. A little bit here and a little bit there. I'm not sure if it's got vitamins in it but it's still good for you. It makes for variety doesn't it. And life does need variety. Variety is the spice of life, as my…"

I watched as his large, expressive, desperate eyes glazed over for a moment as he looked within himself. I saw a hint of wetness and prepared myself for the inevitable, but, for a wonder, he managed to pull himself together and carried on talking.

"…yes, variety, it's good for you. It makes life exciting doesn't it? Routines are just shackles aren't they? When I worked at the Oak I didn't have a routine, I was everywhere. I know I had duties but that's not what I mean. And I know I had normal working hours but no two days were the same. I was here, there and everywhere – fetching, carrying, greeting. Meeting people, there's no routine in that. I met a Sultan once. He gave me a fifty pound tip. Now, that's variety. Fifty pounds. Not like here, there's no variety here. I suppose they try but it doesn't really work. Trying isn't doing as my Sandra…"

He crumbled and I watched him cry into his toast, the wetness in his eyes becoming a flood - mingling with his beloved jam. A pathetic figure, I wanted to throttle him. At least one morning a week I have to put up with his whining, snivelling, self-pitying, desperate tears. At least they don't last too long, not these days. That is the way with Barnes, one minute he is fine and is telling you at length about how Princess Diana smiled at him or the Earl of Marlborough let him drive his Mercedes and then the next minute he is sobbing into his food, lamenting the loss of Sandra. I try not to get angry with him. He is so weak.

I remember when he started work here. He arrived on a Sunday and then didn't come out of his room until the following Friday. Daniels said it was the shock. The others had met him as he moved his things in and had said he was pleasant and talkative. I was not able to meet him on the Sunday, owing to prior arrangements, but I had gone to see him first thing Monday morning, immediately after breakfast. I had gone down to his floor to welcome him - part of my duties - and could hear him screeching through the walls. I stood and listened for quite some time, trying to decide whether to knock or to leave him in peace. I had made the effort to come down and see him and I had made the decision to speak to him – what concern was his mood to me? My knuckles even rested on the cheap wood of the door. But I could imagine the combined words of Newcombe and Daniels: inconsiderate, inflexible, insensitive. I would leave him be. I surprise myself sometimes with my tact and decorum. I tried again on the Tuesday and could hear a keening whimper, like that of a dog pining for its master. Again I waited, but decided it was perhaps too soon. On the Wednesday morning, I could barely hear anything, just the occasional sob, as I pressed my ear up against his door. I still thought it best not to knock – I didn't want to disturb his loneliness. I considered my duty to welcome him discharged and did not return to his door. When he did finally come out and I met him in the corridor, he was ashen faced and raw-eyed, and he said:

"My wife left me, you know."

I was taken aback; shocked by the sheer openness of the man. I had only just met him. Pleasantries hadn't even been exchanged. I had only just retrieved my hand from the entirely proper handshake that comes on first meetings. His hand was clammy and it clasped onto my hand for longer than I thought necessary. Later, when I smelt my hand, I deduced that he had been masturbating. Between the tears. I recognised the smell from when I had been in love. I am not the only one in Pottergate who now washes his hands after an encounter with Daryl Barnes.

"Welcome to Pottergate. I'm looking forward to working with you."

"Thank you, thank you. I'm glad to be here really, it just gets too much eventually. I had to get away you see. She got the house and the car. I couldn't get to work. I just gave them to her. My sister told me to see a solicitor but I wasn't interested in all that. I've met many a solicitor in my time and I don't care for them. And besides, it wouldn't be right

17

after all this time. It's all for the best you know. A clean break, you know. I thought she might come back if I gave her everything."

The whole thing was entirely peculiar – I soldiered on.

"I'm sure you'll be a very valuable member of our team. What job will you be doing exactly? I wasn't involved in the selection panel so I'm not entirely sure, although you will come within my area of responsibility."

"Oh, your responsibility? I'll be working in…erm…hospitality, yes, I think the hospitality section. Or is it housekeeping? My sister thinks that will be good for me, to have a bit of familiarity. I used to work in a hotel you see. I was a night porter. I loved it. I met all sorts of famous people. Have you heard of the Earl of Marlborough? I worked in a very nice hotel. The Oak Priory. Have you heard of it?"

"No. Good, I'm sure your experience will come in handy. Having spoken to Mr Newcombe, I'm assured you will take your job seriously. There are some here who do not. It is my job to keep them in line as best I can. I thought it prudent to have a quick word with you before you commenced your duties. A second interview in a way. Newcombe will be interested in what I have to say. Presumably you will take the last week as holiday? Unless you were sick of course but I am not aware of a general practitioner having visited the premises. Some people here at Pottergate have to be coerced into doing their jobs and it is very time consuming. I assume I will not have to hold your hand, as it were?"

"Oh no, I'm very experienced. I was very good at my job. I enjoyed it. My wife was sleeping with another man while I was at work. She got lonely you know. All those nights. I didn't realise that I was neglecting her. I was always very busy at the hotel, there was so much to do and the management relied upon me for everything. I was virtually the night manager. I thought she was happy. But I drove her into the arms of another man. I was making a lot of money, I could have bought her anything she wanted. I would have taken her back but she didn't really give me the chance. I gave her everything. I would have…"

That was three years ago and he still hadn't shut up about it. Our conversations followed at eternally unchanging cycle. But yesterday morning, he must have noticed my chagrin because he stopped crying, wiping the tears from his soft, malleable face with the cuff of his jumper.

"It's Christmas soon, do you think I'll get a card? Or even a present? I don't think I'll visit her. I'm sure she's quite happy with her new man, and they wouldn't want me intruding. I'll just post my present to her. Mr Newcombe says I can use his internet and order something for her online. It will get sent to her direct then. To their home. I know the address. Well, it's my old house. Do you think they would want me there? No, I shouldn't think so. Perhaps I'll just stay here. It would be nice to get a card though. Just to show that some people are thinking about me. I'll get one off my sister I imagine. Are you going away for Christmas?"

"No."

"Well, perhaps we could have Christmas dinner together? It would be nice to have company wouldn't it? Everyone likes a bit of company. I'm sure there will be others who'll stay as well. Like last year. They will probably keep us working up to Christmas Eve like last year as well, not that it was really work, but they made it seem like it. Team building they call it. We used to do the same kind of things at the Oak, not that I was ever invited because I was on nights and most of the things happened during the day. I quite enjoyed it last year actually, it was nice to have company. I do miss Sandra sometimes. Shall we have Christmas dinner together?"

I decided to say nothing. Barnes took it for a yes.

"Yes, we'll have turkey…"

I switched off, confident that Barnes would neither notice, nor really care. And besides, she had just entered. 08.24.

Deborah Phillips. Flat 3.

She was hard to miss as she flounced in. I watched her out of the corner of my eye, straining to keep my head still, desperate not to turn towards her. The door banged against the wall as she entered. I have pointed out to Newcombe that this causes significant damage to the wall behind the door, and also to the hinges of the door itself, but nothing is done. Barnes turned to watch her as she entered and he even stopped talking; she pretended not to notice. I could tell that she was enjoying it though. I could see the small smile creasing her lips as she glided towards the food counter. I tried to keep my head tilted away from her, following her with just my eyes.

I found I was biting my nail as I studied her. Her hair was tied back, but I could still see the distinctive dark brown waves within it. It revealed soft, pale skin as far back as her small ears. Her features are – or perhaps were - rounded, except her eyes which were sharp and alluring. Her face prompts the faint reminiscence of a pig, at least to me. There is a small cleft to her chin and her eyes are a pale blue. Her substantial neck dives down into a full bosom that was flaunted to all who would care to see. At least it was only Nash on the food counter. The remainder of her clothing was similar, designed to have the maximum effect on the viewer. In every way, she was and is beautiful. I hate her.

I pulled my eyes away, allowing myself to retrieve my nail from my mouth. I had not bitten too deeply and the mark in the nail faded away quickly.

"My Sandra looked like that when she was younger. Amazing, amazing she was. I love her you know…"

Barnes had his back to me as he stared at Phillips, the turkey and the Christmas arrangements quickly forgotten. His voice had taken on that dream like quality of someone who is really only speaking to themselves.

I got up to leave. He didn't notice.

CHAPTER 3

"**I** saw her at breakfast, probably at around quarter past eight. I can't remember the exact time I was sitting with Barnes."

I try to make the words casual. Nonchalant. I know the little detective is watching me keenly.

"And nothing happened at breakfast?"

"What could have happened at breakfast? Breakfast is breakfast. Cereal. Bacon sandwiches. Orange juice. Coffee. I don't know what you're getting at. I had my breakfast and went to work."

I hear Newcombe "tut" behind me as I raise my voice to the little detective. I "tut" at myself internally for losing my cool. Unless I calm down, this gumshoe will break me. I deliberately move myself back into the deep leather chair, trying to appear cool and calm, just like Thomas. Keep smiling.

"So you went off to work? What happened then?"

By 08.27 I was at work.

I am very fortunate in that I work in the same place that I live. It's a residential job – they come together. Pottergate is deep in the Suffolk countryside. Travel to and fro is not easy if you cannot drive. The nearest village has one bus per day to the nearest town. Newcombe travels for nearly an hour to get to work in the morning. I believe it takes longer on the way home, due to the traffic when he leaves the country roads. He does tend to arrive late and leave early though, so I have no sympathy for him. If he chooses to waste his life sitting in a car listening to mock-intellectual discussion on Radio 4 then so be it. Perhaps he is unhappy at home.

I only have to walk down the corridor from the canteen and I am at work. It takes less than a minute. Indeed, this whole building is my workplace, such is the ambit of my responsibility. Living here is an absolute necessity for me, although I do pay for the privilege. The costs of living are deducted from our wages. Barnes says we are paying as much for the location as the accommodation itself: he speaks on the subject like some sort of authority. Pottergate is a centuries old, rambling archaic building with sprawling grounds and excellent facilities - apparently. Those words must appear in a brochure of some sort. It is surrounded by countryside and the sounds of nature. Before the Trustees owned it, it was a popular hideaway for rich ill people. The seclusion and the tranquillity appealed to them. I'm not sure if it appeals to me, I enjoyed the city. Urban life invigorated me. I am sure I could get a room in the local village for a fraction of the price I pay for this one, but that would remove me from my job here. The others could take advantage of me if I wasn't here to keep an eye on them.

We don't get paid much, after deductions, although I am sure I'm the highest earner of the residential staff. I would very much like to get a look at the personnel files to see for certain. After the Plan is complete, I may well take another job that pays more. The money will do for now. My father is always on hand to help with any additional expenses. We get paid "peanuts" according to Palmer. He used to beat panels in a small garage and got paid more. Enough to buy a whore a week, he says.

I was early. I'm usually fairly early but yesterday I had extra time. I don't really like to arrive at work until 8.40. That is early enough to make sure that I am the first one there but, due to the lazy buffoons that Newcombe chooses to keep here, it means I don't have to wait too long for the first to arrive and for my report to begin. I do not like wasting time. If that silly bitch hadn't been annoying me and Barnes hadn't talked incessantly I might have been able to enjoy my breakfast for a few more minutes instead of sitting in an empty corridor staring at a wall. At least it was quiet. That silly bitch of a woman had whipped me up into a frenzy. I bubbled with rage. The scene kept running through my mind – the way she entered and banged the door, the way she was dressed, the smug smile that crept onto her lips as Barnes looked at her, satisfying her self-conceit and vanity. I was struggling to force down my anger so I thought about the Plan, running it through in my mind. The thought of it made me calmer.

The meeting room was locked so I found a chair and sat down to wait. There was no point going back to my room, I never do that.

I took out a pad of paper and some pens from the drawer in the desk outside the meeting room. I learnt that lesson early on – always keep spare stationery in various locations around Pottergate. I started a new page by marking the date and settled down to wait.

Newcombe arrived at 09.03. He was whistling. I could hear him before I saw him.

"You're late. By three minutes."

"Ah, good morning Stanley, and how are you this fine morning?" His Welsh lilt was filled with happiness and optimism - as it always is. He's a Christian. He must be, because he tells me he reads the Bible.

"None of the other staff are here yet. I have made a note."

"Well, never mind about that. You know we run a relaxed ship here Stanley. And it is a Friday. Everywhere is slightly more relaxed on a Friday. Some places have a dress down day on a Friday you know. Perhaps we'll look into that. It might boost morale. Make a note of that Stanley, we'll consider the policy. As to the lateness, you just make sure you put those details in your log book and we'll review them as normal at the end of the day."

"Dress down day? Some of the people here are constantly dressed down."

Newcombe looked at me, eyebrows raised, and waited. I relented, in order to keep the peace.

"I will make a note of it Mr Newcombe - for all the good that it does. We review my report every evening and yet we never take any action. The absence figures for the last month are astounding. For example."

"Now Stanley…" Newcombe turned towards me. He is a big, broad man with a usually happy face. I believe he is almost of pensionable age but he is robust and lively and this somehow makes him seem younger. However, there was no trace of joviality in his fiery eyes at that moment yesterday. "…we do take the appropriate action. And you know it. Our action isn't always as harsh as you would like, but it is *always* appropriate."

He has that way of staring, eyebrows raised, chest out, full of bravado and power. I think he may have been an angry young man. He hints as much occasionally, when we're having our Sharing Sessions, and his stare suggests it. It generally leaves little room for discussion, but yesterday Phillips had fired me up.

"I just worry that they are taking you for a ride. Taking us for a ride. Some people aren't pulling their weight, Mr Newcombe. That means they are not doing their jobs properly because they think they can escape censure. They do not believe that you will do anything about it. They are slacking. And it's my job to worry about it."

Newcombe placed his giant hand on my shoulder, the weight of it threatening to push my slim frame down. He stared into my eyes, as he always does. I looked away.

"Very true, and what a wonderful job you do. But you can't worry about everything. You have to let me do my bit too. Delegation is the fancy term for it. Now, I think I hear Wendy arriving as we speak so there's one for your report. Try to insert some of those phrases you just used. Your vocabulary is absolutely astounding and is getting bigger every day by the sounds of it. Use it Stanley, use it."

I scowled at his back as he turned to greet Wendy, but I did mark the time in my book. He always speaks like that; grand statements said in extreme earnest. *Use it Stanley, use it!* I wanted to slap him and tell him that I have memorised those phrases, learnt the context. It's so easy to fool people. Newcombe thought he was helping me and he wasn't. One day I would tell him and crush him.

Wendy Daniels was like a whirlwind as she entered. Her voice is high and chirpy, and soars upward from the relatively low starting point that is her head, perched as it is on a diminutive frame, smaller than mine. Her features are small too: eyes, nose and mouth. Despite being small, her mouth is capable of emitting the greatest and shrillest of noises. She is the noisiest woman in Pottergate by a long way. Palmer fancies her. He often says he would like to throw her around his room like a rag doll, show her a good time. She is that small, even I could throw her around like a rag doll, but I wouldn't have the same intent as Palmer. I often think that Newcombe could kill her if he hugged her as hard as he could. He could squeeze the life out of her. Unfortunately, I could not and he does not.

"Good morning Nicholas," she screeched as she entered, "and good morning to you Stanley, first to arrive again."

I didn't say anything. Daniels is one of the most senior members of this establishment and I have to show proper respect. I suppose I am becoming good at "keeping my peace." It is difficult though, especially considering her superiority. She should be setting a good example, not turning up late. I underlined her name in red. I resolved to give her a special mention when I made my daily report to Newcombe.

As I finished underscoring her name with an abrasive red line, the others started to arrive, so I followed Newcombe into the meeting room that he had just opened. I retreated to a corner of the room to make my notes on the rag tag, ill-disciplined bunch as they entered and assumed their positions. I found that I had a lot of things to note down. Not one person had turned up on time and three people had arrived without due regard to the H.P.A.D. - the House Policy on Appropriate Dress – which I wrote. I tried to catch Newcombe's eye to alert him to the fact but he ignored me. Typical Newcombe, always ducking the hard issues. This place would be different if I was in charge. Not that that will ever happen, they keep holding me back. The Trustees don't like me. Newcombe called for quiet. At least everyone settled down quickly. Sometimes they can take an age, especially Palmer – the idiot. He would be the first out of the door if I were in charge – thrown out like an old rag doll.

Everyone was sitting in a semi circle, staring at the great master as he prepared to speak – his arms out in the air, like some ironic, incompetent crucifix before the amphitheatre. Newcombe arranges the chairs in this way so that everyone is looking at him, so he can look everyone in the eye, so that he can be the centre of attention. The room went quiet. I refuse to become part of these despicable, pretentious "team meetings" and I so remained in the corner, noisily shuffling my paper when I sensed that Newcombe was about to make a dramatic and important point. Newcombe did try to bring me inside the semi-circle once but I refused – it is not really fitting of my status. I cannot enforce policy if I am too close to my colleagues. That was the reason I gave him; it sounded valid enough. Besides, I told him, these team meetings are an American influence and I cannot abide them. I think he agreed.

Newcombe began his morning routine:

"Well good morning everyone. It is lovely to see you all, bright eyed and bushy tailed, as they say. It really is. Now I don't know about you but I am in a wonderful mood today. I don't know why, I just woke up this morning in a particularly good mood. The joy of nature was shouting at me this morning and I loved it. I said to my wife, 'This is going to be a great day. I know it.' And now I see you and I am convinced that it is the case."

Newcombe is one of the few members of staff who live off-site. Maybe that is why he is in such a good mood – he doesn't have to see the poor state of this place twenty four hours a day, seven days a week. I do. It does not make for great moods. I have to live in the context of his incompetence.

"Now Daryl, I was very impressed with the work you did yesterday. The standard of the accommodation since you arrived has been exceptional. I know I have said that before, but it is true again. Maureen, our cleaner, said that very same thing to me yesterday. She said you were working wonderfully as a team since the new arrangement started and she wanted to thank you for all your good work. I understand you're on some of the residential rooms today. I'm looking for a similar effort again today. Can I count on you?"

Barnes wriggled in his seat, as pliable and gullible as a new born puppy, desperate for attention, lapping it up. I marvelled at him, being able to take a compliment from that woman with such enthusiasm after the complaint she had made against him. The Trustees had to get involved.

"Yes of course, of course you can. I was just saying to Stanley in the dining room that I am enjoying my work here, especially since the new rota came in. Very much so. Not that we get enough variety, but we do seem to enjoy ourselves. Well I do anyway. You can count on me Mr Newcombe."

"Note that down will you Stanley, we need to consider how we are going to insert more variety into the day. A change is as good as a rest as they say. I hear what you are saying Daryl and whilst we are somewhat constrained by the nature of the work we do here, we must try to maintain our focus on variety. It keeps us fresh and enthusiastic. In fact, I was just discussing with Stanley the possibility of introducing a dress down day – that would add variety. A very good point Daryl, very good. We will have to consider appointing someone to look into that. Make sure you remind me of that Stanley."

I glared at him as I wrote down his command. Who does he think he is?

"And Zoe, you were doing some wonderful work yesterday in putting together the nutritional manual and food schedule for next year. Now, there is variety! You'll be working on that again no doubt…"

The talk went on: a word of encouragement for everyone, an exaltation to higher and better work. I listened and watched attentively, making any notes that Newcombe decreed, fighting the boredom and anger that threatens to engulf me at these daily meetings. If Newcombe wants variety, he should try changing the record. We hear his voice every morning, saying the same things, the same pleasantries, the same inane plaudits.

"And you, Deborah, have been doing wonderful work on our new décor. It is already looking wonderful but no doubt you will be working wonders yet again. I will be getting quotes for the latest phase very soon and we can then have a meeting to discuss how we are going to present the changes to the trustees."

The ends of my fingers started to go white as Newcombe used *her* name. I squeezed my pen tightly, the ridges digging deep into my skin. Newcombe smiled at her, like some lecherous drunken uncle indulging his perversions. I could see her preening like some peacock at the front of the room. All eyes were on her, even mine, to my great irritation and shame. She smiled demurely at Newcombe and exposed her bosom even further as she basked in his public praise. Flirtatious whore. My eyes bored into the back of her head as anger raged within me. I wanted her to turn round, to see me…to realise, but she didn't. Her eyes were locked onto Newcombe's. My look would have been as good as a confession, but it might have been worth it. I wanted to do it there and then; forget the planning, just rise up and do it. I could have used my pen. I was angry enough. I made a further note about her standard of dress just to pull my eyes away from her. It wasn't enough.

After he had finished undressing Phillips with his eyes Newcombe continued his speech, going round the room, speaking to everyone in turn. He didn't mention me, although he did send an appreciative glance my way. I didn't return the look.

By 09.42 the meeting was finished and the room gradually emptied, everyone setting about their daily tasks. I had 18 minutes before I was due to check on the first employee and therefore I had to sit and wait. I had nowhere else to go. I used to start my inspection at 09.30 but my routine was constantly interrupted by the ridiculously long and useless team meetings. I complained to Newcombe about it. I told him he was interrupting my schedule. He didn't take my complaint seriously. He didn't realise he was impacting on my job. I have to admit that I got particularly angry with him.

I tried not to look at Phillips as she waltzed out of the room, although my peripheral vision registered that she still had the attention of the room. I wanted to stab her in the eye with my pen, and then puncture Newcombe's lung with the same implement – there would be some romantic irony in that somehow. The tips of my fingers were starting to hurt and I thought I heard a small crack of plastic through the bubbling hot blood racing through my ears. Slowly and deliberately, a case of mind over matter, I made a start on my report to distract my attention from her and Newcombe and the Plan and visions of their intertwined bodies – an old rutting pig defiling that preening peacock.

I made a decision – today would have to be the day.

CHAPTER 4

"I was early, so I waited for Mr Newcombe to arrive. He was late as usual. Needless to say, I pointed this out. Mr Newcombe is a very unreliable character, in many ways unpredictable, so I doubt he even noticed."

I wait for this character fault to be assimilated by the little detective and proceed. It calms me as I finally start to rely on my training – misdirection and accusation.

"The others arrived eventually and then we had the usual, boring, unnecessary, inconsequential meeting presided over by Mr Newcombe. The meeting went on, as you would expect; Mr Newcombe likes the sound of his own voice. I then started my inspections."

The little detective is an extremely slight man. Even I tower above him, Newcombe makes him look like a child. His head is shaven in what strikes me as a most unprofessional manner. He has beady little eyes that do seem alert though. His face is pleasant when he smiles, but turns almost thuggish at other times. His clothes are slightly too big for him, with plenty of space between his scrawny neck and his shirt collar.

"These reports, do you do them every day?"

"I do."

"Why?"

"Because I am the House Compliance Officer here at Pottergate House. The H.C.O. I assess the others here to make sure they are meeting House Policy and keeping House Rules. My wider ambit is to ensure that Pottergate is fully compliant with national laws and regulations. For example, I have recently been researching the Data Protection Act and plan to make recommendations to Mr Newcombe in the next few days about how we store and disseminate information. Today's events may delay that somewhat."

Better.

"House Compliance Officer? Oh yes, Mr Newcombe did tell me about that. It sounds interesting."

I have no comment to make so I remain silent.

"Daryl Barnes. Morning meeting

Barnes displayed a good level of attention during the morning meeting. I was unaware of any daydreaming and Barnes is to be commended on his ability to retain his concentration throughout the protracted meeting, evidenced by his ability to field the inane questions put forward at various intervals by Mr Newcombe. It is well known that Barnes sometimes fails to keep his mind firmly fixed on the task in hand, but this new level of effort is to be congratulated. My preliminary view is that Barnes is steadily improving and gradually becoming a valuable asset to the team here at Pottergate.

His standard of dress is acceptable, although I did notice a small smudge of what appeared to be chocolate just inside his left elbow. (Although with Barnes, the smudge could have been anything.) I would recommend that this minor offence be overlooked in view of Barnes' good behaviour so far for the day.

I remain concerned by Barnes' ability to socially interact with other members of the group. It did not escape my notice that Barnes received peculiar looks from other members of the staff throughout the morning meeting, particularly when he mentioned the Earl of Marlborough for the third time. Despite Barnes' hands being in plain sight at all times, I do feel that some members of staff remain uncomfortable in the presence of Barnes, even in a group setting. I would suggest that Barnes be advised as to his future conduct with other employees and exhorted to make greater efforts at genial and acceptable communication.

Barnes was my first visit of the day. He was in Room 3 when I found him. I stood on the threshold of the room and watched him for a moment. He was bumbling. No other term quite fits Barnes so well as bumbling.

The room was in a state. I had been horrified the first time I saw him standing in a wreck of a room. I had berated him for his lack of care. I told him in no uncertain terms that Pottergate would not tolerate vandalism. I remember jabbing my finger into his puny, flabby chest, each thrust eliciting a yelp of desperate defence. I think I scared him. The ransacked apartment looked entirely at odds with the principles of good hospitality management but he assured me, in a pitiful whining voice, that there was a method to his madness. Daniels asked me to give him the benefit of the doubt. I did, reluctantly. Eventually, I did begin to see the system. He stripped the entire room back and then began again.

"It's the secret you see. My first boss told me that and he was right. He ran a famous hotel, the Oak, you know, worked his way up the ranks, right from the bottom. He was a porter to begin with, just like me. I could have been like him. He didn't have any qualifications either. Just hard work. The secret of hospitality management is detail; that was his motto. You have to look at every single detail to make sure it's all right. And you can't do that whilst the room is tidy, because you focus on what is looking good rather than what can be improved. So you have to rip the room apart and then piece it together. I do it all the time now, even at home. I mean, I used to do it at home. He earns nearly one hundred thousand pounds a year for running that place. He credits it all to the system. Sometimes I wish I'd never heard about the system. It hasn't really helped me. I think he would have had me back after all that fuss with Sandra had died down. I wouldn't have minded knowing about it really."

I suppose it made sense. It certainly made sense to Barnes, he swore by it; even though part of him hated it at the same time. He was half convinced that the system had ruined his marriage. If he hadn't had stripped his own marital bedroom back... He couldn't quite process that it might be his slut of a wife or his own inadequacies as a husband and man that brought an end to his conjugal bliss. It might even be the fault of the heating engineer who was having sex with his wife. But Barnes didn't think like that. I suppose it's easier to blame the system. As such, at 10 o clock, the time of my first inspection, I knew the room would be in a state of flux.

He didn't notice me for nearly three minutes, so engrossed was he in his work. He was pulling the sheets off the bed, he was clearing out the draws. He was almost violent in his determination to strip the room back to its bare bones. Something Daniels had said to me before suddenly flooded into my mind. She thought that perhaps Barnes used the system as a way of punishing himself, by constantly reminding himself of his failure to retain his wife. Daniels thought that he was probably thinking of other things when he was stripping the bed. I wasn't so sure. I thought Barnes just liked to use the system because it was a good system and it worked. Daniels said that things weren't always the way they appear. I said that Daniels had made a career out of making straightforward things appear complicated. However, seeing Barnes attack the room with almost a manic type quality, I think I started to understand what Daniels meant. Maybe.

Barnes was really tearing into his task. That would receive good comment. Newcombe would be pleased with that – to see that his place was "ship shape." Despite his obvious personality defects and occasional sexual deviancy, Barnes at least puts in some work around here, not like the majority of the slackers. In fact, once given a task, Barnes is particularly good at seeing it through. A thought occurred to me...

Careful.

"Barnes!" The words were out of my mouth before I had time to think. That was my first mistake of the day – one of many. I cursed myself inwardly at my lack of care. But I just couldn't stop.

He swung his concentrated little eyes towards me. His face was clammy and red, an angry scowl etched onto his face for the instant in which he turned round. He was shocked for a moment, before pleased recognition spread across his face.

STANLEY YOUNG IS PLANNING A MURDER

"Oh, it's you Stanley, I'm sorry, you scared me, I was just getting into my work you see and your voice was so sharp and it made me jump. I was thinking of other things. That's what happens when you haven't got any company, you start to think about things don't you. I wasn't expecting you. I wasn't ready for you. You always seem to surprise me, even though you come at the same time every morning. I always used to be able to forget about things when I was working and, well, I'm sure you know that anyway…"

I ignored virtually everything he said as thoughts spun through my mind. I had always planned to incriminate Barnes, but perhaps he could incriminate himself too.

I moved into the room almost nonchalantly; as nonchalantly as I could when my heart was beating quickly, pumping murderous blood through my veins, sweeping me along in excitement. How to approach this? Blood was pumping in my ears too, making it difficult to think. How had the thought come to me? I don't know. Maybe it was pure cold logic. Every crime needs a scapegoat. A patsy. Someone would have to take the blame for what was going to happen that night. It might as well be Barnes.

"Did you ever feel like killing him?"

I moved slightly closer to Daryl and lowered my voice to the conspiratorial level. One quick glance over my shoulder. We were alone.

"Who?"

"Him. The guy who took your wife. The one she ran away with. The one who's living in your house right now. The heating engineer. Did you ever think about killing him?"

"Stanley, what are you talking about…?"

"Didn't you ever think about it? Didn't you want to get your hands around his throat and squeeze? When you thought of all the things he had been doing to your wife, all the things she had been doing to him, didn't you want to get a knife or a gun or use your own fists and show him that you were the real man?"

"Stanley I don't want to talk about this. It upsets me."

"Think about it Barnes, it's important."

He did as he was told, as he always does. His eyes took on the glazed expression of people who are looking deep within themselves – I didn't need Daniels to tell me that. His sallow cheeks dropped even further, the colour draining out of them. He was silent, but I dared not disturb him. The only sound in the room was that of this meditative slow breathing and my careless, shallow breaths. I could see him delving into his most closely guarded emotions, thinking the unthinkable – a problem that I have never had. I wanted to hurry him along, to bring satisfaction to my own tortured emotions but I had to be careful. Patience.

"£59.95," he breathed at last. It wasn't what I had expected.

"What?"

"£59.95 for a double room. Breakfast included. Two cocktails at £4.95 each and a bottle of champagne at £19.95. £89.80"

"What are you talking about?"

"Paid by card, authorised by signature. S Barnes. Not Mrs."

"Is that how you found out Barnes?"

"£59.95 for a double room. Breakfast included..."

"Barnes...?"

He was staring off into the distance, barely conscious that I was there.

"Daryl..."

I started to panic. Waving my hand in front of my eyes did no good. I coughed loudly. I shook his shoulder. He was repeating his mantra, "...two cocktails at £4.95..." and staring into his desperate, shredded soul. *What a fool I am!* The blood in my ears was pumping furiously now. I had been too hasty, I had ruined it. He wouldn't complete his work and Newcombe would start to ask questions. Barnes would reveal the details of our conversation without a moment's thought – such was his verbal diarrhoea and his desire to please.

I tried to keep calm. Panic. Panic is the enemy. I could feel my feet starting to heat up.

Deal with one issue at a time.

I slipped off my shoes and sat down on the edge of a desecrated bed. The air of the room circulated around my feet, dissipating the heat before it could form into sweat. My mind cooled at the same time. I needed to think clearly. The Plan wasn't ready but I had decided to go ahead anyway. This had not been part of the Plan but now that it had happened I needed to make use of it.

Misdirection is the key.

This could be a motive. Barnes, in a rage as he contemplated being cuckolded by his fat, fleshy wife, decided to wreak vengeance on womankind. Deborah, the embodiment of all that is bad in a woman, was the natural target.

Clever Stanley, clever. Thomas would be proud.

Barnes was still standing in the middle of the room, surrounded by housekeeping detritus. Someone would find him soon. Suspicion would naturally fall upon him when the deed was done.

I put my shoes back on and slid out of the room, closing the door quietly behind me as Barnes continued to chant his lonely mantra.

CHAPTER 5

"You visited Daryl Barnes first didn't you?" the little detective continues in his gentle Scottish accent. I am not a racist, despite what may have happened with Abdul, but I do wonder why he isn't detecting in his own country. I know from my research that Scottish law and English law are vastly different. Is he even qualified?

"Yes."

"What did you talk about?"

"We didn't talk about anything. Perhaps I bade him morning salutations." I pause to allow the little detective time to wrestle with my complex vocabulary – a small hint to show him just the type of person he is dealing with. "I assessed him and made notes for my report."

"Ah, the report. I have a copy of your report here. It's quite detailed. I'm very impressed. You obviously take your role here very seriously. You wrote that Daryl, or Barnes as you habitually call him, was fine when you left him and was working as normal."

I decide not to take issue with Newcombe for letting the little detective have sight of my confidential report. However I see that my report on data protection cannot come too soon.

"He was."

"And what time did you leave him?"

"You have the report, why don't you tell me?"

The little detective smiles at my insolence.

"OK Stanley, it says you left him at 10.28."

"That's right."

"And he was fine when you left him?"

"That is the same question as before and my answer remains the same."

"Are you sure Stanley? Wendy Daniels says something quite different. As does Daryl for that matter."

Daniels. The bitch. How many bitches can this place sustain?

"I'm sorry I don't understand."

"Wendy Daniels said that Daryl was in quite a state when she found him yesterday, round about a quarter to eleven. He was quite disturbed actually. It was a very strange scene all round. Let me know what you think of this. He was standing dead still, in a room that looked like it had been trashed, repeating a series of numbers to himself."

The little detective lets the scenario hang in the air, waiting for some reaction from me. I don't give it.

"£59.95. £4.95. £19.95. Do these numbers mean anything to you?"

"I'm afraid they don't."

"These numbers mean a lot to Daryl. Apparently, the staff here have tried to help him forget these numbers, or at least accept them, ever since he arrived here at Pottergate. Those numbers are quite painful and harrowing for Daryl and he's worked hard to learn to live with that pain. Mr Newcombe and Wendy Daniels tell me that Daryl was making good progress. And yet there he was, for the first time in months apparently, paralysed by his traumatic memories. Do you happen to know anything about that Stanley?"

"Barnes was fine when I left him."

"You didn't say anything to upset him then? No talk of murder?"

What had Barnes said? What did he remember? What does the little detective know? Could I counter his knowledge, alter his perception with a subtle twist? I am pleased to find my brain is working in such an analytical fashion; the mental preparation integral to the Plan has obviously worked. Assess the situation, make the little detective work for his information. He is fishing, I can see the hopeful look in his eyes. Panic is the enemy. Maintain the party line. He was fine when I left him.

"Absolutely not. Why would I talk about anything like that?"

"Something must have happened, Stanley, to make him relapse like that." Newcombe interjects from his chair in the corner. I notice the little detective's eyes flash towards Newcombe, mild irritation displayed. Perhaps there is a tension there that I can exploit later.

"Well, it obviously happened after I had left him at 10.28."

The little detective stares at me. I cannot meet his eyes. That's not because I feel uncomfortable or guilty in light of developments – it's just an issue I have generally. I focus on his head and notice how far back his hairline has gone. That is probably why he has a shaven head. He raises his eyebrows and his brow furrows deeply. The silence stretches.

I give the appearance of thinking. I open my mouth to speak but then close it. The little detective takes the bait and heightens his eyebrows ever further – inviting me to speak.

"I can only assume those numbers have something to do with Barnes' ex-wife...?"

Despite my words being sufficient to construct a fully formed sentence in themselves I have expressed the words in such a way as to suggest I have something further to say. Which I do, but my hesitation will be interpreted as reluctance.

"Yes?"

"Well, I hesitate to cast aspersions upon a colleague but if Barnes' marital difficulties are such that he is capable of lapsing into a trance then perhaps...?"

I do it again and the little detective bites again.

"Yes?"

"Perhaps it is not inconceivable to imagine that Daryl Barnes may have been capable of committing an act of violence."

Newcombe can't help himself, "Daryl Barnes is as gentle a man as you could ever wish to meet."

"With all due respect Mr Newcombe, whilst I appreciate that Barnes' painful past usually manifests itself in masturbatory melancholy it is not beyond the realms of possibility that he could respond differently occasionally."

The seed is sown.

"OK Stanley, let's move on. What did you do after you had seen Daryl?"

Naylor was my next appointment of the day. She is the nutritionist here at Pottergate and spends the majority of her time planning the weekly menus and considering the health of the residents and employees of Pottergate. She also gets involved in food preparation, when she deems that she has the "energy." I find it hard to comprehend that this constitutes a full time job. She doesn't actually get involved in any of the food dispensation. They leave that sort of menial work to wenches such as Nash. Naylor is above these things. She is above most things, treating almost everything and everyone at Pottergate with cool disdain. Daniels spends much of the day with her, giving the senior management position on what can be bought and what can't. Healthy food is expensive and the Trustees are careful with their money. Our money. My father's money.

As I headed back to the canteen area, my mouth started to curl at the thought of spending time with Daniels. In this place you never quite know when you might bump into Daniels – she has an omnipresent quality that is quite an odds with her size zero frame. I told Newcombe that she was like a bad smell. Newcombe congratulated me on the technical accuracy of my simile but, in the next breath, admonished me for the improper use of language to a colleague. Hypocrite.

As I stood outside the wreck of a room in which Barnes was lost in his hypnotic state, I was in a state of constant watchful anxiety in case the small figure of Wendy Daniels should appear and ask me my business. I had concocted any number of plausible reasons which proved ultimately unnecessary as she didn't. From just outside the door to Room 3 I could hear Barnes still chanting away, lost in the depths of remembered pain. Perfect. I waited the necessary minutes out and then headed down the corridor in search of Naylor and Daniels.

I was very careful about the time, ensuring I arrived in the canteen right in the middle of my usual range of arrival times. Daniels notices if I do anything out of the ordinary. Naylor wouldn't notice. She hardly notices anything. She concentrates on her manual, her purchase book, the latest nutritional fads and research. The woman is obsessed by her work. If she's not doing that she's looking in the mirror to see how she looks. Self obsessed? Yes. Vain? Absolutely. I would usually find that level of self-absorption quite attractive in a person – it's a trait I recognise in myself occasionally – but in Naylor it seems wrong. Pathetic somehow. There's no strength in her self obsession.

I arrived at the median arrival time and cursed my fastidiousness – it was wasted.

Naylor was alone, staring at her page and oblivious to her surroundings and my very presence. There were a small selection of foods, in little trays, in front of her but they looked relatively untouched. I found myself staring at her in the silence – wondering if she would even notice if I slipped my hands around her neck and began to squeeze.

"Hello Stanley, right on time as usual." The chirpy, effervescent voice cut through me as I stood guiltily just inside the entrance to the canteen. "Zoë and I are working on the manual. Would you like to help us?"

"I'm afraid not. I'm here to observe, that's all. Carry on and pretend I'm not here."

"But you are here Stanley, and Zoë might find it helpful to run her ideas past someone new. I'm sure she gets tired of just speaking to me. Sometimes it's good to have a new sounding board. Zoë, would you like to speak to Stanley?"

This is one of the reasons that I dislike my visit to Naylor – Daniels' voyeuristic attempts at matchmaking. Naylor is wise, she didn't look up. I didn't look at Naylor either but concentrated on my clipboard. This is always Daniels' game, trying to "play Cupid." She is always getting us to talk to each other while she slips away and watches from a convenient distance with an analytical frown and a smug grin.

I won't fall for it this time, although it annoys me that I have in the past. Daniels has an uncanny ability of drawing people into conversations. She usually gets you when you are relaxed, but I was far from relaxed yesterday – not with the thought of Barnes a few metres away standing in an incriminating state. Naylor isn't even good looking. She is a pale woman, almost albino pale. Her pale blond curly hair is almost white. She always looks ill, the only colour on her face coming from her weak blue eyes and the natural blotchy red of her lips. She is incredibly thin, as if a strong gust of wind would push her over. She always wears trousers and big jumpers or cardigans as if to hide her figure, but I sometimes catch a glimpse of her wrist or her ankle. It is bone covered in skin.

She is nothing like the women that Thomas gets. They are voluptuous and sun-kissed, with a sense of fun and vitality about them.

Naylor doesn't speak much either. I suppose she's shy. I can't ever remember having a proper conversation with her. A one word answer is about all you get. As if I'd want to marry this woman, as Daniels was no doubt thinking.

"Just please get back to your work."

Daniels sighed and took her place next to Naylor, defeated in her licentious scheming this time. Their conversation began anew. I tried to follow it but my mind wasn't attuned to the task at hand. I kept thinking of Barnes. I tried to remain calm on the outside, being careful to note down the odd phrase or comment. I would piece together a report later in the day, perhaps over lunch. I have done it before and no-one has noticed. It's quite easy really. It would give me an excuse not to talk to anyone, although I would like to check on Barnes, smooth things over, allay his suspicions. Panic contended with logic within me. *Barnes could ruin me, or provide the perfect suspect.*

"How was Daryl today, Stanley?"

The question took me by surprise. Damn it, I am never distracted. I might as well admit my guilt. Daniels was on the verge of repeating the question.

"He was fine."

CHAPTER 6

"**M**s Daniels said you were a little distressed yesterday morning."

"I was not. I was fine."

"She said you were finding it hard to concentrate. She said that your concentration is usually perfect."

Circumstantial.

"I was fine. Daniels can't read my mind. Any opinion she may have expressed was just that – opinion, not fact. So perhaps you should change tack in your interrogation technique."

The little detective laughs gently and leans back into Newcombe's deep, leather seat. His large suit crumples around him. I notice that he doesn't have the cuffs of his shirt done up. Some small rebellious act perhaps against the Establishment which envelops him.

"This isn't an interrogation Stanley. You have not been arrested and this is not a formal part of the investigation. You are here entirely voluntarily. You can leave at any time. I'm just trying to piece together what happened yesterday. You do know how serious this is don't you? A girl is dying Stanley. A girl that you have known for years. Perhaps you could call her a friend. Surely you want to help me get to the bottom of this. I've asked everyone the same questions. It's my job."

He lets that sink in, perhaps hoping that I will assert my commitment to his cause of trying to untangle the rather messy events of the last twenty four hours. I don't.

"A few people said you were acting strangely yesterday, that's all. You understand my position right? I have to follow up every lead in order to do my job properly. It would be a dereliction of my duty to do otherwise. You understand that don't you? You're a man of duty. I understand that already. Can you see where I'm coming from?"

"I do understand."

The little detective smiles at me and I warm to him. He is just doing his job. I know the feeling. He is merely PC Plod carrying out his enquiries.

"OK, let's carry on. Tell me about the altercation yesterday during your morning tea break."

He is a bastard.

"That was because of Everett. He was breaking the law."

"Breaking the law?"

"Indirectly."

"How do you mean?"

I take a breath, momentarily dispelling the tiredness pervading my brain.

"European legislation – you may know it as the Working Time Directive – provides that all workers – I won't go into the definition of a worker at this time other than to say that I am satisfied that it does apply to the people here at Pottergate on the whole– should have minimum periods of rest during their working day and week. It is incumbent on the employer to ensure that these regulations are complied with. All Pottergate staff are required to report to the canteen at eleven o clock for the morning tea break. I drafted that policy. Everett was not in the canteen and therefore I could not be sure that he was having a rest break. This could mean that Pottergate, and the trustees who are ultimately responsible for its running, could be in breach of the Working Time Directive. It would be a dereliction of my duty to let that happen. Mr Newcombe should thank me that he is not being taken to the employment tribunal by an aggrieved worker. The damages awarded can be substantial."

The little detective raises his eyebrows and nods a little, no doubt impressed with the range and depth of my knowledge of the law. He frowns as he speaks to me, almost apologetically he says:

"That's all very well Stanley but Peter Everett was resting."

"I wasn't to know that."

"You could have asked. You didn't need to do what you did."

"What do you mean by that? Nothing happened. I found Everett in the TV room and accompanied him back to the canteen so he could complete his regulation break."

It is my custom to stand at the door of the canteen with my check board and count everyone as they come in. I mark them off as they arrive. It is not the most enjoyable part of my job but European Regulations prescribe regular breaks and I am bound to enforce them here at Pottergate.

My inspection of Naylor is generally in the canteen and this allows me to make sure I am ready to perform my duties. I try to station myself near the door at about 10.55 to make sure that any early-comers are noted and recommended for sanction by Newcombe. Late-comers are also recommended for sanction by Newcombe. I do realise that it is almost impossible for the staff here to escape a recommendation for sanction on a daily basis. They need to arrive between 11.00 and 11.01 to escape my wrathful pen. The time span is too short, I know that. But Newcombe doesn't do any sanctioning anyway so what's the point in changing the policy? Besides, I like marking people down.

Yesterday, I found myself at the doorway at 10.51 in the vain hope of seeing Barnes and Daniels.

"There's nothing wrong is there Stanley?" Daniels had asked me midway through my inspection of Naylor.

"Of course not," I answered as brusquely and as professionally as I could muster.

Daniels stared at me for a moment or two, considering me, weighing me up, before standing and saying:"I'm just going to check on Daryl. I need to have a word with him about something. Can I leave you here with Zoe? Have a chat and I'll see you at breaktime."

With that, she left the canteen and headed off to find Barnes. I desperately tried to think of something to say to prevent her going but nothing plausible would come to mind. Thomas would have thought of something. I was helpless as she went to discover Barnes in his hypnotic state and perhaps uncover the existence of the Plan.

Out of the corner of my eye I noticed that Naylor was watching me. I turned my gaze upon her and she immediately looked away, almost flinching as if she had been violated in some way.

I went and stood in front of her, bending down to try to look her in the eye. I generally avoided doing such things, but the Plan was in action now and I needed to go through with it. She continued to look at the cuff of her knitted jumper.

"I hear there have been intruders in the area recently. Nash – one of the serving ladies in the canteen – told me that they have been trying to force their way into people's houses and rooms. They're raping and pillaging everything in sight. Be careful tonight. We all need to be vigilant."

She didn't say anything or give any indication that she was listening. She just twisted the cuff of her jumper between her thumb and forefinger. Her thumb nail was tattered and bitten.

"Just be careful and make sure that any unusual activity is reported to Newcombe. That's very important. Can you do that?"

She wouldn't answer me, I knew that, but the seed had been sowed.

I moved away from Naylor and left her to consider my warning. I needed her to lay a false trail for me but I had no particular wish for her to get hurt. And who knew how far Barnes would go when consumed by lust. Testimony from Naylor would be compelling.

I found myself standing near the door of the canteen. I was anxious to see Barnes. I wanted to see him bumbling down the corridor, back to his usual idiotic self, prattling and whining as he went in search of a bit of company. Barnes, however, didn't come. The minutes whirred past as I looked out for him. I barely registered the others as they started to filter into the canteen although I did have the presence of mind to tick them off.

Newcombe and Phillips arrived together. My eyes traced her self-indulgent path across the room. Newcombe fetched her a cup of tea, befuddled by her feminine wiles, and they sat down to "chat." I noticed that Newcombe positioned himself so he could get a good look at her cleavage. Palmer and Shaw arrived soon after that, but no Barnes. By 11.04, only three people had yet to arrive – Everett, Daniels and Barnes. My eyes were stuck to the door, not even the presence of Phillips could draw my eyes away. Finally, Daniels arrived.

"Stanley, I've taken Daryl to his room, I think he's a bit upset. He's having a lie down. I'll tell Mr Newcombe. Are you sure nothing happened when you were there? Anything that might have upset him?"

Daniels was clearly suspicious. Even I have to admit she is quite a perceptive woman. She has never liked me. She thinks that every piece of upset or controversy in this place has me at the root of it.

"He was fine when I was with him. He carried out his duties in his usual manner – thoroughly but with too much chat. Perhaps he was thinking about his wife. That usually sets him off." I managed to force those last words out, although they are terse and abrupt. I need to be clever and consistent. "Is he resting? Tea break is between eleven o clock and half past. It is essential that he has the regulation thirty minutes of rest. It's the rules."

"He is resting Stanley, don't worry."

I knew she didn't believe me, and I knew she would convey that to Newcombe and he would ask further questions. It would be best if I wasn't there. I thought quickly, desperation breeding ingenuity. I needed a distraction.

"Have you seen Everett?" I asked Daniels as she moved into the canteen.

"No sorry, I haven't. I'm sure he'll be here soon."

It was already 11.06 and everyone was accounted for, except one. Peter Everett.

Daniels made her way into the canteen, sharing a few words with Shaw and Palmer as she headed towards Newcombe. I suspect that Daniels is having an extra-marital affair with Shaw; they share inappropriate glances throughout the working day. Dirty bitch. Palmer stared at her bottom quite openly and gave Shaw a look with raised eyebrows as she wandered past. Shaw shook his head in a resigned way. Within a moment, Newcombe and Daniels had their heads together. I stared at them, wondering when the moment would arrive when they would involuntarily flick their eyes towards me. I needed a distraction, I needed to get out of the room. Everett. I was gone.

I found him sitting quietly in the TV room, staring at the box without any thought of his designated break. The TV room is designed to aid the social aspect of the work here. Most people live and work in different places: we do not. Most people have at least two groups from which to draw friends and acquaintances: we do not. Therefore, it is doubly important that we at Pottergate get on. It is essential to our wellbeing that we have friends. The room is laid out in a manner suited to the convivial spirit. The seats are not in rows, they are arrayed in a semi-circle in front of the huge screen. Like a family home, not a cinema.

It is here where I have carried out the majority of my planning. I have carefully harvested every grain of information in an effort to plan the perfect murder. Thomas has taught me so much. He has taught me how to be a hero. In this room, we have bonded. We have become co-conspirators. In this room, we have become friends. And it is here that I find Everett.

Everett is a giant of a man, as broad as he is tall. His hands are huge, so big that my hand was completely enveloped in his handshake the first time we met. Not that there was any strength in his grip; on the contrary, it was limp and weak. But there was something in the coarse, hardened skin of his hands that hinted at the great strength in them. I knew he could break the bones in my hand if he chose to. But he didn't. The thought of it probably didn't even cross his mind. Or if it did, the idea of it didn't cross his face, much to my immediate relief. That was just over a year ago. He is the newest member of staff and, to be honest, I don't know him all that well. He is extremely quiet, quieter than Naylor I should think.

He is a giant of a man, although sometimes you have to look twice to realise it. Sometimes it's as if he's not there at all. He has this habit of melting into the background, so much so that you can actually forget he's there. And when you actually become conscious again of his pure size, you realise that it's like not noticing the obelisk standing on your front lawn. I said that to Newcombe once and he was disproportionately impressed. I didn't tell him I had read it in a book the night before. I first read the word "obelisk" in an Asterix book and didn't know what it meant. Why would they put such a difficult word in childrens' books? How can a child be sure that the picture on the page corresponds with the words in the bubble? There are some cheap tricksters in this world.

I don't like him personally, Everett that is, I think there's something creepy about him. He has a side parting in his hair and wears glasses with thin golden rims – they are far too delicate for his large face. He's the only one who works here who has his family hanging about all the time. Not that he has his own family, but his brother is always coming over and making a noise. He brings his wife and kids and they just run around the grounds shouting nonsense and breaking things. He doesn't say much to them either – not that I see anyway. He just sits, sometimes with his little niece on his knee gently stroking her tiny, weak back with his huge, tender hands. They don't seem to mind him not talking, they just carry on as if he is. His sister in law could talk Nash into the ground. I hate her even though I don't really know her.

I find it hard to make allowances for him. I considered him as a likely accomplice once. With his brute strength he would be able to break someone's neck like a normal person would snap a twig. He is surprisingly light on his feet for such a big man too. He works in the gardens, making sure they are well kept. Even in autumn, when the ground is littered with leaves, you can't hear him coming, not even when you are trying to be surreptitious under a conspiratorial tree. And the bugger doesn't even flinch when you shout at him. He just looks at you with those dark, sad, magnified eyes until you leave him alone. At least Barnes whimpers and gives you some satisfaction.

He was just staring at the screen. The television wasn't even on. I have to admit, I got very angry, very quickly. I wasn't sure if it was the Barnes debacle or the flagrant disregard of expensively thought out European legislation but as I stood in the doorway for that brief second, sweat beading in my armpits, blood pumping in my ears, anger pulsed throughout me. I could see that Everett had noticed me but he didn't look up. I could see him staring at me out of the corner of his eye, his great shoulders hunched down into his body, his right leg shaking slightly. My ragged, desperate breathing was the only noise in that deathly quiet room. Maybe it was the fact that he was breaking the rules, maybe it was the fact that Barnes now had a power over me, maybe it was just the nervous tension of the day – who can say?

I got angrier, and I snapped.

CHAPTER 7

"**A**s I said; nothing happened. I accompanied Everett back to the canteen so he could complete his regulation break."

The little detective looks at me as he leans across the desk. His eyebrows are raised, creasing his brow. It's hard to tell where his eyebrows end and his head starts. Policemen should not have shaven heads.

"Nothing happened? You accompanied him back to the canteen? You make it sound placid and good natured."

"It was. Everett is a reasonable fellow and he accepted that he had made a mistake when I pointed it out to him."

The little detective's voice turns hard.

"Stanley, you have a talent for understating your actions. It makes me wonder whether you are telling me the whole truth, rather than just your version of it. That worries me Stanley when I have a girl fighting for her life and no-one knows what happened to her. Mr Newcombe, perhaps you could tell us what really happened."

There is a pause. Dramatic of course.

"You threw a chair at him Stanley." Newcombe's voice wafts over my shoulder, tinged with anger and embarrassment and perhaps a little sadness.

Perhaps I had.

"I did not throw a chair at him. I raised the chair in order to demonstrate my point – my responsibility for Everett's wellbeing - and the chair then came out of my hand."

Now Newcombe starts to get angry: "The chair did not slip out of your hand Stanley, you threw it at Peter Everett. And then you chased him into the canteen, screaming at him and trying to hit him. It was disgraceful. I haven't seen you get that angry in many years Stanley. Demonstrate your point indeed."

I am losing control of the situation, I can see that. They are after me. My heart starts to beat as they set about their character assassination. I want to speak, to defend myself, to diffuse the situation, to insert a smart, witty comment like Thomas would. They don't give me the chance.

"Peter Everett is a big man, Stanley. What kind of anger would it take to scare a man as big and powerful as Peter Everett?" the little detective poses a question that I assume to be rhetorical. "You have problems controlling your anger don't you Stanley?"

"No I do not. Anger is a tool. Sometimes it's necessary."

I am getting angry despite myself.

"Do you think you needed to get angry with Peter? He was only watching TV. He was resting."

"It is policy that everyone should assemble in the canteen for their break between 11.00 am and 11.30 am. Everett was breaking the rules."

"OK, you're a stickler for the rules, I can understand that. It's your job as a "compliance officer" or whatever it is you call yourself, but was it really worth getting that angry with Everett? Shouldn't you have been a little more temperate, more reasonable?"

Temperate. I like that word. It sticks in my tired brain – enticing me somehow. Temperate. I will write that down. Why am I thinking about nice sounding words when I should be concentrating? It sounds like a dreamy word, something that Shakespeare would have used.

"Yes, perhaps I should have been calmer. More temperate, as you say."

"So, why did you get so angry? Was there anything else playing on your mind?"

Damn. I have fallen into that one. He has cornered me quite skilfully. I have allowed him to do it by my mental slackness. If only I wasn't so tired, I could beat him. I know it.

"There was nothing else playing on my mind thank you."

The little detective resumes his relaxed seating position and places his feet up on the table. I wonder how Mr Newcome will react to that. The little detective stares at me, his sunken eyes relentlessly considering me, searching out my guilt. The little detective is good I now realise, a worthy adversary.

"So, what happened after that? Who was next on the rounds?"

"No-one was next."

"What do you mean?"

"Mr Newcombe and I had a few minutes talking about Everett's ill-discipline."

I can hear Newcombe shuffling in his seat behind me, as if he wants to say something but doesn't have the authority to cut in. Ha, at least this day is teaching Newcombe a thing or two about humility. The little detective hears him shuffling and nods for him to speak.

"Well, that wasn't exactly what we were speaking about Stanley now is it?"

"As far as I'm concerned it is."

"As far as you are concerned Mr Newcombe, what were you speaking about?"

"Stanley and I had quite a detailed discussion about *his* behaviour, and *his* ill-discipline. What Stanley did to poor Peter Everett was quite unacceptable and Stanley and I discussed that in no uncertain terms."

The little detective looks at me, considering me. He is trying to look analytical, trying to make me believe that he is thinking deeply, clearly, perceptively, but I know he isn't. He is looking at me and not really thinking at all. It is all a game, an act, an attempt to make me believe that he has discovered some crucial element of the evidence that will incriminate me. I smile back, a knowing smile.

"You seem to have a habit of re-writing history Stanley. That worries me. If Mr Newcombe hadn't been here to present the other side of the story, you would have led me to believe that…well, no matter. Let's move on. How long were you with Mr Newcombe?"

The glaring incongruity of Everett always hits me, even when I am angry. He is such a big, powerful man and yet he is so easy to intimidate. It is easy to scare him, to the point where you have his entire body shaking and his eyes welling up with fearful tears. And yet his face never changes. His face is like rock. I don't think I've ever seen an ounce of emotion on it. He could squash me like a flea had he the guts and the requisite rage. He is so big and powerful, and his silence should be menacing, but it isn't. He has never scared me, not even once. I scare him all the time, however. He has always been scared of me, I'm sure of it.

I first discovered his weakness when I went out to play tennis with Barnes, one Saturday morning. The court was covered in leaves. My game is built upon judging the bounce of the ball, adapting to the spin and being one step ahead of my opponent. I have studied the wrist action of the Australian Pat Rafter in quite extensive detail in order to copy his game. I have always admired him as a player. At my best I believe I could have given Pat a game. Not that I needed to be at my best that day. Playing Barnes is easy. He is so slow around the court, lumbering around with his droopy cheeks flapping in the wind. And if he does manage to get to the ball he generally lobs it into the net or smashes the ball out of court. Or misses the ball entirely. I have beaten him the last thirteen times we have played. In fact we have only played thirteen times. I beat him in straight sets last time, flashing the ball past him with consummate ease. It was almost boring. Barnes was puffing around the court complaining about his age, the quality of the courts comparative to the Oak, the way Sandra used to hit her backhand - but generally seeming to enjoy himself. He kept smiling and chatting between points. I eat my banana, drank my energy drink and tried to focus on recovery – ready for the next point. I tried to wipe the smile off his face too by crashing winners past him at every available opportunity. He kept trying to speak to me during the rest breaks between games. In the end I had to move my chair further down the court.

Everett is the only one of us who works six days a week. I could see him in the gardens, filling the bird bath with fresh water or something. There I was standing up to my knees in autumnal debris and Everett was filling up a basin for flying rodents. I could not, and still cannot, believe it. He jumped so much when I shouted his name that he nearly knocked the solid stone bird bath over. That was a microcosm of his character.

Everett cleared away the leaves, and then evenly swept out the gravel after we had had a little chat. He did it well, despite casting furtive glances at me every few minutes as I sat on my chair watching him. The match was delayed by seventeen full minutes. It would have been quicker but Barnes kept trying to speak to Everett – asking if he was OK – and it slowed him down. I had to tell Barnes to be quiet; it was my duty as match referee. As for Everett, I could see what kind of slacker he was, doing half a job. He has never once failed to clear the court since then. Every Saturday, whether I am playing or not, the court is pristine. All you have to do is be firm with people and they are able to do their jobs quite well.

The whole incident must have upset Barnes because he blubbed to someone and I was called into Newcombe's office first thing on the following Monday. Newcombe gave me the great "I Am" speech and sent me on my way. I was banned from using the tennis court for a month which required significant amendments to the System. It was worth it though because I had learnt a valuable lesson – Everett was pliable. And he wouldn't say a word to anyone about anything. He could be used.

Just a few months later and I was back again – having to confront Everett about his indiscipline in the TV room. Yet again, I was forced into being firm with him.

These thoughts ran through my head as I stood before Newcombe's desk - again - called in to explain my actions.

"We have been here before Stanley." Newcombe let the statement hang in the air, the familiar harsh look upon his face. "It is unacceptable. Entirely unacceptable. We pride ourselves here at Pottergate on being a friendly, supportive, helpful unit. We do not tolerate bad manners, aggression, intimidation or anything of that sort. You are guilty of everything in that list."

"He was breaking the rules."

"Damn you Stanley," Newcombe screamed at me, as he leapt out of his chair, banging his hand down upon the table and glaring at me, "don't you dare. You know you are in the wrong so do not try to defend yourself. What you did was unacceptable. Be warned Stanley, I am seriously considering your position here and I have already made the necessary phone calls."

I gulped. Newcombe was angry. Properly angry. That angry young man within him, mellowed somewhat by age, erupted. I had goaded him sufficiently. He had never considered my position before. The thought of it terrified me. No-one had ever been made to leave Pottergate. Abdul had left of his own accord, technically. If Newcombe had made the phone calls already, I could be out before the day. I could lose everything – my job, my apartment, my colleagues, my opportunity to implement the Plan.

What would my father say?

He had helped me to get into this place. He had used all his influence after the Abdul incident and after the incident with Phillips and the delivery boy. He had never mentioned it directly but I knew it was him. He had some sort of hold over Newcombe it seemed, although I'm not sure what. Perhaps just monetary. He would be disappointed. In fact he would be angry. Very angry. Worse than Newcombe.

"I'm sorry, Stanley, I shouldn't have cursed. That was wrong of me. I apologise." Newcombe had sunk back into his chair, a defeated look upon his face. "What do we do with you Stanley? You create problem after problem. I do so want to help you."

I wondered if he wanted some sort of response, but I was unable to speak.

"I want a written apology to Peter before the end of the day. And then you will hand it to him and you will apologise personally. And you will mean every word. That will do for a start. We'll see where we go from there. In fact, do it now."

"But I'm supposed to see…"

"Do it now."

CHAPTER 8

"I was with Newcombe for about fifteen minutes. Much of that time involved him shouting at me with considerable amounts of rage. I have long suspected that Mr Newcombe might have anger management issues."

The little detectives ignores my attempt to further undermine Newcombe's character. I imagine that Newcombe is already a suspect. Christians always become suspects – there is a presumption that they hear the voice of God in cases such as this. Instead, the little detective sighs irritably and asks:

"And after that?"

"I went back to my room to write a memo to Everett. I wanted to clear up the confusion that led to our disagreement."

Newcombe and the little detective share a quick look, but I let it pass.

I was sitting at my desk before I could think clearly. I was staring at a blank piece of paper, attempting to write to Everett. Newcombe had said I should apologise, but it wasn't easy to form the words, especially when I knew I was entirely in the right. Newcombe is so biased, he holds everything against me, and forgives everything of everyone else. I was so angry at the injustice that I wanted to cry. I could feel a faint wetness across my eyeball, as if the tear were gathering strength. I would not let it out. I would not give in to Newcombe and his threats. I would stand up to the bully.

Besides, the initial fear induced by Newcombe's threat had quickly turned to anger. How dare he consider my position? How dare he threaten me? He had made the necessary phonecalls had he? What did I care? Why should I care about that? He is nothing but an inconsequential, power-hungry, self-obsessed, impotent social worker who can't give this place the necessary leadership. I would complain to the Trustees. I would tell my father.

My father.

If Newcombe had called him he could be on his way already, strapped into his expensive car and driving with that furious speed that was so common to my childhood. I never once asked him to slow down – that would have been pathetic. My father cannot abide pathetic, helpless characters. He admires strength. Perhaps that's why he intervened in the Abdul incident. However, he had warned me after that particular misunderstanding. One more incident he had said and I would have to move on. He had something else lined up, of that he had left me in no doubt. Something less pleasant. Less salubrious. Less expensive.

I sat at my desk and considered the consequences. Everything would change. Pottergate had been my life for nearly five years. My job, my home, my duties, my friends – all of that could disappear within an instant.

How dare Newcombe do this to me? I give more to this place than he could possibly imagine.

I would not leave without a fight. I would not go meekly. I would not be bundled quietly into a car like Abdul was, head down and defeated – never to be spoken of again. Thomas wouldn't give up and neither would I.

Thank goodness I had decided to implement the Plan. That would be my legacy to this place. To Newcombe. All I needed was to ensure they let me stay the night.

I just had to hope that my father was not on his way, or that Newcombe had been bluffing.

I tried to turn my attention to the letter to Everett. It was virtually impossible. My mind kept slipping back to the Plan. My eyes kept sliding onto my wardrobe.

My wardrobe is small and compact. On top of it there is black suit carrier that is gathering dust. I use it for business trips, although, if truth be told, I haven't used it for a long time, so wrapped up in my duties have I been. Another reason to leave. The wardrobe has ten shirts all neatly arranged. Each night, I take the shirt from my back, and if I have worn it only once, I place it on the right hand side. Each morning, I take from the left. I add a new shirt every Christmas, and throw away the oldest one so as to continually refresh my collection. Some of my shirts are nearly ten years old. There is a small label inside each one, recording the date of purchase. If it is the second time I have worn the shirt, I place it in the wash basket outside my door and it is laundered. The bottom of the wardrobe has two drawers. The first drawer contains various t-shirts and jumpers. I do not need many because I only use them at the weekend. I don't bother to change of an evening. I find that looking smart helps concentrate the mind.

The second drawer contains three pairs of trousers, a pair of jeans and one pair of tracksuit bottoms. Another pair of black trousers is currently being washed. I wear them for five days and then have them washed. I also get a new pair of trousers every Christmas. And throw the oldest away. Trousers tend to wear out quicker than shirts. I rarely need a new pair of jeans or tracksuit bottoms, so I get them as and when I need them.

But, behind both drawers and positioned carefully on a small wooden runner that makes a handy shelf stands a small notebook. It stands upright, held in place by a small piece of blutack that comes away without a noise.

Every evening, when I am sure I will not be disturbed I carefully pull the drawers out, conscious at all times as to the noise made. I gently pull away the notebook from its hiding place and check that it has not been disturbed since the last time I used it. Then I replace the drawers, and after checking that that hallway is clear, I retire to my desk and begin to plan.

I never look at it during the day, but I was sorely tempted as I tried to write the letter to Everett. It would have just given a small shot of comfort. It would have reassured me that my life was not a futile procession of frustration and ineptitude. All I ever wanted to do was help people, to help people be more like me. But some people are so difficult to help. They are so reluctant to better themselves. And people like Newcombe are the worst. They accept people in their frailty. They make concession after concession. They do not allow me to help others. I could work wonders with Barnes if Newcombe would let me. That book, *that small notebook*, would allow me to demonstrate that something could be done. People could be helped, even if one person had to suffer for the sake of the rest. Tonight, I would make this place better with just one small jab of a knife. Easy.

I was so tempted to take the book out, just to skim the pages, but I dared not. I would look at it after dinner, remind myself of the intricacies of the Plan and put them into action. Tonight. I could only hope that my father would let me stay one more night before he took me away. Surely fate, or God, or whoever, wouldn't let me down.

Hastily, I got something down for Everett and left the room. The thought of carrying out the Plan burned within me. I felt I needed to urinate, so excited was I. I tried to force it down. I needed to remain calm.

CHAPTER 9

"**H**ow was lunch?"

"Lunch was fine."

"Do you have a system for eating lunch as well? Same as breakfast?"

"Yes."

"Do you want to tell me about it? What did you have?"

"I had potato gratin, salad and southern fried chicken. That was the meal of the day. That was what I had. That is my system, I have the meal of the day. Occasionally there are some meals that I don't like and I am able to use a wild card and have any meal of my choice. I only have ten wild cards a year. I am not a fussy eater so I have only used three this year. I make do. I didn't think much of the potato if that is what you're going to ask next. I believe potato gratin should be made with cream and milk. Yesterday's meal tasted as if it was made with just milk. That is typical of this place. Newcombe does like to save money wherever possible. I believe he may be engaged in fraudulent economic activity."

"Stanley…"

Harsh tones come from behind me, but I don't care. I am too far-gone, too involved to care.

The little detective looks at me, a small smile creeping onto his lips. I detest him. I can see that he isn't interested in Newcombe. He's after me. This aspect of the Plan – misdirection, deception, plurality of suspects - is failing me. "You can be pretty mean when you want to be, can't you Stanley? It makes me wonder…"

I know the wretched little man is itching for me to ask what he is wondering about. I will not do it. We both know exactly what he is wondering. He does a lot of wondering for a detective. I make the silence my friend.

"Tell me what happened at dinner."

Idiot. He is trying to be methodical and yet he has missed a step. My movements between leaving my room and reaching the canteen. And it isn't dinner, it's lunch.

The letter for Everett burned in my pocket as I headed down the stairs from my room. I wanted rid of it as soon as possible. The lies made me feel ill. Newcombe had won his small victory. I had said everything he would want to hear. Perhaps now he would let me stay. Perhaps my father – if he really was on his way – would turn his car around and return to work.

I took the steps quickly, eager to reach the canteen and throw the letter of apology into Everett's face.

As I reached the corridor leading to the canteen I saw her.

She was oblivious to my presence as she stood looking at a blank wall, considering a small bolt of fabric. Her face stopped me. It inspired rage within me even at a range of thirty metres. I wanted to race past her, but I couldn't. She held me.

Why wasn't she in the canteen with the rest of them? A small pang of disappointment shot through me as I realised that she wouldn't be there to witness my act of rebellion – the disdainful way in which I intended to toss my letter of apology into Everett's face.

Her wavy dark hair was pulled back into a ponytail. The waves continued under the small band that held her hair in place and down her back, coming to rest just below her shoulders. It was a familiar look, indeed, to me, every part of her is familiar. Even from this distance I could see her bottom lip being unconsciously tucked beneath the top one. Her look of concentration. I cursed my eyes for admiring her, but they would not stop.

She held the cloth up to the light and I saw her in profile. Her body is desirous, being curved and shaped in a way that cannot fail to attract attention. Her top half was covered in a voluminous pashmina, but I knew what lay underneath well enough. I have thought about those breasts at length – they have haunted me. Her heavy shoulders and the pronounced bulge of her womb – all covered up but no less visible to my careful memory. Her body. It held my attention as I followed it down to the floor, past the tight skirt that hugged her bottom and caressed her short yet shapely legs, ending in bare feet that would leave that faint impression of warmth on the cold floor when she changed position.

I felt my trousers growing tight. I wanted to touch it.

Only her hands are incongruous. In the midst of the aquiline beauty stands the arid desert of her hands. They are raw and callused; dry and cracked: a faded red that tells of screaming crimson in days gone past. Bitten down nails, surrounded by constantly flaking skin at the end of her fingers. Every inch of her demeanour speaks of pleasure and gratification, except those hands. Those hands repulse me. They also enlighten me and I am the only one to see it. Others see her full bosom, her welcoming thighs, her come-to-bed eyes and nothing else. But there is more. Those raw, damaged hands reveal more, something extra. If only the people with their admiring eyes could see past the allure, they would perhaps see what lies beneath – the hard, callused soul of the woman. The deliberate showmanship, the uncaring attraction that wreaks havoc and indiscipline. The lack of care, the lack of safety, the lack of thought and of discipline and of rationality. I have seen those hands work – on herself, on other men – on one other man. The pursuit of pleasure at the expense of all else. I have seem them work unconsciously during one of Newcombe's protracted meetings as her mind wanders onto other things. I have seen the dry skin crack at the top of her palms when she works her fingers after a period of distraction. Her hands don't bleed; they ever-so-slightly ooze. The hint of red is ever present. It screams at me. The hands remind me why I hate this woman, it is because she works at her indiscipline as much as I work at my discipline. She could let them heal, but she never would allow it. Those hands reveal the real her; the planning, calculating self.

I stared intently at the hands without really seeing them. Rather, her hands were in my mind's eye, scraping roughly down my bare back but consumed in the sensation of overwhelming smoothness. I can see the dots of red scattered on my back as she scrapes me and pleasures me into an agitated nirvana. She tries to dig her gutted nails into the grooves between my spine, but they have little effect. I am hurting her but she can't hurt me back. She is screaming, half pleasure and half pain. She tries to touch my face and I lash out. She does scream then and I hurt her more as she tries to placate me...

"Hello Stanley." I looked up to find Phillips staring directly at me, not one metre away; a playful, quizzical look on her face. Her breath carried, it was mint. "Have you come to inspect me?"

Her voice is soft and her eyes were open to their maximum width. Most people would be unable to speak or move, caught as they were in the grip of that combination. She makes the word "inspect" sound slightly rude, like some cheap gag in a Carry On film.

But not I. Her voice sent a surge of hateful adrenalin through me as I thought of her hands on my face. I was close enough to grab her, to crush her, to take her. She was close enough to touch me. I harshly rearranged my trousers, hurting myself, on the verge of what felt like a snap, a rupture. I did not even countenance the idea of embarrassment, despite the fact that she has seen me. I was ashamed and glad at the same time.

"No I have not." I snapped at her. "If you haven't noticed it is one o'clock and therefore it is dinnertime. You should be in the canteen, eating. It's potato gratin today Phillips. Don't miss it."

I tried to step past her but she moved to block my path.

"You missed my inspection today. Is something wrong?"

She tilted her head onto one side; playful, sexy, sensuous.

"Nothing is wrong Phillips. I had other duties to attend to. That's all."

A small smile curled onto her lips, "You always call me Phillips, why not Deborah? Why not Debbie, or Debs? You can call me anything you like you know."

I found myself staring deep into her eyes. Her voice was soft and warm.

Before I knew it, a soft arm with a callused hand had snaked its way closer to me and was gently pulling my tie out from under my jumper. I jerked back. I could see the mischievous look in her eyes. I recognised the look of sexual desire, I'm not sure how because I don't know much about it, but somehow I know that she wanted me. Right there, she would have done anything I asked. I wanted to slap her, hard and full in the face. I wanted to send her reeling down the corridor. But somehow, I could not. Instead:

"It isn't proper. You should be working. No, you should be eating. It isn't proper."

"You are always so proper Stanley. Always thinking about work. Always thinking about the time. Have you ever thought of doing something totally crazy? Like skinny dipping? I went skinny dipping once, it was wonderful. Cold ice water does wonders for your skin you know Stanley. It tightens it. Do you see how smooth and tight my skin is? Would you like to touch it?"

She squared herself, leant back and gently pulled the pashmina away from her neck. It dropped, already forgotten, to the ground, as she stepped towards me. I was presented with an expanse of smooth, pale, white skin. I could see her neck, perfect except for a faint dark shadow that I could barely see but I know is there. The neck dropped away into the body, and then the body gladly curled out into large, pert breasts, half displayed by a low cut, fitted top.

I wanted to hit her, I wanted to hurt her. I wanted to touch her.

Involuntarily, I found my hand was sliding towards her. My left hand lay dormant, clutching to the desperate normality of my clipboard as my right hand ventured into the unknown, slowly inching its way towards her.

Perhaps my hand was too slow for the flaming passion that burned within her because she reached out, grabbed my hands and yanked it towards her. The hard, grated skin of her hands broke my reverie as it scraped violently against my soft skin. She jammed my hand against her breast, trying to push it down under her top. That despicable hand held mine hard against her body. I could imagine the dry, inflamed skin cells starting to mingle with my own. I managed to pull my hand away. I had to jerk hard because her hands are strong and did not give up their grip on me easily.

We stared at each other for a moment. My face was painted with shock, hers was daubed with anger.

And then she span away without a backward glance, nor a shred of regret.

I wiped my hand on my trousers. The thought of heading back to my room to change them flitted across my mind, but it was soon replaced by anger.

I stormed towards the canteen, rage boiling within me. The bitch had lured me in. She had humiliated me. I felt sick, absolutely sick. I wanted to stop in the hallway and wretch, I felt so dirty. To be touched with those hard, corrosive hands. I needed to shower.

The canteen was much as it had been only a few hours earlier, albeit a little fuller. I didn't recognise anyone though, I couldn't tell you who was in the room. Only Everett. I found him and approached him slowly, anger burning within me. Everett looked up timidly as I approached his table. He was sitting alone. He tried to keep his head down as I approached, although he was staring at me through his eyelashes. His timidity irritated me further.

"I'm here to give you your apology." I stood before him and found my voice to be calm and level. He raised his head towards me, slowly and fearfully. "Open your mouth."

Everett did exactly as I told him without a moment's hesitation. His mouth sat agape as I stood before him. I took the written apology out of my pocket, folded it carefully and shoved it deep into his gaping mouth. Hard and fast. He didn't flinch, despite the trickle of blood that flowed out of his mouth. Part of me was disappointed as I whirled away,

Who next?

I could see Nash on the counter. For the first time in all my time at Pottergate I went towards her voluntarily. Almost gleefully.

I did not see the commotion behind me, as those around started to react to what had happened.

"Hello again Stanley. I don't usually get the pleasure of seeing you twice in one day but Sarah is off sick so I'm standing in for her. What a nice shirt. It makes you look dashing. The colours suit you. Don't get any potato on that lovely tie. Oh, if I were twenty years younger…"

I didn't know what I was saying. No, I knew exactly what I was saying.

"If you were twenty years younger you leathery old bat, I would stick this tie in your mouth so you couldn't scream and then repeatedly stab you with this knife until your blood flowed freely enough to cover my southern fried chicken."

CHAPTER 10

"**M**rs Nash was pretty upset after what you said to her."

The little detective lets the statement hang in the air, waiting for me to elaborate. Pretty upset indeed. I bet she was hysterical, screaming in some melodramatic fashion. I look the little detective in the eye and dare him to underplay me.

"Do you often make threats like that?"

I need to think clearly. The little detective is highlighting two instances of aggressive behaviour on the same day that Phillips ended up in hospital. Everett and Nash. The evidence is stacking against me. Perhaps the Plan had been implemented too soon. I'm clearly not ready. I had been so angry. That encounter with Phillips was extraordinary.

"I will answer both parts of your question. One, I do not usually make threats like that and two, and indeed, I do not make threats at all."

The little detective smiles at my answer, acknowledging that I have cut off his next question before he has even had the chance to ask it. I am proud of the answer.

"You see, Stan, I'm struggling to understand you. You're an intelligent guy. You know this place inside out. You know the consequences of breaking the rules. Mr Newcombe had just spoken to you an hour or so earlier about your behaviour and then…you threaten to stab Mrs Nash and you assault Peter Everett - again. From nowhere, you turn.

"It seems to me that you were quite rational when you wrote the memo to Peter. I've seen it, it's short and concise, but it is clear and reasonable. It said, *"Dear Mr Everett, I apologise for the misunderstanding earlier. I fully acknowledge that my behaviour was unacceptable, although allowances can be made in the face of such great provocation. Let us put this behind us and move on. Kind regards, Stanley Young,"* or something along those lines anyway. I wasn't inclined to read it too closely – it was a good few minutes before Wendy Daniels could coax Peter into allowing her to take it out of his mouth. It's a good note though, an apology without an apology, the kind of words and sentiments that sum you up. So you were obviously thinking straight, when you were in your room at least. Maybe you're a little angry, but you can still think, make decisions, identify a consequence, shift the blame and all that. But by the time you reached the canteen, you are furious. You threaten Mrs Nash, you hurt Peter yet again – two crimes in and of themselves. So what happened between your bedroom and the dining room? What or who made you so mad?"

So he hasn't forgotten. He hasn't missed a step.

"Nothing. Nothing happened. Nothing made me mad."

"Anything to do with Deborah Phillips?"

"No."

"You didn't see her?"

"No."

"What if I told you that I have evidence that you were speaking to her in the corridor?"

Who? Barnes? Everett? Daniels?

"I'd say that you were lying, or that you were mistaken or that you have an agenda."

"It's none of those Stanley. It's the truth. You spoke to her in the corridor. I know it for a fact. What happened?"

What to do? Come clean or maintain the position? *Think you idiot. What would Thomas do? Smile, that's it.*

I smile – an innocent mistake.

"Oh, I forgot. Now that you mention it, I did pass her in the corridor as I was heading to the canteen. I can't be expected to remember every person I pass in the corridors of this place. She said a few words to me, I said a few back. It was nothing. It slipped my mind. I forget what the words were really."

"You didn't argue?"

"No."

"She didn't do anything to upset you?"

What a question. Her being alive upsets me. But that isn't the right answer. My smile doesn't slip.

"No."

"And you didn't do anything to upset her?"

Pulling away from her hands? The look of distaste and hatred upon my face?

"Of course not."

"Why did you keep her pashmina?"

The words hit me like a violent bolt of realisation. The image floods back to me. Before heading towards the canteen I had picked up the discarded pashmina, the one that had been draped around her vast bosom, the one that I had touched only a few moments before. I had shoved it into my pocket. It had created an obvious bulge in my trousers that made it difficult to walk. I didn't even realise I'd taken it. How could I have been so stupid?

Think quickly. What did I do with it? Where is it now? I can't remember.

"I...I...thought I should pick it up and return it to her, Phillips I mean. The floor was dirty so I didn't want to leave it there."

Stutter and hesitation, the most obvious indicator of guilt and dishonesty.

The little detective leans back in his seat. He can see that he has me rattled. He is enjoying his moment. And I, the protagonist in this pashmina related scenario, can't even remember the key details. Where is it now?

"Is that why you handed it to Ms Daniels?"

That is what I did with it.

"Yes. I knew she would be able to return the garment."

"That's very nice of you Stanley, especially as you don't seem to like Deborah Phillips all that much."

Motive. He is getting at motive.

"What do you mean?"

"I just mean that everything I hear and everything I have seen indicates that you don't really like Deborah Phillips. You could even go as far as to say that you hate her. You have a daily complaint about her, at least one. Everyone else here at Pottergate knows it. You have a problem with her."

Now we get to the interesting stuff. The rest had been pre-amble, now we are heading into the pressured investigation. I have to rebuff this. One of the key tenets of the Plan is giving the appearance of being indifferent to the existence of Deborah Phillips.

"It's not true. I treat her in just the same way as everyone else here at Pottergate. I give her no special attention or extra notice."

"Really? What did you and Ms Daniels speak about at your meeting yesterday afternoon?"

I refuse to answer. I want to plead the Fifth Amendment but that is part of the constitution of the United States and is clearly inapplicable. Only idiots use that sentence in England. This is motive, one of the key ingredients of the little detective's case against me – along with opportunity. I need to keep him away from motive. The motive is supposed to be sitting against Barnes and Newcombe and possibly Palmer.

"Nothing important."

"No mention of Deborah?"

"Perhaps in passing."

"What else then?"

"We may have discussed the paintings she has on the wall, or her favourite subject of all, feelings. That is what it is usually about."

"Hmm."

I look to the floor and urge the little detective to move on. He lets the silence continue for as long as he feels necessary. Only Newcombe's excessive breathing – everything about that man is excessive – breaks the silence of the room.

Lunch passed quite nicely, the satisfaction of my previous actions blotting out my disgust towards Phillips and my actions towards her. The memory of my involuntary erection shames me. To distract myself, I kept replaying my victories over Everett and Nash. They were sweet in the memory. The southern fried chicken tasted excellent and I savoured it. I even practiced my descriptive speech. It was succulent and juicy, crispy on the outside. It smelt of...I don't know, I could not translate that aspect of my dinner. I took my time to think about it, it was pleasant. I knew it would be the last time that I would be eating southern fried chicken at Pottergate.

Whilst I was gathering my dinner – I had to serve myself after Nash ran away from me – I noticed that Everett had left the canteen also. Such is the man, I had no idea where he would go.

I kept looking at the door, expecting to see Newcombe storm in at any moment. And my father perhaps. I knew that word of my actions must have been spreading around the building. If Barnes had seen, or Palmer, the whole building would know before 2 o'clock. Thank goodness Daniels or Shaw hadn't been in the canteen when I battled with Everett and Nash – I would have been packing my bags already. There were probably in an adulterous love tryst somewhere in the building. But Newcombe...he should have been on the rampage.

To my surprise, Newcombe didn't appear and my lunch hour dwindled away happily. I tried not to notice anyone else in the room as I concentrated on my southern fried chicken and on writing a report about my failure to inspect Phillips as per my usual rota – I laid the blame firmly against Newcombe.

At two o clock I was due to have a meeting with Daniels. That soured my mood a little and I was tempted not to go, but in the end, with consistency of movement uppermost in my mind, I decided that I ought to attend.

Daniels, owing to her lofty position here at Pottergate, has a rather nice office. Not as nice as Newcombe's office of course. It's small, but nice. The walls are painted in gentle colours; the furnishings match and are soothing on the eye whilst the furniture is arranged so as to be comfortable and informal. On each wall, of which there are four, hangs a picture depicting the four seasons. Summer is bright sunshine beating down on lush, green grass whilst a little boy throws a Frisbee for a golden retriever to retrieve. Autumn shows a multitude of semi-naked trees, in various shades of brown. On one tree, there is a hint of a squirrel, looking for a place to hide his food in anticipation of the winter ahead. Winter shows rolling countryside, bedecked in white whilst spring shows a similar area but this time resplendent in green and ready for the romantic frolicking of the new born lamb.

She forced me into examining the pictures over many months to come up with those particular descriptions.

She has told me before that each picture can represent a person's character. She says I am like autumn: dour and resigned to the onset of winter, but still with a hint of warmth. She says I am perhaps like the squirrel, hoarding away its treasures so that they are safe. She says I am like the trees because they perform their roles with alarming regularity, controlled by the forces of nature and abdicating all choice to fate and destiny.

I think she is a bitch.

There was something odd about Daniels' manner as I entered her office just after two o'clock yesterday. I immediately deduced that she knew all about my altercation with Peter Everett. I expected her to bring it up immediately, but she surprised me.

"Have a seat Stanley. Would you like a cup of tea?"

I took a seat. "Is it two o clock yet?"

"Yes it is."

"In which case, I will have a coffee, strong but with plenty of milk. Decaffeinated in my usual mug."

The two o'clock meeting with Daniels is the only appointment of the day where I am prepared to arrive late. I like to drag my feet as I head towards her office. It annoys her. I often like to invent some "emergency" that requires my attention as I'm heading to her room. The more trivial the better, especially as I explain the need for my immediate involvement in the most earnest tones imaginable. That really irritates her. My other favourite is to ignore something extremely important on my way to the meeting and then to suddenly "remember" it half way through our meeting. That really winds her up. Like that time I saw Palmer speaking to Everett's young niece in the corridor near his room. She leapt out of the room that day. Hilarious. The little girl was fine in the end, but still, Daniels was furious.

She took her time with coffee, as always.

Daniels has a number of pictures on her desk: many of the people that I don't know, and perhaps never will. I know one of them is her husband, but I'm not sure which. It could be the bald, shifty looking one or the dark haired, Jewish looking one. I try to draw her into conversations about her family sometimes but she doesn't give much away. I try to bring Shaw in the conversation as much as possible. I sometimes refer to how good looking and strong he is and then cast obvious glances at the picture of her husband – a sad counterpoint whichever of the men in the picture happens to belong to her. She tries to ignore me. She doesn't have children, of that I'm pretty sure. Her husband probably can't bear to touch her. Perhaps she can't have children. I have tried to broach the subject. She is one of those people that like to turn the questions around:

"How are you Wendy?"

"No, how are you Stanley?"

She finally came back bearing a tray with two cups and a small plate of biscuits. I waited for her to get settled. If she had been talking to Newcombe she gave no immediate indication of it.

The silence stretched. Daniels often says she isn't afraid of silence. I think she's not afraid to take a generous salary from the Trustees whilst doing very little to justify it. Yesterday, I made the silence my friend.

I busied myself with the mundane in order to extend the silence. I took my cup, carefully selected a biscuit, tried to find a comfortable position in my chair, anything I could think of. I sipped my coffee frequently, burning my top lip in the process, and tried to wait her out. The room was deadly quiet, with only the occasional slurp and the ticking of the clock intruding upon the psycho-analytical silence. I desperately wanted to stretch it out, but finally, I could wait no longer. The opportunity to goad her became irresistible.

"I suppose you want to talk about this lunchtime."

"Not just this lunchtime Stanley, the whole day."

Why is her voice so calm?

"I was just trying to do my job."

"Stanley, it is not your job to abuse our canteen staff. It is not your job to upset our other members and it is certainly not your job to go manhandling our groundsman as he tries to relax and watch some TV."

Ha ha, her voice became sharp. How could I provoke her even further?

"Please don't be angry with me."

When I become circumspectly penitent she usually gets irritated. She knows I am putting it on, and she knows I know she knows. She screeches. It never fails.

"I am angry Stanley because this isn't on. You cannot do things like that and you know it. You do know it don't you Stanley?"

"I was just trying to do my job. Everett was breaking the rules. He should have been in the canteen with everybody else. How are we supposed to know he is relaxing unless he is in his designated relaxing place? I apologised to him didn't I?"

I kept my voice level, adding that conciliatory reasonable tone that says "Hey, what could I do?" and was incredibly amused to find her becoming shriller by the second.

"You call that an apology? You shoved the apology into his mouth and made it bleed. Poor Peter is very distressed. And Mrs Nash…well, she has had to go home with the shock. How dare you speak to her like that?"

"I was joking."

"Don't give me that claptrap, Stanley. Do not try to weasel out of this one. Stop using that bloody voice and speak properly. This is not a game."

"Why am I always the one in trouble? I only try to keep to the rules, that's part of my role here after all. And you shouldn't have said "bloody" in your professional capacity."

"Rules? You want to talk about rules? You broke the rules Stanley. You are always so keen to point it out when others break the rules so what of today? You broke the rules by manhandling Peter. You broke the rules by abusing our staff. What do you say about that Stanley? Tell me about your bloody rules."

I couldn't keep the smirk from my face, even as I spoke, actually meeting her eyes.

"They broke the rules first. I had to break the rules to make them see they were breaking the rules. Everyone breaks the rules around here. It was for the greater good. Sometimes you have to meet fire with fire, if only to make people realise that they are in the wrong. I call it the Re-assertion of Perspective. Like the short, sharp shock treatment. The whole management here could do with the same. You lot have no sense of discipline. The meetings here are a joke, no order nor structure. And you pretty much just let everyone do what they like. It's like...I suppose it's like working in a zoo, if that helps you get the picture. Just let them roam free like animals, doing whatever they want. Phillips can do whatever she wants and you never say a word to her. I try to keep the rules and I get a telling off."

"Phillips again! Why does every conversation we ever have bring us back to Debbie?"

My good mood started to crack, just a little, but I managed to keep my voice like the Reasonable Joe I was imagining myself to be. At least I think I did.

"It comes back to her because she is a bitch. All she does is swan around this place as if she owns it and you do nothing about it. You should slap her down, you should make her listen, you should make her realise that this isn't a holiday camp and that sometimes we have to get some work done. I would do it if you'd let me."

"Calm down Stanley."

I realised I was standing, glaring down at her. The small table sitting between us was rocking gently, having been knocked by my leg – no doubt as I stood violently. The coffee swirled precariously in the cups, a millimetre away from escape. My fists were clenched, my nails were biting into my palms and my face was red. Wendy stared calmly back at me, as if I were not towering above her like some barbarian aggressor.

"Please sit down Stanley, there is no need to be aggressive."

So much for my good mood. So much for appearing indifferent to Phillips.

"Stanley, please sit down. You don't want me to call Owen do you?"

I sat and waited, a deathly scowl on my face.

"Have you spoken to your parents lately Stanley?" She was calm now, and sipped gently at her drink as she looked at me. I hate her.

"Why do you keep calling me Stanley, Wendy? Do you need to say it at the end of every sentence? Is this what you have learnt from your Amateur Psychologist book? How are you Stanley? Have you spoken to your mother Stanley? Let's talk about Debbie Phillips Stanley. Please stop calling me Stanley. It does not breed a sense of intimacy and trust, it will not disarm me and make me open up. It will not build up a sense of familiarity thus allowing the free flow of ideas and emotions between us."

She stared at me, eyebrows slightly raised.

"Have you been reading up?" The hint of the "Stanley" was still hanging at the end of the question.

"I saw a documentary a week last Thursday. I thought of you."

"You still have your different days then?"

"Of course, you know I do. Let's not get into that again. I will say the same things as I always say and you will say the same things as you always say."

"Well, quite. When is your next "phone" day?"

"I'm not sure. I'm sure they are coping without me."

"I spoke to your mother yesterday and they are very keen to hear from you. They did try to ring you last week, although you didn't answer your phone. They were disappointed."

"I was busy and she isn't my mother."

"They said they were hoping you might go home for Christmas, see the family."

"Christmas is a very busy time for me. I'm not sure I'll make it."

I wondered if my father was on his way.

"Can I go now? We both know this is pointless. I'll be gone within the week. I know we are supposed to meet until three but there doesn't seem any point. Besides, I have things I need to attend to and no doubt Newcombe will want to speak to me."

"You want to go?" She looked surprised.

"Yes."

"OK, you can go. Mr Newcombe doesn't want to see you. He's spoken to your father again."

I couldn't help but ask.

"Do you know when he's coming?"

"We're not sure. When he can get himself free I suppose."

He is very busy. With all that work and fishing and the hunting. Daniels must have noticed the expression on my face.

"You can go."

CHAPTER 11

"Your father will be here soon."

"People have been saying that to me for the last twenty four hours."

"I'd like him to sit in on our chat if that's OK with you?"

No it's not okay. Why doesn't Newcombe say something? He's supposed to intervene in situations like this. That's what he gets paid for. He'd intervene for anyone else.

"How long is this going to take?"

"As long as it takes Stanley, we still have half a day to account for, and some of the night too. It's likely that Deborah Phillips sustained her injuries sometime in the night, rather than this morning I mean, before you let me know that I'm stating the obvious, so we need to account for everyone's movements."

"No-one else's interview took this long. Palmer was done in about twenty minutes, This is harassment, it's police brutality, it's false imprisonment, it's against regulations."

"Your story is just so much more interesting than anyone else's Stanley. A lot happened to you yesterday. You were quite conspicuous. Who do you normally see after Ms Daniels?"

"Everett."

"Didn't you think it might be inappropriate to see Everett after all that had passed yesterday?"

"No."

"Why not?"

"It's on my list."

"Did you go straight there?"

"No."

"What did you do?"

He knows the answer already, so why does he bother asking.

"I went to my room. I didn't do anything, before you ask. There was some time before I was due to see Everett so I went to my room."

I had thirty three minutes before I was due to see Everett. In fact, I would have to leave a few minutes early in order to find him so it was even less. He could be anywhere on the grounds. He doesn't keep to a timetable, only the timetable of nature or some claptrap like that. Palmer came up with that one when he compared Everett to Tarzan or David Attenborough or someone. In fact, I think he actually said Richard Attenborough, the famous thespian, and I had to correct him. He's the father of David I think. Palmer called me an anally retentive sphincter. I have no idea where he learnt those words.

66

Everett does have one timetable that I can always use. For some reason, he is absolutely insistent on having a cup of tea at regular established intervals. Or coffee. I generally respect a man with a system. I myself allow myself only 5 cups of coffee per day, but I am not too prescriptive as to when I take them. Everett's insistence as to timings is particularly rigid. At eight thirty, with breakfast, he will have a coffee. At 10.45, it will again be coffee. Lunchtime, it will be tea. At 3.15 in the afternoon he will have tea again. After dinner he will have a coffee. It really is quite unyielding. He will refuse to work unless he has taken his coffee break. Not that the break amounts to much because he gulps the tea down so quickly. He must burn his mouth.

I had tried to make him change his morning coffee break to coincide with the House coffee break, but he refused. I raised it with Newcombe. He did nothing. I wrote to the Trustees but they didn't even send me a reply. Therefore Everett has two extra breaks throughout the day. He stops for a leisurely two minute coffee break whilst everyone else is working hard. I find it astonishingly unfair.

The canteen have a little flask prepared for him every breakfast and every lunchtime, prepared by Nash or whichever harridan of hell that happens to be on the counter at the time.

I love the days when they make a mistake. You ought to see his face when he gulps down a cup of coffee in the afternoon, when the canteen should have given him tea. It ruins his whole day. He can barely function. I'm sure he was on the verge of swearing last time. It is usually the highlight of my inspection and I am often praying for it to happen. I pray for a new girl to join the canteen staff so she can make the seemingly innocuous mistake. I'd love to see Everrett get angry again. Newcombe backed him up – as he always does – and arranged for someone to buy Everett a new flask.

I sat at my desk and stared at the wardrobe. Today was to be the day after all. No backing out now. My actions with Everett and Nash – and Phillips for that matter – had forced my hand. I wanted to look at the book – to remind myself of the intricacies of the Plan. I needed to make sure I was prepared. And yet I could not. I never look at it during the day – it is against the rules I have set myself. I will only open the book at night, it is safer that way. You never knew when someone might just turn up and knock on your door. Abdul used to walk in at all hours, never once knocking. So I always wait until night time. I carefully creep out of bed, check the corridor and then remove the two draws at the front of my wardrobe. I generally devour the book for an hour, savouring it and adding to it, no more though, despite the burning desire to continue. All the time I am paranoid that someone will see my torchlight. Someone occasionally patrols the corridors. They don't patrol every night, but still,

I need to be careful. It is everything to me, that book, it has been my reason to be for the last eighteen months. But it could also prove to be my undoing. If anyone were to find it, or if anyone were to barge into my room, whilst the book was in my hand, wardrobe draws strewn across the floor, that would be it for me. Abdul did it once, although he didn't realise what I was doing. He told Newcombe I had been masturbating. I made sure Abdul left Pottergate soon after.

I knew the Plan was ready– it contained all the necessary ingredients. But would I be ready? Could I do what needed to be done? That was the real question.

I had been putting it off for the last six months, waiting for the right moment and using the time to refine the Plan. Throughout that six months the nagging feeling within me had grown, the fear that it might all come to naught. The events of the day had forced my hand. Thankfully.

I desperately wanted to get the book out but I dared not. I forced myself to suppress the desire. I am good at that. So, for twenty nine minutes, I stared at the wardrobe, longing to unlock it but being disciplined enough not to.

CHAPTER 12

"I didn't do anything. I can honestly tell you that I didn't do anything all the time I was in my room."

"So you just waited for three o clock to come around?"

"I left my room at four minutes to three. Everett is sometimes hard to find."

"You told Ms Daniels that you had some business to attend to."

"That was just an excuse."

"A lie?"

"No, an excuse. Don't put words into my mouth. It is unprofessional. You know as well as I that there is a clear distinction between an excuse and a lie. If I had meant to say the word "lie" I would have used it."

The little detective smiles, seemingly amused. He is always smiling. I am getting tired of this. He thinks he is superior. He thinks he is playing a game with me, taking his time until he reaches the inevitable result – his victory. I hate the little detective, with his Scottish accent – why doesn't he go back to his own country – and his shaven head. I want to smash his little face into the hard wood of Newcombe's desk. I want to place my hands around his scrawny neck and squeeze as I look into his bulging eyes and see the fear as it develops. I want him to know that he has no power over me. I want him to know that I can beat him. My shoulders tense, anger straining to burst forth.

He is beating me and I can't stand it.

"Did you find Everett?"

"No." I say with clenched teeth. Anger racks through me in waves. I want to hurt him, but I can't.

Everett was nowhere to be found. I searched through the entire grounds but could find him nowhere. It was like he was hiding from me. I suppose I could understand that, after all, I had been a little mean to him throughout the day. But, his work should have been paramount. I had been mean to him in the past and he had just carried on as normal, pottering around the grounds as if nothing had happened. It was strange.

It got stranger still when I headed for the patio, eager to intercept Everett at his scheduled tea break. I had to be there at exactly 3.15 because Everett would gulp the tea down in less than three swigs. It often took longer for him to pour it than to drink it. Perhaps he had been a builder in his previous life, I have heard that they did that kind of thing. Builders' tea, that's what they call it when they wolf it down. As well as overcharging you for work. They all do that.

I paced up and down on the patio and waited for 3.15 to come. The flask was already on one of the tables, prepared and delivered by one of the canteen staff. I waited, rather impatiently, for 3.15 to finally arrive. It did, but Everett didn't. I watched the fifteenth minutes tick away on my wristwatch. The surprise that rippled through me stopped my pacing. Creatures of habit do not change their routines lightly. Perhaps Everett was dead or had been unavoidably delayed. No, he was hiding from me.

I sensed an opportunity.

Everett had had a strange day, he probably wasn't emotionally stable. I could use this. People could see how he had been visibly tipped over the edge. Using him as a suspect wasn't within the Plan – his character was too stable – but why waste an opportunity to spread suspicion a little further?

I weighed up the risks. What if Everett arrived back? What if he was running a few minutes late? What if I was caught? What about the Plan? What about my father? What about her?

I hurried to his tool shed. It wasn't strictly his tool shed, it was Pottergate's tool shed, but everyone referred to it as belonging to Everett. He is the only one who uses it after all. Shaw goes in there occasionally when Palmer can be persuaded to do his job for a change, but other than that it's pretty much Everett's domain.

He wasn't there either. I searched the entire hut just in case, searching in places he could never have fitted, but he wasn't there. I leaned against a worktop and wondered what to do. Could it be so convenient? I wondered if Everett was with Newcombe at that moment, getting me into further trouble. It didn't matter. I didn't have to worry about that anymore. The only thing I needed to worry about was getting caught and that wouldn't happen. The Plan wasn't perfect but it was perfect enough.

Everett kept a box of latex gloves in the hut. He would wear them for particularly difficult tasks such as cleaning out the drains. He didn't like getting his hands dirty, a strange characteristic for a handyman. I took a pair for later and slipped a pair on while I searched through the hut.

I needed a knife and I found one. It was an old bread knife, nestled inside one of the first drawers I opened. It was pretty blunt, but that would serve my purposes nicely. In fact, after theorising about the difficulties of getting a knife in my planning, it turned out to be surprisingly easy – the shed was full of knives and screwdrivers, any number of deadly weapons. I could have taken any number of Stanley knives – I saw the beautiful irony in that – but decided against it. It could be interpreted as a clue.

The bread knife was long. I had to slip it down the inside of my trousers, resting gently against my thigh. I know what the forensics experts can do these days so I wrapped the knife in a plastic bag before sliding it down my trousers. It made a slight bulge and my leg rustled when I walked but it would have to do. I could hold my clipboard beside my leg and hide the bulge. The rustle would give me away though. I would have to be lucky. Fortune favours the brave.

With the evidence procured and the clue laid I left the tool shed and headed back to the big house. The garden was thankfully clear, the patio still empty. The house was busier, but I managed to avoid everyone, sliding through the corridors and up to my room. It was 3.27 as I re-entered my room for the second time that day, a most unusual occurrence. I hastily pushed the knife and bag under my bed, wedging the knife in amongst the wooden slats that held the mattress.

I was surprisingly calm.

I wanted to check and recheck that the knife wouldn't fall down but I didn't have time. I had to get to Palmer.

CHAPTER 13

"**D**o you know where he was?"

"No."

"He was in his room."

"Oh."

"Are you seeing any kind of link developing? Daryl Barnes was taken to his room after a session with you. Yvonne Nash had to go home after lunchtime yesterday and Peter Everett blocked himself in his room all of yesterday afternoon. All linked to you, Stanley. And yet you keep feeding me this absolute crap that everything you did yesterday was reasonable and proper. I don't know what to believe about the things you're telling me. I get this strange feeling that you are missing things out. Perhaps you are telling me the facts. You're leaving your thoughts and feelings out. You're not telling me the context. That can give a false picture you know Stanley. I just get the feeling that you are playing with me Stan, you are giving me the broad brush strokes and not much else."

"I am telling you the truth."

"I hope so Stanley. How was Palmer?"

"You seem to know my movements better than I do."

"Perhaps I do."

I was a minute late, I needed an excuse.

"Ah, Stanley me old mate, how are you? Come for a good old chat? What shall we talk about today? Girls? I knew a girl once who was so posh, she didn't say she was coming, she used to say she was arriving."

I have heard that joke exactly seventy eight times. I decided to keep count after I'd heard it five times. When he gets to a hundred I'm going to report him to the Trustees for sexual discrimination. We'll see what Newcombe thinks about that.

"Have you seen any blacks lately? Have I ever told you that joke about the Queen and the black man's willy?"

"Yes Palmer you have. Please don't tell me again. I will have to report you to Newcombe again. There is no place in this establishment for racism, sexism, ageism…"

"…jism…"

"…or anything of that sort. Please don't interrupt me again."

Shaw was there, sitting quietly. He smiled briefly at me but didn't say anything. I wondered if he took a furtive glance at his watch. I needed to explain my lateness, what had Newcombe mentioned this morning in briefing?

"Now, I understand that you are supposed to be fixing a shelf in the laundry room." *Time to take a risk, fortune favours the brave.* "I have been to the laundry room and you are not there: you are here. I noticed that the shelf in the laundry room is still hanging off one hinge or whatever you call them…"

"…bracket…"

Neither Shaw nor Palmer balked at my lie. I had got away with it.

"…yes, bracket. Can I ask why you haven't done the work? Newcombe will be very interested to know."

"We can't do it. Haven't got the tools. Have to get contractors in. Shame, terrible shame. I've spoken to Newcombe and he says we have to get the contractors in. That's what he said, he said it to me and Owen heard him."

Owen Shaw is Palmer's mate. He rarely leaves his side. He is a great big hulk of a man with blonde hair and blue-ish eyes. He is the very image of a Nazi, albeit not in character. Shaw, with his rather gentle ways, I can almost tolerate. Almost. His lack of work ethic does irritate me somewhat. They were sitting opposite each other, playing cards of all things. Palmer probably noted my upraised eyebrow.

"Newcombe said we could pass the day as we liked. He said that we have to get the contractors in so there was nothing we could do. We were going to look at the drains but I think it's going to rain and Newcombe thought it best if we wait until a better day is forecast. It never rains but it pours eh Stan? Do you want to play? You've got a good poker face I tell you. You've either been hit with a poker or you've got one stuck up your arse."

Palmer shot a cheeky grin at Shaw, seeking approval for his latest joke. Shaw smiled blandly and Palmer beamed. Shaw doesn't really like me, I can tell, despite my being fairly indifferent to his existence. He was personally invested in the Abdul situation and he has not been able to forget it.

"I shall be writing that down. Insults of that nature are not acceptable. Newcombe will be hearing about that."

"Oh he won't worry. I heard he thrust a poker up your arse this morning anyway for what you did to Plastic Pete. Why did you have to do that anyway? You should just relax a bit. Come on, come and play cards."

I glared at Palmer and sat down in a chair in the corner of the room. Palmer looked at me expectantly until he realised that I would not play. He shrugged his shoulders and carried on.

He kept shouting "snap" and various intervals and throwing his hand down on the pile of cards in the middle, even though they were playing Gin Rummy or whatever it's called. Shaw kept smiling blandly, humouring him. I didn't note that down although I was tempted. Idiot.

CHAPTER 14

"Palmer was fine. I shall give you the intimate details if you require. As I entered the room, Palmer was sitting with his back to the door, opposite Owen Shaw. They were playing cards on the table between them. Palmer was wearing a grey v-neck, long sleeved t-shirt. He had the sleeves rolled up. His face was its usual red blotchy colour, his nose the same bulbous, veiny monstrosity that it usually is. His hair, as always, was close cropped and receding. He turned as I entered the room, turning his upper body to an angle of..."

"That's enough Stanley..." Newcombe's voice cuts into my diatribe, bringing a smile to my lips.

The little detective stares at me, matching my smile.

"A remarkable memory for detail."

"How can you tell if any of that is true? I could have made it up."

That's it, be cheeky, be cocky, be confident. Remember the training, remember Thomas.

The little detective doesn't answer the question: "Mr Newcombe, perhaps you could order us some coffee. Stanley must be thirsty, and I certainly am. Would you like some coffee Stanley?"

I look at my watch, it is well past 4 o clock. Well past my usual coffee drinking time. I have a coffee every three hours – not on the dot though, that would be crazy. It would be better to say that I restrict myself to no more than a coffee in every three hour period of the day. Caffeine is bad for you. Reports differ but it is generally accepted that any more than six cups of coffee or tea per day is bad for you. Some reports actually say that two cups of coffee is the ideal, but that would be impossible – I like coffee too much. I suspect that I am addicted to the caffeine but I quite like the fact, it gives me an edge, it makes me interesting. A small Romanian woman who was here for a few months many years ago used to call me the "Coffee Man." I liked it. I didn't like her.

My first cup comes at breakfast, the next at morning break, the next at lunchtime. My fourth comes at 4 o clock when I sit down to write my daily report. The final drink of the day comes sometime after dinner, no later than half past seven. Otherwise it keeps me awake and I find myself thinking about her, and sometimes I can't control myself and I feel ashamed for days afterwards.

"I'll arrange it," Newcombe says as he slips out of the door.

The little detective resumes his seat, leans back into the lush, leather chair and pulls his mobile from his pocket. He writes a text message, not looking at me once. Not even a glance.

I watch him do it, knowing the little detective is trying to play games with me, trying to unnerve me. I wish I had something with me, like my clipboard, anything that would allow me a distraction. Unfortunately I don't, so I watch the detective as he plays with his phone, each tap on the keypad eliciting a beep. Otherwise the room is silent, punctuated only by the series of short but infuriating beeps, like Morse code. The beeping starts to irritate me, and I feel the anger rising within me again. Why doesn't he turn the volume off? It must drive him mad. Unless he's turned the volume on just to irritate me. I'll bet he does this all the time – to antagonise his victims.

I can't give in to it. I close my eyes and try to breathe, concentrating on that, instead of the continual bleeping. My hand starts to cramp as I realise it is clenched. It is a struggle to force my fingers away from my palm.

Eventually, after what seems like hours, Newcombe arrives bringing a tray of drinks. I open my eyes as I hear the door opening. I realise that the beeping has stopped. Indeed, the little detective is sitting forward in his chair, no sign of the phone, looking at me. Newcombe places the tray on the table.

"This is tea." I state the obvious.

"Oh, I am sorry," Newcombe says as he looks at the little detective – not me.

"Not a problem Mr Newcombe, I like tea."

I wonder whether this has been an elaborate ploy to irritate me further. He wants me to lose my cool so he can trap me. I decide to let it go. I will drink the tea, just to spite him. I take a cup from Newcombe's proffered hand. He serves me after he has dealt with the little detective although before himself. This is Newcombe trying to show off his Christian servitude. I despise him.

"When is Stanley's father due to arrive?" the little detective asks.

"Another hour or so, I should think."

"Fine, well, we might as well continue," the little detective says as he sips his tea, "let's have a look at your report Stanley."

I glare at Newcombe.

"Was anything wrong yesterday Stan?"

Stan, no-one calls me Stan. The little detective has done this on a number of occasions now. My "mother" made the mistake of calling me Stan once. She doesn't do it any more.

"No, I was fine. I keep telling you."

"I know you keep telling me but when I look at yesterday's report – and then I compare it against the reports for the last few years…I don't know, there is just something about them. They lack focus, they seem distracted, there isn't the usual scathing detail."

I smile.

"I was in a good mood yesterday and most people were behaving themselves. Besides, it was Friday and Newcombe always tells me I should be more lenient on Fridays. I don't understand why, but he seems to think it's important, so I do."

"OK fine. You were in a good mood. How would you explain what you did to Everett? No, don't answer that, it's not important now. You were in a good mood. Maybe I'm misinterpreting the report then?"

"Yes you are."

"And maybe your concentration was elsewhere. Ever write anything else Stanley?"

The book.

I carefully removed the drawers to the wardrobe after checking the hallway to see that it was clear. My heart was beating – how do they say – ten to the dozen. I am usually nervous opening the book, but yesterday it was unbearable.

The clock in my room had only just clicked over to 21.00. I had watched the numbers change for the last few minutes, desperate for time to go quicker. The day had passed so slowly, every minute grinding slowly around me, testing my patience and my murderous desire.

After I had finished with Palmer, a time which couldn't come quickly enough quite frankly, I had headed back to the meeting room to finish my report. The inspection of Palmer had proceeded in the same way as it always does – with his constant attempts at joviality – usually concerning penises, breasts, buttocks and the like. I ignored him and made my report as best I could before making my escape.

I was watching the clock then as I prepared my report. I am usually so engrossed in my job that I am still writing when Newcombe taps me on the shoulder and reminds me about our daily meeting – usually scheduled for 4.45pm. Just a few minutes to go through my observations before he heads home and I clock off. I often give him a smile which is returned. We share our best times together in those moments. Yesterday, there was no shared smile and my report was less than half its usual length. I didn't smile, but then neither did he.

I followed Newcombe to his office where he told me to sit down. Told me. He usually asks and I usually accept, but yesterday he told me in no uncertain terms that I would be sitting down, and I did. I sat meekly, flimsy report in hand, like some pathetic, impotent individual.

He didn't say much. He sat hunched over his great, expensive table, silver cufflinks catching in the artificial light. His eyes locked onto mine. I was able to return his gaze. Just.

"I am very disappointed in you Stanley."

Your disappointment means nothing to me Mr Newcombe.

"Your actions today have been entirely unacceptable."

They are only unacceptable to you because you are weak, unable to embrace justice and fairness.

"I have spoken to your father and we have decided to defer action until next week. Use the weekend to gain some perspective."

He decided and you agreed – you are pathetic.

"Do not think that your behaviour will be forgotten over the weekend. We will pick this up again on Monday."

After what happens tonight, you won't be interested in my small misdemeanours. Your career will be stained. Enjoy your weekend.

"I don't want to discuss your report. I don't think you are in a position to be able to comment on other people's behaviour. It would be hypocritical. Just leave it on my desk. Have a good weekend Stanley, think upon your actions. I will."

Screw you Newcombe.

As is entirely predictable on a Friday, the canteen was serving fish. No-one has yet offered me a satisfactory explanation as to why we eat fish every single Friday. Nash says it's something to do with fishermen returning to port on Fridays. Newcombe suggested it might have something to do with the feeding of the five thousand but I think he was joking. Barnes said it had something to do with Muslims. Daniels said it might have something to do with Elizabeth the First or some other Monarch wanting to boost the fishing industry. Palmer said it was something to do with a female conspiracy involving an increase in vaginal odours towards the end of the week. I am not sure that any of them are true, especially not Palmer's.

I ate my fish and chips alone. No-one seemed to want to sit with me. Barnes was in his room, as was Everett. Naylor was quiet, Phillips picked at her food and disappeared after only a few minutes – she hardly ever eats anything on an evening. Palmer shouted a few things at me across the dining area but I didn't respond.

I thought about the Plan as I chewed methodically through my food. I am not silly enough to make myself chew a mouthful of food a particular number of times, but I am conscious to masticate properly. I say conscious, but actually it's rather unconscious. I can think freely during this time. I considered my failings of the day. I had done many of the things I had told myself not to do. The Plan was only as good as its execution. But, on the plus side, I had managed to upset Barnes and Everett to such a degree that they had to go to their rooms. That could work in my favour. Cooped up in their rooms, distressed and upset. Perhaps upset enough to lash out, to commit murder? I could use this, I could cast suspicion on them both. Perfect.

Dinner finished and I filed into the TV room. Again, it was sparsely populated. I chose a documentary channel at random and settled down to look within myself. For over two hours I was undisturbed as I gave the impression of being interesting in huddling penguins.

Phillips was in the room and I kept the corner of my eye on her. She played with her hair and rubbed her exposed legs as I tried to concentrate.

I yearned for nine o clock to come.

CHAPTER 15

"**N**o Detective, I rarely write anything else, perhaps the occasional letter home."

The little detective gives me a knowing look and shakes his head, almost imperceptibly. He changes the subject.

"I just can't quite reconcile the discrepancies between your account of yesterday and everything else I've been told. Let me ask you again Stan, was something wrong yesterday? Anything to upset you?"

"There wasn't anything wrong. I did everything I normally do. I'm sorry if my report wasn't detailed enough for you, detective. I'm sure it was detailed enough for Mr Newcombe. He didn't mention anything of note when I met with him to discuss the report at the end of the day."

"We didn't really discuss the report though Stanley did we? In fact, I didn't even look at it. I told you that. We had other important things to discuss – like your behaviour yesterday."

"My behaviour was fine. It was entirely consistent."

"Consistent with what?" asks the little detective.

"With my previous behaviour."

Damn. The words are out of my mouth before I can stop them. What a fool. Do I want to be caught?

"What a strange turn of phrase. Why would you use the word "consistent" when referring to your own behaviour?"

The little detective stands and moves around the table to me. He stares at me intently. I cannot answer, I am struggling for a plausible excuse. I keep smiling though.

"Consistency. That makes me think – perhaps you were consciously trying to be consistent, to be as normal as possible – to avoid attracting unnecessary attention. Is that what you were trying to do Stanley? If so, you weren't doing a very good job. You stuck out like a sore thumb. I suppose the question is why."

My smile slides away. Within an instant he has changed the tempo, increased the intensity. He is moving into areas that I had planned to keep away from. My training is counting for nothing. I am weak. I am useless. The Plan is worse than useless. I deserve to be caught.

"Do you like Magnum P.I. Stan?"

He has me.

The blu-tack holding the book upright against the back of the wardrobe came away easily, without a sound. I cradled it gently in my hands and retired to my desk. I caught a sight of my face in the mirror. I looked guilty. Strange that, I hadn't done anything but such was my determined intent that I could feel the guilt seeping into me. And the satisfaction. Soon the bitch would be dead.

I started at the front cover and devoured every thought and consideration built up over eighteen long months.

How to do it? How to do it? I had considered every conceivable possibility.

Should I make her swallow plastic bags full of cocaine and punch her in the stomach until the bags burst? I would have to punch her pretty hard. Just like they did to Lieutenant Dan Cook, one of Magnum's closest friends, when they lured him down an alley by pretending to be from headquarters. Would that leave a mark? Where would I get the cocaine from? Could I get that in the local town? Could I find some shifty looking character in the local pubs and clubs? That was only the pilot episode. Should I club her over the head and drown her as occurred in Episode 2, Series 2, "Dead Man's Calling"? Should I run her down in a car when she goes out for a jog like Mr Eto, the Al Capone of Hawaii, did to Carol Ann Little, his mistress? But Phillips doesn't jog, as evidenced by her fat, flabby thighs. And I can't drive. My father isn't as sympathetic as the dead father that we never see in the film "Rainman." I am not Dustin Hoffman, although Palmer kept laughing at me once he'd seen that film. Should I kill her with one punch like the martial artist in episode 1, series 1 who kills just after blinking? Should I make it look like suicide, like in Series 2, Episode 3 where Henry Ellison makes it look as if Sarah Clifford has driven off a cliff in her car? When Magnum asks the dead woman's niece why Sarah Clifford was killed, she says: "Because a man loves me and I don't love him, therefore he will destroy me."

Quite apt in a perverse sort of way.

So many ideas from a family show. My father and "mother" were delighted I'd fallen in love with Magnum P.I. They think it's good clean fun, but they obviously haven't seen into the dark heart of the show. My mother doesn't like the addition of the prefix "step," despite being my father's third wife. She won't last, I'm certain of it.

Could I somehow lock her into a steel container in the hot midday sun so that she dies of dehydration? No, that would take too long and the British climate is not really appropriate. That entire episode was preposterous. Series 1, episode 2, "Thank Heaven for Little Girls and Big Ones Too." A bunch of little girls want to steal and return a rare painting and they manage to con both Magnum and Higgins. Simply preposterous.

Should I kill her with a machine gun? Should I put a bomb in her car?

Should I shoot her in the face with a shotgun? One of my favourites. The shot from the gun obscures her face entirely. What a fitting end that would be for Phillips – her vanity wiped clean away.

Should I deprive her of her vital medication so that it would look like natural causes? Should I jab her through the heart with a scalpel?

I had received the first series almost three years ago. I don't know why they got it for me, I think they thought I'd like it. I did, a little, but it wasn't until *she* arrived that I started to immerse myself in it. My parents were amazed when I rang them to ask for the second series the following year. I told them I enjoyed the comic tales and Magnum and TC and Rick, friends from Vietnam who now live in Hawaii. I think they were pleased.

The second series was fertile too.

It started to reveal the most common weapons. Knives and guns. Stabbings and shootings. Should I kill her in a knife fight? Make it look like self-defence? Should I force her to take a drugs overdose? If only I could see her personal file I might be able to see if she has a drug dependency problem. Should I set fire to her room? How about I just strangle her? That last one has a strange appeal and I have experience of it. Ensign Healey, who had appeared in the pilot episode of Magnum PI as a good guy, re-appears in Series 2, episode 8 and strangles a girl on the beach. He has sex with her as well, although I'm not sure if he does that before or after she's dead. Of course, I wouldn't engage in the sexual intercourse, but the thought of having my slim fingers around her delicate neck does have a certain appeal. Magnum is thrown off the scent too by the previous good nature of Ensign Healey. *That* would be my tactic. My character is generally without blemish. Most people would agree that I was in the right on most occasions when trouble has come my way. That would add real credence to my tales of innocence.

Like Thomas would say, "*What me?*"

I pored through the pages, savouring each plot, soaking up the twisted machinations that had dominated my life for the last two years. I would have to destroy the book the next day, I knew that. It would be the last time that I held it. Tomorrow, I thought, it would be all done. My greatest act.

Before I knew it, 10 o'clock had come and my usual bedtime had passed. I dared not stay up any longer. There was every chance that someone would walk past my door, spotting the telltale light seeping out from under my door. I therefore replaced the book with reluctance. I almost kissed it.

I made my preparations for bed and waited.

CHAPTER 16

"**I** do like Magnum P.I."

"So do I. Excellent show. I used to watch it a lot when I was a kid. Did you watch any last night?"

He knows. He knows everything.

"No."

"What did you watch?"

"Some nature programme or other," I say quietly. "Penguins I seem to recall."

"Any good?"

"Informative, yet entertaining."

"Any killing in it?"

"There is always death in the natural world. Survival of the fittest. Natural selection. It cannot be avoided." The words don't have my usual bite.

"Death. You seem to be fascinated with it. Anyway, I think we've played around for long enough Stanley. What did you do after your "documentary" session?"

"I went back to my room."

"And did what?"

"Read my book."

"Which book?"

"The New Guide to Golf."

"You don't play golf – why would you read that?"

"I may not actually play golf but that is not to say I'm not interested in the theory of it. I'm building up to actually hitting a ball."

"Implausible," the little detective snaps. "That's a red herring. Tell me what you really did."

"I read my book."

"You did not." The little detective starts to raise his voice. "What did you do?"

"I read my book and went to sleep."

"You didn't go to see Deborah Phillips?"

"No."

"You didn't call in on Daryl Barnes?"

"No."

"You didn't wake Patrick Palmer by banging on his door?"

"Of course not."

Just after ten o clock, I readied myself for bed, following studiously my usual routine. I lay still on my bed, clothed but covered to the chin by my duvet. It was extremely hot, but I dared not lower the covers. What if someone were to enter? What if someone to pop in for a chat? I would be undone. I listened tensely to the sound of activity around the building as it gradually slowed and eventually disappeared into the sleep that comes over a place as well as people at night time. By eleven fifteen it was quiet, but I dared not move. Appearances can be deceptive.

At 11.30, I slowly climbed out of bed, releasing a wave of hot air from under my duvet as I did so. The sudden loss of heat from about my body made me feel monetarily faint. I put my hand out to steady myself. I noticed that my hand was trembling. It must be the heat, I thought to myself, causing dehydration which results in some small degree of shaking.

After a moment it passed and I slipped quietly out of my room. I made my way quietly through the empty corridors of Pottergate until I reached Barnes' door. I knocked gently. There was no response. I knocked louder. The noise sounded excessively loud in my ears, reverberating around the empty corridors. Nothing. I steeled myself to knock again when I heard movement from beyond the door. After a moment or two, Barnes opened the door and stuck his sleepy head into the corridor.

"Stanley?"

His voice was quiet and concerned and not a little confused. I could see a suggestion of soiled, droopy pyjamas through the crack in the door. He looked even more pathetic than usual but I felt no compunction in doing what I had to do – to effect the Plan.

"Good evening Barnes. I'm sorry to disturb your sleep. I realise it's late."

"What time is it?"

"Approaching midnight."

"What are you doing here?"

I realised that he was speaking almost like a normal person – using normal length sentences and getting straight to the point. His fatigue had deprived his mouth of its usual verbal flatulence.

"This is rather awkward. I'm not entirely sure how to phrase what I am about to say..."

"Yes?"

"This evening, in the television room, I was watching a documentary about penguins. Phillips was the only person in the room. There was a segment of the programme where two penguins were seen to mate quite tenderly. Penguins tend to mate for life. Phillips turned to me and said, 'I wonder if Daryl Barnes makes love in such a fashion.' I didn't reply of course."

Barnes was dumbstruck, just as I expected him to be. He thinks only with his penis and his testicles. It doesn't matter how fantastical or nonsensical the story is, Barnes' penis will not pass up an opportunity.

"She said that?"

"She was rubbing her fat legs at the time."

Barnes almost began to salivate and I wanted to slap him as a punishment for his gullible stupidity.

"What should I do?"

"I think she wants to see you. Tonight. I cannot be certain but the way she said what she said suggested, to me at least, that she would be prepared to have sexual intercourse with you on the premises in the next few hours."

"I'll go straight round. I'll go to her room. I'll..."

"Wait Barnes. Not yet. Give it fifteen minutes or so. Play it cool. Find her at midnight. I'm sure there's something romantic about that. I'm sure that's what she'll want."

Barnes nodded vigorously, like some sort of automated toy.

"Barnes, forgive me if I go too far here but..."

"Yes?"

"I hear she likes it rough. She likes to be dominated. She likes to play hard to get. Do you understand me?"

"Oh I do Stanley, I do. I know exactly what you mean. Oh yes, indeed. I think I know where you're coming from. I can..."

"Barnes!" I interrupted him. "Go freshen up."

Barnes ducked inside his room without a further word and I sighed with relief. Barnes would incriminate himself without a second thought. If Phillips could demean herself to allow that flaccid excuse of a man to defile her then Barnes would be bang-to-rights, as they say. If not...well, the Plan accounted for that eventuality.

I headed to the next corridor and found the door to Palmer's room. I stood outside for a moment or two, trying to estimate just how long Barnes could wait before the burning lust within him made him head for Phillips' door. Not long, I thought. After a moment or two, I pounded on Palmer's door loudly and then quickly snuck into a store cupboard across the corridor. I nestled in beside a vacuum cleaner and waited.

A moment or two passed before Palmer groggily made his way into the corridor. He looked about in a bemused fashion before turning to re-enter his room. Fortunately, he heard footsteps from around the corner and waited.

Barnes hurried into view a second or two later, hastily doing up a creased shirt.

"Who are you, the midnight rambler?" Palmer asked as Barnes hurried past him.

"Sorry Patrick, can't stop, can't stop, I've got business to attend to. Sorry."

Barnes hurried past without stopping. Palmer, for once, couldn't think of anything to say. He watched Barnes disappear around the next corner and turned back to his room.

I waited until the opportune moment and quickly let myself out of the store cupboard and bounded across the corridor. I managed to get my foot in Palmer's door just before he could close it. At the last moment I realised that I should –to maintain plausibility – have been wearing my pyjamas. I hoped Palmer wouldn't notice.

Palmer was surprised again and said: "Stanley, who are you, the midnight rambler?"

I ignored his recycled comment.

"What's all this noise? It's two o clock in the morning. I'm trying to sleep and all I can hear is you bashing and banging around."

Palmer smiled and the reference to the time seemed to pass him by. Hopefully, he wouldn't think to check. I knew he couldn't resist the lure of my loaded words.

"I haven't been banging anyone. Chance would be a fine thing. Might do a bit of bashing if you leave me alone. Goodnight dickhead."

I moved my foot as Palmer slammed the door.

Phase 2 complete, I headed back to my room.

CHAPTER 17

"Where were you between the hours of eleven and twelve last night?" the little detective asks. No, demands. He is "turning up the heat" as they say in criminal circles.

"Asleep."

"And between the hours of two and four this morning."

"Also asleep."

I returned to my room, climbed back under the covers and wondered what Barnes would be doing downstairs. The thought of what it could be both tantalised and repulsed me and, with a supreme effort of will, I managed to remove my mind from the thought of his clammy little hands trying to leech their way onto Phillips' rounded hip.

I considered the Plan. Reciting it over and over again to keep my mind occupied.

At exactly two o clock I would leave my room and head to the store room at the back end of the building. It would be open, Barnes always leaves it open despite numerous instructions to the contrary. This is where the cleaning products are kept. Barnes always loiters there at the end of the day, hoping to get the cleaning lady alone, just like before. He hasn't realised that she has been warned. He always leaves it open after doing whatever it is that he does in there when he realises that she isn't coming. Maybe he enjoys the thought of being caught. There I would find some special bleach that is used on the pine flooring in one of the offices. After slipping on some latex gloves I would take it and make my way across the ground floor to where she has her room. I had calculated that this short trip would take exactly twenty three minutes as I negotiated the noisy floors and the creaky stairs in a pre-ordained route. I would slide into the room, banking on the fact that she never locked her door either, despite Barnes' earlier intrusion, smother her quickly with the bleach on a clean white cloth that I had stolen from the canteen a few days before until she became groggy and quiet. Then I would quickly, although not so quickly as to not fully appreciate the moment, slide the knife into her heart until she was dead. This should take not more than four minutes, perhaps four and a half if her rib cage should prove tougher than expected. The knife –Everett's knife - I would leave sticking out of her chest. The bleach would be hidden in one of the draws of Newcombe's desk.

By three o clock I would be tucked up in bed, ready to sleep like a baby.

CHAPTER 18

"Let me ask you one more time Stanley. And please, do think very carefully about whether you wish to lie to me. It will not go well for you if you do." He pauses for dramatic effect. Picking up tips from Newcombe I see. "Did you visit Deborah Phillips at around 2 o clock last night?"

"No."

"Did you have sex with her and then kill her?"

"I thought you said she wasn't dead."

"Try to kill her…"

"No."

My stonewalling tactics obviously frustrate him. He starts to pace the room. I am getting the better of him finally. One key tenet of the Plan is having mental and intellectual superiority over the investigating officer.

"Sometimes I wonder about you Stanley. Did you just wake up this morning and decide to be as difficult as possible or are you always like this? All I want is the truth. I just want to find out what happened to Deborah Phillips. And I know you know. Did you try to kill her?"

"No."

He sits down again and abruptly changes tack.

"Tell me about your relationship with Deborah Phillips."

"I don't have a relationship with Deborah Phillips."

"I have evidence that says that you did."

They couldn't have done the tests that quickly. They hadn't even tested me. This must be a bluff used on all the men.

"What evidence? Forensic?"

"Anecdotal mainly, for the moment, although forensics are working on their side of things as we speak. Everyone I have spoken to today tells me that you have been obsessed with Deborah Phillips for the last two years. In fact, ever since she arrived here."

"That's ridiculous."

"Is it? I'm not so sure about that Stanley. Even your personnel file mentions it."

I spin to face Newcombe, relieved to be able to break away from the gaze of the all knowing, smug faced little detective. I hate him. I am furious. "You showed him my personnel file? That is against the rules. It is a breach of data protection. It's a breach of confidentiality. I'll report you to the trustees. It is a breach of the employer – employee relationship. I'll take you to the employment tribunal."

To my great irritation, neither Newcombe nor the little detective respond. Newcombe shares a glance with the little detective and then meets my stare. He knows I will drop my eyes within a few seconds, and I do.

The little detective speaks.

"Do you remember Magnum series one, episode six? The one where that movie agent kills his actress girlfriend with a shotgun but makes it looks like suicide?"

I have to return my attention to the little detective.

"Why are we back on Magnum P.I? I thought this was a police investigation, not a movie review."

"Just humour me please Stan, do you remember it?"

"Yes I remember it. He doesn't kill his actress girlfriend, he kills another woman to make it look like his actress girlfriend is dead. He shoots the other woman in the face with a shotgun so that it's impossible to make out her face. Why?"

"Oh, no reason. It just made me think of it, you know, the events of yesterday. It's all very strange isn't it? Tell me again about your relationship with Deborah."

"I don't have a relationship with Phillips. And I resent the way you have linked the discussion of suicide with my so-called relationship with Phillips. I will tell you again, for the sake of clarity and your police report, I do not have a relationship with Deborah Phillips. I don't much like her but that's about it."

"You don't like her much?"

"Not much, no."

"And that's all is it? You were just indifferent. Bordering on dislike. You didn't like her much. No strong feelings either way then?" The little detective shrugs his shoulders and throws up his hands as he speaks, attempting to convey the nonchalance in his words.

"No not really."

The little detective stands up sharply and glares at me across the table. His voice though, is calm.

"You see Stanley, everything I have heard and everything I have read over the last few hours suggests otherwise. I have heard the same word over and over again: "obsession." Now, the word obsession does not allow for indifferent feelings, it is an extreme. You either loved her or hated her, or perhaps you couldn't decide."

I slid in, wondering desperately if my courage would desert me at the last minute. The door was open, as I had hoped. I had been prepared to try to pick the lock, despite not knowing how. I had procured a hair pin and a credit card some months before to cater for the eventuality.

Fortunately, these were not necessary. I touched as little of her door handle as I could in the circumstances. I didn't want my latex glove to smear Barnes' fingerprints. They must be all over the room. Forensics would have a field day, finding Barnes' DNA in amongst all the blood and guts. I thought again, would my courage hold? But no, as I took the first steps into her small room, almost identical to mine in its shape, although polarised in its style, I could find no fear, or doubt, or trepidation in my heart. All I had was the cold, hard ball of anger that had been within me for eighteen months or more. I was ready.

Her room was cold, so much so that I could see my breath. Her window was ajar, wide enough to let in the cold and suck out the warm. The window blind flapped gently. The room was in disarray with clothes and books and make-up strewn everywhere. I had to pick out a route to the bed, striding uncomfortably to get from one clear patch of carpet to another. I moved silently, like an assassin.

She, like her possessions, was strewn. Despite the cold she was laying across part of her duvet, the right side of her body totally exposed to the cold air, protected only by a thin, silk negligee that hugged her curves. The weak moonlight cast just enough light for me to see her right nipple. It was erect against the silk.

I came close to her, I could see her breathing. Her hair was free-flowing for a change, curling and waving its way across the pillow that held her head. Her breathing was shallow and I instinctively knew that she wasn't asleep. A brief moment of panic engulfed me.

As if by some ironic and malevolent timing, she opened her eyes and looked at me. Not a flicker of surprise crossed her face. No sneer of derision contorted it. Her face remained as it was when I walked in, perfect in the dim moonlight. Only her eyes had moved.

I expected her to cry out, to ask why I was there, to make some reference to Barnes and his earlier visit, to ask why I was carrying a knife. But she remained silent and just gazed at me. I knew the timing was right – there would be no better time to straddle her and plunge the knife into her throat or her chest, or perhaps hack indiscriminately at her exposed body. The Plan urged me on, a gathering force within me.

But the outside of my body was deadly still, with only my shallow, quick, panicky breath giving the lie to my statuesque appearance. The bottle of bleach and the bread knife were held in my immovable arms, my reluctant hands. I could not move, despite the strength of my previous conviction. The internal, desperate, vitriolic urging could not move me. Like a trap her eyes held me, deadly still.

I don't know how long I was looking at her before she gently lifted her shoulder from the bed, in such a sleek movement that I barely registered it in the dark, and slipped the thin strap of her negligee down her arm. Another movement freed the captured side of her body from the duvet as she revealed herself to me. I took the sight in, and she let me, as she lay there. Slowly, as if not to alarm me, but entice me, the other strap came down and she slipped the whole flimsy article off her body. She laid still, glorious in her luscious, delicious nudity. My eyes caressed her body as only eyes can. I drank her in, from the shapely leg to the firm, rounded dome of the breast. My eyes flowed where her body flowed and dipped where her body dipped. She continued to stare straight at me, her lips slightly parted as a small sign of the desperation that inhabited her. The cold goose bumps forming all over her smooth skin were a stark counterpoint to the heat that pulsed through me. Heat of such a kind that that I had never experienced. Heat that seared my bones and frazzled my mind, burning my neatly arranged plans in a torrent of lust and love and whatever lays in between, and melting my cold, hard hatred with the uncontrollable temperature.

A slow hand crept out from that perfectly formed body and found mine. She touched the back of my latex covered hand with her tough fingertips. I dropped the knife and the bleach and peeled off the gloves. She touched me again. The calluses met the smooth skin of my hand for the second time in only a few hours. I flinched as the vague memory of repulsion slid across my consciousness. But my consciousness was in control no longer. My subconscious desire had surfaced and I could not fight it. For eighteen months, I had dreamt about putting my hands around her neck and now here I was, placing my hand into hers, and feeling a thrill that I could never have hoped to have achieved by killing her. This was anticipation, excitement: the thrill of impetuousness, of passion unrestrained.

She pulled me on to her bed.

CHAPTER 19

The memory of just a few hours ago is vivid and strong It is almost as if I can still feel her on my fingertips, taste her on my lips. The memory of her scent is overwhelming.

"Can I have some water please?"

"No Stanley you cannot. Now tell me about your relationship with Deborah."

"Stop using her first name. I know what you're doing. You're using her first name to make her seem like a real person. You want me to understand the real, personal tragedy."

"You're a very clever man Stanley and I apologise for playing mind games with you. It's what we learn in our interrogation training. I can see that approach is too crude for you. But you have to understand that this is very important. A beautiful young woman is fighting for her life and we need to get to the bottom of it."

"I don't understand why you think I have anything to do with it."

"OK Stanley, I'll level with you. There are a few reasons why I'm interested in you. This may not be nice for you to hear but I can see it is the only way we can get information out of you. We've been playing games for long enough. I should have levelled with you from the start, then maybe you'd have been more straight with me. You are one smart man after all. I'll tell you everything."

I returned to my room in a daze. I wasn't really conscious of anything around me as I made my way through the corridors of Pottergate. It was all a blur.

What had I done?

The thought crashed upon me as soon as I closed my bedroom door and returned to my normal world of control and self-discipline. Regret is not an emotion that I am overly familiar with.

I didn't regret for a moment the things I had done to Barnes or Nash or Everett over the years– they were necessary. I had never felt anything approaching repentance towards Abdul – he had deserved it. Even my father's third wife – the one who asked me to call her "mother" – had never received an apology from me and my father said I had been lucky to escape prison for what I did to her.

But this was different.

"One, it became quite clear after seeing Deborah this morning that she had recently had sex."

I sense that this is the denouement.

"Obviously, the lab tests will confirm that but to be honest it was quite evident. I'm sure you don't need me to go into the details. Now, a girl doesn't often have sex and then kill herself, unless of course she's been raped…"

"You don't think…"

"Let me finish Stanley. It was also clear from viewing the body that there hadn't been a struggle. She had no marks, cuts or abrasions. Apart from the obvious ones of course. The old ones. And no-one had heard any noise. A girl screaming in this place would wake everyone. So if she had been raped, then why no noise? Perhaps she had been gagged? But no, her mouth was clear – no bruising, nothing. Perhaps she was drugged, but I doubt that somehow. There was some bleach in her room that may have been intended for that purpose but I don't think it was used. Lab tests will confirm in due course I suppose. I'm pretty sure the sex was consensual. That was my initial gut feeling and knowing what I do now, I am absolutely convinced."

When she touched me, it felt natural and exciting. I succumbed to her every wish, her every prompting. She directed me and I complied willingly. I savoured the moment, her touch, the feel of her, the look of her and ignored the hypocrisy of it all. Her small stubby toes, her fat thighs riddled with cellulite, her over-generous hips, the swell of her womb, the slight bristle of hair under her armpits, those hands: just hours before they would have caused rage to bubble within me. But then, in her cold room, naked and sweating and hot, they added to her allure.

But when she called me "Stanley" something changed within me. I knew it was illogical but I felt her use of my name was too intimate. She had violated me.

"So, then the question becomes "who." It had to be one of the men here overnight wouldn't you say given the timing of the incident? That counts Mr Newcombe out. He was at home with his wife. Owen Shaw wasn't here either, he works shifts and wasn't on. So that leaves only one other."

"You are a very trusting little detective. It is well documented that wives lie for their husbands when trying to cover for some heinous act. I wouldn't necessarily trust the word of Mrs Newcombe."

I can see that my attempts to sully the character of Mr Newcombe have failed. However, a thought occurs: "What do you mean one other? I take it you mean me? What about Barnes, Palmer or Everett?"

"Barnes, I suppose it could have been him. He is obsessed with sex – that's fairly obvious. But, I just don't think it was him. I don't buy it.

He's not the type. Lecherous certainly. But murderous? No, I don't think so. He's quite a weak little man really."

"But..."

"But what?" the little detective asks.

"Nothing. I am just not particularly impressed by your powers of deduction." Although I am actually. Barnes is weak and couldn't do murder if his life depended upon it. But I must continue to be aggressive, as the Plan dictates.

"Help me out then Stanley."

I can see that I am going to have to do the little detective's work for him.

"It is well known that Barnes' wife left him for another man. I am sure he has plenty of pent up rage about that. And wasn't he in some sort of trance yesterday as he recited those numbers? Who knows how unbalanced he was by the end of the day? I wouldn't be surprised if he hadn't decided to take out his frustration on Phillips or Naylor or any other woman he could locate. I would have thought he would have been a prime suspect."

The little detective sits down again and smiles at me. He steeples his fingers and I scorn his clichéd posture.

"You want me to suspect Barnes don't you?"

"It's not a case of "want." I am indifferent to his fate. I am just interpreting the facts with an analytical mind, something you seem incapable of doing."

"Did you know that Daryl Barnes went to Deborah's room last night and propositioned her for sex?"

Finally, this information is revealed.

"Another significant clue I should think. You have your man, detective," I say in a congratulatory tone.

"He says you put him up to it."

"It's a lie."

"Is it? He told me you came to his room and told him that Deborah wanted him."

"I didn't do that. Although you haven't mentioned the time that this incident was supposed to have occurred, I can assure you that I was asleep."

The little detectives smiles at that. Cheeky.

"If you're interested..."

I am interested but dare not show it.

"...she told him to go away."

"I cannot fault her taste."

The little detectives smiles and moves on.

"Patrick Palmer, now what about him? The perfect suspect I suppose, given his past record. Deborah is a few years too old for his taste I imagine but in this place, maybe you take what you can get."

I am still smarting from his refusal to point the finger of guilt at Barnes. Daryl Barnes truly is a pathetic excuse for a man. He was supposed to force himself onto her. Too weak to do even that. Now to Palmer...

"A sexual deviant on the premises at the same time as a sexual crime is committed – it's compelling."

"Yes, I would have gone for him had it not been for him being disabled Stanley."

"Such comments would not be well received by the Equalities Commission. Disabled people – if that's what he really is – can achieve remarkable things."

"How could he have done it exactly? He's paralysed from the waist down. If he had been the one, he would have left evidence all over the room. I don't want to be "un-PC" again but he would have certainly have left tyre tracks. And I suspect, the sexual act is beyond him."

Damn. Palmer should have been a prime suspect but had been dismissed without a thought.

"He told me you knocked on his door at 2 o clock."

"I did. He was making a racket. I think he may have been speaking to Barnes who passed him in the corridor – probably on his way to see Phillips."

"And it was definitely 2 o clock in the morning was it?"

"Of course."

"If you say so. OK, Peter Everett. He could have done it I suppose. He's certainly mobile and strong with access to knives, etc. The knife that was used on Deborah appears to have come from the shed where he keeps his tools."

"Bang to rights then, as they say. Also, he was quite distressed yesterday."

"Perhaps. But for some reason I just don't buy it. The guy barely registers anyone else's presence. Have you ever heard him speak? I haven't. I had him in here for about half an hour earlier trying to get him to speak and he wouldn't say a word. Sometimes I didn't even know if he was following me. No, I stand to be proved wrong, but I don't think it was him. He seems to have the mental capability of a child, he is most probably a virgin. I would be most surprised if he is subjected to any sort of sexual urgings at all. No, I just can't see that one. So that leaves you I suppose."

Everett swept aside – just like that. Silence is key now.

"I'm sure you know Stan, from all your research, that people kill for three reasons mainly: love, lust or hate. Which one applies to you Stanley?"

"I didn't kill anyone. Is that a formal accusation? You don't have anywhere near enough to charge me."

"Well, I haven't got to the third thing yet."

"What third thing?"

"The note of course."

Unexpected.

"She was clutching it when we found her. Do you want to know what it says? I've got it written down here."

He delves into his pocket and pulls out a small piece of paper, neatly folded. I doubt very much it is the real note. The real note would be bagged for evidence. He's copied it out for effect. He unfolds it with deliberate painstaking slowness. He reads it to himself, shakes his head and then speaks, pulling the words of Deborah Phillips out of her dying mouth and into the present: "Stanley, why didn't you tell me you loved me before you left?"

The little detective lets the words hang in the air, looking directly at me. He knew all along. So why the pretence? Why the game?

"Stanley, no games. Did you have sex with Deborah Phillips last night?"

I will not answer.

"Stanley…"

I occurs to me that I have failed. The Plan has failed. Or perhaps I have failed the Plan. I am too weak, too much of a failure. I am a walking clue. They are going to prosecute me for murder and I will plead not guilty. The jury won't believe me because I am not a credible witness – lacking in emotion and visible regret - and they will send me to prison.

There is no choice now…I have to be compliant and penitent.

"Yes I did."

"Did she ask you to stay?" Newcombe's voice floats into the tense conversation. I had almost forgotten he is there.

"Yes."

"But you didn't."

"No."

I couldn't stay. I was so worried about getting caught.

"You think I killed her don't you? You're going to lock me up. You're going to tell my father."

A small look of sympathy flickers across the little detective's face.

"Mr Newcombe, could you tell us a little about Deborah Phillip's past please?"

Newcombe looks doubtful, but starts after a little reassuring nod from the little detective.

"Deborah is a...troubled young lady. She had a difficult upbringing, abused by an uncle from an early age and for a number of years. Her parents are wealthy, very wealthy, but they lived a privileged lifestyle that didn't always include provision for a child. Her parents were both busy people and were constantly jetting around the world on business. That's not to say that they didn't love their child, because they clearly did. That is clear from meeting them. They were just busy. They regularly left her in the care of her mother's sister, a woman who had no children who welcomed her presence as a pleasure. The aunt was very good to Deborah and was, in many ways, more of a mother to her than her actual mother. But the sister's husband enjoyed Deborah also, but for very different reasons. The uncle abused her, repeatedly and severely over a period of six years before he was finally caught.

"Deborah was warned not to tell and so didn't. She was scared, both of the physical retribution that would follow, the pain that would be inflicted upon the family and the risk of not being believed. Make no mistake, this Uncle was devious and cold. To sustain an abusive relationship like that for over six years, within a close family framework, required a vindictive and devious streak as wicked as any you have ever seen. He was an absolute controlling force. Absolute.

"At first she screamed and cried when forced to stay at the house of her uncle but of course, being gripped with fear as she was, she couldn't reveal why. Not many parents see beyond the histrionics of their child and Deborah's parents were no different. They just thought she was being difficult. Eventually she realised that crying would do her no good and so she went along meekly. The same attitude started to show itself with the Uncle. Ay first she tried to scream and fight, and would no doubt cry herself to sleep but by the end she was just lying there and taking it. She could see no other way. Eventually, she became unhinged and, in some strange way, she started to enjoy it.

"How can I explain this? She started to associate the abuse she got from her Uncle with love. It was the only time she got any affection or attention. I suppose he said some nice things, conditioning her, telling her that he loved her, and eventually she bought into it. She even defended him when she was questioned by the police. I'm not supposed to say this kind of thing in my profession but she was absolutely screwed up.

"When he got arrested she was cut adrift, the aunt couldn't bear to deal with Deborah any longer. Deborah's parents were appalled but didn't really know how to deal with the situation. Deborah was more isolated and lonely after the abuse stopped than she had been before, at least as she saw it. She tried to kill herself not long after and has been trying to kill herself ever since and has tried it here once. That's why she's here. We've been trying to help her, and we thought we had made progress, until now…"

"You mentioned another incident like this…" the little detective asks.

"Yes, a few years ago she was caught with a delivery boy in one of the store rooms. She is an attractive girl and I suppose we should have watched her more carefully. She was caught in the act."

"By whom?"

"By Stanley."

"And what happened then?

"She tried to kill herself that night, but we were ready for it and we managed to stop her."

The events of that day start to come back to me. I had been following her, watching the coy looks she sent at the delivery man. I knew something was going on. The delivery boy was just a callow youth, driven by his dick. I knew his type. I watched her as she sat watching him. She draped herself across a chair in the canteen, watching as the delivery boy toiled with the sacks of supplies. He nudged his workmate occasionally and blew out his lips as he traced Philips' fat legs - which she had carefully exposed by arranging her skirt. I followed the curves, wanting to touch them and knowing that she wasn't even thinking of me.

I was secreted behind a pillar in the dining room, deadly still, barely breathing. I watched as she suggestively drew her hand across her breast as she locked eyes with the delivery boy.

I slinked back behind the pillow, fighting anger and lust in equal measure. I wanted her and yet she was betraying me. I leaned my head against the hard texture of the pillar, scraping it violently but slowly against the rough surface, trying to concentrate on the pain. It hurt.
I steeled myself for another look around the pillar and found her gone. The room was empty. I stepped out – frantic. Where was she? What had he done to her? What was she doing to him?

I raced around the room, searching for them, desperate to put a stop to it.

I heard a noise, coming from the store cupboard.

I crashed through the door and found them.

He, with his trousers around his ankles and his bum showing, grunting like a pig. Her, pushed up against the wall, moaning with pleasure, cracked, raw fingers curled around the collar of his shirt.

He dropped her as I barged in and hastily began pulling up his trousers, until he saw the knife. I wasn't sure where it had come from or where I had picked it up, but there it was – in my hand. My eyes told him that I was ready to use it. He had frozen, trousers half way up his legs, staring at me in fear of his life. He was tensed as if he expected me to lunge at him at any moment. I nearly did until Phillips caught my attention.

As if she had not been dropped to the floor, she leaned back against the wall…lifted her skirt and…touched herself. All the while she stared at me. My eyes locked onto hers. My peripheral vision registered the slow, hesitant escape of the delivery boy. The knife dropped from my hands as I moved towards her.

She spoke as she reached climax, so quiet that I barely heard.

"Do you love me Stanley?"

"I hate you."

Her tears mingled with her orgasm as she raced out of the room. I barely knew what to do.

"She slit her wrists that night." Newcombe carries on speaking, bringing me back into the room. "Not very well though. The scars are clear enough but she didn't do herself too much damage. We were able to treat her and we kept her under constant supervision for almost a month, until she had calmed. It was a number of weeks before we were able to establish the full facts, after the delivery man confessed all to his workmates and a complaint was made against Stanley."

"Was any action taken?" The little detective asks.

"No, I believe Stanley's father dealt with it."

"How?"

"I don't know for sure. I have the feeling that Mr Young paid the delivery man off and the matter was dropped. Mr Young was firmly of the opinion that Stanley had done nothing wrong."

"I was just doing my job."

"Stanley, you don't work here. You live here." The little detective's voice sounds quite tired, as if he didn't want to deliver the news.

"I am the House Compliance Officer."

"You aren't any sort of compliance officer. They gave you that title to shut you up, to give you purpose. You're here because you've got issues. They read your reports to monitor you – your anger comes through into them. You're just like all the rest. Barnes, who can't get over his wife leaving him. Palmer, the disabled simpleton with a history of child abuse. Everett, the mute – who knows what has happened in his past? Naylor, the anorexic and Deborah Phillips, the suicidal nymphomaniac. And right next to them is you: the aggressive obsessive compulsive."

"I am not."

He is talking nonsense. Trying to unsettle me.

"What happened with Deborah Phillips Stanley?"

"Nothing happened."

"After you had had sex?"

"I left. She tried to kill herself, Newcombe has already told you."

"Maybe."

The little detective leans back into his chair wearily.

"This looked so simple when I arrived Stanley. Here we have a mentally disturbed girl with a preponderance towards self-harm, a multiple suicide attemptee who is found with slit wrists and other horrendous wounds that I won't detail. There is no great mystery in that. But then we find out that she had recently had sex, that adds another layer of complication. But Mr Newcombe explained that away quite easily, it was just a case of finding out who did it and then rounding out the facts. It's not against the law to have sex with a girl who willingly consents. It had to be you Stan, from the outset, and yet you were difficult from the very beginning. I suppose you didn't know about the note. I have had to drag information out of you. Mr Newcombe warned me that you could be difficult so I was prepared. It made me wonder though, whether you had something to hide. Then we have to consider your obsession, and that makes me think even more. Why is this man being so difficult? And then, in the back of my mind, I start to wonder if it wasn't suicide at all. What if it had been made to look like a suicide?"

Newcombe is shocked, "You're not suggesting…"

"Why are you here Stanley? In this place?"

"I came here to be House Compliance Officer. My father secured the position with the Trustees." I answer meekly.

"Wrong, your father didn't secure a job for you, he bought a room for you. Why did he do that?"

"I don't know."

"Sure you do, it's because your father sent you here. And why did he send you here? Come on Stanley, think about it, remember. What about your mother? Does that ring any bells?"

"She's not my mother?"

"You strangled her didn't you? You put your hands around her neck in a fit of rage and squeezed. Do you remember? Do you remember?"

"I didn't kill her."

"No Stanley, you didn't. If you had, you wouldn't be in this nice country house, paid for by your father, living with a collection of other idiots and retards who just happen to have rich families."

"I really must protest…"

"Mr Newcombe please be quiet. I am speaking to Stanley."

"My father said it was OK, I didn't mean to do it. They forgave me."

"Forgiveness? Did you ever forgive Deborah Phillips for not loving you in the same way that you loved her?"

"I didn't love her."

"Sure you did Stan, you just didn't quite know it. You have to be in love to write a book about someone."

The book. The Plan. He has it. All along, he has had it.

"I can explain that."

"I'd love to hear it."

The little detective waits.

Newcombe clearly has no idea what is going on.

"Mr Newcombe likes me to write using my imagination, it is something I am not always able to do. The book is just an example of me trying to use my imagination."

"You'll have to do better than that Stan."

"What is this book?" Newcombe can't help himself.

"This is a book all about the death of Deborah Phillips. It's a series of thoughts, musings, plans – everything really, that can be used to kill Deborah Phillips. And it was written by Stanley Young. He calls it the Plan."

"Oh Stanley…"

"It's all here Mr Newcombe. He'd planned to cast suspicion on others – Daryl Barnes, Patrick Palmer, Peter Everett, even you. He was going to plant some bleach in your desk draw. He took a knife from Peter Everett's shed. He'd tried to unsettle Daryl Barnes throughout the day and then he arranged for Barnes to visit Deborah in the middle of the night to ask for sex. He'd tried to create a tenuous alibi by knocking on Palmer's door and feeding him false information about the time. But the real clincher was that he was going to make the murder look like a suicide all along."

"I can't believe…" gasps Newcombe.

"Oh believe it, Mr Newcombe. It's all written down in this little notepad. He's been planning it for years, gleaning wisdom from Magnum P.I. of all places."

"But…" Mr Newcombe's religious sensibilities still can't take it in.

"There are no buts Mr Newcombe. This is the easiest piece of detective work I've ever had to do."

I cannot give it up.

"Why would I write about killing someone and then kill them in exactly the same way? Someone obviously found the book and tried to frame me."

"I don't think so Stan, this book was pretty hard to find. It took us a little while but I knew there would be something in your room to help me out. You really should have destroyed this, this gives you away entirely."

Does it now?

"I didn't kill her."

"She committed suicide," Newcombe interjects. "She must have."

"Page 17 Stan: how to make a murder look like a suicide, inspired by Magnum P.I. I am very impressed Stanley, in a macabre kind of way. You made the killing look so authentic. You had everyone here believing that she killed herself."

"She did kill herself."

"Stanley," the little detective shouts for the first time in our entire interview, "do you deny that you were obsessed with Deborah Phillips?"

"No. I suppose I must concede that point."

"Did you go to her room yesterday night?"

"Yes."

"With the intention of killing her?"

"Yes."

"Did you have sex with her?"

"Yes."

"And then you tried to kill her?"

"No. In the end, I couldn't do it."

"I don't believe you Stanley. I believe you executed your plan perfectly."

I have him.

"There is a clear dislocation of logic in your thinking."

"Which is?"

"If you think that I had sex with Phillips and then killed her by perfectly executing the Plan then why didn't I finish the Plan off? Why didn't I plant the knife where I had intended? Why didn't I use the bleach and then plant it in Mr Newcombe's desk? And most importantly of all, why didn't I kill her properly?"

I let the little detective digest that thought.

"If I was thinking clearly and killing in cold blood, wouldn't I have finished off the Plan, executed it fully? If I had lost my nerve however…that would explain everything."

The little detective's eyes narrow.

"Oh, you are very clever Stanley. Very clever indeed. An inherent contradiction – I see it."

I smile at the little detective. I can see him thinking. Weighing the odds. Eventually, he reacts cautiously, as I had expected him to.

"I'm going to have to arrest you Stanley for attempted murder. You understand what that means don't you?"

"I understand."
But I continue to smile.

***

Lightning Source UK Ltd.
Milton Keynes UK
UKHW020347131118
332242UK00003B/152/P

THE FOGGING

Tom and Clara are two struggling academics in their mid-thirties, who decide to take their first holiday in ten years. On the flight over to Indonesia, Tom experiences a debilitating panic attack, something he hasn't had in a long time, which he keeps hidden from her. At the resort, they meet Madeleine, a charismatic French woman, her Australian partner Jeremy, and their young son Ollie. The two couples strike up an easy friendship, and the holiday starts to look up — even to Tom, who is struggling to get out of his own head. But when Clara and Madeleine become trapped in the maze-like grounds of the hotel during the fogging — a routine spraying of pesticide — the dynamics suddenly shift, and the atmosphere of the holiday darkens . . .

LUKE HORTON

◆

THE FOGGING

Complete and Unabridged

AURORA
Leicester

First published in Great Britain in 2020 by
Scribe Publications

First Aurora Edition
published 2020
by arrangement with
Scribe Publications

A catalogue record for this book is available
from the British Library.

ISBN 978–1–78782–489–8

Published by
Ulverscroft Limited
Anstey, Leicestershire

Set by Words & Graphics Ltd.
Anstey, Leicestershire
Printed and bound in Great Britain by
TJ Books Limited, Padstow, Cornwall

This book is printed on acid-free paper

For Mum, Dad, Jess, Antonia, and Albertine

1

They took the evening flight, so the plane was full of people trying to party the six hours over. Whole rows of early-twenty-somethings ordering drink after drink, sharing their iPhones and earbuds around, and laughing uproariously. When Tom turned to place them, their flushed faces were green in the reflection of their screens. Either that or it was young families watching movies — groups of one kind or another.

In the row ahead there were three young men, each six-foot-something, dressed smartly in button-down shirts and chinos, with combed-back hair flopping forward, square jaws, and squared-off hairlines across broad necks. They looked like ex-high-school football stars on a night out, or like mannequins that had come to life. They drank cans of beer and Bourbon and Cokes, and flirted shamelessly with the female flight attendants, who, by and large, appeared receptive to it. Every now and then, one of the young men would lean in to whisper something in his friend's ear, and they would convulse with silent laughter, the whole row of seats shaking under them. They were oddly intimate with one another, Tom thought: forever touching and cradling and even kissing each other's heads as they laughed. He craned to see them communicating with other passengers via the seat-to-seat chat on their screens, but couldn't make anything out. They seemed to be egging each other on, pushing each other to be bolder, ever more risqué in their exchanges. Then they would shake their heads and convulse with laughter again, with their fingers pressed into their eyelids, at either the things they said or the things being said in return.

By the time the turbulence hit, though, all three of the young men were asleep, and the cabin had fallen quiet. And Tom had become complacent. He'd had two beers and two Valium and had finally fully relaxed. Directly after the Valium and the beers, which he'd ordered in quick succession and drunk as fast as he could, he'd felt better than relaxed, he felt transcendent. Just for a short while, as the alcohol interacted with the pills. A woolly, dull kind of grace, settling thickly over his ringing nerves. He'd looked over at Clara, who was asleep, and he'd swelled with feeling: he loved and was loved. Everything in the cabin was immaculate and vivid: the soft curve of Clara's upturned cheek, rising and falling minutely as she slept; the breathing bodies all around him, shifting their weight in the low light; the pale, finely textured moulded plastic of the seat backs. Soon, of course, he dropped down from these heights, plateaued, and, eventually, found he was close to sleep himself. Then, with the first yank off course, he was wide awake again.

His legs went first. They began to spasm, strangely — violently. This was new. Then came the sweat. The inevitable sweat.

slightly yellowed white ... had ... sun ... her in that
dress for a long time — several years, at a guess

★ ★ ★

Through the turbulence, Tom tried meditation.
He tried deep breathing exercises. He settled on
the kind of combo of the two that he often fell
into — a bastardised technique that he had
worked up over the years, and which probably
did neither of them justice. It involved repeating
the mantra he had been taught while holding his
breath for as long as he could, letting it out as
slowly as possible, and then holding it out for
as long as possible before taking another breath
— sometimes swapping out the mantra for
counting down from ten instead. It produced a
pleasurable physical sensation, as his stomach
contracted and his fingertips and legs tingled,
became weightless, and lifted off from the rest of
his body. When this happened, he would try to
picture the anxiety, the excess energy, running
out along his limbs and exiting through his
extremities. But none of it ever really worked.
Right now, it had calmed him a little, perhaps
— his grip on the armrests felt less violent — but
it wasn't stopping the spasming, the sweating.
Nor was it blocking out intrusive thoughts,
wasn't distracting him from what was happening
to the plane, or to his body. Not for more than a
second or two. So he also tried holding on to
certain images or scenes.

One of these images, which, each time he
managed to grasp it, he tried to detail more
finely as a way of holding on to it longer, was of
Clara earlier that day. She had been wearing a
dress with a print of large blue flowers against a

faintly yellowed white. He hadn't seen her in that dress for a long time — several years, at a guess. It looked good on her, but it was the way she'd moved in it, the way she'd appeared at the door when he got home, excited, and disappeared back into the house, moving swiftly through the rooms, still packing, that made him think of it. How different she'd seemed.

As in real life, the Clara in his head had a few cotton threads hanging down the short sleeves of the dress onto her arms. She had cut the sleeves back when she got it and never bothered to hem them. He focused on these. How many, how long, the freckles on the pale arms beneath. They were in the kitchen. He curled his fingers around the threads, tore them off, one by one, as he had wanted to do ever since she'd cut them. Sometimes at this point in the fantasy — he lost it, it floated back up — her dress would slip off, too, somehow, and she stood naked before him. He could not picture her well like this. Then they had sex, on one of the kitchen chairs, like they had never done in real life. He could not picture her well like this, either. He couldn't picture either of them well like this. He had to redo the scene several times to get it right: how it might actually work, technically, without the usual embarrassments, and in any other scenario than in their bed, or, perhaps once a year, on the couch. But against the fear, against the sudden jolts and drops, against his legs shaking uncontrollably, convulsing really, trying to helped.

When he wasn't able to hold on to images or scenes such as these, he squinted. This was

4

better, he found, than completely closing his eyes, where, in the darkness, things too easily catastrophised — the lurching, the overcorrections — and also better than having them fully open, where he could see what was happening to the plane, their once wonderfully stable, sturdy-seeming plane that had run fixedly through the air, like a train along invisible tracks towards Denpasar. Squinting, there were things he could focus on without seeing too much: the upholstery of the seat in front of him; the screen, now blank, mounted upon it; the tray table stowed beneath that. Through the curtain of his eyelashes, all this swam in filmy, vertical lines.

In contrast — he could just make out — Clara's face was frozen in an expression of delight. Her face was turned to his, but she was looking out from the corner of her eye down the aisle, towards the front of the plane, as if she had woken and turned to say something to him, found him asleep, and her thoughts had drifted — or perhaps she had become distracted mid-thought by the escalating turbulence. Clara had always loved turbulence. It was a strange thing to say about her — because these days she manifested it in no other part of her life, as far as he could tell — but she had a daredevil streak. Turbulence brought it out. It was the same side of her that had thrilled to rides at theme parks when she was a kid on the Gold Coast. She had gone on one ride during their time together (that he could remember) — the Big Dipper at Luna Park — and, coming off the ride, her face was changed, her eyes dilated, like

5

he was sure, if he could see them properly, they would be now.

He had forgotten this about her, like he had forgotten quite how much she loved to travel until he'd got home that afternoon. Up until then, the trip had hovered over them like some awful thing neither of them could quite face, rather than something they were looking forward to — which it had been for a few days when they booked it. After those first days, whenever they did talk about it, they weren't sure they should even go. They certainly had no money for it. But Tom's mother had had Frequent Flyer points up for grabs — and one of his half-sisters did, too, it turned out in the end. She had three kids now and wasn't going anywhere soon. So they'd had easily enough points for return flights, and then the money began to feel almost like an excuse not to go. It just doesn't seem like the right time to be taking a holiday, Clara had said. He'd said, It never seems like the right time.

But when he came through the door that afternoon, and she'd disappeared back through the house, she was clearly excited. She was talking fast. She told him everything she had packed so far, everything she'd organised, how the key was under the pot in case Lena wanted anything in the house while they were gone, and how Helen was watering the garden for them. Helen had seemed frailer, she'd said, pausing for a moment. They should do something for her when they got back: bake her something, do some work around her house, yard.

Helen was their one friend on the street.

6

They'd met her when she had mulch she was giving away and they came up the street with a plastic tub each, and she was out the front, wanting to talk. They'd never had a friendly neighbour before and didn't quite know how it worked. The tubs had been filled with old drafts of their theses. One tub each, filled with hundreds of pages, which they'd emptied into the recycling bin on their way out. Now, let's fill these with something useful, Clara had said.

After finishing the packing — Tom took about five minutes, wedging into one corner of the suitcase an armful of clothes — Clara took the dress back off, said she was just seeing if she might want to wear it over there. Tom said she looked nice in it. She'd probably end up wearing shorts and T-shirts the whole time like him, she'd said, rolling the dress up into a ball in her hands.

Clara loved everything about flying. Airports, crews, fellow passengers. These things occupied her, exercised her to a degree that was always surprising to Tom. She was like that when they first went travelling, all those years ago, when they went off for ten months and spent so much time in international airports: Singapore, de Gaulle, Frankfurt. They hadn't exactly been frequent flyers since then — there were trips to her parents' place on the Gold Coast, and two weeks in New York once, for her research and to see some friends — but she was always the same. So quietly content, observing it all. It was dumbfounding to Tom, whose nervousness spoiled any pleasure he might have otherwise derived from it, but he admired it about her. Sometimes he thought he

7

loved her more in these public moments than at any other time. He loved seeing her through the eyes of others — her self-possession, her manners — but also the world through her eyes, seeing what she looked for. In the airport it was moments of awkwardness in the system, mostly, or moments of communion. The confusion at check-in kiosks and bag drops, the immediate rapport between strangers. The quiet, shared humiliations of the security check. And then, on the plane, the infantilising condescension of flight attendants, and the response by passengers to this — all the minute, touching gestures of resistance and acquiescence. They didn't discuss it much. They didn't need to: he saw it in her face. They had read the same books. Just this week — he for a class he was teaching next semester, she for a paper she was giving in August — they'd both been re-reading their copies of *The Poetics of Space*. Dipping back into them, at least.

Meanwhile, the panic was chewing his insides, but it was not escalating. It had maybe even tapered off a little. It had something to do with the turbulence, how consistent it was now, the firming sense it probably wasn't going to get any worse than this, the sudden jolts, the listing. His legs were spasming still, his thighs mainly — outwards and then in again. But the sweat had not become a flood; he was merely sodden in the usual places. And he was still shimmering, pulsing so hard he imagined it would have to have been visible to others if the cabin lights weren't dimmed: the panicked blood swelling his veins. But it was dark. No one could see the shimmering. No one

8

could see anything. Not even Clara, who was so close to him. Maybe that was helping, too.

★ ★ ★

The turbulence subsided, but it wasn't until they broke through the clouds and he could see the lights of Denpasar that he properly relaxed. He was flooded with endorphins. He was drunk with relief. He drummed on his knees and stretched out his legs and slid down his seat, and he looked over at a sleepy-looking Clara, who was staring into space. And, perhaps for the first time, he was truly excited about the holiday.

Inside the airport, they made their way through long halls and vast carpeted rooms that were more like the floors of an empty office building than an airport. A golden Buddha in one corner and a *canang sari* every once in a while — one on a windowsill, one on the floor — were the only signs of the country outside.

On the other side of customs, they were met by a teeming crowd of men pressed against a barrier, jostling for position. They walked up and down the line, looking for their names on the boards the men held above their heads. They found their names, or his — they had mistaken Clara for his wife — and the shuttlebus driver, a short, smiling man, jumped up and down to clear the heads and shoulders of those in front of him and point the direction out.

They emerged from a tunnel into the heat. The unbelievable heat. Even at eleven, twelve, whatever it was in local time. It was so hot Tom wondered how anyone could stay out in it for more than a moment, and yet here were dozens of people moving through it calmly, or just standing around in it in groups. His eyeballs stung; his nose burned when he breathed. Fleetingly, for an instant, the press of it, the lack of oxygen, gave him that pause, that sudden falling sensation — like a sudden drop in air pressure — that always preceded a panic attack, but did not itself always become one. Panic's presentiment. But he didn't panic; he turned to Clara. She was beaming at him. He found himself beaming back.

The driver had brought his son with him, or his nephew maybe — to show him the business, he said. Although the son was silent, the driver was upbeat and charming, but his English wasn't good, and they quickly ran out of things to say. Tom and Clara's lack in this area became palpable, and Tom was reminded of how bad they were at this kind of thing. No doubt other tourists made up for the limited shared language with all kinds of banter, but neither of them was a voluble person, and especially not with strangers. Being here had loosened them up, he could feel that, they were excited, and they were doing their best to show it, to be responsive — expansive, even — asking the driver questions about his life and his work, about his son, but they kept coming up against the language barrier, and soon the shuttle fell silent. Tom concentrated on the passing scenery, which was by turns grim and exotic, familiar and strange, derelict and bustling: crowded city streets; lamp-lit night markets; flashing billboards that were much like theirs; and the concrete

10

foundations and hanging wires of buildings going up on rubbish-strewn blocks. And everywhere, scooters whipping by with multiple people on them — couples out on dates, children out late clinging to the waists of mothers, one with a woman and a child behind a man driving. Then one with a dog.

Near the hotel, the driver had another go and came quickly to the point. What will do you while you're here? he asked, finding their faces in the mirror.

As little as possible, said Tom, jokingly, looking at Clara. She looked back. Oh, he tried again, nothing much. We'll probably just stay on the beach or by the pool most of the time, I guess.

Tom knew this was not what the driver wanted to hear, so he explained that they were only in Sanur for a week or so, and Ubud for a few days after that, and that they were very busy at home and wanted to spend as much time relaxing as they could.

Yes, yes, said the driver, but maybe . . . Maybe later you want to see the temple, go shopping, go to Seminyak?

Maybe, said Tom, and when they arrived, the driver gave Clara his card. She was saying to the man, Oh wow, that sounds great, thank you so much, and then the man drove away, and Tom, gathering the bags, heard her gasp. He turned to see why. It was clear enough. They had arrived in paradise.

From its profile on TripAdvisor and Booking-.com, the place had looked impossibly beautiful, with implausibly charming pools and gazebos

11

and grottoes and ponds and traditional thatched-roof bungalows rendered in Mediterranean colours, amid tropical gardens that wound through the grounds and out to cabanas on the beach. It was the perfect mix of old-world charm and modern comfort — the shots of inside the bungalows showed crisp white sheets and traditional-patterned bedspreads piled high with pillows and littered with pink petals under canopy frames and mosquito nets, pebble-encrusted bathrooms and terraces decorated with wooden statues, and antique writing tables under the honeyed, prismatic light of bamboo lamps. That light alone. Under that light, Tom thought, I would have to be changed. They read every review to check there wasn't something the photos didn't show, some hidden flaw, but nothing of consequence came up — maybe a couple of them said it wasn't quite what it used to be — and now here it was, in the flesh, looking every bit as good as in the photographs, if not better. For here you could feel the heat and hear the sea and smell the fragrant air.

They checked in and were shown to their bungalow, which they loved everything about, including the hidden extra room with two antique daybeds that was enclosed in glass and encircled by dense green foliage, and which you got to through a low, shuttered door that initially they'd thought was a window or a cupboard. Then they followed the sound of the sea to the beach.

It was very late, now. No one else was around, and everything was closed up for the night. On the sand, greyish in the moonlight, maroon banana-lounge cushions lay stacked up in piles. They sat in one of the cabanas — something they'd looked forward to especially — and enjoyed a cool breeze coming off the water. The water was low and still and pale. From somewhere nearby came the hollow clatter of wind chimes. A couple of dogs drifted over, looked up at them, and moved on.

2

The first morning, while Tom slept, Clara went for a walk, which she told him about when she got back.

She'd gone out to the boardwalk and headed north, past markets, a turtle rescue, and fish stalls on the beach. She could see, ahead of her, the long curve of the coast: several white lengths of beach extending north, one big hotel looming over the rest of the low-rise coastline, and, off in the hazy distance, the thankfully inactive-looking volcano. She took short breaks from the heat in air-conditioned shops and 7-Eleven-type stores, which were blindingly white under fluorescent strip lighting, and whose aisles were full of strangely flavoured snack food — Chicken Wing Pizza crisps, Pepsi-flavoured Cheetos — a selection of which she brought back with her to the room. One of the shops was full of beautiful but over-priced antique woodwork — lots of monkeys, phallic lingams, and long flat faces missing ears or noses.

Not keeping track of time, she turned back only when she got tired and hungry, but on the way home had stopped in at a museum dedicated to a German painter who had lived in Sanur in the twenties and married a famous Balinese dancer. The painter, Kirschler, who had returned to Germany in his final days, established the museum of his work before he left. The paintings were mostly

14

portraits of the dancer against idyllic, expression-istically rendered Balinese scenes.

She was topless in nearly every one, Clara told Tom, as she handed him the brochure.

Still in bed, Tom read the brochure and made jokes about its poor grammar and confusing design, while Clara changed into her swimsuit. The way the biography of the artist made a point of noting, in parenthesis, that at this time women in Bali mostly went topless: was this a sly nod to the reader about the painter's attraction to the woman — that she had great tits? Or just an awkward way of explaining why she was topless in most of the paintings?

Clara was laughing. I think it's a romantic story, she said.

Is it?

Or . . .

What?

Really gross and creepy.

It's so hard to know.

★   ★   ★

After breakfast, they lounged by the pool and read their books and dropped their bodies into the water for cooling. Squatting on the edge of the pool were two large bronze frogs. Through their upturned mouths, through nozzles that sat on their lower lips like lolling tongues, water arched up in the air and cascaded into the pool. It made a pretty pitter-patter that lulled them, in the heat, into a pleasant stupor.

Along the other edge of the pool, both in the

15

early morning and late afternoon, there was shade from the overhang of the restaurant pavilion's roof — this they had seen in the photographs, too — and under the water, running along a curved platform, there were stone stools with seats the shape of waterlilies, so you could sit in the water and drink cocktails in the shade. Later they would do this, they said. Now, it was time for the beach.

From spindly-trunked trees a canopy of leaves and tangled branches shaded the restaurant tables and the boardwalk, and reached across the boardwalk to meet the roofs of the cabanas, so Tom and Clara could walk through the grounds from the pool to the beach without catching any sun. Inside each cabana were two bamboo couches and an armchair around a glass-topped coffee table — except the cabana at the end, which had a dining table. They had blinds that could be dropped down each side, or three sides, for privacy, while keeping the side that faced the sea open, which was how they were set when they reached them.

The beach itself wasn't much to speak of. With white, raked sand and flat water stretching shallowly to a reef, it was pretty, if unspectacular. The water was well suited only to sitting or floating around in, which was okay by Tom and Clara — that was all they required of it.

From the shade of the cabana they looked out at the sunbathers on the beach and the few people crouching in the water near the shore. Every so often, further out, people motored by on jetskis, usually in pairs. Tom wondered if,

16

with another sort of partner, Clara might have been convinced to do something like that — if, with someone else, she might be the kind of person who would hire jetskis while on holiday in Bali and spend the afternoon carving arcs through the surface of the placid water.

They ordered juice. Then, when an elderly couple relinquished their banana lounges, they took their towels and books and drinks and set up in front of the water.

With freckles and skin cancer in the family, Clara had a strict no-sun policy, and she set to work spreading the umbrella above them. Tom picked up the menu and leafed through it, although he had done this several times already. After dealing with the umbrella, Clara sat down, put on her wide-brimmed canvas hat, and began applying sunscreen to her legs, squeezing out onto her knees high piles of the thick paste and methodically, in circular motions, rubbing it from her knees down to her ankles.

Clara didn't like herself in a swimsuit. She thought she had a big arse and flabby arms, and her fear of the sun meant she was anaemic-looking all year round. So she wore a towel around her waist much of the time, and often a rashie over the top of her one-piece, and she spent no longer in public than absolutely necessary. From behind his sunglasses, Tom watched her arrange herself on the banana lounge, tucking the towel under her bum and pulling it up over her breasts. She then pressed her hair behind her ears and focused on her book.

When they'd first met, it occurred to Tom,

17

Clara had had hair much as it was now: shoulder-length and brown — her natural colour — most of the time gathered into a ponytail, with some of it inevitably escaping the ponytail and reaching the nape of her neck. Or perhaps it was blonde when they first met. Or black. In those first years, it changed colour a lot. It seemed forever in the process of being grown out, her natural brown meeting the peroxide halfway down. It was green, too, briefly. And pink, very early on. She'd had a shaved head, a pixie cut, and for a while a more boyish kind of cut, with curls falling around her ears. Then a bob, which he had never liked — it was too severe, it looked like a wig — and, for years, long hair with bangs. But now it was back to how it was all that time ago, except with a premature grey streak he thought he sometimes saw, under certain lights.

People found Clara attractive, he knew this. She was rarely the most beautiful woman in the room, in the classical sense. Her face was round, fleshy — those big cheeks — and her nose was a little bulbous, so from certain angles her nostrils could appear large, slightly flared. She could look vaguely piggish. But at other times none of this was apparent at all, apart from the cheeks, which were irrepressible, and, Tom thought, very cute. Her attractiveness crept up on you, surprised you, or it had him; even after some time, he hadn't seen it consciously, he just knew he wanted to be around her, until one night he realised what had been there all along — desire. Some saw it much quicker than he had, admittedly. But she was mutable. She could look

18

as sexless as anything, and then do something small, look at you a certain way, or do something as simple as get up from the table, and all of a sudden the jeans she was wearing were not shapeless at all, but hugged the curve of her hips, or her inner thigh, suggesting the possibility of sex in a way that all the short skirts in the world could not. She looked better dressed down than up, usually — she, they both, didn't really do dressed up — but she could be transformed by clothes, a shapeliness appearing suddenly where there had been none.

She had become more attractive as she got older, too, he thought. He hadn't known her then, maybe he had seen a photo or two, but he felt sure that at eighteen she was nothing on her twenty-five-year-old self, which again was nothing on her thirty-three-year-old self. It was hard to say exactly why. Her features had become more defined as she had aged, more distinctly her own, and this suited her — perhaps that was it. The crow's-feet around her eyes. The laugh lines. All of this seemed to reflect her character, so that she embodied it more fully and seemed more authentically herself now her features had matured. The maturity of her looks seemed to affect her demeanour, too, which had grown more self-assured over the years. People warmed to her quickly. He always noticed this, because it was in a way that they never did to him.

Not being classically beautiful had been a good thing for Clara, Tom decided — in contrast to say, Emily, Clara's best friend, who was very beautiful and must in some ways be forever and exhaustingly conscious of her beauty. It might have had nothing to do with it, but Tom wondered if, had Clara been more conventionally beautiful, she would have turned out the same — if she would have been as relaxed, even nonchalant, about her appearance, as comfortable in her own skin as she was. She was not without her neuroses, of course, but when she wasn't in the sun on a beach, for instance — her least comfortable place — she could be impressively unselfconscious. She was almost, at least to him, preternaturally comfortable in most situations, and untroubled by the way she might appear to others by sitting like that or standing that way or by wearing those clothes or by what her hair was doing. He would look over at her in a crowded room, on some special occasion, and she would be alone against a wall, looking vacant, her mouth agape. She burped loudly — a teenage party trick she had never grown out of — and he had seen her pick her nose in public, unrepentantly.

There were several other people on the beach, on lounges either side of them and on a wooden platform on the sand, and one group of people — two women and two men — on towels directly in front of them, close to the shore. One of the women in this group was stunning. Tall, olive-skinned, dazzling white-teeth smile. She had long black hair that shone in the sunlight and breasts that bobbed up and down every time she laughed, which was often. She was glamorous — like something out of an Antonioni film — and here, in this hotel, with its Mediterranean theme, he imagined for a minute that they were on the Amalfi coast somewhere. Then the group left, and Tom turned his attention elsewhere: a statuesque, grey-haired woman by herself, smiling lazily with her eyes closed to the sun; a young family with a Balinese nanny, the parents ignoring their toddler as she played in the sand behind them with the nanny hovering above; and a couple of very tanned women a few lounges over who looked like they'd had work done. Lips too fat, cheeks too taut. This made Tom think of porn, and he fantasised for a moment about what he might do with a woman like that — a woman that he didn't love.

★ ★ ★

They didn't go to the fish stall for lunch like they thought they might, but to a warung a little way down the road from the hotel. Of all the warungs, it had the best ratings on the apps. There was no air conditioning at Little Monkey — it was one small room opening out to the street — but the beer was cold, and the food was good. The monkey theme ran throughout, with toy monkeys and plastic bananas hanging from rafters, motorised waving monkeys on the counter, and a ceramic monkey with a large erection behind the bar. All the staff were smiling young men, and Indonesian hip-hop played through two small speakers on the bar. The other diners were all tourists: Europeans; Brits; a grizzled, red-faced man eating by himself who Tom guessed was Australian.

21

Tom drank two steins of Bintang with lunch — they were so cheap — and they went to his head. He felt good. Heavy, exhausted, but buzzed. Clara seemed in good spirits also, enjoying her nasi lemak and taking everything in — the street life of the tourist strip and the world of the young men at Little Monkey. Tom was thinking how good they were together, how happily they spent their time — not speaking much, not needing to. How comfortable and easy it was, when it was good.

Clara was interested in the tsunami evacuation signs that were dotted about. They had come across one on a path in the hotel, and another out on the beach. After she had finished eating, she pointed to one across the road. A small, rectangular, orange sign on a stake driven into the ground, pointing the way to go and showing a figure in white running up an incline away from a wave curling at their feet. She wanted to follow them one day while they were there, see where they led.

Maybe I could come back here and do some research, she said. Become an expert on Indonesian planning and get funding each year to come back to Bali. She chuckled, then looked less sure. I wonder if people do that — base their research on places they'd just quite like to go?

Ha, he said, feeling mostly that talking was harshing the vibe.

At the counter, he became confused with the currency, how many zeroes he needed on the end of the number — three or four or five. Clara came to his rescue, which was good, because he felt light-headed. He loved the paper money, though. The illusion in the profusion of notes, their multiplying zeroes, of such wealth. But no, that was wrong. They *were* rich. Here, now, the illusion, which the wad of notes so loudly dispelled, was their poverty.

★ ★ ★

They had sex twice that day; it was a long time since they'd done that. The first time was after they got back from the beach. They were on the bed, naked, lying on towels, and Clara, with her face turned away, looking at something on her phone, reached over and took him in her hand. The second time was after lunch, when he followed her, a little drunk, into the shower.

Afterwards, while she went out, with her hair still wet, to scout for nearby beachside places for dinner, he lay on the bed with a book on his chest, his phone in his hand but screen-down on the sheet, and his eyes closed.

He was thinking about their early days again. Something about them being overseas together again after so long, doing something new, seeing Clara out in the world, was triggering all of these memories. And he had such a bad memory — the anxiety. Alcohol too, probably. Although he didn't drink anything like he used to. Of his childhood, he thought he remembered, all in all, about five things, and most of these he suspected he'd only imagined himself into from photographs or stories told to him by his parents.

He couldn't remember what he was doing the day he and Clara had first met, either, but he remembered where it was — in Fitzroy, on the corner of Johnston and Brunswick streets — because he was rarely in that part of the city, precisely for the reason that he might run into people he knew. She'd been with Trish. Trish, ever loud and eccentric, wearing a tiara and a fake-fur leopard-print coat, and leaning on a cane, her leg in a cast after a bicycle accident she'd had while riding home drunk from a party one night. Trish was a friend of friends, whose exactly he couldn't remember — the Miller Street house maybe. She was dominating the conversation like always, and she only introduced Clara to him passingly.

In his recollection, Clara stood in the shadow of her friend, literally hovering on the periphery of the conversation, like a child might while waiting for a parent to finish their conversation and keep going down the street. What words had they exchanged? Barely any. She seemed sullen and pale. Bored. And he was slightly annoyed by her presence — wasn't enjoying having his awkward conversation with Trish overheard by a stranger — but Trish carried the whole thing by talking nonstop, inviting him to a party, and then telling him about the accident and waving her cane about, almost hitting a man in the face with it as he walked by.

When they spoke about this first meeting, Clara remembered it differently. She remembered Tom as the aloof one. Thought maybe he was a snob. Nevertheless, she had known they would become friends eventually, she said. Not just from that meeting, but from the few other times they ran into each other around then. They were just the same sort of people, she said. He didn't know what she meant by this exactly, but he'd agreed, because somehow he had felt the same thing. Even though at the time he was suspicious of anyone who was close to Trish — she was so much, how could you bear to spend any kind of time with her? — there had been something there, it was true.

He hadn't gone to the party, of course, and after one or two brief run-ins, he didn't see either of them for months, until he took a room in their house. He hadn't wanted to, initially, but the room was cheaper than most, and he badly needed a place. There, his wariness about Trish evaporated. She was a lot, but she was kind, and he was impressed by her. The way she made her life into a series of fascinating encounters and hilarious anecdotes by sheer force of will. Plus, she smoothed over every awkward social moment, so you could essentially hide in plain sight with her. So many times out she had become his shield. He knew the chances of coming under any real scrutiny while Trish was around was slim. He thought Clara liked this about her, too. But Trish also pulled Clara out of herself. She was more fun around Trish, more open, more liable to reveal things. To drink more, stay out later. She once said Trish was her joie de vivre, as if she wouldn't have any without her. She quickly added that he was too, of course.

Clara brought someone home once, during those first months in the house, and that was when Tom noticed it. He was jealous. He started wondering where she was when he got home and

25

she wasn't there. The house had a strange dynamic. It was like they were the parents and Trish was their difficult teenager, whom they loved but had to forbear, deal with her tantrums and worry about, and fret over when she left the room. When they exhausted the topic of Trish — her boyfriend woes, her drug intake, how she was getting any work done at university — there was little to say. But it was nice, the two of them pottering around the house, doing chores, cooking meals for each other, with Danny, the fourth housemate, occasionally joining them and making it feel slightly less embarrassingly obvious what was happening between them. But in this way, they became something like a couple before anything had even happened.

He found himself, in those first months, masturbating to the thought of Clara slipping into his bed without a word. At the thought of wordless, almost mechanical sex. Sex where she took him inside her like she was adjusting herself, getting comfortable on the bed. Sex that was seamlessly integrated into their movements around the house, enacted like any other activity, like picking up a book, or making tea. He fantasised about pulling up her dress and fucking her while she was cooking, that sort of thing. And it had something of that feel about it when it actually happened, after a night out together with Trish and talking in his room afterwards. She simply got into his bed and shuffled over. And that was that.

They never spoke about it, their relationship. They didn't need to. It unfolded in front of them naturally: each step taken and decided through opportunity and necessity, and confirmed by him privately with a little thrill he felt, a shiver through him, which he thought he concealed from her successfully. A long weekend away at her parents' place while they were out of town — an early time he remembered well, them lazing around in towels, playing house — then he was going camping over summer and did she want to come, and then a re-evaluating of their lives at the start of a new semester and deciding they needed their own place, to get more serious about things — not their relationship, they meant studying, working. They also wanted to be less distracted by Trish and all her drama. They had had enough of that house. They did all the cleaning, most of the cooking. Danny had moved out, and they'd never found a good replacement. Plus, the house was on a main road, and two lanes of traffic thundered past all day, leaving grime on the windowsills. And if they moved further out, they could maybe afford — just — to rent a place alone.

But then the idea of travelling came up. Maybe, instead of getting serious about things, they should do the opposite, they said, getting excited. They could go overseas for a year. Clara wasn't enjoying her arts degree much and was thinking of giving it up altogether if more shifts came up at the nursery. She could save up over summer. Tom had some savings, and could borrow money from his parents, and was more than happy to defer his degree for a year. Maybe that was the better idea, before they got serious about things. Before they were locked into a new lease.

Looking back, it all seemed so natural, so inevitable. From the moment it started it was like they had always been together, like they were an old couple, not two people in the first bloom of love. Which, at the time, had been a huge relief. Sometimes, though, he'd worried about that. Worried that it pointed to some essential thing that was missing. Maybe it wasn't relief he had felt after all, but resignation, he'd think. But he didn't think that now. Not today, on the bed, directly under the struggling aircon, waiting for her to return with several dining options, each within walking distance.

3

The next morning they emerged from the path and from between a pair of semi-effaced putti to find a woman trawling a boy of four or five through the blue-spangled water of the pool, which, the previous day, they'd had to themselves. The boy was giggling and saying, To the frogs, Mummy, to the frogs, as she struggled through the deep end. Tom and Clara settled into their banana lounges, the woman smiled up at them, and Tom watched Clara smile back a strange smile that seemed more a mirror of the other woman's than her own.

It was only midmorning, but the heat was already intense. The sun bore down upon them with such ferocity that the pebble-encrusted concrete around the pool seemed to wither under its force. The reflected light was blinding. Tom found his sunglasses and put them on. A Balinese woman in a sarong with a maroon sash around her waist appeared with three juices on a tray and put them on a table. As she left, Clara ordered juices for them, too.

Soon a tall, skinny man in wet shorts appeared and dived into the water. He came up grinning broadly as the boy squealed to escape his grasp. That's when Tom learnt that he was Australian, but she was French. She was saying, Non, non! as he came after her, too.

When the woman and the boy got out of the

pool, they sat on the lounges nearest them. The woman, who looked as if she was about to lie down, instead gathered her long hair behind her ears, and, squinting, turned to Clara.

Is your room mouldy? she asked.

There was a beat as Clara, behind her book, registered being spoken to. She lowered the book. No, our room's not mouldy, she said. Is your room mouldy?

The woman twisted her hair into one big plait, pulled it around her shoulder, and let it unfurl down her front. She then lay back in the lounge and pulled on her sunglasses. It was, she said. Two different rooms were . . . The third room, it was okay.

Oh, said Clara.

It was okay, but — she spoke quicker, turning her face to the sky and perhaps closing her eyes behind her sunglasses — it was annoying to move each time. And then I found them spraying disgusting toxic shit in our room, which I asked them not to, actually.

Really? Clara put her book down and pulled herself up the banana lounge. What stuff? Insect spray?

The waitress returned with their juices. Tall, brightly coloured drinks, full of ice. Tom sat up and apologetically removed things from his table — his cap, book, towel — for her to set them down.

Yes, the woman continued, her voice lowered as the waitress returned to the restaurant. This huge fucking can was on the dresser when we came back to our room. They use it in all the rooms, every day. I asked them not to use it in our room. I complained to the front desk. I don't want Ollie to be sleeping in a room full of toxic fumes. Merde. He has a bad chest.

Tom looked over at Ollie. A vaguely pudgy, gentle-looking kid, he was not paying attention to the conversation. He had an iPad out, drawn very close to his face, presumably due to the sun.

I guess our room does smell of something, now you mention it, Clara said. I thought it was just, like, cleaning products . . . I haven't seen them use it, though.

They do it when they clean the rooms, when you're out, the woman said, growing angrier about it as she spoke. You wouldn't know, unless they leave the fucking can in the room!

Wow, Clara said, and there was a pause in conversation as they considered the problem.

Clara had allergies, and other strange ailments and symptoms that had never been satisfactorily explained. A stubborn rash on her upper thighs. For weeks, every night she rubbed cream into the inflamed, pimply skin and he would walk into the room while she was doing it and pretend not to stare, her white legs pressed flat and wide against the bed, her unshaved pubic hair tightly curled. The thing above her lips, like an echo of her upper lip drawn on, a possible fungal infection that was a mystery to her doctor, and which meant they couldn't kiss for a while. Also, iron deficiency, possible IBS.

Tom had nothing like this. He had an anxiety disorder, and he was perpetually exhausted from this and insomnia, but he could eat anything,

31

rarely got sick, and, unlike her, was entirely complacent when it came to the chemical threats around them in the house: the black mould in the bathroom, the asbestos in the roof. For some reason these dangers gained no purchase on his anxieties. Perhaps because they were things that could be fixed, but the fixes were expensive or involved a lot of work, so it was easier to just pretend they weren't there.

Not that Clara was alarmist about these things, and ultimately she took them in hand — convincing the landlord to re-enamel the bathroom tiles, and repainting the ceiling herself She was sensitive to smells; she was always catching whiffs of things he couldn't detect at all, or not for ages after her, like the time a house a few doors down were polishing their floors, or when the tip caught on fire a few suburbs over. All her senses were stronger than his. She tasted burnt garlic in her food, heard all the mumbled things on television he didn't catch, could read signs on the highway hundreds of metres before him. He had always meant to get his eyes checked, but he couldn't be sure if it wasn't just exhaustion that made things swim right in front of them or lines blur in the distance, unless of course he was short-sighted as well as long. He couldn't afford lenses, so he put off even finding out.

The man — who had been floating on his back while the women talked, kicking off the sides of the pool with his long legs — joined them finally and stood over his family, drying himself and casting a shadow that fell over the legs of his son and over Tom's feet, too.

The two women were talking about mould now, about its effects on the lungs of children, but in a pause in the conversation he interjected apologetically and introduced himself, and introductions were made all round. They were Jeremy, Madeleine, and Ollie. Jeremy made to shake hands with Tom, but, as he came towards him and leaned down, he got his foot stuck on Ollie's banana lounge and dragged it with him a little, sending the iPad onto the tiles.

Papa! cried Ollie.

Idiot, Madeleine said, not quite under her breath.

Jeremy scooped up the iPad. It seemed okay. He handed it back to the boy. Crisis averted, he said, grinning at Tom.

★ ★ ★

Back in their room, Tom laughed about the rude Frenchwoman and her bumbling husband, but Clara was not amused.

I like them, Clara said.

Yeah, yeah . . . they're fine.

He was naked at the bathroom mirror, working on his hair, which had become impossibly frizzed and uncontainable. He was wetting it and patting it down with his hands, which worked — while the hair was wet. Clara was on the bed, flipping through the channels on an old TV that sat on a bamboo cabinet in the corner of the room. He gave up on his hair, stepped back into his wet shorts, and pulled them on.

I guess we're going to see them everywhere now, he said.

33

And they did. On the way to the markets, outside warungs they'd chosen for lunch, out on the beach. It was Tom's intention to keep them at arm's length, at the level of the passing nod, and he assumed Clara would want the same, but she was being warmer than that. She seemed glad to be making friends, and by the end of the third day she had a loose arrangement to meet Madeleine at the cabanas for breakfast.

Not sleeping well in the poorly air-conditioned room, Tom came out the next two mornings to find them all eating breakfast — banana pancakes, nasi goreng, eggs, pastries, large platters of fruit.

Madeleine held court, talking about her research (she was a cultural historian specialising in women's history); flat prices in Paris as compared to Sydney, where her sister lived (which were shocking to her), and as compared to Melbourne (which were slightly less so); and about Ollie (the complications of her pregnancy, his chest problems), in muted tones, or in code (third-degree T-E-A-R, postnatal D-E-P) if he was around.

Jeremy didn't speak much, and he moved around the place quietly, too. He was always ducking his head, as if to dodge door frames only he could see, and, although he was mostly nimble, if he moved too fast he became clumsy, comical. But he beamed readily, at Madeleine, at Ollie, at Clara and Tom, too, and engaged happily with everyone he came across — hawkers, the women selling massages on the beach — while also following Madeleine's orders and keeping Ollie entertained with board games, frisbee on the beach, or by

34

drifting around with him in the shallow water. When he came back, he sat next to Madeleine, and she arranged him so she could lay her legs over his lap. Then he would stroke her legs as she talked. At one point, Tom saw him absent-mindedly raise one of her feet to his lips and kiss the joints of her toes. They were painted fluorescent orange.

For Tom, it was all too much. He wanted slow mornings. He wanted to stay so long in one spot they got hungry again and ordered the next meal there, too. He wanted to read his book. He did not want to make small talk. When he tried, he said stupid things, or distracted, awkward things, and received looks from Clara for them. She made excuses for him — said he was always preoccupied. And this was true, but he wasn't relaxed about it. He couldn't relax, and relaxing was the whole point. All he wanted was for two weeks what they'd never really had before: a proper holiday. And they'd picked Sanur because it was quiet; people called it 'Snore'. Of course, he could see where they'd gone wrong there, now — because of this reputation it was popular among young families.

But beyond that, beyond Madeleine and Jeremy and Ollie, who weren't awful, he had to admit (and sometimes it worked out well for him — with Madeleine and Clara talking for hours and Jeremy asking little of him, he was left relatively alone and could slip off and lie in the shade somewhere and try to nap), it was still too much: too much noise, too much accommodation of other people. Too much everything. He needed time. He needed peace. He was exhausted. More exhausted than he felt at home. The humidity wasn't helping. He seemed to shed his body weight in sweat every few hours. It was triggering, too, the heat. He couldn't decide half the time if he was starting to panic or was just overheated.

Plus, he was still coming to terms with the flight. The turbulence. How he'd simply . . . disintegrated. It had been a while, and he had been half-hoping — pretending, at least — that that was over.

So he continued to be disparaging about them, while Clara defended them both.

★ ★ ★

I think he's funny, she said.

They were at dinner — a tiny, one-room warung on the corner of a busy intersection that was open on two sides to the street. On one side it overlooked the main tourist strip, forever congested with honking pick-ups and snaking scooters, and on the other opened onto a dark side street that led down to the beach. This was a popular parking spot, with scooters and motorbikes starting up continuously and thundering past.

Under hard lights, Tom and Clara sat at a small plastic table on gleaming pink tiles. It was their fifth day now, and Clara had taken to wearing the same thing each day — not shorts after all, and not the floral dress she had tried on at home, but a big loose-fitting cotton thing with pockets. It was a pale, faintly marled grey that turned darker in patches with her swimsuit underneath, and she wore it with sandals and a floppy red canvas hat that, by squashing her hair down, had the strange effect of making her face and ears appear bigger beneath it. There was something carefree about the outfit that told Tom she was enjoying herself. That she was happy. He would have liked to have been gratified by this, but something about it annoyed him. He was in a bad mood, it was true — the exhaustion, their new friends — but there was something about her attitude, her happiness here, that felt like a rebuke, even a rejection of him. It had nothing to do with him, her happiness — how could it, if she was enjoying herself so much and he wasn't? It was all about Madeleine and Jeremy and Ollie, and he felt dumped for more interesting people while also pathetic for being so transparently jealous.

. . . and, actually, they have a good relationship, she was saying. Madeleine loves him, you can tell. She's kind of play-acting, being grumpy like that all the time. She's actually one of the happiest people I've met in a long time, I think.

Sure, okay, I don't really care about the state of their relationship, Tom said. He was running his fingers along his eyebrows, collecting and inspecting sweat.

No, but you're always making comments about how she comes to a place like this and complains, or is ordering Jeremy around —

She is kind of bossy, is all I said. And when she's not being bossy, she's draped all over him and complaining about the mould in their room or the water pressure or whatever . . . in this incredible pl —

Mould is bad for kids, she's just concerned about her little boy . . . who is very adorable, you have to admit that, at least?

He's cute, he said, looking down at the menu.

They've had a difficult time, though, too, Clara said, more carefully.

Really, how's that?

She was telling me about how hard it was with Ollie . . . when he was young. That he never slept.

I thought there was something in him I recognised.

Madeleine said he woke up all through the night, and ended up in the bed with her all the time. So they co-slept . . . but it was long settles every night, and still lots of waking up . . . with Jeremy sleeping on the couch for, like, years. She said they had become enmeshed, or something.

Enmeshed?

Yeah, enmeshed. Something her psychologist said. I'm not sure what that means, she didn't really explain. But she said she ended up spending a lot of time away from Jeremy, with Ollie at her mother's in Léon, weeks and weeks away, even though everything was okay between them, and he was a good father and everything . . . She said that was the only way she could stay sane, that her mother calmed her down . . . and things slowly got better, Ollie started sleeping through the night, but it took years.

Sounds tough.

Yeah. But they got through it . . . And now he sleeps like an angel.

Seems so.

There was a pause.

I wonder if we'd have an anxious, bad sleeper, Clara said. Surprisingly, Tom thought, without a trace of irony.

Holding her gaze, he dragged in breath.

I guess the whole thing is such a lottery, she continued . . . who they become, whose genetics they get . . . God, I hope we don't produce another academic.

Ha, he said.

The water they'd ordered with their food five, ten minutes ago hadn't arrived. He had sweat still stuck to his back from the walk. He was wearing a linen shirt — the kind that, when worn in, was perfectly suited to hotter weather, but before this point was scratchy. The shirt was before that point. And he knew it was wrong, it wasn't their fault, it wasn't about *them*, but he was irritated by the people at the restaurant. The pace of everything was so slow. The woman who had taken their order had disappeared, and there was no one to ask about the water.

There was no one else dining in the restaurant, either, other than a large Australian man with a tiny Balinese woman, eating in silence under the coruscating lights. He had probably paid for her services, Tom thought. They had seen something like this being negotiated the day before at lunch, at another warung down the road. A late-middle-aged Australian man waiting with a vaguely officious-looking woman in a suit, and then another woman, dressed less urbanely than the first in a long skirt and a T-shirt, arrived, trailing a boy. The whole thing was openly discussed, with the man, crudely, it seemed to Tom, negotiating the terms of the agreement, and then patronising the boy — I'll come and spend some time with you and your mother at your place? And you show me around? How does that sound? Sound like a good deal? — and the boy looking baffled.

More scooters started up outside. They were teenagers, two per bike, with their helmet visors up, hooting and throwing back their heads. One of the scooters looped around the road dangerously as it gathered speed.

He was painfully hungry now. He felt faint from fatigue. Words from the menu still in his hands swam a little, but they often did that. At the base of his scalp, in the cavities between the neck muscles along his hairline, his head itched. It stung under his fingernails as he scratched at it, but he couldn't help himself. He desperately wanted to go back to the hotel and take a long shower.

Where the fuck is everyone? he said.

She'll be back, Clara said, now preoccupied with her phone.

He looked around the room as if he was in a busy restaurant trying to catch someone's eye, but there was no one in the room, so it was pointless. He was willing someone to materialise and realise they'd left them out there too long.

What happens when someone wants something quickly, though? Or *now?*

Clara looked up. Her face had that pale look she got when she was unimpressed, her expression set a little more firmly, both eyebrows ever so slightly raised.

You know, at first, of course, it seems so gracious and charming or whatever, they are so *beautiful*, and *discreet*, especially with everything they have to put up with, all these arseholes, and how hard they work, and what we are doing to their country and everything . . . but then . . . I don't know. You don't get that? Does everything have to be *quite* so painfully relaxed? All the time?

He was still whispering, but his whispering had risen in volume a notch or two. There was music playing, gamelan, from the kitchen, but it was low, and no doubt the other couple in the restaurant could hear at least some of what he was saying.

You're being a shithead, Tom.

Fine, I'm being a shithead.

A racist one too, even.

Racist, he scoffed. But the word bit. It punctured his outrage, and, just like that, it collapsed.

Okay, fine, he said sarcastically, but without conviction.

He looked down at his phone. He could feel her scrutinising him. Shame pressed against his face.

It was true that he didn't usually allow himself to get angry. The impulse was there, but he controlled it, swallowed it back down. He couldn't remember the last time they'd had something that might be considered a proper fight. They bickered in passing and let it drop. Usually he didn't have the energy. He needed things to be okay at least with them; if there wasn't that, then what was there? But he'd felt it rising in him and had to let it out. Maybe he'd moved up into

41

another gear, like an overtired toddler, become so tired and hungry he was furious. But it was over now. He'd done that, he'd let it out, and the usual shame had descended over him.

And Clara knew he hadn't *really* meant that about the people here, surely; he spent so much of his time saying how incredible they were, but of course he wasn't going to bring it up again to backtrack on that. Still, it did seem now that she wasn't looking at him or speaking to him.

The food arrived soon after that. Tom felt himself become almost theatrically ingratiating, needlessly rearranging the condiments and glasses on the table for the waitress to fit their food on there, too. Then they ate in silence. He asked Clara how her food was, and she said good. He said the sate ayam was actually really good here, and she agreed, the food was good.

They carried their silence back to the hotel. He liked to pretend, when this happened, that it was a comfortable silence they were sharing, and, although he was concealing stomach cramps, which were worsening, as if there was concrete being poured into his stomach and folded in with his blood, he pretended they were simply strolling home after a nice meal — contented, full, enjoying each other's company without feeling the need to speak. He had to do this, because otherwise he became enraged.

She was much better at silences than he was. She could go on forever. It was always he who had to cave. He would let the silence deepen for as long as he could, but ultimately he would back down and puncture it with some innocent-sounding question, ask if she'd seen something he was looking for — his phone, the bottle-opener — and she would respond to the question, sometimes reluctantly, sometimes readily enough, like nothing had happened, and, usually, this was enough for it to pass. Except when it wasn't, and she resumed the silence and didn't talk to him for days on end, which had happened a few times — the worst time when they were travelling, all those years ago.

He was thinking a lot about that trip now — now they were overseas together again. It was as if, when they'd broken up for a while, and she was living mostly away from him, he'd boxed up those ten months and relegated them to some dusty corner of his memory where there was, he had convinced himself, nothing of interest to him. And he'd left them there ever since, untouched, even though they'd been back together for so long.

Now, it seemed, he was interested. He kept remembering new things. It seemed like it had happened to different people. She was twenty then, and he was twenty-two. He had to remind himself of that. At the time, they had felt so jaded and old — certainly not like young people exploring the world, which, of course, they were.

At the hotel they trudged past reception where the woman who had checked them in was on shift, sitting at a computer behind a tall bamboo counter. She smiled and called out goodnight, and Tom smiled back, waved, said, Lovely night, and turned to see Clara's face still closed against them both.

Back on the bed, and still not talking, Clara

flipped through the channels again, finding nothing but Indonesian versions of the same game shows and reality TV they had at home.

Tom drank a beer and read his book, but he couldn't concentrate on the book and picked up his phone. He scrolled through Instagram. Then, using his best neutral tone, he said: Do you remember our other holiday pals?

Clara didn't respond straightaway, and, for a moment, he wondered if she was going to ignore him completely. This was an unspoken rule, that they respond to each other. Ignoring him completely would make it something else, something they might need to acknowledge.

Who? she said, finally.

In Thailand, he said, feeling a rush of gratitude and trying not to show it in his voice.

No?

The Swedes. You know, the sweetest people on earth.

Oh . . . yeah.

She was looking up at the ceiling, now, and he followed her gaze. Beyond the mosquito net, there were ornate cornices that were glossy with varnish and many-tiered and so intricately carved it was hard to make out what they depicted. Flowers? Angels? Animals?

I loved them, she said.

They were very sweet, he said, relaxing completely now. Dumb, though. Or maybe just naïve. Like they'd lived a very sheltered life and this was their first time out of the village, or Stockholm or whatever. She got heatstroke, and we visited her in the hospital.

44

Oh yeah. Clara clicked her tongue against the roof of her mouth, and began exploring her teeth with it.

He was so excited when he found us and brought us to visit her, he said. Like we were their oldest friends. Do you remember that? She was so happy. So grateful. It was very weird.

It's strange, she said, after a moment. I remember that, but nothing else about it. I mean, I don't remember the hospital, at all . . . it's like a dream . . . Just her very, very red, very, very happy face.

And it was only, what, ten years ago?

Twelve, I think. No, thirteen. Two thousand and six.

He kept making bad jokes and getting all sheepish and embarrassed and blaming it on his English, he said.

They were young. He was sweet.

He *was* sweet. They were both were. Lovely. We just had absolutely nothing to say to each other, that's all. He recommended books to me. Strindberg, I think. That was good.

Clara changed the channel again. Have you read Strindberg?

Not yet, no.

He looked down at his book, and then back up. How about Marco, in Paris, remember him?

Oh God, of course. I will never forget him.

You know who he reminds me of, just a little?

She looked at him. No, who?

Non, Ollie, *non!* he said. His impression was terrible. He laughed.

Don't be ridiculous, she said.

45

4

France was around five months in. After Thailand, Laos, Krakow, Berlin, but before England, New York, Mexico. They spent about a month there, mostly working on organic farms. WWOOFing, it was called — Willing Workers On Organic Farms — and the idea was you exchanged labour for food, lodgings, skills. They stayed in three places, with three families, all English — where were all the French people, they wondered — and only one was anything like what they'd hoped it would be. The other two were disasters, although one of these disasters had little to do with the farm. And then once, between stints, they'd stayed with Marco in Paris. That was a disaster, too.

Marco ran a squat on the outskirts of the city, far south of the thirteenth arrondissement. They were given his email by a friend, Tess, who gave it with trepidation.

He is intense, she said, Full on, and she fixed them with a look that suggested a gravity her words could not quite convey. She tried again: He was in a bad place when I was there. But who knows, maybe he is doing better now.

They took note of this and would use him only as backup, they decided, if they had time to kill between farms, which, in the end, they did have — a week in fact. He was receptive to their email, and they turned up one afternoon to find

46

him alone in the courtyard of the squat, an old factory of some kind, sitting at a picnic table with a laptop, in front of a fireplace fashioned out of bricks and corrugated iron.

The squat was nicely set up. The fireplace, the picnic tables, plants in pots scattered around, raised garden beds full of herbs and staked tomato plants heavy with fruit. A clean, light-filled kitchen with benches made out of recycled timber. People had put effort into it, and recently, but it was strangely quiet now, as if everyone might return at any moment and the place would spring back to life, but it never happened. There was only Marco.

Marco was an unkempt, ruggedly handsome man, kind of timelessly aged, with piercing eyes and long black curls streaked with grey, which were permanently entangled in a scarf hanging loosely around his neck. He was charming, kinetic, and he welcomed Tom and Clara with a winning smile and immediately made plans.

A dinner was proposed for later that evening, and he would take them to the markets and show them how to source free food. They would pay only for the fish, and he would teach them about Paris as they walked. Tom and Clara were tired after travelling — to get there from south of Lyon had taken three trains, and then it took a long time to find the place so far beyond the nearest station — but they could not refuse him, and they set off.

On the way to the markets (the oldest markets in Paris, Marco said), which were a long way from the squat — a walk, a train back into the

47

city, and then another walk away — Marco pointed out a street where barricades were erected during the commune, and later a cafe where André Breton and Philippe Soupault read pages from their experiments in automatic writing that would become the book *The Magnetic Fields*. He was impressed that Tom and Clara knew who Breton and Soupault were, too impressed, and embarrassingly pronounced them the most cultured guests they'd had in a long time.

Usually, we have only stupid fucking students, he said, snorting snot back up his nose. People who only want to fuck and get wasted and who don't care about anything like culture or art. There are so many morons everywhere, he said. Culture is everything. If you are cultured, you understand some real things about life, understand the value of work and struggle and resistance and love.

Marco got worked up like this easily, of his own accord, his thoughts inevitably drifting back to the same grievances — it happened several times during their trip to the markets alone — and when he did, his speech, which was already quick and agitated, became more so, and the snorting worse. He made them nervous. Tom could tell Clara was nervous by her over-eager smile, her forced receptivity to Marco's talk — it was so rare to see her strike a false note — and for Tom the nervousness was compounded by the dawning realisation that Marco had designs on Clara.

At the markets, they bought fish, dumpster dived for vegetables, watched Marco extract free bottles of wine from an initially sceptical-looking merchant as he packed up his stall, and returned home, listening the whole way as he talked. Their good cheer was an effort to maintain, but they both sensed the importance of keeping him happy.

Prompted by a discussion of certain recipes and his culinary skills in general — that, despite its reputation as a nation of food-lovers, most men didn't cook in France, while he was a fantastic cook — Marco asked Tom how Aboriginal people separated domestic roles according to gender. Tom was studying history and must know these things, he said.

Surprised by this, by the misunderstanding of his degree — he had readings on urban history with him as part of his degree in architecture and urban planning, not history — but also by the sudden swerve in the conversation, the way Marco demanded this knowledge from him, Tom laughed awkwardly. He explained that he had not studied Aboriginal history or culture in any depth — not since high school, at least — and admitted, guiltily, that he did not know much at all about gender roles in Aboriginal nations. Marco did not hide his disappointment, indeed he evinced shock — a shock that was ludicrous in its performativity, but which nevertheless had the desired effect — and Tom found himself bumbling through an incoherent explanation about the secrecy of certain aspects of Aboriginal culture, the idea of secret men's business and secret women's business, which westerners were not allowed to know and out of respect did not pry into, but the whole time he was speaking it felt like a cop-out — he knew it sounded like one — and it was accompanied by a sinking feeling that he had fallen into a trap. Regardless, he did feel ashamed. Even though he suspected the question had been disingenuous, designed only to humiliate him, he couldn't help but think Marco was right, that he should know more about Aboriginal culture, and that he was every bit the arsehole he sounded like in that moment.

Clara saved him, distracted Marco by talking about something else, asking him questions to get him back on the tour-guide tack, and then, as they walked, she found his hand. He didn't know why he still remembered that — maybe because she never did things like that. But she found his hand, and they walked hand in hand, while he smarted and sweated in the third arrondissement. Maybe, he thought now, it was only to signal to Marco that she was loyal to her boyfriend.

The turn against Tom, then, was sudden and vicious, but not unforeseen. The impasse over his knowledge of Aboriginal gender roles was one warning sign. Another was the obviousness of Marco's crush on Clara. He lavished attention on her and complimented her in a way that was transparently seductive, pouring his tour-guide facts and charming grins upon her with ever more intensity. It didn't seem to trouble her much — when they went to bed the first night, Clara laughed about it, said she found Marco ridiculous — but it gave Tom a sense of impending doom.

But it was the guitar that took the blame.

The squat was once a music-filled place. This was evident in various ways. Adjacent to the courtyard was a long, single-storey building that faced the street. Once the factory office, it now served as an open-plan kitchen and dining area, and there was a small riser built into the far corner of the room. It had a single, limp mic stand on it and bits of gaffer stuck to the carpet. And there was Derek, one of the only other people they met during their three days there. A tall African man with dreadlocks down to his waist, Derek came to rehearse in the basement, which, when they followed him down there, turned out to have several rehearsal studios built into the space, all carpeted and soundproofed and fully wired. Derek was friendly, soft-spoken, and on good terms with Marco, although his responses to Marco's efforts to engage him in conversation were muted, bordering on perfunctory. For his part, Marco was clearly pleased to be associated with this musician in the eyes of their guests, and he boasted about his friend's talents and his success in the underground music scene.

The guitar Tom had spotted the moment they walked in the place, a blondwood acoustic guitar resting on a stand in the corner of the kitchen. The first night, after their fish and wine, and after Marco had finally gone to bed, Tom came back down for it and took it up to their room, a mezzanine floor in the main factory building, where a double mattress lay under slanted, frosted glass and the diffuse yellow glow of street lights. Tom didn't want to play the guitar in front

51

of Clara, but he badly wanted to play it, so he did, quietly, while she read.

The next day, in the afternoon, after they got home from their visit to the city — to be tourists, to visit the Louvre, to buy baguettes and cheese and climb the Butte Montmartre to the Sacré-Cœur — Marco wasn't around. In their room, Tom played the guitar again, and Clara read and worked on her laptop, until, finally, they heard Marco downstairs, whistling to himself and calling out to see who was home. They roused themselves and clambered down from the whiteness of their room, through the darkness of the warehouse, and into fading daylight.

But Marco wasn't much interested in them. He was expecting a visitor, a woman who was a dear friend of his and whom he respected greatly, he said, as she was a true champion of revolutionary art and artists in Paris. He was in high spirits and was setting out a cheese plate for her, making much of the goats' cheese and a tiny bottle of black truffle oil he had bought, and he had sourced more wine.

When she arrived, Juliette was warm and vivacious. At least a decade older than Marco, maybe more, with similarly grey-streaked hair tucked into a scarf around her neck, she exuded cultivation and charm, but, unlike Marco's, her charm was not aggressive — it seemed to come at less of a cost, and her conversation was easy. She expressed interest in Tom and Clara, their travels, their work and studies, and was kind and affectionate to Marco, whom she had obviously known for a long time and whom she indulged and faintly patronised, as if he was a precocious, sometimes errant, child.

In turn, Marco treated Juliette with great reverence. He played the attentive host and deferred to her on all things, and went to great lengths to pump her up in the eyes of his Australian guests, telling them of all her great work in social justice and arts organisations and her championing of squatters' rights and, again, revolutionary artists in Paris. He was lighter with her around, more playful, he enjoyed playing the child, but inevitably his anger bubbled up, encouraged by a kind of hammy petulance he affected with her that, as a mask for his real anger, continually worked its way off. When this happened, she shot him looks that quietened him back down.

Juliette did not stay long, an hour at most, but Marco drank several glasses of wine in that time and was noticeably affected when she left. He tried to detain her, to drag her back into conversation by bringing up scandals and people from their past and imploring her to tell their guests about them, but she extricated herself. Tom and Clara extricated themselves also — they were tired after playing tourists all day in the city, Tom said, chuckling like an idiot and demurring when Marco suggested more wine — and retreated to their room.

Later, Clara went to use the bathroom and Tom could hear voices — Marco's and hers — in the kitchen. And then a crash. Slow to move, listening for signs she was okay, Tom had only reached the ladder when she appeared beneath him.

Marco had intercepted her. Implored her to drink more wine with him, told her he wanted to make her dinner — but only her, because he didn't like Tom, who was ignorant of his own country and a fascist for playing the guitar by himself in his room and not entertaining the house. If you can play, you play for the people, he said. Music is to be shared. Tom was a fascist and a philistine. Marco switched manically between the two registers, she said, between the tactics of seduction and accusation: he had more wine for her, more fish he would cook, he liked her because she was discreet, didn't talk too much . . . and then he changed tack and attacked Tom again, over whom he became venomous, spittle flying from his mouth. Eventually — when it became clear she was not going to sleep with him — he picked up a wooden chair, smashed it on the concrete floor, and left the room.

Clara said they had to leave. She was not surprised he had come on to her — that was bound to happen, sooner or later — but his rage, the way it rose so suddenly in him, was suddenly huge, irrepressible, convinced her they had to go. They couldn't be sure what he might do, next time.

In the morning when they left, it was quiet. They didn't know if Marco was up yet, waiting for them — in the kitchen perhaps, or out in the courtyard — and so, instead of making a run for it through the front, they searched for an exit at the rear of the building. Walking through, they found abandoned bedrooms with mattresses on the floor, other empty rooms with the ceilings caved in, and finally a back door leading out to a

54

rubbish-strewn yard choked with weeds. There was no back gate that they could find, but there were cardboard boxes and crates lying around, and they stacked those up and scaled the wall.

There followed a few anxious moments after this, while they stood at the bus stop, wondering if they should keep going, look for the next stop — they weren't even sure where the bus would take them, and he had only to look out the front door to see them down the road — but the bus arrived, and they were gone.

Tom took the guitar. He felt it was the right thing to do. He travelled with it to the next farm, and the farm after that, where he taught Benjamin Henderson the chords E, A, and D, and then left it out in the rain one night and the wood buckled and split. He gave it to Ben, before they left for America. He felt the boy deserved it, after the weirdness between them, and because of Ben's horrible parents, who had no interest in music at all.

Thinking about it now, Tom felt these times might be his and Clara's best times together, when in opposition to other people. Their parents, people in worse relationships than theirs, arseholes of one kind of another. It made them feel better about themselves. Closer to one another. At least we're not like *that*.

He had been humiliated by Marco, in front of Clara, but she didn't make him feel that. She glossed over it, and he was so grateful for her then.

5

They met Madeleine, Jack, and Ollie for lunch at the warungs. They joined them in the cabanas for breakfast. They sat around the pool at dusk and ordered cocktails and sipped them slowly, watching Ollie in the shallow end, on the tiles, as the sun finally slipped behind the tiered roofs of the private residence next door and the temperature dropped a few degrees. Madeleine and Clara had made a pact to try every cocktail on the menu at the hotel over their stay, one a night, and to order them everywhere else they ate, although often they were so bad Clara's sat barely touched in front of her.

Tom found he was relenting. He had no choice. He was not escaping them. Clara and Madeleine's friendship was deepening. He could see why. Madeleine was not like Emily in many ways, who was sunny, upbeat, while Madeleine was droll, but she filled the same space, somehow, took Clara away from herself; by dint of her strength of character, her forthrightness, her volubility, she made Clara forget herself a little — which was the only way Clara could enjoy herself, Tom thought, except when alone with him, when they sat within themselves but drew comfort from each other's proximity. Trish had done this for Clara, too.

Clara was famed for her mildness. For a reticence that people took for meditative and therefore found calming, reassuring. She was the one wanted in an emergency, the one friends looked to when they disagreed on something, the authority that was appealed to, as if they were all children and she their unflappable matriarch. Paradoxically, this made her nothing like Tom's actual mother, who, although wise and clever and often penetrating about things, was nothing if not flappable. Although she would have been wounded to hear it, and perhaps with good reason because in an actual crisis she could surprise them all and be calm and clear and crucial, no one wanted her in an emergency because they assumed she would be a mess. She was known to shriek with horror at the slamming of a door.

To varying degrees at different times, Tom had found this authority of Clara's infuriating. It was an illusion, largely, he felt. A function of character. She was routinely accepted as an expert on subjects that in reality she knew no more about than most people, and on certain subjects, much less than him. But it was her calm judgement they appealed to, her equanimity. Her economy with words made the words she did utter seem more important, more deeply considered. Her take was often the longest to come, but, because of this, it seemed to carry more weight and was taken as some sort of final word. What was that really based on? How slowly her mind moved? A reluctance to express herself? Of course, when he wasn't grumpy about it, he was proud of her, this status she held.

Madeleine had responded to this in Clara, saw that she took what one said seriously, gave things due consideration. That she was rigorously fair. It made Madeleine feel confirmed in her own feelings to bounce them off someone like Clara. And she enjoyed having an authority she could appeal to. She was always turning to Clara when Jeremy and she were having their little fights, over who had to pay for the drinks, or whose turn it was to take Ollie to the hotel bathroom — Ollie was scared of the bathroom, it was dark and hidden away behind the restaurant. The arguments were in jest, Tom was pretty sure. Jeremy certainly laughed along with them. But Madeleine was so deadpan and brutal it was sometimes hard to tell. But Clara adjudicated effortlessly. It's Jeremy's turn, she'd say. You've only just got out here after putting Ollie's swimmers on. Or, Sorry, Mads, but he is right. You've been sunning yourself out here and doing fuck-all for ages. And they'd obey immediately. Pretend to sulk about it, like teenagers.

For her part, Tom felt Clara was a little too readily amenable to Madeleine's takes on everything. Madeleine had strong opinions on global politics, for example, and Clara seemed to agree immediately with everything she said. Not that he found her opinions unreasonable most of the time. Her takes seemed clear-eyed enough. It was just Clara's eagerness, her ready trust. It all seemed a bit quick. But Madeleine had come on strong. Clara's approval, he could tell, flattered her. And maybe Madeleine did this — needed a friend on holiday, someone else to talk to. Yet Madeleine didn't know everything about them. She didn't know about Clara's capacity for gloominess, how her hesitancy could turn to coldness, didn't know about her silences.

She didn't know, either, how they lived. The state of their house. How, back in Melbourne, they lived in squalor. That the dishes got done, but rarely made it back into cupboards or drawers, or that Tom and Clara's clothes lived permanently in two huge piles on the floor. Or that their whole house was grotty; nothing seemed to make it clean, no matter how hard they scrubbed at it. A structurally unsound Californian bungalow sliding into the grass, the house was almost comically dishevelled, and you warmed to it for this, but it also wore you down. A gap between the steps and the front door widened weekly, as if each shrank from the other, or as if the responsibility placed upon them was too much for them to bear. Most things inside the house were original condition or hadn't been updated since the sixties — walls a sickly yellow, skirting boards Myrtle green, broken Bakelite chandelier light fittings, latch windows with frosted glass, and hardwood floors that were excavated some time ago and, after living under carpet for so long, were blackened in the corners with glue. The lino in the kitchen was deteriorating along the seam down the middle of the room, showing more blackened floorboards underneath, and the Formica benchtops were so stained and burnt that cleaning them only wore away further the patches of colour that remained.

The grot seemed to infect the atmosphere in the house. Their motivation to clean it only ever weakened, and they let things slip until they were living permanently with large cane baskets full of dusty, dirty clothes in the hallway, grimy recycling tubs overflowing in the corner of the kitchen, toilet rolls and beer bottles stacked up the walls, and, in the bathroom, a monstera with spiderwebs in its roots and spattered toothpaste on its leaves. It didn't bother them until it did, and then they'd have cleaning days, and it would look okay again, for a week perhaps — grotty still, but pretty enough, with flowers on the table and benches clear, but it didn't last. They were too busy to clean regularly, and anyway they were too disenchanted by the grot, they didn't have the energy to face it. So they tried to ignore it.

★ ★ ★

Around the pool, among the remains of Ollie's dinner crowding the small round tables — his half-eaten pizza, his mostly finished chips — Madeleine was talking again about motherhood. The subject seemed inexhaustible. Clara encouraged her, though, seemed curious about it all. She was asking her about childbirth.

You forget the pain, don't you? she was saying. There's some sort of biological response, a hormone, that makes you forget it all, so you'll do it again? I heard that somewhere . . . Or is that a myth — the patriarchy telling us to shut up about it?

Absolutely it's a fucking myth, Madeleine said. I remember every excruciating moment of Ollie's birth. And she looked over at Ollie, sitting in the pool next to his father, his legs dangling over the

60

underwater ledge between the shallow end and the deep.

I don't, said Jeremy. It all feels very blurry to me. I was in shock, I think. He brought his long legs up slowly out of the water, scooping up Ollie's legs with them, who giggled. But I'm glad, he said. I don't need to remember all of that, thanks.

But that's because you had nothing to do, darling, except stand around and watch, Madeleine said. Men are superfluous by that point. Not that you didn't help me, mon cœur. Just by being there. Of course. But *I* was working, I was concentrating harder than I ever have on anything in my life. I remember every fucking second.

Clara was chuckling. Kind of bobbing up and down in her lounge. Oh well, she said, that's better anyway, maybe. It seemed strange when I heard that, that the only way the human race survives, reproduces itself, can bear to go on, is through some kind of wilful forgetting.

Maybe we *do* do that, as a society, Madeleine said. Yes, that is true. But non, non, non. Merde. It's not women forgetting how much it fucking hurts.

Jeremy shot her a quick look, presumably about all the swearing in front of Ollie.

That is a good phrase, though, actually, 'wilful forgetting', Madeleine said.

Thank you, Clara said.

Can I use it, maybe?

It's yours.

They laughed.

Tom registered, while he tuned out Madeleine

61

and Clara, that he only ever thought about parent-
hood abstractly, as if he was still in his twenties
and it was a long way off. He had always taken it
for granted that he would be a father, most likely,
at some point in his life, but he assumed that, like
him, Clara knew they were in no position yet to
have children. Their jobs were too precarious,
their incomes too low, their lives too disorgan-
ised, too full of things they were struggling to get
done so their lives proper could still begin. They
were barely functional. They could hardly clean
up after themselves. They didn't need another
thing that made all that harder.

He had never seen Clara clucky as such, although
she was a good aunt to her sister's daughter,
Annie, and was good with children generally.
They responded to her, her lack of condescension. She asked them questions that other people
didn't think to ask and listened carefully to what
they said in reply. This was true with Ollie, too.
She talked to him about things that mattered to
him, tried to understand why he didn't like the
food when it was served to him, was it texture,
colour, smell, and they had an ongoing thing
about the scooters and bicycles that were around
them all day, who could spot the most from any
one position, what were their best ones, colours,
styles, makes, decals. They had certainly never
openly discussed having children, not since the
early days, when maybe it was only a subject for
discussion because it was hypothetical, and only
really about getting to know each other. Maybe
he was in denial about all that and she thought
about it all the time — who knew? They were

careful to avoid sex at certain times each month, he knew that much.

Madeleine was comparing French and Balinese attitudes to children, and admiring the Balinese's understanding of consent and boundaries. Their own children have wonderful lives, she said, despite everything, and western children love the Balinese, you see grown men and women communicating with kids from across the room, silently, laughing, pulling faces. They adore children, but they don't feel the need to touch them, ruffle their hair, bend them to their will. There is respect, real respect.

Tom looked over at Ollie, who was now watching his legs move under him through the water, treading only on the blue tiles as he waded backwards into the deep end, his fair hair dark as it stuck against his brow. But quickly, Tom stopped paying attention to what everyone else was doing. He was trying to empty his mind, breathe deeply, relax as much as he possibly could into the banana lounge, and see if he could locate and relax very specific muscles in his body. He was distracted by a song in his head — the refrain 'These songs of freedom . . . all I ever had' going round and round — and a host of other things he was thinking about, or trying not to think about: his tax, an email from a student he had yet to respond to about the extremely late submission of her final essay, ordering another drink. Also, a list he was making about his mother. All the things she was scared of, and which of these fears he had inherited, or maybe not inherited, but assumed: thunderstorms; flying; spiders; showing her body under any circumstances, but especially in a swimsuit (perhaps the only thing she had in common with Clara); socialising, especially if playing the host; death. Most of them reasonable enough, too, he would argue.

Although he didn't have her astraphobia. In a storm, his mother would not only switch off every powered device in the house, turn off the power at the wall, and pull out all the cords or get his father to, she would also retreat to the safest part of the house — by her reckoning the hallway — and cower on the floor in the darkness with the dog, with whom she had a special affinity at such times. Like the dog, she would emit moans corresponding in volume to the intensity of the flash of lightning or the clap of thunder. This was one of her fears he had learnt to scorn while growing up, but, as she grew sicker and he grew older and his own fears loomed larger, he tried to be kinder to her about it. Still, he remembered swanning around the house with sweaty palms, trying to prove to himself that he wasn't scared.

★   ★   ★

That night Tom and Clara watched the film about the tsunami. They found it in the hotel's DVD library. It was a pirated copy, recorded on camcorder, the camera occasionally bobbing about, and it was greenish around the edges, which removed them a little from the action, but at the same time made it more dreamlike, nightmarish. The big scene was quite close to the

64

start, the tsunami sweeping over the coastline and into hotel grounds much like theirs. It was a challenge for the filmmakers, because it seemed to move so slowly, and, in some ways, it was unspectacular. Just a mass of swelling water. Also, because it was so big, the scale of everything got strangely corrected in your head, as if you wouldn't allow yourself to see it for what it really was, so you kept thinking they were tiny, miniature — those buildings, those trees, all that outdoor furniture.

Then the camera plunged under the surface of the water, and it all sped up, things whipping by, and the violence became clear. The sound effects helped, and you saw Naomi Watts being struck by various things churning around her in the water. Although the film became less engrossing after this scene, as it followed the aftermath of the tsunami, it was a gripping enough story, based on true events. Tom knew Clara enjoyed this kind of movie. He did, too, up to a point, but he didn't want to be scared like she did. He had never liked horror movies. She seemed to want everything to be more intense in movies. Bigger, scarier. He was just glad he could laugh at it and pretend to be unaffected by the emotional family reunion at the end.

Afterwards, they turned off the light, and he put his hand on her thigh as they got comfortable in the bed. He thought she might be asleep, but then he felt her pick up his hand and clasp it in hers. After a few minutes, she put his hand back down on the bed between them and fell asleep.

6

The next morning, Tom arrived at the cabanas to find Clara comforting Madeleine. She was sitting beside her on the couch, rubbing her back, looking up at him warningly, and saying, She's smart, Mads, she'll know to get out before it gets really bad. He couldn't think who they could be talking about.

It was Madeleine's sister in Sydney. Madeleine and Jeremy had visited her before their trip to Bali, which was really just a short holiday tacked on to the end of their visit to Sydney because — like Clara and Tom — they'd never really taken a holiday like this before. They spent all their summers at a family holiday house in Paros. Madeleine had only been to Southeast Asia once before, when she was young and the family visited Thailand — whereas her sister, Cece, had been to Bali many times and told them they had to go while they were so close.

All this Tom had learnt that first morning they'd met them all by the pool, but now it turned out that Cece had an abusive partner. He had held her by the wrists, slapped her, thrown coffee at her, and once refused to let her out of the car. Yesterday, Madeleine said, Cece had written her a cryptic email suggesting something new had happened, that she was close to leaving him, but didn't know how to do it — their daughter was only three, and she didn't have any kind of support network in Australia — but this morning she was back-pedalling on the whole thing, saying yesterday was one of her fasting days and she always gets emotional when she doesn't eat.

It's so strange, Madeleine said. Everything seemed okay when we were there. Yes, he's an asshole, alright . . . but for the most part he was on his best behaviour, because of his history, I suppose, and because we threatened not to visit at all because we didn't want to spend time with a man who hit my sister.

Clara, looking at Tom, said it reminded her of what had happened with her friend Trish, and she told Madeleine the story of how, several years ago, Trish had held on in an abusive relationship for way too long, and partly because of children, too. She told her about the time in the mountains when Trish sprained her ankle while pregnant, and Simon did nothing to help her, and what happened in Rome — also while she was pregnant — and how he made her walk everywhere and wouldn't let her catch a taxi. Simon wasn't physically abusive, it was emotional, psychological, Clara said. It was all about control. Cece, like Trish, it sounded like, was being gaslighted by this guy.

What is this actually? asked Madeleine.

When someone manipulates you into thinking you're going crazy, that everything is your fault, Clara said. That's what it was like for Trish. She couldn't do anything right, he criticised everything she did — how much money she spent at the supermarket, not just the brand of butter she

67

bought but what size packet, the way she cut up her vegetables — every trivial thing. It was *her* fault that he was so awful to her all the time. If only she did things the right way, everything would be fine.

Oh God. How awful to have a man like that in your life, Madeleine said. We feel crazy and stupid enough already, no? She was laughing weakly, her face still pale with concern.

But it was like what you said about Cece, Tom said, trying to join in. Whenever we were around, everything seemed okay, you know. We never had any idea what was going on. They seemed fine.

They did *not* seem fine, Clara said. I had an idea! You just . . . hope she'll get out, or it won't get any worse. I don't know.

Exactly, said Madeleine.

I always felt so conflicted, Clara said, stroking Madeleine's back. Sometimes people just want to be heard, of course, they don't want advice. They don't want to be told what to do. And of course people need to make their own mistakes and everything. She readjusted herself on the seat, smoothing down her dress with her free hand. And, Christ, who is to judge other people's relationships anyway? Who's to say what is a good or bad relationship? Or a good or a bad man? Clara looked at Tom, innocently enough, he thought, as if to include him in the conversation. It's such a low bar, she continued, and yet, it was my responsibility, my role, as her friend, to tell her to get out, wasn't it? I could never quite get it right, the response to her and her problems, she was never happy with what I said.

If I was simply sympathetic, she could tell I was holding back opinions, and if I gave opinions, she would argue with me about them, and even though she has left him now, and freely admits I was right and everything, we're not really the friends we used to be . . . I don't know, it's so hard.

Tom had no idea this was the case with Trish. He thought they still talked all the time.

Skilfully, Clara brought Madeleine around, and, soon, as Tom picked at the plate of pastries that sat in front of him on the table, talk moved on from Cece and her custody issues in Australia and returned to a subject they'd touched on before, child care and how it compared in the two countries. Madeleine felt Cece would be better off in France as a single mother, especially with her nearby, even though Madeleine's experience with the French child-care system had been mixed.

The pastries were much better in Luang Prabang, Tom was thinking. Much better than the soft croissants and stale scrolls that came with breakfast here every morning, and which sometimes tasted of rancid oil or butter or had an ant or two crawling on them, but which of course he still ate. He couldn't remember much else about Laos. They went there second. After Thailand and before Europe. The pastries, the baguettes, the colonial terraces lining the streets, how sick they had got there from eating street food. But Madeleine's accent, the force of her opinions, the way she said *non* so definitively when she disagreed with someone, had reminded him of something else that had happened to them there.

69

They'd hired bikes for the day, to see the streets lined with French patisseries and coffee shops and then to follow the curve of the Mekong, which was wide and slow there, as it skirted the city, with marinas full of beautiful painted boats. After eating baguettes and cheese at a patisserie — it was such a novelty after a month in Thailand, a country without 'real' bread — they were navigating their way through the streets to the river when they accidentally rode through the gates of a private residence or a hotel or a compound of some kind. It had looked just like any other street at first, with low, shuttered, white-washed buildings either side of a paved road, but there were the gates they had passed through, and then a hulking figure — who, from a distance, seemed like a frail old man, waving to them perhaps — appeared from one of the buildings and steamed up the drive towards them, shouting. They put on their brakes, but the man didn't slow down, and, when he arrived, he tried to pick up Tom's bike while he was still getting off it and turn it around.

The man was old and had an enormous paunch, but the rest of him was wiry and strong. Tom tried to restore civility, to engage the man in conversation, to explain that they were lost, and then to at least insist on his own dignity — to insist on turning the bike himself and walking back up the drive at his own pace — but the man would not allow it, was so incensed that he dragged Tom's bike all the way back through the gates with Tom still half on it. The force of the man's anger, the way he could not be reasoned with, was so unstoppable, stuck with him. He wanted to do something to him — even now. Like he did to Marco. Get him back, somehow. For his violence, his self-righteousness, his misdirected rage. For the way he had humiliated him.

★ ★ ★

Jeremy and Ollie came back under the shade of the cabana. Madeleine was talking about cross-disciplinary work now. How she was working with an illustrator on a cultural history project on French abortion laws and the trickiness of these collaborative relationships. How someone always seemed to need to be in charge, to take the lead, how it had become clear that she was the leader of the project and the illustrator just wanted to be told what to draw or else do the whole thing himself, which was disappointing to her.

Ollie, with a slick of watermelon across his cheeks, his beach hat pulled hard over his fore-head, wanted her attention.

I hear that you want to speak, Oliver, mon cherie, she said, in a practised tone. I acknow-ledge your desire to speak next, but we are talking, please, and she finished her thought. Then she gave her attention to Ollie.

What do you want?

Maman. Les tortues, Maman, he said, tugging ineffectually at the strings of his hat.

She turned to the others and sighed. Should we all go? We can see the turtles on the way down to Mick's place, no?

She was referring to a famous resort further

down the boardwalk that, sometime in the early 1990s, was the location for Mick Jagger and Jerry Hall's wedding. Clara had seen an article about it somewhere. The guest list had included Bowie, Sting, Chrissie Hynde, all sorts of people, some of whom were rumoured to have bought properties in the area or to still visit the resort. The place was so exclusive that there was no listing for it on any of the apps.

They decided on the resort, then the turtles, and they set off south along the boardwalk, running the gauntlet of the masseuses sitting under the trees on deckchairs and crates. Clearly, these women were not allowed to enter the grounds of the hotels or approach people on their beachfronts, so they had to yell across to people as they came out onto the beach. As a result, they were uproariously loud all day long, laughing among themselves and shouting at each other and over to potential customers in a way quite unlike anyone else around.

Tom had flown relatively under the radar of the masseuses, but Jeremy, of course, was well known to them. As they left the hotel grounds, a couple of women followed, and Jeremy laughed and bantered with them happily as they asked countless leading questions designed to circle back around to massages and other services and goods they could provide. They could arrange anything, of course — boat rides, jetskis, trips to the textile factories — and Jeremy answered their questions diligently but ironically, enjoying the entrapment from which he had then to extricate himself. They laughed, too, showing that they

72

knew that he knew but it didn't matter — knowing, perhaps rightly, that all this could still land them custom, in honour of the effort they put into the game. But there was a limit to their efforts, and eventually they dropped away, securing the promise of another chat tomorrow.

Tom was glad to have avoided it, but he couldn't help admiring Jeremy's easy banter with the women, and their ease with him — how happily everyone played their roles and then transcended them, transcended a situation that could only ever have made him profoundly uncomfortable.

★   ★   ★

For hundreds of metres down the boardwalk they passed one resort after another. With Ollie they made a game of comparing each new resort to their own and giving them ratings overall. Very few were as ramshackle and beautiful as theirs; most were newer and more expensive-looking, but ugly. Even so, most of them had one or another enviable feature, mostly to do with pools: more pools, prettier pools, larger pools, pools that extended further out to the boardwalk and the beach and were lined on either side with well-stocked bars.

Then they found it. Like all places of great exclusivity, there was little to see. No signage, no pools. But neither was it walled off; just a low, whitewashed stone wall that opened discreetly at one point onto a narrow white-pebble path and green lawns. Everything else was hidden behind a stand of trees — black-trunked, Japanese-looking deciduous trees that stood starkly against the plush lawns extending deep beyond them. They stood and stared at it a moment, and then Jeremy broke the silence by saying it looked like the kind of lawn that was made to be passed out on, and Clara and Madeleine laughed.

One villa could be seen through the trees, after all, Tom noticed, off to the side: a simple, squarish double-storey dwelling, also Japanese-looking, with a bottom floor open to the elements. This seemed to fit the bill. Serviced, secluded, with perhaps its own pool on the far side, cut into the lawn. Tom could see Rod Stewart dropping in for drinks at a place like that, Robbie Robertson and Martin Scorsese turning up in shorts, ready for a game of doubles. Models walking around it naked.

The place had an uncanny quality, a feeling that was accentuated by how little there was to actually see. How tantalising those lawns were — lawns that gave away nothing, but which stretched endlessly beyond the screen of trees to some imagined paradise. Was it the thrill that maybe they'd catch sight of someone famous? Or was knowing these people had once been there enough? The invisibility of the super wealthy. Exclusivity and privilege present, detectable only in the expanse of perfectly maintained, under-utilised space. The green lawn so green, so soft, so eerily empty.

★ ★ ★

On the way back, they went to see the turtles at the rescue — poor, apparently injured creatures of varying size and colour, including a couple of

74

huge specimens, which were stuck crawling over each other in tubs on the beach, but were nevertheless saved, presumably, from painful deaths in the ocean, asphyxiated by bin liners or tangled in sixpack beer holders.

Ollie had a lot of questions that none of them could answer satisfactorily, and there was no one in particular that seemed the right person to ask. Instead, Jeremy pulled out the frisbee, and Tom and he and Ollie played on the beach near the turtles while Clara and Madeleine went off to the market.

It was another cloudless, hot, humid day in a seemingly endless run of such days, and, after a few minutes of playing, Tom was sweating profusely. They began ducking under the shade of palms and mangroves between turns. The sweating put him on alert, but it felt good to be sweating from exertion. To have an excuse. None of them was particularly good at frisbee, although Jeremy could send a frisbee incredibly long distances beyond the reach of Tom's arms. Ollie was a good sport and threw himself into the game. He was easily impressed by the pseudo-trick throws Tom and Jeremy came up with — behind the back or between the legs was about the extent of it, although they managed passable forehands occasionally, too — and he ran at full pelt after the frisbee no matter how far away it was, sitting on the sand or in the water, the fabric of his rashie stretching tight around his middle.

Near the trees, the sand was raked into piles, and, imperfectly hidden beneath the sand, Tom could see rubbish — plastic bottles, cardboard, napkins, glass — which he took as proof of what he had heard, that they simply raked the rubbish under the sand every morning.

As they played, Tom and Jeremy talked about Jeremy's work. He was a boom mic operator for a TV company. He had done it in London first, after film school in Sydney. It was always easy to find work doing that, he said — his height helped — and he could do his own film work on the side, but he'd more or less given up on that now. He had worked with a few big names, Vincent Cassel, Marion Cotillard, although he didn't really meet her, and he had no notable gossip. Juliette Binoche was nice, he said. Treated everyone on set the same.

Then they talked to Ollie about Bali and the turtles and the boogie board he wanted to buy at the markets and whether or not it would be any good or a cheaply made knock-off.

Jeremy took Ollie's hand as they walked back to the hotel the long way, via the street, and he talked to Tom about parenting. He talked about the hard first months — first years, he grinned — how it never really gets easier, the goal posts keep shifting, but that you kind of settle into it, and enjoy it more, maybe, the more confident you become doing it, the less often you think they might die from some stupid mistake you'll make.

He laughed and then grew more serious. I think, he said quietly — although not quietly enough that Ollie could not hear it, Tom thought — I had postnatal depression myself after he was born, for a while there.

Tom half-laughed before realising Jeremy

meant it. Before remembering what Clara had told him. Oh, he said. Men get that?

Oh yeah, it's pretty common, Jeremy said, and Tom felt foolish. Foolish, and that his tone had not been sympathetic enough. That he might just have shamed Jeremy there for a second, or like it might have seemed he was mocking Jeremy, which he hadn't meant to do at all. His temperature was rising again.

We went to couples counselling, Jeremy said. They took it pretty seriously. It was good. It's something they're good about now, everyone's postnatal mental health. They understand how tough it can be, on everyone.

That's good, Tom said, and they let it drop.

They trod carefully over potholes on the sidewalk, and Jeremy put Ollie on his back as they took a short cut through an empty lot strewn with rolls of wire and crumbled concrete blocks. There was a sign indicating the firm in charge of security for the lot, and, Tom gathered from the symbols on the sign, warnings of jail time for being caught stealing from building sites.

How about you? Jeremy said as he put Ollie back down at the entrance to the hotel. Do you think you and Clara will have children?

I don't know, Tom said, and couldn't decide what to say next. He had become incredibly conscious of his body. The rhythm of his walk, or lack thereof; how he now had to hold it steady, his pace, effortfully. But thankfully he didn't need to say anything else, because Ollie had started talking about going to the beach, and soon they were back at the pool, where they found Madeleine

77

and Clara in banana lounges with untouched cocktails between them on a marble table.

Tom was happy to see them, happy to see the pool. Sweat was prickling his skin, sprouting down his spine. He sat for a moment on a banana lounge, unbuttoning his shirt deliberately, not rushing his movements, breathing deeply as inconspicuously as possible, counting to ten in between each breath. Then he felt something brush his elbow, and he was back on his feet.

It was Clara's hand, reaching out sleepily from the banana lounge, her sunglasses on and her face partially covered in a muslin cloth. She wasn't looking his way, she was nodding at Madeleine, who was saying something about the highly varnished woodwork penises they'd seen at the markets, bunches of them in bowls as keyrings, bottle openers. How graphic they were, how anatomically correct.

Clara's hand hung in the air for moment, as Tom dropped his shirt on the banana lounge, took three steps towards the pool, and split the surface of the water.

Only as he pushed through, skirting the sky-blue tiles at the bottom of the pool, his eyes closed against the chlorine, did he allow himself to feel the shame. They were in Bali; he was allowed to sweat. No one would wonder why. And Clara was allowed to touch him. But he was caught off guard. It was the wrong moment. Besides, he couldn't think of the last time she had done something like that — displayed affection publicly. It was always him, and it was always brief. A quick press of her shoulders with his hands; a hand slipped around her waist for a moment while passing. Only in private were they physically close. On the days when they both worked from home, they fell into each other in the hallway often, exhausted, standing perfectly still for minutes at a time.

7

One happened at the end of a longish walk into the city, to visit the State Library. There was microfilm there, historical newspapers he needed to consult for his thesis. It was November, one of those suddenly very warm days you weren't yet expecting, the sun high and blazing, and he was already a little overheated. Ahead of him in the street he spotted Emily, walking in his direction. She had seen him, was smiling and waving. He had no choice but to greet her. He waved back.

She hugged him — a long, warm hug that sank his face deep into her hair. He worried about his clammy hands, worried about his body odour, a slight stickiness he detected in his underarms, but there was nothing he could do about it now. Her hair, long, shining, strawberry blonde, was pillowy against his cheek. There was a hint of vanilla about her, but her hair smelled of nothing so much as health and cleanliness, as if, instead of some product she used, this was simply the smell of incredibly healthy hair.

She arched back from him, still holding on to his arms, although more loosely now, and looked into his eyes.

How are *you?* she said, and for a moment, like always, he was dazzled by her eyes. So big and blue and clear, Emily's eyes had a depth and a segmented complexity that other people's eyes simply didn't seem to have. Forever wet-seeming,

her eyes gave her the appearance of being constantly on the verge of some emotional outpouring,
as if her capacity for feeling, for sadness, compas-
sion, for great pity, was something she was only
just managing to contain. Beneath her eyes, in
the shadow of her bangs, along the ridges of her
cheekbones, there was a faint patterning of freckles; these he couldn't remember seeing before,
but must have. Then tips of white, good teeth
between slightly parted lips, and a strand of hair
that clung to the corner of her mouth. He tried
not to look at that.

Emily was always like this. Very warm, very
affectionate. She was very beautiful and very warm,
and people loved her because she directed this
beauty and warmth at you with an intensity of
attention that was deeply flattering. It was always
brief, this attention, because she was in much
demand, and always busy, but this only intensified its effect, as well as the sense that it was
being snatched away from you too soon. Snatched
away cruelly — like good fortune, like actual
warmth — and guided upon the next person,
who didn't deserve it as much as you and for
whom you felt a moment's hatred.

But Tom had become cynical about Emily and
her shows of affection. He had suggested to
Clara, perhaps Emily's best friend — he had
introduced them, but she was clearly now Clara's
friend, not his — that there was something suspect about the whole thing, something pathological.
For instance, he asked her, had she ever noticed
how Emily, after she had made such a big deal
about seeing you, the long hug, the need to know

81

how you were, what you'd been up to, and all the talk of catching up properly and all the rest, often didn't speak to you again for the rest of the night? And then how when you parted ways there was another big, essentially empty to-do about having you around, et cetera, pleading with you as if it meant all the world to her, but it never happened? It was all just for show, he said. It was a performance, a seduction, and one that exposed a neediness on Emily's part, to have everyone think well of her all the time. She needed everyone to be in love with her and she needed to feel she was a good, attentive friend — while doing very little of the work of real, actual friendship — so she could move on to whomever she really wanted to talk to in the room. It was contrived, political. It was public relations. Why did she need everyone to love her so much? She was insecure.

Clara told him he was being ridiculous. More than ridiculous, a shithead. Like she had in the warung. It was what she called him whenever he said things like this. It was shorthand for an assessment of him she had delivered in full a few times, and thereafter abbreviated to just the name: that he only ever saw the worst in people. That he assumed people to be acting with the worst possible motives, from the very worst impulses. That he was paranoid, and this made him mean. All that shit in his head made him capable only of shit thoughts, she said.

It was an assessment, and a name, that he tried to laugh off, but it stung. It didn't stop him thinking those things about Emily, of course, and half-hating her for it — as a good, loyal friend, Clara was bound to defend her. What he had noticed, though, was that even though he had come to expect it, the big greeting from Emily and nothing more, until perhaps much later in the night when they were both drunk and they might fall into an argument about something stupid, he still felt the burn of it, the jealousy, and the desire for that attention so quickly withdrawn. That was the worst part of it. That he still fell for it, every time. He wondered if others felt the same way about Emily, but he had never broached the subject with anyone else, because he didn't want to draw attention to the way he felt about her, didn't want people thinking about Tom and Emily and their relation to one another. Plus, no one would agree, he was sure, because everybody loved her.

People loved her also, Tom thought, as he withstood her gaze on the street, tried not to wither under it, for the simple reason that it reflected well on you to be seen with someone that beautiful, made you feel like you might be beautiful, too, or that there was something special about you for having a friend who was. As she approached him and flung her arms around him, for example, he was hyper-aware, without taking his eyes off her, of people watching them. Noting their closeness, her apparent affection for him. There was a certain grace that was conferred upon him by simply being in her presence. How immediately apart from everyone else it made him feel, to be the subject of their envy. But how preposterous at the same time. How ashamed. To be so easily taken in by it, so susceptible.

They determined they were going in the same direction. In fact, to the same location, more or less — she was meeting Esther at the cafe on the terrace of the library. She pressed his arm with both hands, one final gesture of affection as she untangled herself from him, a chunky bangle dropping down her arm, and together they moved up the street.

Weaving in and out of the stream of pedestrians coming the other way, steering around tourist huddles and clots of teenagers in school uniforms, she asked him about his research. He gave the briefest account of it, deflecting the question by shifting the focus onto her own research.

Oh, don't ask! she said, raising her palms in the air and dropping them back down. Everything Emily said was like this: emphatic, deeply felt. When she texted him, which she used to do when they first became friends, the messages were littered with exclamation points, trebled question marks, signed off with long trails of kisses and hearts and elaborate emoticons that he often found indecipherable.

I'm asking, he said. You have to tell me.

Well, she said, sighing dramatically, I have bitten off more than I can chew, basically, I think. And she paused and looked down at the ground in front of her feet.

How so? he asked, before being forced off the curb for a moment by three teenage boys with backpacks coming the other way.

It gave him time to take stock. His underarms

had fused. There was a stickiness elsewhere too now, along his spine, on his chest. And although he dared not test it with his fingers, he felt sure his fringe was stuck to his forehead. Silently, invisibly, he inhaled deeply and held it for as long as he could before letting it out. It wasn't so easy while walking fast. As he held in the breath, his hands pulsed.

I mean, surely that's how it feels all the time, at least to some degree, he said, rejoining her. It does with me.

Yes, I guess so, she said. And it's just early days and everything. But I think I've been overly ambitious trying to be all cross-disciplinary about it or something, bringing in sociology, psychology, now neuroscience, and critical theory of course . . . at the moment Lacan, who is doing my head in . . . 'Preserving farness, nearness presences nearness by nearing the farness' . . . 'Though never present, the thing is not absent.' I should have just written about roundabouts!

Well, you are, aren't you? Just going deep on roundabouts?

Too deep! she laughed.

Emily's research, as he understood it, which he didn't very well, or couldn't remember as well as he should, although they had talked about it many times, was something to do with street design and mental health, or social cohesion, or something like that. Whether living in streets that ran along rectilinear grids was better or worse for mental health outcomes than living in streets and suburbs that followed the natural contours of the landscape, or organic streetscapes that were not planned at all. Or that's where it had started. The focus on roundabouts seemed relatively new.

He was monitoring himself. As he deep-breathed, his heartbeats seemed to come in pairs, the first of each a suspension, an extending out, and the second a drop, a stepping down, further into his body. These he tried to really feel. Feel his body rising and falling naturally as it moved along the street, as if in there some-where, deeper within his body, was a place he could retreat to and escape the pulsing. He didn't feel anxious, didn't feel panicked — his heart rate was relatively stable — but he knew if he didn't cool down soon, he would begin to. He couldn't think about it. He needed to keep the attention on Emily.

This helped in a couple of ways. It was distraction — concentrating on Emily's work, her answers to his questions — and in this way related, he thought, to mindfulness, as far as he understood it, which wasn't well. He had considered taking a class on mindfulness once, downloading some guided meditations, but had instead chosen to learn transcendental medita-tion, thanks to a recommendation from a friend, which he understood to be the much more intense of the two. At the time he reasoned the severity of his condition called for drastic measures. But he found it surprisingly easy to do — it was in essence a simple technique, once you got past the pseudoscience and spiritual nonsense that came with it — and he enjoyed it, practising it twice a day for twenty minutes, in the morning and the early evening, as instructed. He'd kept it up for several months, until he hit a busy period of teaching and dropped it, after which he never took it back up again. But one couldn't do transcendental meditation while walking down the street, or not while holding a conversation.

Keeping Emily talking also meant the pressure was off him. By keeping her thinking about her own work, she would pay less attention to him, look at him less often, and he wouldn't have to try to formulate cogent responses to any questions she put to him. If only he could escape. But she knew now where he was going, so there was no way out. The somewhat contradictory alternative would have been to have a longer walk with her. He could keep her talking and it would break, finally, like it always did, in its feverish way. He would grow hotter and hotter until, somehow, it crested and broke, and, without noticing the change, he would no longer be anxious at all, and almost instantaneously quite cool.

You'll get there, he said.

Maybe! she laughed.

They fanned out either side of the agglomerate of people in front of Melbourne Central and fell back in step.

I have found my straw man at least, I think, she said.

Oh, good . . . who is that?

She told him about the straw man, some city planner from the seventies who made a specious link in a book — which most people weren't aware of, admittedly, but which seemed to represent the consensus thinking on the subject — between the roundabout and mental health.

He ignored class and race, and glaringly, she said, failed to acknowledge that the real problem wasn't the way cars were directed around suburbs, but that suburbs were built around car use in the first place. She became exasperated. Once that is corrected, so many other problems go with it! she said. Communities would be more cohesive, and mental health stats, of which there was a modest drop in suburbs with non-rectilinear layouts, would fall off at a much faster rate.

He agreed, and, although he had become a little confused about her position on roundabouts, whether she was pro roundabout or anti them, he struggled to think of other questions to ask her. They moved on to other things, mainly Clara, how she was going with her studies, her sewing. He joked about the wonderful jumpers he'd now be forced to wear.

But no, seriously, Emily said, I'm so glad she's doing that. It's so good to have something else to do. I mean, of course Clara already has other things — she is such a good cook, and gardener, she loves bushwalking, doesn't she, hiking — but something new, maybe, is good to get into, too.

Yes, Tom said. It's great that writing a thesis has made her so depressed and broke she's started sewing her own clothes.

He was enjoying himself, but he was being betrayed by his body. A river of sweat had opened up along his spine and was soaking into the waistband of his jeans. He tugged at his shirt, to let air in, swiped discreetly at his forehead, dreading it sprouting from there, too, where it was hardest to conceal, but he was losing the battle, he could see that. There was little chance of it just passing, now that anxiety about the anxiety was in play.

The heat of the day wasn't helping. Light glanced off buildings, flashed off the pavement, cut into his eyes from windows. He was wearing a light jumper, but he dared not take it off. The sweat was surely visible through his shirt. But it was only another thirty, forty metres and then they were there, crossing the street to the library and moving through the tables on the terrace towards Esther.

Esther, long-legged, stylish in her work clothes, looking so much more grown up than the girl he saw on weekends at parties and shows, got up to hug them both. Tom leaned in from a distance.

Can't stop for a coffee? Emily asked, putting down her bag and taking a seat opposite her friend.

From their seats, they both looked up at Tom, and he struggled not to flinch. But the way they looked at him. How strange it was. How slow. How dreamy. It was as if they were suspended in time, or the tape had been slowed down, and he could watch it in slow motion, the stretch of their smiles across their faces. Their wondrous, easeful smiles. So beautiful they were almost grotesque.

I should get in there, really, he said. Been putting it off for too long . . . If I find what I need quickly, I'll come back out and find you.

No worries, Emily said, pouring herself some water from the bottle on the table. We're not going anywhere . . . Esther's just finished, and we've both got the day off tomorrow — we might

89

have drinks next, who knows! she laughed.

Drinks! Esther said. Very here for that.

He ducked in under the awning and through the cafe into the foyer of the library. It was cool and dim and reverberant in there. It had vaulted ceilings and marble floors and air-conditioning, and, although it was a public space and wide open and busy, people streaming through the main doors and in and out of the foyer in various directions, he felt better.

He wondered if he might be okay now, in the air-conditioning, in the anonymity of the collections. He moved through the many rows of tables, which were mostly empty, to the front desk. The woman at the counter directed him to the microfilm room, and he was making his way there when he realised it wasn't passing, after all. He wasn't calming down. He would need to find a bathroom.

Inside the cubicle, he took off his jumper, his shirt, pulled down his jeans, and sat on the toilet with his eyes closed. It was cold in there, his shoulder resting against marble that stung his skin. But it would take time for his temperature to drop. He would need to calm down first. Sweat slipped down his chest. He sat back up, wound toilet paper around his fist, many times over, and ran the wad down his chest, across his forehead, along the length of his spine, around the inside of the waistband of his boxers, and under his arms. The paper was sodden. He dropped it between his legs into the bowl, rested his head back against the wall, closed his eyes, and concentrated on the breathing exercises he had been taught. There were no distractions now. Each heartbeat was sick and sharp and racking. Against his eyelids pulsed a greenish, mouldering red.

He breathed, sweat sprouted, he sopped it up as it came, and, after some time, after twenty, thirty controlled breaths, counting down from ten in between each inhalation and exhalation, and throwing in the mantra every now and then for good measure, he shivered. His heart rate had slowed. The pit of his stomach — which, before, had vanished and been replaced by a terrible dragging sensation, as if each time he inhaled the air escaped back out through a stomach that had been slit open — was back. His blood had withdrawn from his skull.

The exhaustion he felt now was almost as overwhelming in its intensity as the panic had been. He had fallen into a kind of stupor — a heavy, pleasant, drugged kind of state. He had no strength. He opened his eyes, but could not keep them open. His whole body was leaden, as if, if he didn't concentrate on holding himself up, he might slip off the toilet seat to the floor.

After he didn't know how long, he finally pulled himself together. First eyes open, then upright on the seat, then standing to inspect his shirt. There was a line of sweat running down the back, and two more patches over his ribcage, but the biggest spread was from his underarms, the half-moons running over the seam onto the front of the shirt, and far down both arms.

He put the shirt and jumper back on, blew his nose, wiped at his underarms one more time, and left the cubicle. He checked himself in the mirror. It took a moment for his eyes to focus, but then he saw that while his fringe was wet and clinging to his forehead and his face was blanched white and at the same time faintly blotched — a weak, cell-like pattern bloomed in patches over his skin — fundamentally, as long as no one peered at him too closely, looked into his hugely dilated eyes, he was okay.

Carefully he walked back into the library. The room hummed and rustled. Everything in the room seemed so finely wrought: faces in concentration, pale necks bent forward, the dark wood of desks and shelves. A row of arched windows along one wall glowed dully with soft, whitish light, like in a cathedral.

Then, back through the foyer, under the Corinthian columns, out into the sunshine, sunglasses on, speeding up now, feeling stronger, and home.

★ ★ ★

It was bad around that time generally, he acknowledged. There were a few incidents, some sudden exits. But for some reason that day in the city was among the most memorable. Maybe because it involved Emily, the beautiful girl he'd known before Clara. The girl who had always made him feel uncomfortable, who he always had to prepare himself to see. But he had started teaching then, too, and was barely making it through classes.

That was when he finally spoke to his GP and

got put on SSRIs. Started seeing a psychologist. He lasted about four or five sessions with the psych, about a year on the meds. After the first few days, when he was able to get back off the couch, he felt fine on them. His sex drive, already low, vanished completely, but he slept better, and overall he was maybe less anxious. On balance, he probably had fewer outright attacks.

But then he became worried about his liver. The SSRI he was on had an association with liver failure; while on them he was required to have his liver checked every six months. He continued to drink, and occasionally he felt a pain in his side. His test results were clear, except that one corner of his liver was fatty. Apparently it was common enough, but one corner of his liver had gone to fat. He was going to stop drinking, start running, get off the meds. Of the three, getting off the meds was the only one he managed. He barely noticed the difference.

8

The next day was what Tom thought of later as the best day. Later. When everything was ruined and the holiday had taken on a significance to him that he could not have anticipated.

They had settled in. The bad flight was way behind him, the next flight was a whole week away, but, more than that, he was having a good time. He had warmed to Jeremy, he had warmed to Madeleine and Ollie. No longer was he just being well behaved, putting up with them for Clara's sake. No longer was he feeling anxious around them, either. They had broken the ice. They were friends now.

It reminded him of what it used to be like, being on holiday with friends — something he had not done for a long time, but which was once such a regular feature in his life. Weekends away, whole weeks during summer camping by the beach. Looking back, these times seemed to have stopped suddenly, but that couldn't be right. Surely the end was gradual — so gradual he didn't really notice it. Why *had* it happened? He knew and he didn't know.

In truth, being with Madeleine and Jeremy reminded him what it was like to have friends in his life in any way. This had stopped, too, somehow. He made calculations. At twenty-two he had maybe four, five good friends. At twenty-eight, fifteen, twenty. At thirty-five, one

— or two, if you counted Clara.

He remembered how, very early on with Clara, sometime in those first years, he had become hung up on the idea of friendship. It embarrassed him now to think of it, and yet if he was honest, he still nursed many of the same doubts and questions he'd had then. What it means, how it is done. He obviously banged on about it a lot because one day Clara presented him with a book she had picked up from an op shop called *A Friend Is Someone Who Likes You.* She thought it was sweet, funny; she was only gently mocking him. But he had been humiliated by that present, and he was as embarrassed thinking about it now as he was then: that he was preoccupied with something that was so obvious there was a children's book that explained it to you in the very title. Of course, he thought then — and still did think, privately — it wasn't actually as simple as that. Simply liking you did not make someone your friend, not in any meaningful way. People could 'like' you and not see you one year to the next. In what way was that friendship?

At the time, when Clara had given him the book, they were part of a tight little group, people from university, mostly, and a few of Clara's older friends from high school who had also moved to Melbourne from the Gold Coast; Tom had happily let his hometown friends go when he moved to the city. Perhaps because of this, because they were her friends first, he always felt slightly on the outer of this group. He was uptight, paranoid. Everyone else — it was girls mostly and a couple of guys, boyfriends of the girls

95

— seemed to see each other more often than they did him, and he wasn't sure quite how this happened. But he knew he wasn't always easy to get along with, he could be argumentative, prickly, and he always suspected he was tolerated rather than liked. Back then, he was often like this, moody, unpredictable. He slept about as badly then as he did now. He had a reputation for saying things most people wouldn't — and to people's faces, too. Certain people called him 'acid tongue'. But he couldn't handle the injustice of people walking around oblivious, not knowing what everyone thought of them. So he told them. An early girlfriend had said if there was a song about Tom, it was The Smiths' 'Big Mouth Strikes Again'.

When they first got together, he and Clara would argue all the time about the smallest things, and did it everywhere — in front of her parents, in front of his — but he'd put a stop to that. He was agreeable, now. Mild. Quieter.

He'd been trained in the art of argument by his parents — trained to take offence, rise to the occasion, take the bait. To be thin-skinned and sharp-tongued. And it wasn't good for him. He'd agreed with his therapist about that. He could give, but he couldn't take. Besides, if his parents were how you turned out if you kept up with all that, he wanted no part of it.

So he was pleasant, now, and polite. You could just do that, it turned out: swallow it back down, roll with the punches. It was an anti-anxiety strategy, too, of course. If he could just not care about things so much, they wouldn't piss him off or stress him out or make him paranoid, so he

96

was trying to let things go. It might all come out in other ways, of course, like in your legs on a plane or in your hands as you raise your cup to your lips, but he was working on that.

After the present of the book, he'd dropped the subject of friendship, kept his thoughts to himself, and, over time, the preoccupation waned. Besides, only a few years later, when they were no longer in contact with most of the people in the old group, it became a moot point, because they suddenly found their people. A big, messy, amorphous group, introduced to them mostly by Trish, who was a girl who could go out on a Friday night and have a whole new gang by the end of the weekend. And, for a couple of years, they were busy with art openings, gigs, parties, spontaneous all-nighters. There was drugs, lots of booze. It felt late — he was twenty-seven, she twenty-five — but they'd had a quiet, supposedly studious, but in truth lacklustre period after their trip overseas, some of which had been especially lonely for him, as she had spent time away from him, and they entered this new world with a hunger they recognised in each other, but did not discuss. He was happy for the distraction from the PhD, which he had just started, but was already loathing, and she was yet to start hers, so had the time.

But it was short-lived. As quickly as it bloomed, it withered. Certain key people moved overseas — instigators, party-throwers, the glue between groups within the group — a few had kids and moved to outer-ring suburbs. By then, Tom himself had to knuckle down and get on with his research, Clara was finishing her honours thesis, and no one seemed quite in sync anymore. And something that had been so effortless, the spontaneous nights out that moved from openings to restaurants to bars to lounge rooms, even backyards the next morning, something that took no arranging at all, no need for texts or Facebook invites, became something that took work, was difficult to line up, and was never as satisfying. It felt prematurely nostalgic, elegiac, vaguely sad. Very few of these people actively kept in touch, and soon they hardly saw anyone.

He was aware this wasn't the full story, and others might tell it differently. And he knew that if he'd kept going to the shows, the art openings, he would've kept seeing those people; it was as simple as that. That the anxiety played a part in this was something he found hard to acknowledge. He had concealed it even from Clara, as far as he could, and he spent so much time covering for it that he had himself half-believing the lies too: that he was just busy; that he had too much work to do; that he was old now, needed to knuckle down; and, to Clara, that he didn't even like those people anymore.

Clara did better. Some of her older friendships endured, and the small group that had formed around Emily — Paula, Celia, Thuy, Chris — remained her friends, and by extension his. It came more naturally to the women of the group, friendship, it seemed. To talk on the phone, meet for drinks, coffee. The gendering of it was depressingly predictable. Not once had a male friend suggested anything like this.

He still had Barry, of course. Barry he saw because they played tennis together, itself something they had taken up semi-ironically as the classic buddy thing to do, but which soon became the most significant and regular contact he had with anyone. Barry was a leftover from the big group. But Barry didn't go to parties much anymore, either; he worked long hours on the weekend in a bike-repair shop. As the only job he'd ever really enjoyed, he was doing all he could to hold it down. He was on a health kick, too, not drinking, and he'd lost weight. But he was still depressed, most of the time. Before Barry stopped drinking, they'd sometimes had a beer or two afterwards. Very occasionally it became five.

Being with Madeleine and Jeremy brought some of the old times back. All those times he'd forgotten about, when they'd spent whole days, whole weekends, with people without a second thought, as if it was the most natural thing in the world. It reminded him how much he liked it. How much he missed it. But he was rusty. Rusty as hell. He felt like he hadn't spoken about himself to anyone in years — someone who wasn't Clara or his mother or his therapist or Barry — not if he could help it, not in anything but the most cursory way. But Madeleine was insistent. That he not dodge the question — about his research, his teaching, what growing up the son of an architect and an artist in a small Victorian town was like. He found himself clearing his throat a lot. Telling them rambling stories that didn't go anywhere, as if he had forgotten how to tell a story that made sense, that held shape

— what it was about a story that kept people's attention. Besides, his childhood seemed so quaint to him, like he was telling stories of some incredibly distant past.

One story he told was about his father's architectural practice. How he'd semi-retired to the country when they were kids, but of course had started back up and designed people's houses around the place, and how he would later, when he finally did retire, take them on tours, showing them his work, the few houses around the area that stuck out so obviously as architecturally designed. There were a lot of driving tours, as Tom's mother got sicker, and got out less. They were, by and large, ugly houses, he told them. Ostentatious eighties builds. Busy proto-McMansions or too-big luxury beach houses with spectacular views. They'd be sparkling and bloated, with marble and stainless steel, ridiculously broad decks, and white curving roofs poorly mimicking the waves beneath them, like budget, mini Sydney Opera Houses. That was what led him to urban planning, probably, he said — although he wasn't sure this was true at all. All that vanity. How do we kill that?

The others laughed along with his take-down of his father's work, although they were somewhat distracted — by Ollie, by orders arriving, the general busyness of the boardwalk — and he had felt embarrassed for a moment for going overboard, for going so dark, laying it on a bit thick, and he decided he would not talk so much from now on. It wasn't even true, what he had said. His father had designed as many nice houses

100

as he had awful ones: the A-frame; the eco house now reclaimed by the national park; some early, uncompromising geometric houses after Roy Grounds in the seventies. The bad, later ones were a reflection of the tastes of his clients when he moved to the coast as much as his own. But his embarrassment faded quickly in the general atmosphere of good cheer, and later Jeremy picked up certain threads while they played frisbee, asking about his half-sisters, his mother, her art, and, more tactfully, later after a few drinks, her illness. What a person with emphysema could and couldn't do.

But it wasn't being able to talk about himself that he enjoyed particularly — he had no good answers to their questions, nothing interesting, or cogent, to say — it was that he was comfortable around them. And once all the preliminaries had been taken care of, once all the getting to know one another was out of the way, they could all sit around and talk about nothing. Or not talk that much at all. Eat; chat; watch the comings and goings along the boardwalk from their vantage in the cabanas; stare out at the water, grey and flat, but also glittering, reflecting the sun back into their faces; watch the prettily painted jukungs launch from the next beach over, the bigger catamarans heading off to the islands; and drift in and out of one another's experience of it all. Madeleine continued to dominate conversation, but this meant that the rest didn't need to worry about it so much. A dynamic had established itself. And even she had quieter spells. Being a constant source of distraction, Ollie helped. He required some sort of attention so much of the time. But Jeremy was easy to be around, too, and the longer Tom spent in his company the more he liked him, the more he was happy, not resentful, to be spending his days with him.

Jeremy was as easygoing as he was quiet. It helped set a certain tone. He was also discreet. Tom had the feeling he could say whatever he liked around him, didn't have to be constantly on guard or worry about being funny or clever or whatever, because Jeremy himself didn't. Perhaps this had something to do with the fact that they were on holiday together. These were people he would never see again. It was freeing. After a tense first couple of days, when Tom did his best to avoid spending any time alone with Jeremy, he found he looked forward to seeing him each morning at breakfast. He was earnest, perhaps, mostly, but he had a sly wit that became more pronounced the longer you spent in his company. He didn't try too hard, wasn't a performer like Barry, which Tom decided was a good thing. His ego did not demand an audience, or competing wits to spar off, which was the default mode of most of Tom's male friends. In fact, Jeremy made no demands. But he wasn't entirely passive, either. He seemed to sense when more from him might be needed to make things run more smoothly, or to change a mood, but he did this without reluctance or any apparent sense of obligation. Tom wondered how much of this was the effect of being with someone like Madeleine. They seemed so perfectly matched: Jeremy happily leaving most of the social energy to her, but remaining present enough to pick up the slack when needed, as if he was as perfectly content being quiet as he was talking. Tom was slightly in awe of this quality, and then, increasingly, of Jeremy in general.

But most importantly, Jeremy was at ease with himself. Self-consciousness or anxiety in others repulsed Tom. As much as he tried to empathise, as much as he dreaded exactly this kind of judgement of his own anxiety, he found himself eye-rolling inside, thinking: just, like, pull yourself together. People who were comfortable with themselves didn't look at you the same way, with the same sharpness. They weren't constantly making appraisals. Their self-possession could be infuriating, but on balance it was better than the alternative, and anyway, this was unlikely to happen with Jeremy, who had not a whiff of smugness about him. His physical presence, which at times scanned as apologetic, and clumsy, made this impossible.

★ ★ ★

On the morning of the best day, they had breakfast together at the hotel, under the thatched roof of the open-air restaurant. Looking up at the roof from their table, they saw the dustier, though more richly golden underside of the woven panels, which extended in a steep pitch to a small opening at the top that showed a square of blue. From the underside of the roof and between exposed beams hung paintings, mostly large-scale works, in a wide range of styles — works reportedly donated to the hotel from the many artists who had stayed there over the years. Some of them looked like this might have been the case. There were several moody, airbrushed portraits of women with complex, variegated hairstyles wearing reflective visors that looked like they had probably been painted in the eighties. But some of them looked suspiciously like the kind of art you found everywhere in cafes and hotels in Bali: that odd mix of the grotesquely sensual and jokily surreal that often featured monkeys or gorillas engaged in human activities, like riding motorbikes or surfing or smoking joints or holding paintbrushes and pallets and wearing berets.

Some talk at breakfast was about this, both the styles of art prevalent in Bali — they told Madeleine and Jeremy about the Kirschler museum — and the authenticity of these supposedly donated works of arts from the many esteemed artist guests of the hotel over the decades. They had to be discreet about it, as there were only a few other people at tables around them, and the waitresses — the few women they saw each day and whom they had now begun to recognise and talk with more freely — were constantly on the floor, serving and clearing up after the guests. They would hate for them to think they were mocking the hotel.

Madeleine was of course friendliest with these women. She knew a couple of their names now, Eka and Inten — or Indah maybe — and there was talk of a play date with one of their sons, who was of a similar age to Ollie. Tom admired this about Madeleine, how she made the most of the people around her, made herself a little community wherever she went. And he admired more generally how comfortable she and Jeremy were with the Balinese people, as far as they were encountering local people — almost exclusively in service to them. Clara was comfortable, too, with these interactions, in her understated way, but Tom found he couldn't relax into it, these transactions that over days morphed into relationships; he felt he was either overdoing it the whole time, and getting things wrong, fussing too much, or trying to be cool about it and becoming paranoid that he was being rude.

Other topics came up. Brexit — what the French thought about it, and about the British in general — then Jeremy's French, which Tom told them he admired. He had always regretted not learning another language.

Your French is so good, he said.

It's okay, Jeremy demurred.

No, he is fluent, you are fluent, Jeremy, Madeleine said, holding on to Ollie's arm while she popped the cap on the sunscreen.

Maybe.

Yes, you are. He is fluent, but not bilingual.

Fluent, but not bilingual, Tom repeated.

Yes, of course. He can speak it, he can hold conversations, but maybe he can't write an essay in French, or give a lecture, maybe.

Okay, I hadn't made that distinction, Tom said.

It is not maybe the dictionary definition of it, but yes, of course, he is fluent. You are fluent, Jeremy. But not bilingual.

Madeleine applied the sunscreen to Ollie's arms, pushing up his sleeves while he chewed on a piece of pineapple and stared vacantly into the distance. The piece of pineapple appeared in his open mouth, worked its way towards the front, looked about to fall out, then fell back into one of his cheeks. Tom found all this very endearing, the way food quietened Ollie, the way it occupied him. How hypnotised he was by it. The absentness of children; the way they were permitted to just disappear.

It was a pleasant way to start the day. Tom was exhausted — he still wasn't sleeping well — and he had his sunglasses on. They were effectively outdoors, so he did not feel self-conscious about that. He ate all of his eggs and toast and tea and several other things from the baskets of pastries and the plate of fruit that came with it, even if none of it was especially fresh or particularly high quality. It was serviceable, it was free, and he felt like indulging himself.

For most of the breakfast, when he wasn't eating, mostly from the plate of fruit, Ollie agitated for another a game of frisbee on the beach, and finally they did that, while Madeleine and Clara stayed behind, moving with their books and phones and towels from the restaurant to the poolside lounges.

It was another sparkling day out on the beach, cloudless, the sun climbing fast, but not yet too sharp, the beach starting to fill up. The boardwalk was bustling: men walking together in traditional clothing — sarongs and small, square hats — brilliant and immaculate; hawkers carrying coconuts in tubs on their heads; schoolchildren on bicycles; tourists wandering by, looking dazed, sizing up the hotels and their beachside frontages as they passed.

The couple with the Balinese nanny were back out on the beach. The nanny had the child building sandcastles with a bucket, while the mother, in a nearby banana lounge, looked up occasionally from her book to comment on her progress. The father was behind them, flat on a timber platform in the shade, shirtless, looking at his phone. One of Ollie's wilder throws landed on the sand in front of the man, and he did not flinch.

Not long into the game, the woman strained to find her husband in the shadows behind her.

Come over here, love, she called, gesturing to the lounge beside her.

He did not respond.

Come over here, she said again.

She turned back, and, again facing the sea and her daughter, she called back to her husband flatly, loudly, all the sing-songiness gone from her voice, and her Australian accent more pronounced each time, Get off the Insta, love, get off the Insta. She said it several times more, less and less good-naturedly, but it had no effect on her husband. He did not move or reply until maybe fifteen, twenty minutes later, when Tom and Jeremy and Ollie had finished their game and were leaving the beach. Then, in one slow, graceful motion, he rolled off the platform onto his feet and trudged sleepily over to his family.

It became a running joke.

They got back to Madeleine and Clara, and Ollie nuzzled into his mother's armpit and rubbed his head all over her breasts, while she held her phone away and above his head to continue

107

reading. Tom settled into the banana lounge between her and Clara, who was reading her book, and Jeremy took the next one after Madeleine.

Tom got out his phone and checked his messages. Mostly things from the university, nothing important. He opened Facebook for a moment, but closed it again immediately, opened Instagram instead, and, looking around him, wondered if he should post a pic. Now didn't seem the time. Madeleine was holding Ollie at arm's length, while he bounced against her arm, pressing up to her and whining softly.

Because you're a big boy, that's why, she was saying.

I'm not a big boy, he moaned.

You're not?

I don't feel like a big boy.

You don't?

He grinned and spoke louder: I feel like a teenager, Maman! He clasped his mother's hand delightedly at the thought.

Madeleine laughed and looked over at Jeremy, who raised his eyebrows back.

Jeremy had been following various sports on his phone, on silent. He'd walk over to Tom occasionally and show him things, replays, turn up the sound for a second. Or he'd send Tom links to clips, and Tom would turn it up and the sound of commentators shrieking players' names over and over would disrupt the women talking. But they had all begun sending each other things, after their morning chats. Madeleine's were all job openings at European universities. Jeremy's were news articles, mostly, things they would read in the afternoon and talk about at dinner or the next morning: George Pell, the never-ending #MeToo revelations, US politics, the Mueller Report, potential Democratic candidates. Madeleine and Jeremy were invested in US politics. They listened to podcasts on the subject and had strong opinions, knew all the leading Democrats' names, backstories, chances.

Tom read the odd thing, tried to keep up, to learn about the new contenders. Clara was interested while they talked about it, but not enough to read the articles. She had never been particularly concerned with politics, or even current affairs. She was caught up in her research, her reading — right now, on finding ways to link the writing of Elizabeth Grosz to her research on public art on highways — even if she was determined she wasn't working while away. She wasn't on social media much, either, only using Instagram, and that was mainly to stay in touch with friends she no longer saw much of. She rarely posted, herself. She was one of the few people Tom knew who seemed genuinely uninterested in sharing any of her life via social media. What she was interested in was people and their lives, whoever happened to be around her. She prompted long stories from Madeleine about her family and sisters and her work, what life was like in Paris, or Léon — where Clara and Tom had stopped through once, on the way to a farm — and when she spoke of her own interests, it was about the lives of the people around them in Bali, or the way these lives were organised. Like the tsunami evacuation system and the signs she saw around the place.

One day, she said to Madeleine, I want to follow them and see where they go.

You should. Or maybe we could all go, said Madeleine. You should do some research here too, next time.

Maybe I will, she said. I found a PDF of a map. An evacuation plan.

You could do some interviews, Madeleine said.

Yeah, but who with? Clara asked them.

No one knew.

When Tom checked his phone again, he saw that Jeremy had sent him an article on 'Bernie Bros' — how the term was offensive to the diversity of his supporters — and Madeleine had sent him a job ad from Goldsmiths, but Tom didn't open either of these. He was scrolling through Instagram: brutalist architecture; art on the walls of the Guggenheim, more at MOMA; a couple of urban planning accounts showing plazas and aerial views of urban centres, scrolling too fast to see where they were; a photo of Trish's dogs, two greyhounds, lying on blankets either end of a couch, looking equally contrite (this had seventy-seven likes, including one from Clara and one from Emily); some old friends, two couples, with their kids around the outdoor sculptures in the gardens at Heide; another old friend against a whitewashed wall in Crete; a couple of memes, only one of which made any sense to him; a New Yorker cartoon; a selfie of a girl he had never met in person, who was ten years younger than him at least, in a bikini on a beach somewhere; Barry's latest shot from the bike shop, a selfie with an old party friend, Ira, looking thinner and greyer, but most surprisingly wearing spandex riding gear, Barry's thumbs-up in the foreground, clearly having taken the photo without Ira knowing; a sponsored post about R U OK? Day coming up (Fuck you, Tom thought); and one from Clara yesterday he didn't know she'd posted, of a corner of the hotel gardens. It was a perfectly symmetrical shot that framed a bright-green pergola, with a bench and table inside it that were painted powdery pink. Rampant bougainvillea cascaded down either side, and intersecting white pebble paths ran around the perimeter. It had forty-seven likes.

A shadow fell over him. It was Jeremy. He leaned in, serious-faced, and whispered, Get off the Insta, love, get off the Insta, and Tom found himself giggling uncontrollably.

★   ★   ★

After lunch they went to see the fabrics. Jeremy had the number of a driver who had offered to take them to a batik factory. He and Madeleine were thinking of taking something back to France with them, sarongs maybe, as presents for Madeleine's family.

It was a picturesque drive through the country-side, valleys full of terraced rice paddies, choked pockets of jungle, food markets full of people eating, groups of men working in bare feet among concrete foundations and timber frames, and others alone, resting on their haunches on the side of the road, smoking and watching the shuttle as it passed.

The factory itself was underwhelming. It was set up for tourists — the rugs and sarongs and throws bright and busy, not the beautiful faded pastels of the fabrics they saw people using as hangings and tablecloths everywhere around them on the streets. They were also expensive, and Tom and Clara quickly lost interest and wandered out to watch a couple of women working at a loom under a corrugated-iron roof in the dirt. Tom wondered what they were being paid and if they were just for show, if any of their work actually made it into the warehouse behind them. He felt stupid standing there watching them and also complicit in their exploitation, and he wanted to leave.

The weather had changed. It was suddenly dark, and he peered out from under the roof as the first big drops hit the ground. The others appeared — Madeleine had found kids' clothes in one section of the huge warehouse and had bought Ollie some board shorts. And then the sky opened up.

They huddled under a tattered awning outside the factory, waiting to be collected. The rain dragged the branches down on trees, thundered against tin, painted the tile roofs a glossy terra-cotta. Tom felt sleepy, lulled by the intensity of the rain. Everything had succumbed, everything seemed glad for it, was having its thirst quenched.

A wind had picked up. The fabric across the awning had come away from the frame in places and was flying up into air. It was letting in water towards the back, and the water flowed across the pavement and over Jeremy's thongs. It's leaking, he said, his head not far from the sagging green cloth. He manoeuvred himself and Ollie out of the water's path and closer to Madeleine, putting his arms around her waist.

No one said anything for a moment; they had been made mute by the rain. By its suddenness, the heaviness of it, as much as anything.

That's how you know it's a roof, Clara said, finally.

Tom guffawed.

Jeremy and Madeleine looked at them.

What? Madeleine said.

Clara looked embarrassed. Frank Lloyd Wright, she said.

What about him? Madeleine said.

That's what he said, Clara said. When a client told him the roof was leaking. *That's how you know it's a roof.* All his roofs leaked. When another client complained that he was being dripped on at his desk, Wright told him to move his chair.

Jeremy and Madeleine laughed, and Ollie did, too, exaggeratedly. He was clawing at Madeleine, trying to climb up her body.

Of course, Rossi said that a building wasn't finished until it collapsed into the ground, Tom said. Jeremy nodded at him slowly.

* * *

Back in Sanur everything was sodden, but the rain had passed and the sun was back out. Clara and Madeleine went to their rooms, and Tom went with Ollie and Jeremy to the markets. Jeremy had caved and agreed to buy Ollie a boogie board. They're so cheap, we'll just give it to someone before we leave if we can't take it with us, Jeremy said. Ollie chose one that was blue and white, with red stripes down one side and a picture of a man on a surfboard, emerging from a wave's barrel. 'Shred' was written down the length of the board in a kind of retro computer font. On the way back, Ollie began to mope and lag behind. It had been a long day. Jeremy said he *would* put him on his shoulders, except that he was carrying the boogie board and all their stuff — bags, water bottles.

Unless, of course, he said, turning to Tom, Tom could carry all this so I can put you on my shoulders?

Or, Tom said, surprising himself, I put Ollie on my shoulders, and you carry all the boring stuff?

Ollie giggled, and they stopped at a railing, Tom crouched down, and then lifted him into the air. He was surprisingly heavy, but they didn't have far to go. Tom held the boy's shins close to his sides and staggered forward into a light run. Ducked and weaved around trees and awnings and people on bicycles coming down the street, as Ollie cackled and clenched his knees around Tom's head and yelled back down what he could see in the distance.

They spotted Clara and Madeleine at one of the restaurant tables with drinks in front of them when they got back, facing out to the sea, which was metallic now in the dusk. Way out beyond

114

Lembongan, which was a fine line of grey in the distance, the storm front was moving away.

The women watched them approach in silence. Tom could tell Clara was surprised to see Ollie on his shoulders, but she was grinning, as if she couldn't help herself.

Getting in shape, he said, lowering Ollie on to the ground.

He had a sweat stain all down the front of his T-shirt, and his fringe had stuck to his forehead, but it didn't give him pause. Clara reached out to him as he aired his T-shirt and rubbed his wet back with her palm. This time, he didn't flinch.

★ ★ ★

After showers they regrouped for a drink by the pool, then headed out again to a BBQ chicken place Clara had seen was rated highly on the apps. They took a taxi. They had tried nearly everywhere within walking distance now — everywhere that had a rating of four stars or more. But Ali's Golden Chicken was the perfect choice, because it was the kind of food Ollie would gladly eat.

It was six-thirty when they arrived, and the sky above them had turned lilac. They had beers and Cokes and waters and ordered nearly everything off the menu. It was a tiny place, with a rotisserie in the kitchen and one on the street, and room for only one table inside and a few others in the courtyard under trees, which is where they sat. The menus and the walls and the uniforms of the staff were all in the same gold and red. They devoured the food — plates piled high with fried chicken wings and drumsticks, sides of mash and chips and corn on the cob and mac-and-cheese and jugs of gravy — and they washed it down with more Bintang and more Coke.

Ollie was giddy with joy, giggling and growling like a monster as he ripped into the skin of his chicken. He talked nonstop. Told them stories of everything he had seen during the day, some of which they had all seen, and some of which they had not. How much was imagined was hard to tell. Boys his age zooming past on motorbikes, a girl surfing the waves while they played frisbee, whom neither Tom nor Jeremy had seen. Clara encouraged him, wanting more details, which he never tired of furnishing. By the time the girl got on her motorbike, put on silver goggles, and drove off in a cloud of smoke with her surfboard under one arm, they were clapping.

After Ollie was asleep, Madeleine and Jeremy crept back out for another drink. It was the first time they had done this, but everyone was caught up in the mood, and they were nearing the end of their time together. In two days they would part ways — Madeleine, Ollie, and Jeremy to the Gili Islands, Tom and Clara on to Ubud.

At tables on the sand, under the warm glow of the bamboo lamps and candles on white tablecloths, they ordered beers — although in the end Clara declined, said she was too tired, alcohol would put her to sleep, and ordered a soda water — and they toasted to themselves, to having a successful holiday, having *any* sort of holiday. They joked about coming back next year, coming back every year.

And we'll be introduced to your little bébé, Madeleine said. A boy, too, I think it will be, and they'll become the best of friends, and we'll see each other every July, and they can play together while we sit by the pool and drink. Yes? Or you both get jobs in Paris, or Europe somewhere, and we see you there instead, take research trips to Greek islands?

Tom and Clara laughed along, deflected the kids thing by making self-deprecating comments about how they'd never get jobs in European universities, they hadn't published enough, but they agreed to it — Oh fine, they said, we'll do it — although Tom noticed that Clara would not meet his eye.

9

It was one of those nights when everything felt more vivid. There was no chance of sleep because everything, including him, was monstrously, throbbingly alive. Maybe it was that the moon was full. The room was mostly dark, but he could tell the moon was full because, through the shutters, it cast six bright bands of pale-blue light against the bed and the walls.

He turned onto his other side, faced the air conditioner. The unit was loud, but he could still hear things above it: crickets, frogs, the shrieking of other creatures, birds of some kind, monkeys maybe. Something big scampering across the roof of a nearby bungalow.

He got up. Tiptoed to the door and found the iron ring-pull. The porch was in darkness, but beyond that everything was bathed in the same bright, but kind of washed-out blue. Short, bare trees and tropical flowers were motionless and finely detailed against the grey sand. He wanted to lie down on that neatly raked sand, so soft and cool-looking, but he dared not do this — who knew what was crawling around there at night — so he stepped out barefoot onto the path and looked up at the sky. Looked for the moon, but now it was hidden. The upper reaches of the tallest trees above him moved a little in some higher breeze, and he looked around for the monkeys, but there was no sign of them.

He followed the path towards the beach. The restaurant was dark and still, the boardwalk was dark and still, all the signs and all the people packed up for the night. The beach was cooler, the merest breeze, but it was not inviting. He worried about rubbish, about stepping on a needle that had yet to be raked under the sand.

He turned back and went the other way, all the way back through the grounds to the entrance of the hotel and the curving white-pebble driveway. There, outside a row of low-lying buildings set off from the entrance to the hotel by a knee-high rope fence — they had peeked into these buildings one day when a door was left open to see a mess of mattresses, sheets, and towels in plastic — a woman was getting onto the back of a motorcycle. He recognised her from the hotel. She had served him breakfast at least once, brought drinks over to the pool. She was in jeans and a T-shirt now. Her traditional clothes — her uniform — were hanging in the room with the mattresses maybe. If she saw him, there was no acknowledgement. She got on the back of the motorbike, folded her arms in front of her, and rested gently against the man's back, and they drove off.

He went back to the room. Pushed open the little cupboard-sized doors that led to their secret room with the daybeds. He picked one, lay down, and looked out at the wall of green that shielded the room from other guests. He thought of taking a look at one of the job ads Madeleine had sent through to him, but he didn't have the energy left to get his phone from the other room.

119

He didn't really want a job, anyway. A permanent job. Being an uncontracted sessional was a nightmare in many ways, but it was his nightmare, and he had found his place in it. He could do without a whole new set of things to worry about.

The whole thing was too depressing. All the hope people like Madeleine had for them and their 'careers'. The word career itself was exhausting. The reality was that he had no great love for his field, no real interest in pursuing it, no projects he was excited about embarking upon, no ideas for a book proposal. He wasn't angry about the whole thing, not anymore; he was simply jaded. And ashamed. All the effort, all those years of research and writing, and peer assessment by experts and editors of journals no one had heard of. All of it going into something whose only real justification was the perpetuation of itself. The need to publish. To have published. So you could support a claim to a contract, which in turn helped the funding cause of the faculty and the university. But not, primarily, so your work would be read. So you could contribute anything real. No.

He wasn't an architect, a builder, a planner, a designer — someone who had any influence on the built environment or our negotiation of it, now or in the future. He was someone who wrote about these things. Someone who, if he ever wrote a book, which was less likely with every passing year, would write one that no one would read. Possibly almost literally, no one would read his book. Surely there was something more worthy of his time, what was left of his energy.

In light of this, Clara's attempts to get out of it, to find something else to do besides being an academic, a writer of books that were not read, a worker in an industry that had fewer jobs every year, seemed sensible. But she had never found the right thing. Organic gardening, landscaping, a ranger for the national parks . . . she'd had many ideas, some of which were accompanied by short bursts of enthusiasm that inevitably petered out. It didn't dishearten her. She knew she wasn't without talent; that it had never been honed strongly in one direction or another seemed to be okay by her. Sometimes he wondered if one of her greatest talents was to be so magnanimous in the face of all of that. To be basically untroubled by not having one great calling or whatever, however silly the idea sounded when you said it out loud. She tried things, they ran their course, and she moved on to the next one. She had downgraded these ideas for alternative careers as time went on, and as she found more work teaching and more success getting her work published — found herself to be, after all, a talented academic who wrote things people, in fact, wanted to read. And, rather than escape hatches, they became hobbies that ran alongside her research: pottery, after his mother had taught her some things; photography; sewing. Things that made her precarious work and her interminable doctorate bearable. While he stuck to his one thing, his only thing, terrified that it might not work out because he had no idea what else he would do if it didn't. He didn't have anything else, but even if he did ever think of pursuing other things

121

— once there were musical aspirations, but nothing ever got off the ground — he knew he would be too scared to actually go through with it, to switch so late in the game.

But he liked teaching. Or he did now. The first time he thought he wasn't going to make it through the semester.

That first class was an introductory, survey subject on urban history, which he had taken himself four years earlier, but barely remembered a thing about. He was given a week's notice. He took beta-blockers and Valium before every one of those twelve classes.

It was made worse by the fact he had a difficult student that first time. A tall, fleshy, vaguely unkempt twenty-year-old called Brendan, who carried around with him an apparently empty backpack and a scuffed-up notepad full of scrawled notes and doodles. His presence in the room was disruptive from the beginning; everything about his demeanour suggested boredom and hostility. The way he arrived late and shuffled noisily through the tables to his one friend, Sheila, an alert and sly-looking young woman who smirked at Tom nastily through class. The way he then sat slumped in his chair with his hands in his pockets most of the hour, staring at the ceiling, the notepad sitting untouched in front of him on the table — when he wasn't passing it back and forth with Sheila and sniggering.

Each week, Brendan's attitude would be an undeniable yet silent presence in the room until close to the end of class, when he would snap out of it as if from a nap, or as if, suddenly, he had reached the absolute limit he could take of all this inane bullshit. He would take over completely then, and, while still staring at the ceiling or the door, drone out a long diatribe on some very minor technical point of contention — the efficacy of early modern bastion forts against cannon fire, for example — or on something big and discursive and obliquely insulting, like the hopelessly romanticised version of Jane Jacobs v Robert Moses that was being taught in the class.

Tom was repeatedly caught out of his depth on these subjects, his knowledge not extending far beyond the readings and, if he was lucky, a few other, half-remembered points he had picked up over the years in other subjects — he had forgotten so much, it seemed. But he managed to keep up with Brendan intellectually at least, he thought. He managed to hold his own, and sometimes he was able to successfully mount counterarguments, or, better yet, use Brendan's rants as the basis of class discussion, assigning to sections of the room opposing positions, which sometimes, miraculously, seemed to go well. As far as he was concerned, anything that got them talking, for even a few minutes, was a win; making it through the hour each week was such a task. But Brendan never softened up. He remained as begrudging and mute and suddenly overbearing as ever.

Brendan was late with assignments. He feigned surprise when they came up, and when he got them back and was marked down for his lateness, his lapses in expression, his grammatical errors, the lack of referencing — although Tom was too scared to mark him down too strictly — he waved away the marks, claimed to have done the assignments in an afternoon.

In the second half of semester, the students gave talks on their research essay. Nothing too formal. Tom wasn't going to force them to put together PowerPoint slideshows or even, if they didn't want to, get up in front of the class. His increasing desperation to get them to like him, to get them onside, made him wildly flexible with most assessments — and this one was worth so little, he couldn't care less how they approached it, although getting to ten minutes was important to him because it was time off the clock.

When it was Brendan's turn to speak, he looked around the room, like always, as if he'd just woken up.

Oh, that was today? he said, although they had been going through the roll alphabetically, and Tom didn't really think this was lost on him. He dismissed Tom's offer to move his talk to the following week, however, and got up from his desk.

I don't have anything ready, but I'll do it now anyway, I guess, he said, and he ambled through the tables to the front of the room.

May I? he said, gesturing to the whiteboard, and he uncapped a marker pen and began drawing on the board. It was a complex diagram, and messy. Tom noticed that he held the marker in his fist, like a child. The class sat in silence for several minutes while he finished. During that time — Tom pretended not to notice — Shella was watching him with something like malicious glee.

124

Brendan's talk was rambling and convoluted, but Tom could not deny that it showed an impressive depth of knowledge and an ability to connect disparate facts across centuries and disciplines (in a talk on the contemporary town hall, there was something about wheat-eating as one of the causes of sewage problems in the Late Middle Ages, which Tom wanted to stop him to explain but didn't dare). He used the entire whiteboard to illustrate his points, drawing several diagrams of alternative street layouts in Australian country towns, and then roamed the room authoritatively while he spoke, occasionally rubbing his temples or grumpily pushing his fringe out from his eyes — the only signs he was more nervous in front of the class than he let on. He even stared out the window for a portion of it, thoughtfully, as he tried to pull it all together at the end, which he struggled to do, stammering a few times through his closing remarks.

When he finally finished, after almost twenty minutes — Tom had raised eyebrows at him a few times at twelve minutes, then fifteen, but was ignored — Sheila led the class with an ovation, while holding Tom's gaze meaningfully, as if to say, See? *That's* how it is done. Tom remembered trying to return to her a similarly meaningful smile, an indulgent smile, hoping to convey to her that the kid had been a touch over the top, of course, but sure, it was entertaining, and, not to worry, he was not threatened by him — in fact, he found the whole thing mildly amusing. And he could see how this infuriated her.

At the end of the second-last class for the

semester, as the students filed out of the room, Tom wished them well on the final essay and felt an overwhelming sense of relief. He was elated. It was finally nearly over. In the break, he would sleep twelve hours a night and not leave the house for a week. Then he would snap out of it and mark everyone's work.

He gathered his things, moved through the chairs and around the large tables that crowded the room, and saw something underneath one of the tables on the floor. It was Brendan's notepad. Brendan had left early, like he always did, with Sheila following him — by this point Tom wondered if they were romantically involved — so there was no use chasing after them, they were long gone. He pocketed it. But not before looking inside. He almost didn't, but he couldn't help himself. He reasoned he had to be sure whose it was, although he knew that notepad well. There were very few actual notes, of course — mostly pages of doodles and several pages of chat with Shella. Several of these chats mentioned Tom and the class, as he suspected they might. This class is stupid, Brendan had written. Ugh, I know, she'd replied. He doesn't know anything; the guy's an idiot; so annnooyyying; you should be teaching this class; I should be; ha ha.

Tom wondered if he should just bin the notebook — surely Brendan attached very little importance to it himself and would not miss it — but in the end, he didn't, because he relished too much the opportunity of presenting it back to Brendan the following week.

You left this behind last week? he said, as

126

diffidently as possible, although his hand was visibly shaking. And Brendan, blushing, not meeting his eye, took it off him without a word. It was everything Tom had hoped for. *He* was the grown-up here, and he had claimed the moral high ground by overlooking Brendan's bad-mouthing of him and the class, by being gracious and mature about it, and also by giving Brendan a break by maintaining the pretence — which Brendan clearly knew to be a pretence; after all, his name was not on the pad — of not seeing what was written inside it.

Brendan's major essay for the class, worth 50 per cent of the subject's overall mark, was, like his earlier reports and his talk, an undisciplined polemic that roamed freely from topic to topic and made, in the end, no coherent argument. Or not one Tom could easily fathom. Tom was at a loss with how to mark it. He was privately glad it was a mess, and thus probably couldn't be given a high mark, even a mediocre one, but he also feared Brendan might dispute the mark, or complain about him if he didn't reward him for being the smartest person in the class. He might expose Tom as the fraud he was as a teacher, or at the very least give him a scathing student evaluation — although that was probably coming either way. In the end, he passed it on to the coordinator of the subject to mark, his supervisor, Henry Ales.

Henry smiled when Tom told him about Brendan and, when he read the essay, agreed with Tom's assessment of it — that while this was obviously an impressive mind, he had a long way to go with his academic writing, and what he had handed in could not really be called a research essay at all. There was so little proper referencing, and it would have to be marked accordingly. Henry told him not to worry, he would deal with it, and that Brendan would be given the option of failing or rewriting the essay for a pass. Inside, Tom rejoiced. He never did find out which option Brendan had taken.

It wasn't a good start, and the next few semesters were almost as bad. Beta-blockers and Valium before class, frequent trips to the bathroom during the hour to guzzle water, wipe himself down, and huge relief and drinking too much once it was over. Unshakable exhaustion. Sometimes, at home, he caught Clara looking at him with something that was probably concern. But over time, he no longer needed the beta-blockers or the Valium, and, eventually, teaching became his favourite part of the week.

He was lucky for a few years to have the same subjects each semester. This built his confidence; he knew the material well and needed little preparation. And he began to establish a good rapport with his students. He increasingly received positive, even glowing, student evaluations — he was still a pushover — and he enjoyed the feeling of being an authority that was appealed to, of having an opinion that was taken seriously. More seriously, usually, than the students' own.

Teaching had been so fraught for Tom at the start, he believed, because he let it be so intimately bound up with his sense of self-worth, so bound up with his ego. He remembered asking

Henry about it once — panicking about the first class, but trying not to let it show — and Henry saying something about it being a performance, in a way, a version of yourself that you presented to the world when you taught. But Tom couldn't seem to do this, mask himself in this way; he was right *there*, vibrating on the surface. And when he had been challenged by Brendan in that first class, it was as if Brendan, and then the rest of the class — which Brendan's attitude had swept through and infected — had seen him for what he really was, which was mediocre at best, and, at worst, incompetent.

He knew he wasn't impressive, then, as a tutor. His nervousness was palpable in everything he did, and his all-consuming anxiety meant that most of his knowledge was wiped clean from his brain before he walked into the room. But in these classes, it was as if his legitimacy was being challenged not just as a teacher or an academic, but as a person, and he felt himself crumbling under the challenge, under the scrutiny. The avalanche of anxiety that he just barely kept at bay with medication, and sometimes was not able to under the strain of Brendan's hostility — having to spend ten, fifteen minutes in the bathroom, or walking the halls, vibrating, trying to calm down, while the students did readings in the room — felt like the dissolution of his very being, a sense that everything he normally considered to comprise his most essential self was being dismantled. And he was left exposed for the ridiculous, insubstantial person that he was, in truth.

Sometimes he felt that there was nothing more

to him than a kind of quivering thing. He pictured, for some reason, a candlewick, which appeared upright and substantial only because of the material around it — his feeble defences — but which, if the wax was melted down around it, was really nothing more than a piece of limp string lying in a puddle. And he hated it, that he was so vulnerable to this kind of attack, that his sense of self-worth was so flimsy, so fragile, but he didn't know what he could do about that.

He thought, too, that his classes were as bound up with his sense of self now as they were then, but for the opposite reason, in that having the respect of his students, their admiration even, was one of the only things that made him feel good about himself. His ego was as fragile as ever. If he came home from class and felt that things hadn't gone well, if he came home and didn't feel entirely confident of his students' respect and admiration, fretting that they did not laugh at this or that joke, or seem quite convinced by his explanation of some important or complex argument, or readily agree with his opinions on things — if, in essence, he didn't feel his ego stroked — he would fall into a pit of self-loathing. Why was he so vulnerable, so *deeply, pathetically* vulnerable, to the opinion of others? He visualised himself then in a different way, unoriginally, as a structure built from matchsticks; the merest breeze could rip him apart.

★　★　★

About two and a half years after that first teaching experience he met with Henry. He hadn't seen him for a year, since the submission of his thesis. Over that time, he had been doing sessional teaching for the university, contributing papers to conferences, and had even managed, through great, painful effort, to adapt two chapters of the thesis into articles that were published in middling to high-ranking journals. He had become a much more confident teacher over that time. He was not entirely panic-free, but he was better prepared for it, and knew what to do if it happened, knew how to leave a room like he wasn't fleeing. He had started seeing his therapist by then, and had been taught some breathing exercises and some de-escalation techniques.

He had worked for Henry only once during his candidature, in the subject with Brendan. That had gone well enough, he'd thought, for a first time, despite Brendan's disruptive presence — though he had started to wonder about that. The department was obliged, essentially, to offer candidates at least one chance to tutor, and, as he struggled to find subjects to teach each semester and had started finding work in other departments tutoring history, philosophy even — mostly through his secondary supervisor, Rebecca Maynard — he had started to wonder if Henry's unfailingly affable and encouraging tone wasn't masking the fact that he had nothing else for him and probably never would. Not that it was his job to find him work, Tom understood. But to offer him no leads, no introductions, not to email him over all that time with a single opportunity . . . Once the most basic of obligations were met, there just seemed no investment or interest in him at all. The silence was deafening. And he became paranoid.

Did Henry just not rate him as a postgraduate? Or was it simply that Henry's hands were tied — that he was either obliged to give the work to new candidates looking for their opportunities or, when coordinating roles or lecturing roles came up, obliged to go with more experienced and better qualified applicants? Whatever it was, he felt cut adrift. What stung the most was that, as soon as he stopped teaching each semester, he lost not only his desk in the shared postgraduate office, but his email and library access too. How was he supposed to do new research? How was he supposed to pay the rent? It was demoralising to be in a worse position for having your PhD than you were while undertaking it. You finished, and then there was . . . nothing.

As the second year wore on like this, and he was working less and less on his own research and tutoring subjects in fields further and further away from his own, his certainty intensified that the early-career position he'd dreamed of was never going to materialise. His feelings towards his former supervisor, which included gratitude and admiration, became complicated by resentment, and, yes, paranoia. Once, at a conference, he had seen Henry with a major figure in Tom's field across the room and had made his way over to them, and felt sure he saw Henry subtly but firmly, with a hand in the small of his back, guide the visiting professor away from him.

He sent Henry an email. He tried not to sound desperate, but he also wanted to make it clear that he was worried that soon he might have to give up altogether on looking for academic work, and he could do with advice. Henry suggested they meet.

It was a staff-only club in a double-storey Victorian building, which sat conspicuously out of time on a curve of Professors' Walk and in the shadow of seventies-built department buildings and the hulking glass cube of the new arts department. The building was dwarfed, and yet, with its grand, gleaming portico and its ivy-covered walls, it was imposing enough. He was running late and had rushed. He had been hoping for some time to catch his breath and cool down before entering, but it wasn't possible. Henry was standing on the steps waiting for him.

Henry was a tall, wiry, slightly awkward man who looked younger than he was, with a boyish, unlined face and wispy, tussled hair. He had a smirking, almost embarrassed grin that spread across his face slowly. As he approached, Tom watched its progress.

While he'd rushed, Tom had only grown more confused. About how he was meant to feel about Henry, about how he did feel, whether he was grateful or angry. And about how he should act. Should he be frank or supplicating? Earnest or cool? He certainly didn't want Henry to think he expected things to be handed to him, but he also thought that surely Henry had heard of opportunities or had his own to offer that Tom might have been qualified for over the years. On top of that, he hadn't seen or heard from him for a year and the nature of their relationship was unclear. He was no longer his supervisor, he wasn't a colleague, wasn't really a friend — what was Henry to him? The mentor-type figure Tom had hoped he'd found when he was first confirmed and Henry had helped him secure a scholarship had never really materialised. Something about all of this made him nervous in the days before the meeting, and, as he approached him on the steps of University House, he realised he was no clearer on any of it. What he could feel clearly, however, was the heat that had accumulated as he rushed through the campus and how the cool air of the July afternoon was doing little to mitigate it.

He reached Henry and took his outstretched hand. Henry, gracious and warm, turned and guided Tom through the heavy double doors of the club.

They walked through a carpeted hall with pale-pink walls, past glossy bureaus with plastic display cases carefully arranged upon them and by the open doors of several rooms. It was dim in the hallway, but sunlight streamed in through the double windows of every room they passed so that the whole place was bathed in warm, refracted light. Through one doorway, he spotted a small group of people, no one under sixty, sitting around a coffee table taking tea. In another, several uniformed young men were at work setting a long table, one with a white tablecloth in his hands, another with a vase full of flowers.

At the end of the hall Henry motioned through an open doorway to a cafeteria counter, which felt out of place in such a setting, like a cafeteria in the middle of someone's house. Another young man in uniform was behind the counter, a look of professional discretion fixed on his face. He gave all his attention to Henry, and Tom felt it was obvious to the young man that he was only a guest here and not worthy of his deference. In his agitated state, Tom was sure this young man could see more than this, could see the whole situation clearly for what it was. That Henry bringing him here was an act of charity, and that, essentially, Tom was a ridiculous figure, and one who was only just beginning to understand that about himself. Perhaps, Tom thought, this was where Henry brought all his lost causes.

Henry ordered coffee and asked if Tom wanted anything to eat. Tom said, No, thank you — Henry asked if he was sure, the sandwiches were good — Tom said he wasn't hungry, had just eaten, which wasn't true. But to order something, he ordered a tea, knowing it was not a good choice if he wanted to cool down, but he had to order something.

They moved into the dining room, a large, bright space with a bank of windows and an atrium made from many panels of glass along one wall. Through ivy, dappled sunlight splashed over the tables and cast a wide arc of gold on the floor. The room was mostly empty: at one end, three older men were arrayed around a flat-screen showing the cricket, in armchairs pulled in close, and at a table sat several women to whom Henry murmured greetings as he passed.

Henry chose a table in the sun. It was bright and warm, and Tom felt himself squinting painfully as he settled into his chair and turned to respond to Henry's polite questions about what he'd been up to outside academia: his casual work at a local second-hand bookstore run by a famous curmudgeon that Henry knew well, his occasional book reviews in academic journals and newspapers.

Tom was wired. He hadn't slept well, of course, the night before the meeting, despite taking an Ambien and two Valium, and it was only becoming clear to him how weird he in fact felt. How sick. And how out of sync his vibrations were with Henry, and with the rest of the room. He was thrumming.

Henry, he noticed, was squinting, too, though he was facing away from the wall of glass. At first, Tom wondered if this was sympathetic squinting, the way he sometimes found himself taking on the mannerisms and gestures of the people he was speaking to, but then he remembered that Henry did this, squinted and blinked as he spoke, compulsively. It was a tick of his; he did it in his lectures, too. But it had got worse since he'd last seen him, seemingly. Now, while he spoke, he eyes were almost as often shut as they were open, his fluttering eyelids creating two deep creases, like asterisks, where his eyes should be. Of course, it might also have had something to do with how visibly Tom was shaking.

He thought he'd been concealing it well

enough until the drinks arrived. But then, following Henry's lead, Tom poured the tea into his teacup and added sugar and milk and lifted the cup from the saucer — and found he couldn't bring it to his lips. His arm was too weak. It trembled under the weight, seized up, and he was forced to return the cup to the saucer. How much of this Henry saw, as he sipped his coffee, was hard to tell. Tom tried to cover for it, make it look like he'd simply changed his mind about drinking the tea at that moment, but when he looked up at him, Henry was blinking furiously.

The conversation, meanwhile, was as convivial and relaxed as ever. They spoke about the progress of Henry's book on town squares, about a tour of the university for urban planning students he was conducting, and only after what seemed a long time of fairly idle chatter did the conversation turn to Tom's request for advice.

You must publish, Henry said. Publish or perish, they say, and it's true. He sipped more coffee. No one can survive very long without a book or an ARC grant, and they are increasingly competitive. There are a few, of course, who seem to make it through somehow. Dale Patel. He seemed to get through for years without publishing a thing, but that was a bit of a mystery. He chuckled. It is, now, very rare.

Henry asked him how much he had published since he had completed the thesis. Tom told him, and he said, Well, you have to get a couple more in soon, in the next year if possible. Two or three articles in the next year, and you'll start looking competitive.

137

But it all takes so long, Tom said, aware that now he was straight-out whining. To get anything written, for it to be accepted, to do edits, it can take a year for a journal article to appear . . .

It's true, it's true, Henry said, with resignation, and finished off his coffee. He seemed to be thinking about something else now, or struggling to think of something to add. The blinking was less intense, now, and occasionally he opened his eyes very wide, perhaps stretching back out sore muscles.

Henry asked him about papers and was he going to conferences, and Tom said he had been, which was partly true. He had given one or two papers in the last year, at conferences held at the university, but it was increasingly difficult to attend conferences further afield with no funds for it, and recently he had more or less given up on submitting abstracts for consideration. He had never found conferences very encouraging. Had never found the camaraderie he'd hoped for. Instead, he found himself hovering around trestle tables in foyers by himself, eating half-sandwiches and occasionally chatting politely to other postgraduates, who all seemed to be wondering how interested in each other's work they needed to pretend to be.

Tom knew he couldn't drink the tea. He looked down at it, but didn't dare try again.

He decided to bring the meeting to an end. It was humiliating, they hadn't been there long, but he had got what he'd come for now. A feeling had stolen over him. He knew. He would give it up. And he'd decided this, or it had dawned on

138

him, while he was telling Henry precisely the opposite — that, yes, of course, he would keep plugging away, that he had drafts that were coming along, articles under consideration at journals, fellowship applications underway, hope that it would all come together. But somehow he knew it was over. He had his subjects to teach, but any illusion that he was actively an academic, still researching, writing, working on a book, would fall away. How long he could keep getting work without at least pretending to do all this was hard to say, but he felt strangely at peace with it: he would happily do what he could until they cut him off.

He felt sure, too, that this was the last time he would ever meet with Henry. He couldn't feel any anger about the whole thing, the way he was treated — it was just the system, the thing that everyone warned you about, but that you never took seriously because somehow you felt sure that it wouldn't be like that for you, that somehow you would dodge all that and come out victorious, come out with a job. A career. He was resigned; there was nothing Henry could do. It was simply up to him, to press on, to keep pushing, or to stop.

His decisiveness, or his relief, that this was it, the moment he would give it up, seemed to break through all his timorousness, and he found himself picking up the cup and draining it in one gulp. No, he felt no animosity towards Henry. He had obviously felt Tom's email was the kind of desperate gesture that required a sensitive response, and Tom appreciated it, in an embarrassed sort of way. But Henry had nothing for him. Nothing he didn't already know, and he felt stupid for asking to meet with him to find out. But he hadn't wanted to leave wondering — hadn't wanted to give up without at least seeing what Henry might say to someone in his position. And here it was: a round of polite patter.

He wondered how he might extricate himself, but soon Henry had to leave anyway, had another appointment. He paid for the drinks, and stopped and chatted briefly to the men around the flat-screen about the cricket. Then they left.

Out on the steps they promised to stay in touch, keep abreast of each other's work. As they parted and as Tom was walking down the steps away from him, Henry told him to hang in there, that soon there would be generational change, and jobs would be opening up at universities across the country. He chuckled a little as he said it, knowing it to be the chestnut that it was, knowing perhaps, too, that his colleagues weren't giving up their positions any time soon. He reminded Tom to look out for international jobs, too, although admittedly, he said, these were often taken by US academics, who were over-represented in international universities and were taking their jobs too now. He chuckled again.

★   ★   ★

At the time, this all felt more serious than it turned out to be, of course. When Tom walked away from Henry, he was sure that by the end of the year he would be out forever. Thankfully, luckily, Rebecca Maynard asked him to take on one of her classes while she took sabbatical leave, and this led to another class, and then another, until he had two classes per semester, sometimes three, that he was coordinating, lecturing, and tutoring, and he had kept them for the last three years. These could be taken away from him at any moment — and would be eventually, no doubt, with his lack of publications — but he would find something. In his perpetual exhaustion, he couldn't bring himself to worry about it anymore. It would be fine. It would have to be.

But, the shaking. That time with Henry was the first. Before then it was sweating, dry mouth, or the opposite of dry mouth, too much saliva, constant swallowing, and now he had another thing to worry about. It was true that it hadn't happened much since then, a few times not long after the meeting with Henry, a couple of times when he was out and couldn't raise his drink to his lips, but it had been a while, maybe a year or two, until the flight. That was under exceptional circumstances, of course. Becoming anxious during turbulence was no big deal — it was to be expected, at least to some degree. But the violence of it, the shuddering, the convulsions.

His mother shook. Historically, mostly in the hands, but now it was everywhere. Her trembling was the product of her illness and the medication she took for her illness, the cocktail of drugs she was on — steroids, antibiotics, anti-nausea medication, SSRIs, various other medications he didn't even know about. And yet it was her anxiety that led her to self-medicate with nicotine and alcohol in the first place, so in this sense, anxiety had made her shake. What he did remember of it, before the illness, was how jumpy she could be, how fretful. And paranoid. And she had panic attacks; he had seen that. In many ways, they were alike. But *was* he making himself in her image?

The shaking was particularly cruel to Marianne initially because she was a potter, and while it had already become difficult for her to do the physical work of pottery — she had long since stopped wedging clay or using her kick-wheel — she no longer felt confident in her hands. The control was gone. For a while she continued, and joked about it, said she was going through her wonky mug phase — a style of pottery she had always despised. But now she could not do it at all. The emphysema had depleted her to such an extent that she struggled to do things that most people took for granted: bend down to pick up objects, walk through a room. At times, Tom's condition debilitated him in similar ways. Hindered the same basic functions. Like drinking from a cup. And neither of them could breathe deeply. The main, of course not insignificant difference was that, for her, none of this ever passed.

For Marianne, leaving the house was a major undertaking that involved planning, coordination. His own confinement was voluntary, up to a point. When he was not well, many of their calculations ran along similar lines. Would there be stairs? Hills? How much walking would be involved? Any kind of overheating for him had become a trigger. What kind of place were they going to? Where would they sit? How easily could they leave if they needed to? Who would be there? His mother was able to discuss all this, map it all out, make plans for escape. And it was his father who had to do a lot of the work: gather the details, get her into the wheelchair, out of the car. Tom's calculations were private. No one really knew how much of a shut-in he had become, he didn't think. He did a good job disguising things, dissembling. He was working from home because he preferred it that way; he was driven, not someone using work as an excuse to never leave the house. Had he admitted that even to himself, in such a blunt way? Maybe it was being away from it that allowed him to see it more clearly for what it was.

He wasn't sure how much Clara knew. They'd had conversations about performance anxiety in front of classes — about concealing sweat marks, about dealing with stressful situations — and all of these conversations had subtext. But every-thing they discussed fell within the normal range of nervousness that most people experienced, he thought.

Fundamentally, the anxiety that he shared with his mother kept them both from experiencing the world, the built environment, with the ease that people like them — white, middle-class — usually enjoyed. The world as it was designed did not easily accommodate them. There was no architec-ture for anxiety, no planning for it. Of course, mental health was always a stated concern of planners, of architects in their pitches, and it informed so much theory, especially now — neuro-architecture, environmental health. But how much could really be done for people like Tom and his mother was hard to say. For them, it was the fact that other people shared the world that they had to contend with. Indoor plants and adjusting the height of ceilings in public spaces just wasn't going to cut it.

10

The next morning, Tom took his time getting out of the room. When he finally emerged, he took a packet of lime-flavoured chips out to the cabanas and sank into the cushions of a bamboo couch. There was no one around. He was feeling beaten by the heat, and sluggish, like he always did after not sleeping well and then sleeping late to compensate. He did not bother taking the towel off his shoulder, or picking up his book, or peeling his feet from the bamboo floor. His whole face ached. The pain radiated from the corners of his eyes across his cheeks.

The beach was empty. The massage ladies were in their spot, but even they were quiet, and for once the place seemed lugubrious. Perhaps it was just that it was overcast.

Tom was just ordering eggs when Clara appeared, shading her face from the sun and sucking on a coconut with a straw sticking out of it. Sleeping well, as she did every night, and rising early, she had gone for another walk, further north up the boardwalk, all the way to the big hotel that loomed over the beach. She was going to the room, would meet him back out there, she said.

Tom looked out at the water. There was one couple out there, in the shallows — although it was all shallows to the reef a few hundred metres out, and always calm, no more than a ripple ever

145

making it to shore. The couple were bobbing around together, the girl's arms around the guy's neck. They were kissing every now and then and leaning into each other and leaning away again, and something about this movement caught Tom's attention. As he watched, and it became clear what he was looking at, they became more brazen and began — stealthily at first, then quite openly — pressing against each other and moving up and down in the water. Tom looked around. There was no one else on the beach to witness it except two older women who had just arrived at the cabana at the far end and were busying themselves with the menus. He turned back, felt himself becoming hard in his shorts, and pulled his towel onto his lap. After a few minutes, in which time it was clear the woman was bringing the man to completion, holding him close to her and tightly around the neck, the couple disconnected and floated around the water for a while before getting out. Then they sauntered up the beach, surreptitiously inspecting their wet bodies as they walked.

★   ★   ★

Tom ate his breakfast, and then went to the pool to cool off. No one else was around. He dived deep into the crystalline water, skimmed the blue-and-white mosaic that pixelated the pool floor, and came up at the other end. Then he dived again.

There was something about some water, the blueness of it, which always seemed special to him, vaguely numinous. Even this pool water, which was chlorinated, had enough clarity and spangle in its blueness to make it count, while the dull, metal-coloured soup in the bay clearly did not. Perhaps it was the setting, the beauty of the place. And the stillness, save the two golden frogs presiding over it, burbling away. There was something beyond it being merely invigorating or refreshing in the heat — something that made him feel he might come back up, after a long time underneath the surface, somehow cured, made new. Cleansed of all his shit.

What was it that kept this fantasy alive for him? Why did he have it so strongly, every time? Diving into the water at the inlet near his parents' place, his favourite place to swim, where there were mysterious, clearly delineated drifts of colour — turquoise, sea-green, cobalt — he always felt that if only he stayed under a little longer, in the deepest hollow in the sand, or dived back down one more time, truly soaked himself in it, he would come up changed. And, for a moment or two, sometimes a whole afternoon, if he swam long enough, he would feel that he was. His body felt different, his awareness of his limbs altered, his mind soaked, slowed. And then he would think: If I stayed here and did this every afternoon, then I *would* be changed, if only for a few hours every day — at least initially, and perhaps I could work myself up from there.

Now, he merely hoped the water would soak through the pores in his face and leach the ache of tiredness from it. That was all he asked. And perhaps to be able to sleep — if that was within the water's powers.

He lay on a banana lounge for a while, nodded and smiled at several staff members as they drifted past. One woman, one of Madeleine's friends, spoke to him briefly. She asked him if there was anything he required, and he — relaxed and comfortable in the exchange, feeling perhaps the effects of the water — thanked her and told her there wasn't, and was alone again.

He wondered where everyone was. Perhaps Ollie was having a nap, or they had taken him for an adventure somewhere. But he wanted none of them to come back too soon, so he might remain changed for a little while yet.

Eventually, he got up and wandered back over to the cabanas, wanting a couch. He lay down in the shade and closed his eyes.

★ ★ ★

The first thing he knew about it was the sound. It came to him as if from a dream — or something from outside of a dream, something real puncturing it. It was like a mower starting up or a scooter, but when he turned around, he saw two men coming along the path, one in an official-looking uniform, and one wearing a gas mask with a machine strapped to his waist. The machine was something like a leaf blower, but heavier, all chrome, and it billowed out smoke in a continuous thick spray, disappearing plants and trees and paths and outdoor tables and chairs. The uniformed man seemed to be in charge of clearing the area, but he got waylaid by a group coming off the boardwalk into the hotel, the man with the machine was moving fast, and the smoke began drifting rapidly across the boardwalk towards Tom and the cabanas.

He stood up.

Several other employees materialised, including a security guard. As they watched, three young women rushed out from the hotel onto the beach, clutching belongings.

Tom moved over to the security guard, who was keeping his distance, presumably the safe distance, but not moving further away as the smoke rolled towards them. Tom asked him what was going on. What they were spraying.

Smoke, he said.

Smoke?

Yes, yes, smoke. For bugs, flies. He pantomimed swatting flies from his face.

What is it, though?

Smoke, he repeated.

Tom stared at it: the thick white fog was now obscuring pretty much all view of the hotel grounds, reaching high into the treetops, and covering the boardwalk like mist rolling in from the sea, but going the wrong way. Or like dry ice over a dance floor.

He watched it, for a minute or two, and was half-sitting back down when Clara emerged from the smoke, rushing towards him.

She looked stricken.

It's just smoke, they say, he said, standing back up.

It's pesticides . . . chemicals, she said, moving beyond him onto the beach. Nobody told me! I saw it coming under the door, so I went outside, and the whole place was so full of smoke I could barely see. I thought the hotel was on fire. But it didn't smell like fire, it smelled like fucking horrible chemicals.

She held his gaze for a moment, and then backed further down the beach, towards the water. The fog had reached the cabanas now, was engulfing their bamboo blinds and floating out into the air, although it was thinning elsewhere, the hotel coming back into view through the haze.

Tom followed her.

She began talking rapidly: I tried to shut myself in the room, and I went into the bathroom, but it was coming in under the door, in through the louvres, so I had to leave. And then outside I saw someone who told me they were 'fogging', whatever the fuck that means, and it would be over in a minute or two, and she said to stay in my room or go out to the beach, but I was surrounded by it, I didn't want to walk through clouds of fucking pesticides to get out here, so I thought I could get above it, and I went up the stairs of one of the bigger bungalows, but it was up there, too, so I went back down. And then I got down and lay on the path.

Her voice was shaking.

I thought it would rise up, float up, and maybe being on the ground was the best place to be . . . but then I thought 'this is ridiculous' and got up and ran out here . . . I could barely see where I was going . . . it was like a nightmare . . . Why didn't they tell us?

She was close to tears. Tom couldn't decide if she was being absurd by being so melodramatic

150

or if he was being absurd for taking at face value the clearly inadequate reassurances of the security guard.

I wonder what it is, he said, stupidly.

Tom saw then that the two women he had seen earlier in the cabanas were standing nearby. They looked his way.

You seen this before? he asked.

Oh yeah, the closest one said. They do it all the time, for the mozzies.

Nobody told me, Clara said. They didn't come to my room!

The women looked at her.

It's okay, love, said the second woman. Everyone gets caught in it sooner or later. And she laughed.

There it was, then. He was relieved.

Things came back into focus a little after that. Out on the cool, grey sand, the beach was transformed. By the overcast day, by the whole weird thing with the fog. Everything looked plain and uninviting and kind of grimy: the sand with its dark patches, its litter and leaves; the water a dull brownish colour. But everything was alright now, they were fine, and life continued around the place. People were swimming at the next beach along. Hawkers were making their way along the sand, carrying baskets on their heads and eskies full of soft drink. He could hear music from the other hotels and restaurants all around them, and birds singing, as if they had stopped while the fog rose through the trees, but had started up again. A couple of staff were moving around the beach, tidying up tables after people's lunches, straightening banana lounges.

And, he realised, he had remained cool. If he had felt any anxiety at all, he had not registered it consciously. He looked down at his hands. Beaded sweat lay in his palms, but that was it. It was as if anxiety had fizzed on his skin for a moment and evaporated into the air along with the fog. He felt strange, a little disembodied still. Sleepy, but good. Like this had been a test, and he had passed. Everything he had been worried about since the flight — was he simply going to disintegrate now, in front of fear of any kind? Was this his life now? He couldn't trust himself? *Again?* — he could now counter. It felt less urgent, less real. Maybe he was fine after all. Maybe it was a one-off.

Clara was a few feet away, standing still, with her feet in the water. She would stand like that for a few moments, frozen, hovering over the water, staring back at the hotel and the last wisps of smoke hanging in the air, her eyes wide and her mouth open, and then snap out of it and begin pacing again, up and down the beach. Her face was pale, and she kept wrapping her hands around her neck, as if the pesticides she had inhaled had burnt her throat — which couldn't possibly be the case, he didn't think.

He didn't know what to do. He tried, half-heartedly, to catch her eye, and when that failed, he sat back down in the cabana and tried giving her space. He grew impatient quickly. His stomach rumbled. He wanted lunch. He couldn't look at her. Her cartoonishly horrified face. It was too ridiculous. He felt angry, he wasn't sure why. He

152

tried paying attention to his phone. Picked up a menu and leafed through it. But he couldn't concentrate, and he knew he had to do something, he couldn't let her just keep pacing the sand like that, looking so stricken. So he got up with a sigh, and trudged over to her.

As he got close, she looked up suddenly, past him, over his shoulder. He turned and saw that someone was coming out of the haze and tearing down the beach away from them with a child in their arms. It was Madeleine. Tom could see that she was crying and talking softly to Ollie while she struggled to carry him — he was too big, really, he was sliding down her front, while grasping on to her with both arms around her neck. She didn't see them and wasn't slowing down.

Clara went after her.

★ ★ ★

Later, when Clara returned, she went to reception to complain, and the woman was sympathetic, apologised, said they must have missed her bungalow when they were clearing the hotel. But she seemed slightly bemused, Clara said, as if she didn't quite get it. Clara shut herself in the room for the afternoon, doing research, and when Tom came in, she told him what she'd learnt.

He was keen to let the topic drop. He couldn't understand why she was so upset. Yes, it was pesticide, but surely a single exposure couldn't be that bad, and it had cleared from the grounds within minutes. Clara had had her mysterious illnesses in the past, it was true — possible IBS, those rashes, headaches, fatigue — but she'd cut out various foods and the symptoms had mostly disappeared, as far as he knew. And it was true that this might have made her more susceptible, or more wary of coming into contact with toxins, maybe. But still. Besides, she seemed as upset on Madeleine's behalf as anything. Kept going on about the effects of fogging on children, babies. He couldn't understand that either. Surely Madeleine was being way-over-the-top protective of Ollie and his 'bad chest', whatever that meant.

Under normal circumstances, he was sure that Clara would have joined him in mocking this kind of over-protectiveness. Would mock this response to the fogging, even, and would see the hypocrisy in it — that it was okay for them to spray toxic shit all over the island so they could enjoy their tropical holiday pest-free, just as long as they didn't have to get caught in it themselves. But he didn't really care about any of that, he just wanted them to forget about it. For everything to go back to how it was before.

But Clara didn't want to let it drop. Didn't seem able to.

They have no idea if it's harmful, she was saying. There's no studies on it. And I was lying down in it, Tom. For several minutes.

He was half-inclined to ask her again why she had lain down on the ground in a cloud of pesticides, but caught himself just in time.

I'm sorry you had to go through that, he said, unconvincingly.

She was looking at her phone.

He left for the pool.

154

When Clara emerged later that night, she was barely speaking. Tom pretended not to notice. He was enjoying his book and his beer and didn't want to spoil the second-last night of their time in Sanur by constantly rehashing the fogging incident. If she was going to sulk, then he would enjoy the quiet.

He relented, of course, much to his annoyance.

She was lying motionless on the banana lounge next to him, with her eyes closed.

Should we just eat here tonight? he asked.

I don't care, she said.

What are the others up to?

I don't know.

Maybe we should, then, he said, being upbeat, like it was a good idea. Try one of the pizzas.

Clara didn't respond. And she didn't respond when he got the menus from the restaurant, or when he ordered pizza for them both. When the pizza arrived, she perked up a little, told him briefly what else she'd read about the fogging — it was done all over Indonesia and in many other places, and in Vanuatu a few years ago someone died of an asthma attack while caught in it — but after that she went quiet again and spent the rest of the night in silence.

Clara's silences. What he dreaded most.

An undemonstrative person to begin with, Clara could become quiet under normal circumstances — enough so people noticed. Tom's parents had noticed, when she first came to stay. There was a dinner where he was required to explain her afterwards, which he couldn't really do. His parents were gregarious, opinionated — they expected people to join in and keep up — and her muted responses throughout the dinner were taken as a judgement, rejection even, of them as people. He told them something vague, like it was just her way. But she was so quiet even with him sometimes that he didn't always know if it *was* just her way or something else, if something was wrong. They came and went — sometimes they felt like comfortable silences, sometimes not, and sometimes he couldn't tell which they were. For a while she saw a therapist, too. They only ever spoke about that superficially. They had appointments, she hers, he his. They never discussed why exactly, or what they talked about while they were there. It seemed like they were respecting each other's privacy.

Tom had had his periods of silence — mostly as a teenager. He'd remained mute to his parents for two whole weeks once. He couldn't remember why. No doubt it was a flare-up with his father over something that started it — mowing the lawn or some other petty thing he couldn't be bothered doing. And he was generally very quiet for most of Year Nine. Family friends would try to engage him in conversation, and he would give them the absolute minimum he felt he could without seeming rude. He could remember the feeling, the power of silence, seeing how far he could take it. The aura it gave him.

But then, also, he remembered the feeling of not being *able* to speak. That, to begin with, he had found the clichés of everyday conversation painful and ridiculous, but perhaps above all acutely embarrassing. And then when he concluded that the only way to not feel ashamed was to not speak at all, his deliberate silence resulted, finally, in him not being able to engage, even if he wanted to. He lost the sense of how one did it without being horribly self-conscious about it.

Sometimes, he wondered if Clara was still going through something like this — a stauncher, more grown-up version — and this made him sympathetic, made him feel he understood, at least a little, why she might be like that. But her silences were not the same as his. She was not made uncomfortable by silence like he was — or, if she was, she was very good at concealing it. Her social silences seemed to stem from simply not feeling compelled to reassure those around her that she agreed with them about things, but neither did she care to contradict people, so she was quiet. And this could be frustrating, especially if she was silent around acquaintances of his or members of his family, but by and large he accepted it, respected it even — until it was directed at him.

His father had laughed at his explanation for her quietness. Feeling cornered by his parents, defensive in the face of their persistence about it, and having no real explanation to give them for it, Tom had snapped that not everyone felt the need to fill up all their time with constant talk, and, when pressed further, ventured that maybe she was trying to avoid clichés. His father had sneered at that, repeated it back to him and scoffed: *Trying to avoid the clichés.*

And then, during their time overseas, about five months in — when they were in the Auvergne working on a farm — she didn't speak to him for five days, and they essentially broke up. And he realised now he'd never known why, precisely.

11

The Hendersons' had been immediately disappointing. The last farm, the Potters', they'd
loved. There, with its crumbling seventeenth-
century stone farmhouse and outbuildings, they
had looked out each morning from the sash
windows of a barely converted stables over a
wood and a stream. Not only was it beautiful,
but they liked the family and were well treated.
They ate good food every day, produce from the
farm and others nearby. They rose early — Tom
found this part difficult, due to his insomnia, but
he didn't mind as much as he thought he might
— were brought small bottles of beer and bread
and cheese at eleven am for morning tea, ate a
long lunch, were given much less vigorous work
in the afternoons, and often finished before five.
Then had all weekend off.

In contrast, the Hendersons' farm, also in the
Auvergne, sat on a large tract of featureless, flat
land overlooking a road, and the farm buildings
were all new and ugly. The main house — painted
a dirty pink, with an ornate, dark-wood verandah
around three sides — sat low on the land and
was dim and unwelcoming inside.

It became apparent quickly that the Hendersons were using the program in bad faith. Their
farm was more a tourist destination for English
holiday-makers than it was a serious farm, and
this contravened a core tenet of the program,

that the farm be subsistence-only, not commercial in nature. But they did grow organic vegetables over several large fields, in which Tom and Clara toiled daily, hoeing rows under surprisingly sharp autumn sun.

Peter Henderson was a bony, red-faced man, whose affability and jolly facade imperfectly hid a quick temper and cruel nature. It was obvious that he saw the program simply as a way to procure free labour. Unlike the Potters, who were anxious to show them the area — the village with its market gardens and historic buildings and bars and bistros — Peter expected them to work five long days a week, and on weekends too if needed. They only got Sunday free, when he left them to their own devices on the farm, which was too isolated for them to walk anywhere of interest.

Also unlike the Potters, whose food was good and plentiful, Clem lavishing upon them all manner of dishes — many of which she had learnt from French families around her and was eager to try out on her guests — the Hendersons catered to Clara's vegetarianism by merely making more green salad, perhaps boiling a few green beans or carrots. After long days in the sun, Clara ate bread and lettuce and green beans or carrots every night, while the rest of them had chops and chickens and steak and lamb.

There were other complaints. The farm had three bungalows, plain weatherboard buildings that sat in the field behind the house. It was the off-season when Tom and Clara were there, and all three bungalows were empty. On their first

160

day, while being shown around the place, Peter told them that if he found time to clean one out, they could move out of their caravan, and into one of the bungalows. The caravan was dingy and cramped, and, as tactfully as he could over the first week, Tom reminded Peter about the bungalows on several occasions. He offered to help organise them, to clean them up himself — he could do it after work during the week, and they could be in there by the weekend — and was every time given vague excuses. Peter would say there were things being stored in them, or they'd have to think about it, work out which of the three was best for them, and of course it never happened.

While Clara wasn't that bothered about the bungalows, and didn't particularly mind the caravan, Tom brooded. Even though he had always hated caravans — ever since a few childhood sleepovers in them, when he'd spend all night worrying about spiders and hating the musty smell — he told himself, and Clara, that it was the principle of it, that Peter was full of shit, and his outrage fed into other issues he had with their host.

Besides the family — Peter, Pauline, and the two boys, Benjamin and Barry — the Hendersons had a friend who worked for them, Thomas — or Tommy, as Peter called him. Thomas looked much like Peter — ruddy-faced, stooped — and like Peter did not have either the healthy complexion or robust physique of someone who worked on the land. He had followed Peter and his family over from England, when they emigrated four years earlier, and had lived in one of the bungalows for the first year to help them establish the farm, but now lived down the road a few hundred metres, in a cottage rented off a neighbour. Tommy had no wife or family, spent all his time at the Hendersons', and seemed something of an honorary member of the family — like an uncle, or a lesser Peter — someone who was not especially loved by the boys or by Pauline, but who was useful around the place nonetheless.

He was also accident-prone and was the butt of all Peter's jokes — at the time of their visit, his thumb was in a bandage, his nail having being ripped almost entirely off, and he kept knocking it on things and screaming in pain, which made Peter shake with laughter. But he worked hard, within his limited ability, did what he was told, and was doggedly loyal to Peter and the family.

With his constant injury, browbeaten demeanour, and limited usefulness, Tom suspected Tommy was kept around principally to make Peter look good — both as a reflection of his charitable nature, looking kindly upon this unfortunate old mate who was lonely and hopeless, and as someone against whom he could be favourably compared, what with his farm, his family, his money, his luck. Although, it was also likely that Tommy was Peter's only friend. Peter — Tom and Clara came to see — was essentially a bully, and he bullied Tommy as he began to bully them. Although in fact he ignored Clara most of the time and would not meet her eye, except on the Sunday afternoon after lunch when his excessive, possibly inebriated praise over her orange cake began to give her the creeps.

Then there was Ben. Being new arrivals on the farm, Tom and Clara were naturally of interest to Peter's children, who were bored a lot of the time in the flat, bare countryside, unable as they were to venture too far on their own, and having no friends within walking distance. Ben — who was twelve, maybe thirteen — was interested in Tom in particular, as an older boy to play with, learn from. He was shy, but insistent, and would approach Tom silently, with a wry smile on his lips, or appear out of nowhere in front of him, wanting him to play basketball against the side of the house with the makeshift hoop fashioned out of wire.

The games weren't easy. No matter how many times it was wound and reinforced, the wire hoop was too weak, and after a few direct hits it began to sag and would need tending to, which Tom did with a ladder. Then the ball had only to hit the post on an angle for it to disappear into the brambles. So while some days Tom was happy to play, others he was exhausted and sore — not being accustomed to ploughing fields, or manual labour of any sort — and also resentful of Ben's father, and on these days he avoided him, hiding in the caravan and playing the guitar as quietly as possible until dinnertime.

He felt bad. Ben was a nice boy, and — Tom found out about a week in — he was going through a hard time because his father was unwell. But Tom couldn't help it. Knowing he was punishing the boy for the way they were

163

being treated by his father didn't mean he was any more able to stop himself doing it.

There was something wrong with Peter's liver. They weren't sure what yet or how bad it was, but there was a chance it was cancer. Tom and Clara were told of Peter's illness only once they were in the car on the way to a doctor's appointment in the dull regional centre fifteen miles away, where they were promised a few hours to themselves. It came up because the next visit they would be making into town would be for test results. The boys, in the back with them, became quiet as the subject was raised and Peter told Tom and Clara what he knew so far of his diagnosis.

Tom and Clara made the appropriate supportive and consoling sounds, but Tom didn't really feel sorry for him. He hated him — for the way he treated Tommy, for the way he bossed them around and took advantage of their free labour. He had already decided to leave early — there was no way he was staying the full two weeks — and he couldn't give a shit about the condition of Peter's liver. But he could see how much his children loved him. He could see how upset they were about it, and he felt for them. Even if this feeling was undercut by the certainty that they would figure out soon enough that their father was an arsehole. They were still children and couldn't quite see yet how he treated other people, or how he was seen by others. To them, he was still a hero. But it was coming, and Tom relished the thought. If anything, he didn't want Peter to die soon because he didn't want him to become a martyr to them; he wanted him to stay alive, at least long enough for the boys to grow up and see him for what he really was.

★ ★ ★

One day, Peter got Tom to grout tiles in the new bathroom they were putting in — ugly, faux-vintage tiles in French blue, with a pretentious cursive motif in white. He did this with a mixture of resentment and pleasure: resentment that he was being asked to grout their bathroom, which had nothing to do with organic farming, and pleasure because it got him out of the heat and dirt of the fields. He was lazy in the bathroom and sat around a lot and spent most of the time cleaning up after his shoddy work.

After school, Ben poked his head through the window, which Tom had opened for air and light while he worked, and asked him to play basketball with him. Tom told him he couldn't play basketball because he had to grout the stupid fucking tiles, didn't he. Ben was shocked. It was true, it had come out harsher than he had meant it to, more sarcastic, and immediately he regretted it. But he let it stand as Ben laughed in embarrassment and shrank away.

After that, Ben didn't pay much attention to Tom. In fact, he sulked, and on the one day they all had off together — they had a picnic at a nearby lake — he essentially ignored him, which was awkward as it had become assumed that Tom would play with the children on such occasions.

At the end of ten days — they begged off with some lie about the next place needing them earlier than they'd thought — Peter took the opportunity, as he said his goodbyes, to criticise their work. Or Tom's work — he didn't have the guts to criticise Clara.

Clara was a girl, and not expected by Peter to work as hard as Tom, it was true, but she had stopped even pretending she was having a good time at the farm. She had virtually stopped talking to any of them at dinnertimes and other social occasions, and so, presumably, she would have come under fire, too, if Peter could have brought himself to speak to her in that way. Peter thought she was odd, probably, maybe even unstable — that she couldn't be trusted to respond reasonably to any kind of critique of her time on the farm.

Even to Tom he was sly about it, sandwiching his comments between pleasantries, but he let the veil of affability drop from his face and voice when he said he had hoped Tom might have worked harder while he had been with them, but it was nice to meet him anyway.

Tom was taken off guard — he was surprised Peter had it in him to talk so directly to someone like this — and the comments came across all the more unpleasant for being so out of the blue and in such a suddenly changed tone, especially as he stuck out his hand immediately after, his face an awful mockery of good cheer.

There was also an audience: Tommy, who was always on the periphery of conversations being held on the farm, loitering around the edges of all life there. While Tom stood silently, not sure how to respond, but heating up, Tommy became bright red, and led out a short, almost imperceptible gasp of disapproval.

Leave off, Peter, he's alright, he said quietly. Think of all that wood he chopped the other day in the heat. And we did all the top field, didn't we?

But Peter was unperturbed; he could handle Tommy. I have the right to speak my mind, Tommy, he said. I believe it's best to say your piece and tell it how it is.

He was being earnest, sober, like he was duty-bound to speak the truth, as if it was unpleasant, but it was the right thing to do. The self-righteousness was galling. But Tom took his hand, anyway, while concealing great feeling. And although he barely spoke another word to him and barely met his eye, he felt this was too small a protest, too weak a response. He regretted ever after that he hadn't spoken his mind to Peter in that moment — that he didn't excoriate him for his treatment of Tommy, or for exploiting them, tell him what he and Clara thought about him fundamentally, as a person. For Peter couldn't know, not the full extent of it, how much they hated him; he was too confident of his rightful place in the world, his unimpeachability. And Tom had basically just taken it from him.

★ ★ ★

They went from there to a farm a couple of hours away that was run by Jim and Penny, who were younger and hipper and more fun than anyone else they'd stayed with, although not as hospitable and charming as the Potters, and not in as nice a part of the country. They took them into town for drinks at the pub, and they had two nice, less-demanding children, one of whom had a speech impediment and enjoyed talking to Tom and Clara because he wasn't embarrassed around them and it gave him practice.

That was, however, where Clara stopped talking to Tom, while they stayed in another caravan — one less dingy and cramped than the last — and they effectively broke up for a while. Tom regretted now how passive he was about that — how he'd just assumed her silence and unhappiness was about him and their relationship, rather than something else she might have been going through. He made no effort to comfort her or help her. He just pretended it wasn't happening. At the time he was tired, fed up with everything, and felt kind of paralysed himself.

It was especially awkward because, being younger and hipper, Jim and Penny wanted to socialise after work and talk and drink around the table and discuss books and music, and play records — all things they would normally have loved, especially after the Hendersons, but they were in no mood for socialising. Besides, there was something in Jim and Penny's eagerness for all this that felt forced, like a demand, almost as if it was part of the deal of staying there. It seemed as much about loneliness as it was any chemistry between the two couples. They wanted entertaining, and obligatory fun is not fun at all, especially when you have no energy for it.

Jim and Penny were isolated in their new home in France and had only met a few local families they could call friends. Mostly their contact with others was with neighbours, old French farmers who were exacting about farming traditions and had little to offer them besides sharp criticism over the neatness of their haystacks in the barn. Clara did her best and participated — tried, it seemed, to pull herself out of it by drinking and being friendly with Penny. Her silence with Tom, and with everyone else when she could get away with it, was only really noticeable to someone looking for it.

Clara spent most of the time with Jim and Penny being absorbed by the work. Penny taught her to make cheese, and Clara drew intricate and highly precise diagrams and illustrations of the process over many pages in her notebook. She then drew the vegetable gardens, noting the distance each seed was planted from the next, how deep the rows were hoed, which plants were companion planted with which. And after that she took copious notes about all manner of things to do with French farm life: at what time they herded the cows into the barns, the horrible ways neighbouring farmers treated their calves — tying them up in barns and never letting them out and force-feeding them so they would produce tender veal — the correct way to stack hay bales, so many things that Tom felt sure she would never use in her own life.

And she stopped speaking to him entirely. It

happened gradually. He thought. He couldn't really remember. He spent so much time pretending it wasn't happening, to himself, to Jim and Penny, so much time being falsely affable and sociable, solicitous, pathetic, he now couldn't remember what was real and what was fake. She was unhappy, he knew that: bored, lonely, who knows what else. Going through something. But he didn't seem to have the energy to do anything about it. To even acknowledge it. They fell into bed together each night, sometimes drunk from the wine Jim and Penny plied them with. They had sex once, silently, in the dark, once in three weeks, but beyond that, never touched.

And when, at the end of their stay, Clara left for another farm alone — Tom was to return to England by himself a few days later — and Jim and Penny gave them a minute to say goodbye to each other, turning their backs to them at the station and teasing them to Go on! Give each other a hug, they obeyed.

12

The day after the fogging incident was their trip to Lembongan. Organising themselves without speaking — making it to the right beach at the right time — was difficult, but they managed.

There were loose gatherings of passengers under palm trees on the beach, and moored in the shallow bay were several more or less identical catamarans — mercifully robust, modern-looking boats, with rows of powerful outboards. The scene was chaotic, and finding who was in charge was difficult. Tom checked with some people waiting, who didn't know, and then with several of the many men in uniforms — patterned green shorts and white shirts — who were hovering under the shade of a weathered gazebo. But these men all seemed peripheral to the main business of tickets and destinations, and the information he received was contradictory. In the end, however, they got on the right boat and sat next to each other silently in a wooden booth as the boat bobbed about near the shore.

About halfway through the hour-long trip, the seas got rough, and there were looks, nervous laughter, and talk in the cabin, even some whoops. Tom and Clara, who did none of these things, fell wordlessly into each other's shoulders a few times and pulled themselves back up. With nothing to hold on to that was designed for it, Tom tightened his grip on the edge of the table in front of him and the rim of its inlaid cup holder. But gradually it became clear that, although it would remain rough the rest of the way, the boat was well able to handle this kind of battering, and the mood in the cabin lifted. Two crew members came in and lay down on the free benches in the booth opposite them and closed their eyes, while occasionally they were sprayed with foam from the deck where the waves were bursting across the plunging stern.

A middle-aged couple across the aisle and one up from them began talking to the people sharing their booth. They were German, and the younger couple were American. The Americans, in full view of Tom and Clara, were bronzed, good-looking, laid-back, and, the whole time during the rough seas, unflappable in that smug way people who consider themselves seasoned travellers rather than tourists can be. The Germans were chatty, laughed easily, and they asked the young couple many questions, and told them in turn about their son and his girlfriend, who were clearly never far from their minds. The young Americans were receptive enough, the man more so than the woman — she looked sleepy, vague, so settled into her holiday that she was only half present — but he was a talker. He was always meeting people, you could tell, always dragging her into social situations she would rather not be dragged into, but ultimately she held up her end and giggled quietly along with the rest of them.

He was a 'digital nomad', the young American said, smirking, knowing he would have to explain the term for the Germans, and confident in advance of how impressive it would sound to them. He developed websites, he said. He could work anywhere in the world, as long as he had his laptop, and because of this he was staying on for another month while she was going home, back to the states. The girl prised her gaze from the sea and laughed good-naturedly at this with the Germans, who thought it was very amusing that the boy was staying on without her.

I have to go back for college, she said, and the Germans laughed again, although Tom wasn't sure why they found this funny. Then once again they brought up their son, who had been to Bali with his girlfriend last year for three weeks.

The Germans then probed the young couple about different islands to visit and places to stay, and Tom stopped listening. People behind them were talking about the boat ride and different charter companies. Apparently, they were saying, not only were these trips often very choppy, sometimes they were much worse than this, with a lot of seasickness and vomiting, and just last week one of the boats capsized in rough seas, although no one was drowned. Last year, however, one of the boats somehow caught fire and people drowned then, on the longer trip up to the Gili Islands.

The coast of Lembongan appeared. First mansions and luxury hotels nestled in hillsides above dramatic cliffs, then streets of rudimentary concrete and thatched-roofed houses, and then a clot of hotels and bars and restaurants overlooking the water above bluestone and concrete sea walls.

Finally, they reached the beach, and, helped by

the crew, they disembarked and waded through the waist-high water with their backpacks held above their heads. Once on shore, Tom and Clara began to speak to each other by necessity, because they had no plans. After everything, Clara didn't seem angry. Whatever resentment she had harboured was no longer apparent, at least for the moment. Or perhaps whatever it was that was troubling her no longer expressed itself as anger towards him — if that was what she was feeling. It was so hard to know. She was a little quieter than usual, but in the way of someone who had been weakened by something, but was now recovering — a bout of the flu maybe, or Bali belly. She was amenable to his suggestions, and even smiled a little when he began talking about lunch.

Tom was hugely grateful, and he became cheerful, gratingly so — even to himself. They ate at a warung on the main strip by the beach — the food was good, he drank two Bintang in his wet shorts, and she one — and then they meandered. They spotted a temple in the distance and made their way towards it, walked around its perimeter, admiring its faded majesty, and then walked the length of the main strip, looking at shops and restaurants.

It seemed hotter on Lembongan. Although you could see the sea at any given moment — its astonishing blue sparkling so invitingly at the end of every side street, a rectangle of turquoise in the neat earthen spaces between buildings and the street — the heat felt sharper. There was a lack of trees and shade, and no breeze. Maybe that was it.

They picked up a tourist sheet. One of the best things to do, it suggested — and TripAdvisor agreed — was to visit the mangroves in the north of the island and go snorkelling or swimming and lounge in the many bars with beach frontage along the north coast. They decided to walk. But after twenty minutes down dusty, exposed streets, they changed their minds and looked for somewhere to hire a scooter, only to find they were now too far from town.

They had hired a scooter in northern Thailand. Thailand was the first stop of that ten-month trip. Going there first was a mistake, they both saw immediately. They should have put this — the most holiday-ish part of the trip — at the end, not the beginning. They got the whole trip wrong, really. The itinerary, the places they went to. They had had certain ideas. Notions to avoid the same routes that everyone took, the same locations that everyone visited. Avoid the clichés. Culture over comfort.

Clara wanted to go to Krakow because her family was from the countryside around there. He remembered telling someone that in Thailand, that they were going to Poland next, and the guy had said, Oh yeah, great, Holland is lovely. And how perplexed he'd been that they'd go to Poland when Tom had corrected him. But they'd loved Krakow. It was one of the best places they went to, and one of their happiest times. Maybe because it was the first stop in Europe. They loved the intact old city, the pierogi ruskie, the cheap beer. He wasn't sure he had one proper concrete memory from Krakow, though.

Except for the time they'd lost some money on the street and retraced their steps all the way back to their hostel. And how he'd bought an SLR there, agonised over the purchase for several days, only for it to break a few weeks later when they were in Berlin. But the pictures of Krakow were saved, and they were okay. They looked like De Chirico paintings.

But he remembered the scooter in Thailand clearly. Tom had never driven a scooter before, but he wasn't nervous about it. It was easy, and they decided to drive to the next village a few kilometres away and return it the next day. But they took a wrong turn somewhere and found themselves in the countryside, with no one around and very little traffic. The road led them up a mountain, and they struggled up the steep incline, skidding on the rough surface. They ran out of petrol eventually and hitched a ride into town, putting the bike in the back of a ute, in exchange for beer and cash. When they got in that night to one of the only homestays in the village, a newly built, all-timber place on stilts, Clara complimented his driving.

Why did he remember that? Something so inconsequential? But he *had* driven well. It was difficult going, and the scooter was not designed for it, and it was hairy, with the two of them on this small bike that might skid out from under them at any moment, and he had had to meet the challenge, to get them over that mountain, and he had done it — until they ran out of petrol. He'd felt good about his driving, and there she was, saying it, too, acknowledging it

— awkwardly but seriously. Walking along the road now, jungle opening up either side of them, he felt ashamed that, of all things, this was the kind of thing he retained. And not only that, but that these were the kind of things he had in store to help him feel better about himself.

A tuktuk saved them. It came trundling along the dirt road, with two people spilling out the back, yelling to them to jump in. They were British — in Bali for a fortnight, too — and they were sunburnt, grinning, and holding enormous-looking steins of beer. In a pause in the conversation, once introductions were made and basic holiday facts were exchanged and the small talk petered out, the woman looked down at her stein, which she was no longer drinking from, and said, I don't know whose idea it was to get these. The man, large and sweaty and cheerful, with his legs spread wide, looked at her and said, It was your idea, love. And, still looking at each other, they threw their heads back and laughed.

13

He was at a restaurant table on the beach, sipping beer, with his feet in the sand, waiting for the others to arrive. The ubiquitous Wailers played softly in the background, and above him a series of bamboo lamps rocked back and forth in the breeze, casting kaleidoscopic patterns of shadow and light on the raked sand. All of this should have made for a charming scene, but he was ever so slightly nervous. He had sweat back in the creases of his palms.

It was their last night with Madeleine and Jeremy — they were off tomorrow to the Gili Islands, and Tom and Clara to Ubud — and things felt so different now, that was part of it. But most likely it was about Clara, the way she had been since the fogging. He knew he was being insensitive, but he couldn't help it — not then, out on the beach, and not even now. He was trying.

On the beach, it was strange, he'd felt so little. It was as if he hadn't really been present. As if for him the opposite or absence of fear, or anxiety, wasn't normality — or an even keel or whatever, a normal range of emotions — but a kind of emptiness, a void. He was either overwhelmed, agonised, everything in his life excruciating, unbearable, exhausting — or he felt nothing. And he knew this had expressed itself as insensitivity, it was not like he was oblivious to the fact, but it didn't feel exactly like a choice: he'd simply had nothing for Clara in that moment. He knew it was wrong, but he couldn't seem to do anything about it. If he felt anything, it was annoyance at Clara for getting so worked up over something that didn't matter. He couldn't deal with her distress; he didn't know what to do with it; it repulsed him. But mostly, he felt very little. And any sympathy he evinced would be faked, forced, and she would know it.

These kind of pre-social-gathering nerves were not unfamiliar to him, of course. His parents, his whole family were bad at this sort of thing. Something happened to his family in restaurants. They collapsed under the pressure of special occasions. No matter how good their intentions, no matter how determined they were, going into it. Especially if 'the girls', as Marianne called his half-sisters, were there.

Some of this, no doubt, had to do with the messiness of the family. Marianne and Brian felt pressure to display their happiness, and hence prove it to Penny, Brian's former wife, who they assumed was being fed everything by Tessa and Bronte, despite the girls' disavowals of this. And then there was their desperate need for Tom and his half-sisters to get along — which for Tom was essentially a non-issue, because he got along fine with Tessa and Bronte, they were just very different people with very different lives. 'The girls' were sporty, busy, happy. They were politically conservative, after their mother, which Marianne made much of to Tom. She tried to explain it to him all the time, apologise for it, as if it was a big deal to him, which he found irritating, because in reality it rarely came up. All they had to do was avoid certain subjects, which Tom and Tessa and Bronte were much better at doing than Brian and Marianne. They just didn't figure much in each other's lives. Bronte, the eldest at forty-seven, had a family of her own, three kids, and she and Tessa both lived and worked on the other side of the city, so they rarely saw each other outside of family occasions.

Added to this, there was Marianne's anxiety that they should all feel equally included and loved, which no doubt was just her trying to do her best, but which translated into a tacit demand that they perform their gratitude and happiness for her all the time. That was exhausting, and added to tensions. And on top of all of this was just the pressure of all the previous failed dinners, when things had gone wrong somehow, turned sour, and which they'd all had to recover from.

The last time he'd eaten out with them all, he remembered arriving with Clara and spotting his father. He was standing outside the restaurant by himself with an esky in one hand, the other holding his coat collar, pulled high and tight around his throat, and he was shifting his weight from one leg to the other in the cold. He launched straight into it: how the others were inside already, but he wanted to talk to them about alcohol before going in himself, to show them what he had, in case they wanted to run across the road and get some more.

Tom had to stop himself from laughing. The

country retiree overwhelmed in the big city. But it was also true that Tom hadn't thought about alcohol. He'd figured he would order a beer at the restaurant, maybe two, that it would be licensed, and that that was all there was to it. It dawned on him, however, while he tried to make sense of what his father was saying, that for Brian the whole night had a significance and weight that Tom hadn't quite grasped. They were celebrating Tessa finally finishing her sports sciences degree and getting a promotion in the same month, becoming a senior adviser in some section of the Department of Transport, and Brian felt responsible for the night's success.

He showed them what he had in the esky. Two bottles of white wine, two of Prosecco, a cold pack wedged between them. The Prosecco bottles were too tall for the esky, but Brian had just managed to stretch the elastic clasps to their hooks.

What do you think? he asked, looking from Tom to Clara and back again.

Tom weighed his options. His inclination still was to laugh at his father's overzealousness, to tell him to come in from the cold, that they would work it out inside — but this could get him in trouble later. Could get him in trouble now. Brian was edgy, clearly. But if he laughingly dismissed his father's anxiety around how much alcohol they had now, and then halfway through dinner they ran out, or he found he himself wanting more, that might be enough for a flare-up. He wondered also, guiltily — perhaps anticipating a possible line of attack — if the reason he didn't need to worry about these things, like if the restaurant was licensed or not, was because he knew, in the back of his mind, that his father would be prepared, would have these issues in hand. So he fought the urge to be dismissive and took the question seriously, all the while not doubting for a second that his initial incredulousness had been noted.

Tom told him he would be drinking beer, so not to worry about him at least. And Clara, he said, turning to her, would have a glass or two of wine? — she said she would — so two bottles of Prosecco was probably fine. There was what, seven of us? Bronte's husband David was here? — he was, Brian confirmed — and, yes, they were licensed as well as BYO, Tom continued, pointing to the sign on the restaurant window, so he could order beers and the rest could drink the wine. And, anyway, it's just across the road, the bottle shop, so he could always run back over if they needed more.

He looked at his father.

Well, that's what I'm trying to avoid by meeting you out here and discussing it now, Brian said, his thinning, combed-back hair, once ginger and now almost entirely grey, flapping in the breeze.

But that was the best Tom could manage and, feeling the cold now, he pulled open the door to the restaurant and walked in, and Clara and Brian fell in behind him, chatting about the restaurant, a Greek tavern that they both had heard good things about but not eaten at before.

It was busy inside. A cavernous, beer-hall-like

space, the restaurant stretched past arched brickwork thresholds to several rooms beyond, every table crowded with large groups of people shouting across to one another, struggling to make their voices heard above the din. This, Tom registered as both good and bad. It was good in that their table would attract no special attention from other diners; Tom's was a family of boisterous storytellers. His sisters, especially, would no doubt have stories that were long and complicated, stories that would cause many cries of anguished embarrassment, outrage, uproarious laughter. And, now in their seventies and losing their hearing, Brian and Marianne had only become louder. In a small or quiet space this could add another layer of stress to the evening. On the other hand, of course, a busy, noisy space meant hearing one another would be difficult. This in itself could ruin an evening for Marianne, who for weeks after the dinner would lament how the night was spoiled by the terrible acoustics of the restaurant, while Tom would have to assure her this was not the case, that everyone had had a wonderful time.

Brian and Marianne's expectations were always too high. They wanted full table involvement in every conversation. They wanted a communal experience of storytelling and good cheer and laughter, and the ways in which this could be sullied were endless. If one person seemed to laugh less than the others, this was a problem; if certain people could only really hear the people near them, this was a problem; and if any kind of misunderstanding or disagreement erupted, no matter how minor, it became the cause of numerous phone calls and discussions, recriminations, confessions, apologies.

The dread of this kind of tortured fallout meant that the pressure to have a good time, to be *seen* to be having a good time, was intense. It was like a collective madness, everyone coming out exhausted and slightly bewildered that, despite their best efforts, they had got caught up in all that *again* — that they had taken it all on and had cared so deeply about things that, it was clear as soon as they stepped out into the night, were absurd.

On this night, Tom's resolve, redoubled now he had seen the state of his father, had been to not speak much, to be on his best mild and agreeable behaviour. To act as nothing more than a passive relayer of information, work as a force of accommodation and appeasement, and to resist all temptation to rise to the occasion, to take bait, to argue a point. Especially that: to not argue a point.

Tom spotted them at the back of the room, at a table so broad and long it looked half-empty with only the four of them, and, as Marianne waved, and then Bronte did also, they made their way over to them. Bronte, David, Tessa, and Marianne were sitting in a row down one side of the table, and Tom and Clara and Brian sat down either side of them, so that they were all on the same side of the table, which got rethought immediately, but was never satisfactorily resolved, and in the end people sat in clumps, one around the end of the table, and the other across from each other further down, so that everyone still felt too far away from the others.

Waiters worked the room. There were three Tom could see in their corner of the restaurant alone, and one appeared immediately by Brian's side, who Brian didn't see — he was deep in conversation with Tessa about the best parking in the area — making him start. The waiter, middle-aged, handsome, with slicked-back hair and a crisp white shirt, had a certain flair about him. It was easy to see that he enjoyed the effect his performative gestures had on diners. But, thankfully, there wasn't too much of that — he was charming and down-to-business in equal measure, and he seemed highly efficient at juggling the orders and demands of the many tables in his area of the room. Tom thought, on the whole, Brian and Marianne would approve of the waiter, and, seeing they were in good hands, felt a flood of gratitude towards the man.

The waiter handed out menus with a flourish and was jokingly firm with Brian about trying the specials tonight, which you could see, he said, on the board here, pointing above and behind them, and over there, pointing to the other side of the room, but he would take them through them in a moment also. That's when he noticed the esky by Brian's feet. Brian was halfway through gesturing to it himself, having not paid attention to the waiter at all, and not being able to contain himself any longer about the important business of the esky full of alcohol.

Ah! said the waiter. I see you have brought some bottles of something with you, sir.

185

Fantastic. Would you like me to take them and chill them for you?

I don't know, Brian said, his eyes large. He seemed overwhelmed by the question. Frozen. He raised his eyebrows further. Then he laughed mechanically. I think we might keep them here, he said, with a flourish of his own, his forefinger raised in the air. So we don't have to ask someone for them when we want to open another bottle. His smile was self-gratified, but fragile, and soon gone. If that is alright? he said, peering up at the man imploringly, like a schoolboy might at a teacher.

It occurred to Tom that Brian liked his riesling very cold, his sparkling wine, too — at home, they always chilled their glasses — and, with the lid of the esky not quite on, the bottles in the esky would not remain chilled for long in the warm restaurant, and surely this trumped any concern, which was also vaguely insulting to the waiter, he thought, that service would not be able to keep up with their drinking. But he knew not to raise it. He tried to stop paying attention, and, leaning across the table, he asked David a question about the kids and their babysitter and didn't really hear the reply.

That is no problem, the waiter said, holding up his hands. I would not forget you and your family, but if you prefer, no problem. Let me get these open for you. Are we starting with champagne or wine, sir? Or both?

Perhaps the wine, Brian said, staring at the esky again with incomprehension. And we can open the champagne when we feel like it, he said, finally, looking around the table for a sign and apparently receiving some approval. Yes, we'll do that, ha-ha! he said, clapping his hands together.

Absolutely, the waiter said, and he returned moments later with a corkscrew for the wine. He poured the wine, negotiating the cramped space expertly and swiftly, put the bottle on the table, and left.

Brilliant! Brian said. Good thing I brought the esky — this place is full. Then he turned to watch the waiter disappear from the room. Anxious little man, isn't he? All that running around!

He's anxious, Marianne said into her glass.

Tom relaxed a little after that, and, for a while, the night went well, as he remembered it. They ran out of wine, but they bought another off the menu. And Marianne and Brian were having a good time, laughing loudly at Tessa's stories about the various fad diets taking hold of the people in her course and about what it was like to date a 5:2 guy, or a keto guy, or, worse yet, a fruitarian. And Marianne and Brian were telling a few of their own, about the old days, about the seventies, when Marianne had lived for a while on a commune. So, he couldn't remember how it happened exactly. If it was that, after the two beers and a glass of Prosecco, he'd relaxed a little too much, or if someone else had started it, and he'd joined in, or if he'd simply heard his father congratulate himself about the esky one too many times and couldn't help but roll his eyes at his mother about it and his father had caught it. But however it happened, he

187

remembered how his father's change of tone hushed the table.

What would you have done then, Tom? How would you have handled the situation, do you think? he said, his round face flushed from the wine. His hair was now sitting up in the humid room, as if activated by electricity, and, at the ears, it had lifted and curled, just like Tom's did in the heat.

Marianne, searching for an inhaler in her bag, was saying something appeasing and disapproving to Brian that Tom could not quite hear, not only because of the noise in the room, but because, in a way, it was only ever noise — her notes of caution like static bouncing off the hard surface of his father. The others continued their conversations, but quietly, respectfully, pretending — for whose sake Tom wasn't quite sure — that they couldn't hear what was happening.

You would have sorted everyone else's drinks for them, would you? Brian continued. Thought of everyone's preference of drinks and accommodated them? Or maybe just looked after yourself and everyone else could work themselves out? That about it, do you think?

And Tom took the bait, said something sarcastic about how bad it would be if they had to go all the way across the road for more wine. And his father was away, then, saying that Tom had always been like that, thinking only ever of himself, taking everything given to him and offering nothing in return — or something along those lines. Tom couldn't remember because he had wilfully stopped listening or, if he had heard

188

it, had soon blocked it out.

He didn't know why he took the bait, why he always did. In part, the sarcastic response was a defence mechanism, a reflex against the shock of it. By deflecting his father's rising rage, by making a joke of it, he was diminishing it, at least for a moment. But of course, in reality, it only enraged him further. But how else could he respond? Apologise for antagonising him, instantly, every time, hoping to cut him off before he got worked up? Yes, perhaps. But who could do that every time? Who could be forever submissive and apologetic in the face of such a constant threat? The threat of such bewildering rage? And when his father reached his peak, became truly enraged, how was he to respond then? Agree with him? Accept his father's demolition of his character — that he *was* the lazy, ungrateful person his father said he was, who had never done anything but what suited him? Again, probably. And yet, if he wanted to survive as a person, this was not possible. He had decided he would no longer be doing that — apologising. He had learnt that it didn't work, anyway. So this is what he got instead. Flare-ups that upset Marianne and ruined evenings.

But it was over quickly enough, this time. It was smoothed over expertly by the girls, who distracted them both by bringing them each into their own conversations, and, for the rest of the night, everyone simply pretended it hadn't happened. Tom would have liked to have kept on pretending that, but he couldn't because the inevitable phone call came from Marianne the next day.

Her condition had deteriorated since then. A night out like that was less likely all the time. Everyone discouraged it; it was too much hard work. They meant hard work for her — or did they? And so, it occurred to Tom now, that night at the tavern might have been the last one. This, despite everything, filled him with sadness. Sadness that took the edge off his nervousness, distracted him from the persistent clamminess of his palms.

* * *

Madeleine and Ollie and Jeremy arrived first, then Clara, looking wary and a little dishevelled, but still good in his eyes. It was their last night together, and a certain amount of good cheer was being performed that none of them particularly felt. They had chosen a place on the beach that would accommodate Ollie's fussiness. He could order five things and graze: fish and chips, pizza, nachos, noodles, anything he wanted. It came to nothing. And they could sit on the beach and look out at the water and drink.

They had fish that was grilled in front of them, and Clara and Madeleine had cocktails one last time, the running joke now being how bad they were. They were absurdly inconsistent, one virtually non-alcoholic, one way too strong, one tasting vaguely of turps, but they had to keep ordering them, their one cocktail each night, most left barely drunk, because they were so cheap, and neither of them drank cocktails at home, and because maybe this would be the one, the one that was perfect.

These, a 'La Taverna Rose', named for the restaurant, and a whisky sour, turned out not to be. But that did not stop Clara ordering several others, drinking much more than she had the rest of the holiday. Madeleine joined her, but was less enthusiastic. Clara was talking to Tom, but not a lot. It seemed the thawing the day before, during their trip to Lembongan, was only a brief respite. Back here, she had retreated again. Into the room, into herself. It was as if, in Lembongan, she had escaped it all for a day, and now they were back, she was swamped by it again — whatever it was, exactly. Or, of course, she was faking it at Lembongan, had been stuck with him there and was just playing along, going through the motions — although he hated to think that, and it wasn't really her style; she would rather shut down than pretend. But the food was fine, they ordered a coconut with a straw in it for Ollie from a man on the beach, and, under candle-light, the scene was lulling and cool. Tom cooled his palms on his bottle of beer.

They had stopped talking about the fogging. For now, it was exhausted as a subject; they were all trying to regain their composure. After the incident, Clara had disappeared for a few hours with Madeleine, but Tom had hardly seen Madeleine and Jeremy since it happened. He and Clara had gone to Lembongan the next day, and he had only seen Jeremy once, briefly, on the path this morning.

Jeremy took the incident seriously in the moments they'd discussed it, and this made Tom try to take it more seriously, too. Jeremy was outraged on behalf of the women and worried about Ollie's chest — he had been out on a walk when it happened, while Madeleine and Ollie were napping in their room — but he let the topic drop easily enough.

Clara was clearly still shaken by it, but she was consoled by being with the others. She looked beautiful to Tom, across the table. Her freckles had deepened, her version of a tan, and she looked so good on holiday, despite everything, her hair wayward, her shirt open several buttons, probably not by design. Something about all this made her seem quietly powerful, emboldened. As if her moment of vulnerability had only brought out its opposite in her.

Madeleine told them about the play date they'd had that afternoon with Eka's little boy, Bakti. It seemed a good way to give Ollie a positive experience after the trauma of the fogging, she said, lowering her voice a little, as though Ollie, who was sitting right across from her, wouldn't hear her if she did this. Something so he didn't start hating the place or being scared of it, internalise all their stress about it, she said. He'd become very clingy, wanting to be carried all the time.

But he seems fine, she hastened to add, holding Tom's gaze. There's no research that suggests it's worse for children. And she smiled at him, lingeringly, he felt. It was nice, actually, she said, in the end, the play date, although it was a little awkward at first.

Eka didn't seem to realise Madeleine would be coming with them and had taken Ollie's hand and started walking off with him, and Madeleine had to insist that she would come, too, and could tell Eka was uncomfortable about it, she wasn't sure why. To her, it seemed obvious that of course she wasn't going to let her son be taken off by a woman she hardly knew, to who knows where. But she couldn't tell whether it was insulting to Eka that she was coming, too — that she had to chaperone her son, make sure everything was okay — or, it occurred to her later, whether Eka was embarrassed perhaps by the way they lived, their home, and didn't want Madeleine to see it. After a while it was fine, though, she said. They played just like Ollie would with any other friend, and everyone was very nice. They lived in such poverty, she told them, and the kids had mostly broken toys, no doubt things left behind by hotel guests. She thought it was good for Ollie to see how these people really lived, to see them as people, not just waiters and hawkers on the beach, although he had made friends with some of these, too. One old man always asked after Ollie as he staggered past with his esky full of soft drinks.

Conversation then settled on travelling. They were thinking of their day tomorrow, then flying, and flying with children.

You expect it to be awful, and it is, but then it's over, Jeremy said.

I spent six hours pacing the aisle on the way over to Australia the first time, Madeleine said, when Ollie was eighteen months old. Six hours staring at those assholes in the cabin with me, thinking, I'm doing this for all of you, so you don't have a screaming baby in here with you, and they are totally oblivious, even hostile, to this woman hovering around in the aisle.

She looked at Ollie. Do you remember that, darling? she asked, stroking his head, sweeping some of his fringe off his forehead, which bounced immediately back.

I remember watching movies, he said.

Really? Madeleine said. You were very young. What did you watch?

Ollie thought about it, looked around, opened his mouth as if to speak and stopped.

I remem . . . he said, finally.

You were very young, darling. You don't have to remember. What did you watch this time?

No, I remember! he said. Was it *Frozen*?

That's a good guess, Jeremy chuckled. It probably bloody was, you know.

No, I *know*, it was *Frozen*, Ollie said. I remember, watching and lying on Maman — Mummy — with my head on her lap. She loved *Frozen*, didn't you, Maman?

They all looked to Madeleine, as she thought it over.

Oh, darling, yes, of course. I did love it, she said. I loved it very much. And we had a lovely time watching it together, with you sleeping on my lap.

Madeleine was softened. She was sleepy and glad and rocking gently on her hips as she held Ollie to her side, while he cradled the empty coconut.

There was no talk anymore of next year's holiday, how they'd all meet up here next July and do it all again. No more talk of Tom and Clara getting jobs at European universities and seeing them more often, although they did make plans to see each other one last time, in the morning, before they left.

14

Mexico was the last stop of the trip. Perhaps by then, after nine months away, they were just ready to go home, but they were bored in Mexico. They had been so excited about it for so long that it was a surprise to find themselves bored, but they couldn't shake it.

When Tom went to England for a couple of months, Clara had gone to another farm in France, where she learnt all about growing corn, and then on to another, where she found that the woman who ran the place had nothing for her to do. So she did a local cooking class, cooked for the woman, and rode around the muddy fields on quad bikes with her teenage boys.

There was little communication between them during that time, but when they met back up in New York, they were happy to see each other, and happy to be there for a few days, staying with a friend of a friend in Queens. Then they caught a Greyhound through DC, Atlanta, Houston, crossed the border at Brownsville to San Luis Potosí, then Zacatecas City — its cluster of flat-roofed, adobe dwellings appearing out of nowhere over a rise, a glittering, tiered horizon punctured only by church spiers — and then on to Mexico City.

In Mexico City, they stayed in a crumbling hotel, walked crumbling streets, drank in crumbling cantinas with crumbling old men, who, when drunk enough, approached Tom to request a dance with Clara. Clara consented the first three times and danced waltzes in front of the jukebox while the men laughed and clapped, and then had to say no for the rest of the night to every man that came in the place. They walked streets lined with dozens of shops that all sold the same thing — a street for jukeboxes, one for lawnmowers, one for pets.

Then they went to the pyramids, and then to the mountains to house-sit a place in a small village at the foot of higher peaks. There, they walked and explored, and that was where the boredom set in. They were bored with being tourists, bored with the serene, hippy theme that ran throughout everything there, bored with themselves, bored with each other.

Then it was the end of the year, and, for New Year's, they went to a party on a beach a few beaches over from Puerto Escondido. It was their old housemate Trish who had the contact — of course. Some party people she'd met there who could show you a good time. The party consisted of a generator on the beach and speakers pumping out house music, and people doing nangs and other drugs in the sand. They all seemed very young. They found their guy — Louis — who sold them cocaine, and they settled into an evening of smiling back at the dozens of increasingly drunk young Mexican men who introduced themselves and hugged them and tried to get them to dance. There were few girls.

The cocaine wasn't good, they could tell, but they had bought a lot of it — it was extremely cheap — and, encouraged by Louis, they had it all in one session, in a series of long lines. As moisture vanished from Tom's throat, he began to feel very good. They went into the water, up to their knees, as the countdown began, and they held each other tightly, and laughed intensely at the ridiculousness of everything. Then the good feeling drained from Tom's body and nothing was left in its place, and, after looking for Louis and more cocaine and failing to find either, he fell asleep on the sand.

Back in their house-sit, hungover, they were easier with each other, kinder. Clara looked through her notebook and found her cheese-making diagrams from France. She erupted with laughter, and Tom thought he saw tears running down her cheeks. How pointless they were, how stupid, she said. Why had she been so intent on writing it all down, and in such ridiculous amounts of detail?

Who did this? Who *is* this? she said. What was I thinking?

She looked him.

He didn't know what to say.

★ ★ ★

Not long after that, they were home, and not long after that, without either of them knowing it, they broke up, more or less. Clara went to Adelaide for the summer, to visit a friend she'd become friends with mostly on social media and over one drunken weekend in Melbourne. They didn't have a house yet in Melbourne, so she didn't feel tethered to anywhere in particular, and she'd dropped out of her arts degree and hadn't quite decided what to do next. Tom didn't want to go to Adelaide. He wanted to spend the summer on the beach, and then find a new house — or, now, new room — in Melbourne. So he did that, half-expecting the whole time that Clara would ring at any moment to say she was coming after all or, later, that she would ring to say of course she was still moving in with him. But when she did ring, eventually, it was only to tell him that she was staying on in Adelaide — at least for a few months. She was moving in officially to the share house where she'd been staying with her friend and some other people she seemed almost as excited about as the friend. There was no talk of their relationship during this conversation, but they never talked about it. She was doing this, he was finding a room in Melbourne before the start of semester, and they'd just see each other when she came to visit in a few months' time.

He was the loneliest he had ever been that year. Most of their friends were really her friends, and he felt embarrassed relying on them for all social contact. When she came for her visit, he allowed himself to feel how much he had missed her, allowed himself to acknowledge his excitement, which very quickly turned to anxiety. So much had been left unsaid that he didn't really know what was happening. Were they romantically involved, still? Or was she coming to visit all of her friends — of which he was simply one — and merely crashing at his place because that was easiest?

He met her at Flinders Street Station, and they took the No. I tram up Lygon Street, and he sat next to her, sweating and barely speaking. It occurred to him, while he squirmed, that they were re-enacting the final scene of *The Graduate*, when Benjamin and Elaine ride silently side by side on the bus after Benjamin's grand gesture of love at the wedding — a grand gesture of love for someone who is effectively a stranger to him. Tom felt the same way about Clara. That he didn't really know her. Not anymore. Or maybe he had never really known her. He felt that his feelings for her were founded on something so nebulous as to be suspicious. She was so quiet so much of the time that she was like a screen onto which he projected all his fears, his paranoia, and, when things were going well, his complacencies.

He was embarrassed. Embarrassed by how much he felt, by how excited he had been to see her — what a fluster the prospect of seeing her had thrown him into — embarrassed now especially because all of this was so painfully obvious, and embarrassed most of all because her lack of interest in small talk meant he could think of nothing to say. He was paralysed. And, rather than do something about this, say something, she, like always, and in that way that always drove him crazy, followed his lead.

And so, for the whole length of Lygon Street, they sat in silence. Other people got off and got on, held conversations, talked on their phones, were polite to their fellow passengers — a woman helped another woman on with a pram

— while two people who had not seen each other in two and half months barely spoke to each other.

When they arrived at his house, the spell broke. Things presented themselves to be spoken about — the house, his room, the backyard. He introduced her to his housemates, or the one who was home then, Louise — someone he had nothing in common with and who treated him with the formality of a work colleague. But she was someone they could talk about as soon as she was out of earshot. They slept in the same bed, so they had sex. But it never felt clear, to Tom, what was happening between them.

Then Clara went back to Adelaide, and, over a couple of months, they wrote emails and messages that became more and more infrequent, until one day she told him that she was seeing someone. Not only did she tell him she was seeing someone, she told him all about it, confided in him about it, as if they were merely good friends — which, he concluded, maybe they were. The guy was in a band. The band was good, he played guitar, but there were other girls in the picture, and she was increasingly worried about it — never knowing if he was with someone else when not with her. But sometimes he snuck into her bedroom window — Tom could tell she loved that without her saying as much — and when they were together, it was good. All of which enraged him. He did not respond for several months.

By the following December, however, that was over — the guy was a jerk, after all, and was seemingly moving through all the girls in Adelaide in a certain social circle — and Tom and Clara spent the summer together again, like they used to, and things were back to normal. She moved back to Melbourne, they got their first place together, and she finally started the architecture and planning degree she had been telling Tom and Emily she'd been thinking about doing for a while.

Not long after this, they had their great social flowering, when everything was exciting, and all of a sudden they'd been together, on and off, for ten years. And now, of course, it was fourteen.

But what, in the final analysis, could be said about any of it? Had they ever truly wanted to be together — ever made sacrifices for their relationship? Or was it all just convenience? And how to look at what had happened? Was there a break-up and a second shot or was it all points on a continuum — all part of the same one thing, something that adhered to some principle, even by accident, or by unspoken agreement, or misunderstanding? Or was it just all a symptom of a bad culture? A culture they had initiated by refusing to talk about things and that they'd let deepen and ingrain itself and go on for so long that now neither of them knew how to stop it.

You've not been good for my mental health, she'd told him once, elliptically, in an email. That was while she was in Adelaide, he thought, although he couldn't remember exactly. He knew what she said was true, but only in a vague way, without knowing exactly what she meant. He had genera-lised guilt over being what he assumed was a pretty taxing person for someone else to be around. Stress, anxiety, moodiness, denial. Emotional withholding. She certainly had a point. He could not argue with it. He was glad he wasn't like that anymore. Most of the time.

★ ★ ★

They missed saying goodbye to Madeleine, Jack, and Ollie. They weren't at breakfast, and when they got back to their room there was a sheet of paper under a rock on their porch. It showed a confusion of figures that seemed to be all of them plus one and the words 'have a good holiday we miss you' scrawled over them in a young boy's hand.

Clara was still quiet. No doubt, she was missing her new friends. Tom let her have the room, let her have her silence, spent most of the day by the pool, and when in the afternoon he returned to the room to find her not there, he went for a walk himself. Over to the turtles again, where he watched them clamber over each other and up the walls of their green tubs towards him in a manner that was either supplicating or aggressive, he couldn't tell. It was easy to take a place like that for granted. A turtle rescue on the beach. But someone had to actually do it — to tend to the turtles, help heal their wounds, rehabilitate them. Although he didn't know really what this entailed; they seemed fairly low-maintenance at this point, in the tubs. No one seemed in charge at the turtle rescue. It appeared unmanned. But there were signs about what not to do — touch them, feed them, bang on the sides of the tubs — and they were in shade under tarpaulins and leafy trees. He was sure someone would be back soon.

After that, he visited the Kirschler museum. Through richly coloured fabrics, he passed into a cool, spacious, naturally lit room with sets of large, shutterless windows open at each end. The walls were lined with Kirschlers. The paintings were not bad, technically, he thought, although he claimed no great knowledge or eye for art — influenced by The Blue Rider, he thought, maybe, yet figuratively more conventional — but the treatment of his subjects, almost exclusively the Balinese dancer, and the settings were corny.

In the literature Tom picked up from a stand on a marble desk by the door — the same brochure Clara had brought to their room all those days ago — Kirschler was portrayed, or portrayed himself, as a hopeless romantic: someone devoted to the object of his desire; someone who could not help but endlessly paint her. The word 'muse' was used several times.

Tom wondered about the woman and what she thought of this devotion. In the paintings, her expression remained the same. She smiled — serenely or blankly, Tom wasn't sure which — as she danced, stood in the ocean, sat at a table with high tea arrayed about her. Is this how she received his devotion, too? With serenity? Did she indulge him, or did she, as Tom suspected, find it oppressive, being so mercilessly objectified? And why was Tom so cynical about it? Why couldn't he be impressed by the power of this love that they

204

shared, be convinced by all this devotion? Why couldn't he imagine — instead of oppression, resentment, her endurance of this aggressive ownership of her body, the transactional nature of relationships under colonialism — that a deep and abiding love was possible between these people? Maybe she wasn't in bondage, maybe she didn't need this man's money — indeed, she was a celebrated dancer, wasn't she? — and maybe she hadn't sold her exoticism, her body, to him in exchange for a life of comfort. Maybe she was happy, indeed proud, to be his muse, and they lived a charmed life together, a life miraculous in its harmony, despite their cultural differences.

No, Tom thought. Even if she professed all that, even if she claimed to feel it deep within her, he would not believe it.

★   ★   ★

For their last meal in Sanur, they went to a Spanish restaurant. Clara was still not really talking to him, but she assented to going. When he'd asked her where she'd been that afternoon, as they bobbed about, holding on to the sides of the tray of the ute that was taking them to the restaurant, she said she had finally followed the tsunami signs out beyond the tourist strip.

Where did it take you? he asked.

To assembly points, other hotels, she said, dully.

Oh. Right.

There was a pause.

There is no higher ground, she said, eventually. We'd be fucked.

Stepping down from the tray onto a dark street corner, they could see no sign of a restaurant. There was only a scrappy, empty block with a low wall that ran around two sides of the perimeter before crumbling into the dirt. Beyond this were mangroves and more empty blocks. The streetlights of the main street a hundred metres away cast long shadows across pale fields and the tops of trees. Tom checked his phone. The pin suggested they were there.

Maybe down here? Clara said, and she began down a dirt lane towards a weak light emanating from a group of low-lying buildings.

Tom followed, and she was right. A canary-yellow light box that read 'La Mancha' in uncertain cursive announced their arrival.

The restaurant was subdued, open-air, a handful of tables on an unsealed concrete slab under a series of brick archways. It was one of several buildings built in the same style: dark-red brick, ornamental archways, adobe roofs.

Only one table was occupied, in the far corner, by a group of middle-aged men who were talking animatedly in Spanish. One of them jumped up as they arrived, a stout man with a paunch and a knitted brow, but also a quick smile that he trained on them for an instant. He welcomed them to the restaurant, and, from where he stood, motioned to them to take any of the free tables on the floor.

Tom and Clara hesitated. A young Balinese man in whites came out of the kitchen holding several plates of food. As he passed, Tom asked him quietly if the chef was in tonight. The man apologised, but said no, unfortunately he wasn't, he had been called down to Denpasar on business.

Furtively, Tom motioned to Clara that they should leave, and they turned to walk back out onto the street. They were halfway back up the drive when the man with the paunch caught up with them.

Is there a problem? he asked.

Tom couldn't think of what else to say, so he told him the truth: that, since the chef wasn't in tonight, they thought they might eat somewhere else. And then, stupidly, as if he needed to explain himself further, but in fact only making things worse, that they'd read in reviews that when the chef wasn't in the dishes were made by young apprentices who simply reheated leftover food.

The man looked annoyed for a moment, and then smiled, laughed falsely. No, no, no. That might have been true once, my friend, but all the people we employ in the kitchen can now cook our dishes, and they are cooked fresh each night. You come back, and I show you.

There didn't seem any way out of it, and Tom allowed the man to usher them back into the restaurant. He then lavished attention on them in a way that previously, it had been clear, he was not going to bother with.

He brought out menus and talked them through the dishes, even though they were the same basic tapas dishes on all Spanish restaurant menus: chorizo, Manchego, chickpeas, squid. Clara was obviously uncomfortable — she was responding minimally to the man and his entreaties, barely raising a smile for him — but Tom laughed along at everything he said and agreed readily to his suggestions.

When the man left them alone with the menus, they exchanged looks. Tom's look was to suggest there was nothing he could do, the man had run roughshod over them, but maybe it was going to be okay after all. In Clara's gaze, there was no indication that she understood or was sympathetic to him, she simply looked at him steadily for a moment, then looked away.

The owner brought them their drinks, and, when Tom spoke to Clara, he felt he had adopted the man's false good cheer, but couldn't stop himself. He talked up the sound of the dishes, declared the beer delicious, chatted away, wondering if the place, with its outbuildings, all the same brick with the same arched walkways, was a back-packers', or a place that accommodated Spanish tour groups, or what. Clara sipped her wine, which she said was very nice.

The food when it arrived seemed initially promising, but turned out to be mediocre at best. Confirmation that the food had in fact been reheated from the night before seemed to hang in the air: the potatoes were dry, the chorizo was tough, the prawns slightly spongy. That every-thing was drenched in garlic and tomatoes and olive oil helped. They had also ordered too much food. It just kept coming: small terracotta bowls of corn croquettes, patatas bravas, green beans, more chorizo. Clara stopped even pretending to pay attention to the man or his food, and he looked increasingly strained as he returned each time, clear as it was that neither of his guests was eating much and neither of them was happy.

How is it all? he asked, tentatively.

Delicious, Tom said.

Almost imperceptibly, Clara rolled her eyes.

You are not hungry, señora? the man said, turning to Clara.

We're actually pretty full still from lunch, Tom said for her. Seeing her face set like that, he couldn't be sure what she might say if he left it to her to reply.

Finally, the man left them alone.

After that, Tom found himself talking too much again. About the boat ride to Lembongan and how, for a while there, when the sea had become rough, he had started to wonder what they would do if the boat capsized. Wondered how far they would have to swim, or if they could hold on to something from the boat, perhaps, and wait to be rescued. No one had offered them life jackets, and he doubted anyone would come to rescue them in time. Is this what had happened to the people in the accident they'd heard the other passengers talking about? They weren't that far from Lembongan when it got rough. They could see houses and other buildings in the craggy hills high on one end of the island, although distances over the water could be deceptive. Could they have swum it? Some people might have been able to, he said. Those Americans looked pretty fit.

How far was it from shore, a kay? he said. We wouldn't make it. Especially in rough seas.

Unlike Emily, of course, Clara said, abruptly.

What? What do you mean?

She is an excellent swimmer . . .

Is she? I didn't know that about her particularly.

Yes, you did. You told me, when we went camping that time, how she was this little surfer chick when she was a kid, and now could swim, like, fifty laps of the pool, and was this beautiful, graceful thing in the water.

I don't remember saying that, or even if it is true, Tom said.

Clara drained the last of her wine and fell silent again.

He let it drop, but he couldn't figure out why they were talking about Emily. Clara had never seemed jealous of her before. Not that she would let it show, of course. He was very tired. After the beer, and all the effort he'd put into being cheerful, he was spent. He couldn't face an argument. Clara's anger couldn't be about Emily, anyway, not really. But he couldn't figure out what it *was* about, at bottom. He knew he hadn't been amazing about the fogging, but the whole thing just seemed insignificant to him. He couldn't bring himself to care about it all that much. She was so morose, he couldn't figure it out. He would talk to her about it this time, though. He would. Tomorrow, though, not tonight. Tomorrow he would ask her. He didn't know what he was so afraid of.

15

Tom had prepared mentally for a day out of their holiday for the travel to Ubud, but they were there and installed in the hotel in two hours' time, and then didn't know what to do with themselves. It was more expensive than the hotel in Sanur, a bit of a blowout budget-wise, but they'd had to stay there, once they saw the pictures.

Located about half an hour out of town, the hotel projected vertiginously from the side of a deep gorge and hung cantilevered over jungle that was denser and greener than anything Tom had ever seen. At first, it was hard to distinguish much in the mass of green, but the more he stared at it over the coming days, the more things began to emerge: the grassy bank opposite, hidden behind a screen of palms; the silver thread of water far below on the jungle floor; patches of grey sand down there, too, in the shadows; and monkeys, or their wake, as they crashed down the hillside, the jungle closing back up behind them. There was a track high on the opposite bank, sections of which drew into focus for Tom as he watched from the banana lounges around the pool. He could see workers walking along it throughout the day, some riding bicycles, to the site of a new development being raised out of the jungle, further along the gorge — a sprawling complex of concrete foundations running over a swathe of cleared land.

The drive to Ubud had been quiet, frosty even, but they checked in and looked around the hotel a little, finding the infinity pool at the bottom of a winding marble staircase with a view over the jungle, and the mood lifted a little. It was mazelike, the hotel. It ran down the sheer side of the gorge in a series of buildings connected by zigzagging platforms and staircases and walkways, before finally resolving, with a narrow lap pool and massage hut, at the jungle floor.

Besides the marble, the hotel was all dark wood, and when the sun fell behind clouds, the wood and the cavernous buildings and the shade of the palms made the place feel a little gloomy. But the rooms themselves, at the top of the hillside, were light-filled, with glass doors, skylights in high ceilings, white marble floors. Tom was impressed by it all, but there was something about this version of luxury that he resisted. It was cold. There was an austerity to it that wasn't entirely hospitable.

After the tour of the hotel, Clara seemed kind of dazed. She sat slumped on the bed, staring out through the sliding doors to the wading pool and ferns in oversized, glossy pots.

This is where Tasha and Henry stayed, then? he asked, knowing the answer.

Yes, she said.

I thought they mentioned amazing views from the rooms. Why doesn't ours have amazing views? he joked.

I think some of the rooms look over the gorge,

she said, picking up an information sheet and turning it over. There's a spa a few doors down from us.

Want to go look?

Not right now. I'm tired.

He looked at her, and she looked back at him, glassily.

Maybe have a rest, then, he said. We'll go and have a look later.

Maybe I will, she said, already flicking the straps off her dress.

Tom hesitated.

Clara had made that dress. It was one of her early successes. The sewing hobby was suggested to her by her supervisor, Anna Haywood, an intimidatingly accomplished academic who had somehow produced a PhD, twenty years ago, while her first child was a toddler and her second had just arrived. But how? Clara had asked her, for the third time in several minutes, at a supervisor meeting she told Tom about once. Oh, you find the time, Anna had said, finally, when she could no longer avoid the question, and she told Clara she'd written a lot of her first drafts on the floor in the hallway while the baby slept! And then, as they get older, she'd said, there is child care. God knows, no one else was helping. (Why didn't she want to talk about it? Clara had wondered to Tom. Why isn't she proud?) But then she told her, as she picked up papers and moved them around the desk, that you just do it every possible moment you can. And she'd looked at her, Clara felt, pointedly.

While Anna had been a wonderful advocate

for Clara's work, and Clara hung on to her every word, sometimes these conversations were just depressing. This time, at a low point in her resolve about her research, Clara was more honest than usual. She told her: Some weeks, I can't bring myself to even look at it, let alone work on it every possible moment! She'd said that jokingly. Anna hadn't laughed, but that's when she suggested the hobby.

Baking? Sewing? Running? Anna said. Do you run? I run three times a week, an hour at a time, and it's wonderfully mind-clearing — meditative. It gives you time to think. You can work out the problems with the work, get some air . . . You need to do something in between the reading and the writing where you feel productive, but which also allows you time to think. Thinking's half the thing. Well, an important part, anyway.

Clara didn't run and wouldn't be starting, but she could sew. She used to make her own dresses in high school, and she'd sewn other things later, while at uni and living in share houses — a patchwork cover for an ugly but comfortable armchair she'd found on the street one day, some cushion covers. Perhaps she could get back into that. So she'd tried and quickly remembered how much she loved it. It wasn't time to think about other things, though. It was occupying. But that was what she needed, really. She needed something to be distracted by for an hour each day that wasn't research, wasn't the organising of thoughts, material, the endless revision of drafts. It was also something she could talk to her mother about, she joked. And this dress, a patchwork of coloured squares, was one of the first things that really worked. It was light, airy, and, although simple, almost crude in its design and shape, like a child's drawing of a dress, it hung off her frame in just the right way and showed off her lovely shoulders.

Seeing the straps fall off those shoulders now, Tom had the urge to watch her undress fully, but he knew she didn't want him to, so he turned away and went over to the windows. All he could see was the courtyard, bordered by a high sandstone wall that he imagined monkeys scampering over at night. Under the blanket of clouds everything was blanched white. The marble, the sandstone, all surfaces hard and reflective. The large ceramic pots contained the only colour — bright pink and red and orange flowers, green leaves.

What would these places be like without the fogging, he wondered. Filled with all sorts of horrors . . . he didn't know what . . . scorpions, snakes, swarms of mosquitos? Spiders the size of your face?

When he turned back, Clara was lying on the bed, turned away from him, on top of the covers. He went down to the pool.

There was one other guest down there, a young woman, lying on a banana lounge, reading a book. She was shaded by the sail-sized fronds of a palm tree that had grown up and around the pool, as if to give her precisely this amount of shade. The area around the pool was not large. The grand marble steps everywhere took up a lot of space, and there was just enough room for the row of banana lounges off to the side. And the pool itself — while beautifully designed, curving with tiny pale-blue tiles around a water garden, and extending out into the air with a graceful sweep, a bit like a huge jutting lower jaw, Tom thought, or like a pregnant stomach — was not large, either. He could either get in the pool and float about in full view of the girl or sit down quite close to her, and, at the last moment, decided on neither and entered the hotel library instead. Like most hotel libraries, it was disused. It was a mostly empty space with a few rows of tattered paperbacks on one shelf, a few travel guides, a set of encyclopaedias, and a huge ripped and stained coffee-table book on Ubud. He went back outside, the girl was gone, and he settled into her shaded lounge.

He checked his phone. Madeleine had replied to his email about work visas in France. It was just idle chat, daydreaming on his part, but she took everything like this seriously. He clicked on it, and, as he did, his hand spasmed, perhaps from the awkward way he was holding the phone above him on the lounge, angled away from him to avoid the glare from the marble floor. He dropped it, and it fell on his face. He picked it back up and saw that she had sent through a couple of links, one to an article about working in France, another to a page on the embassy website, but then she had written something else, at the end, a kind of a farewell message: Sorry we didn't get to say a proper goodbye! she wrote. It was so lovely to meet you. And then this:

And I really hope everything works out for you two! You have time now to think about what you really want. Both of you. Clara told me everything. It will happen of course (if you really want that), I had a couple of false alarms (!) myself, before Ollie. You are maybe disappointed or maybe relieved, but you have time now to really figure this all out. Actually this has been a good thing for you, I think. You will both realise this at some point. No one wants that kind of awful toxic shit hanging over their pregnancy, or their baby.
Anyway, talk soon xxx

He found himself just staring at it. The lines, the words. Thinking about the tone of it, what might be lost in translation. What she thought he knew but he didn't. What had happened and how, when. The words separated, and then came back together. They made sense, and then they didn't again.

In the end, he put down his phone — it was heavy in his hand, his arm was sore from holding it above him like that — and looked out at the jungle. Wondered if he should take a dip in the pool, after all. Wondered if he could order drinks down here.

His eyes fell on the steady stream of workers coming and going along the path on the opposite side of the gorge, and followed the figures to the trucks and cranes and diggers all in motion around the building site. It would have quite the view when it was finished, the new resort, sitting high on the bend in the gorge like that. What was beyond that bend? More jungle, no doubt. But resorts were going up at an incredible rate, he had read, something like one a week. And they were being cut ever deeper into the jungle so that they'd just be one development after another along here until all the jungle was overlooked by someone sipping drinks from an infinity pool, marvelling at the view, trying to ignore the other resorts either side of theirs and all the other marvelling going on around them. What could you do about that? Not come? He didn't think he was selfless like that. He wanted to see the jungle. He was glad he was here to see it.

★ ★ ★

When he went back to the room, he wasn't sure what he was going to say, how he might broach it. All he knew was that he was going to say something to her, he had to. But he wasn't given a chance, because Clara was gathering her things. She was going for a massage at the 'wellness centre' at the bottom of the gorge, she said, and took a towel and her swimmers and left him alone in the room.

Slipping off his shoes and lying down on the still-made bed, his feet resting on his still-rolled towel, he decided that was a good thing. He could get his thoughts straight. He didn't know how he really felt about it, hadn't given himself enough time, maybe, to figure it out. He felt some anger, yes, but he wasn't sure he had a right to be angry, or not primarily, not as the main thing he felt about the whole thing. He wasn't entirely sure what had even happened. He found himself thinking about her cocktails, how Clara never seemed to drink them. Not until after the fogging, at least.

He began collecting in his hand the pink petals scattered over the bedspread that were within his reach. He put the petals in a neat pile on the bedside table, straightened the finely embroidered gold and maroon bed-runner beneath his feet, and smoothed out the indent from Clara's body on her side of the bed. He rested his head on the high pile of soft pillows and tried to meditate. But he couldn't. He couldn't quieten his hands. He opened his eyes and looked down at them. They were spasming, twitching gently on the bedspread, like they were creatures independent of him. Like they had a life of their own.

16

When Tom woke up the next morning, the room was alive with light. It blazed through the glass doors onto the marble floor and, as he got up and made his way to the bathroom, it flashed into his eyes from all the hard surfaces in the room — the gilt-framed mirror, the marble coffee table, the highly polished dressing table.

It was only when he came back into the bedroom that he realised Clara wasn't in the bed. She usually got up earlier than he did, of course, so he figured she was out for breakfast. He checked his phone. It was nine thirty-five am. He considered getting back into bed; he considered sitting outside in the courtyard. But what he really wanted to do was find her, so he pulled on his shorts and T-shirt from next to the bed and left. He made his way down the narrow path bordered by high bamboo walls that concealed the other bungalows. He passed reception, which was unmanned, and took the marble steps down to the restaurant and the pool, passing on the way a collection of gamelan instruments under a pergola, their mallets lying beside them in the dirt.

She wasn't in the restaurant. No one was in the restaurant. No one was by the pool, either.

He took a swim, sat for a bit on one of the banana lounges, and then made his way back up to their room. Finally, he came across another person, a young woman, the one from the day before by the pool. She passed him on the stairs. Clara still wasn't back in the room, however. He was checking his phone again and thinking she must have gone back to the massage hut, or else she must be in the lap pool down there on the jungle floor — they were the only places left she could be — when he realised their suitcase was gone. All that was left behind were his clothes in a small neat pile against the wall, next to where the suitcase had been. He went into the bathroom. All her things were gone. Every sign of her was wiped from the room. As if she had never been there. He stood quite still for a few moments, in the middle of the room, unable to think what he should do next.

He went back down to reception. Someone was there now. Yes, they had seen her, they said. This morning, around six. She had ordered a taxi, had sat out in the carpark with her suitcase, and was gone by six-thirty. She'd paid half the bill. She was alone and didn't seem in any way distressed.

★   ★   ★

For the next few days, he wandered aimlessly in Ubud, or hung around the hotel, waiting for her to come back. Initially, he thought she'd gone to clear her head for a night and would be back the next day. Or for a night or two, he reasoned, when she wasn't back the next day. She wasn't replying to his messages, and so he emailed everyone he could think of who might have

221

heard from her: Madeleine, her sister Lena, Emily, Trish. Some of these got back to him, eventually, to say she was okay. They were vague on everything else. Madeleine seemed especially vague, for someone usually so forthright. She was probably staying on for a few days elsewhere, needed space, would get in touch in time . . . all of it vague, patronising, falsely sympathetic.

He lay by the pool for hours, lay on the bed. Replayed things: that moment in the room when he thought he might talk to her about it, and the disaster later that night at the restaurant, their last night together. Another missed opportunity.

* * *

They had gone into Ubud, to a restaurant that was hard to get into, and which they had booked while they were still in Sanur. It donated half of all proceeds to setting up schools for Balinese children, employed local youth in the kitchen, and had solid 8s, 8.5s on the apps.

They were dropped off by the shuttlebus and worked their way through the streets. Ubud was very different to Sanur. The streets there were lined with shining white designer outlets — Ralph Lauren, Nike, Le Coq Sportif — and clogged with tourists. Tom was glad for the change of scene. And pace. The busyness, the things to see meant the quiet between them was less noticeable, and it gave them more reason to talk, in an incidental way.

But he was disorientated by Ubud. It had the feel of a city, but he had no sense of how far the streets stretched, and where they were, exactly, in relation to anything else. Were they in the centre of town, or was this just one of dozens of strips that were repeated over and over until you hit rice paddies and countryside, bypasses and freeways? It was much hipper than Sanur. The restaurants, bars, cafes piled on top of each other down every alleyway were more like the ones at home than they were like those in Sanur, where they were all Rasta or nautical-themed.

The restaurant, when they finally found it, ran over two tiny rooftops, with a landing in between filled with people waiting for tables. Diners were crammed into each rooftop, sitting at bars that ran around the perimeter, overlooking the street, or around tables crowding the middle. They were young people, mostly — ten, fifteen years younger than Tom and Clara — in designer activewear, shorts and tops made out of high-tech synthetic material. Although some were dressed up, with glittering jewellery, expensive watches on tanned arms, and there was a small contingent of eco-tourist types in muted colours, natural fibres, and no makeup.

Tom and Clara stood in a line, quietly, side by side, and waited for a shouting match to play out between a guy in front of them in the line and the maître-d'. There was a wait for tables, even for those with bookings, and the guy had been waiting in line with his date for half an hour. The maître-d' told them there was nothing he could do, this was the nature of restaurants, especially busy ones like theirs, while the guy was appealing to him with gestures to his date as if the injustice of a young woman standing out there in the heat might convince the maître-d' to somehow conjure a table for them. After a while, a young woman, a stick-thin American who was half the guy's height and was behind him in the line, piped up and asked the maître-d' why take bookings at all if people have to wait so long? And the rest of her group, several other diminutive women, joined in, and the maître-d's command of the situation began to look less assured.

Just then, a figure appeared above them on the steps, blocking out the lights of the restaurant. With both arms raised in the air, the silhouetted figure leaned down to the crowd, revealing a deeply tanned man wearing an open-necked denim shirt, who was beaming down upon them a perfect, white-teeth smile.

He hollered out above their voices: Hey, hey, hey, hey, HEY!

People fell silent.

Why are we all here? he asked. Huh? Why are we all here?

The rhetorical nature of the question seemed to throw the crowd for a moment, and no one replied. The man let the moment lengthen, but not so long that people had time to recover and say something.

Here in beautiful Bali, on this wonderful day? Huh? he continued. To eat? Yes, to eat. To have fun. To have a great time. Like everyone else. That's what everyone is here for. All these people before you came here for the same reason.

He gestured to the people behind him and turned back.

They are eating our beautiful food, we are donating a large portion of their payment for this food to people in need here in Bali, and we have a wonderful time. This is perfect, no? Yes! Though we are busy. You might need to wait a little while for a table. But! It is a beautiful night, here in Ubud, we are all here together, and this is a beautiful thing.

He raised his hands high into the air, again, perhaps gesturing to the night sky, looked back down at them with his eyebrows raised, seeming to wonder himself if there was more to come, and finally said thank you and disappeared.

The tall guy at the top of the queue said, This is bullshit, and walked off. His date followed.

Twenty minutes later, Tom and Clara were seated at one of the tiny tables, where they pulled their seats in tight to avoid bumping into the elbows and backs of the diners around them. Despite the limited space on the tables, they were romantically set, with pink frangipanis in tiny vases, artfully folded napkins, and candles flickering in low light. It was cheesy, but Tom thought it would have made for a good time to talk, if it wasn't for the cramped space and everything else going on in the room.

The kitchen was open to them, and, not far away, there were flashes of flame and clouds of steam as water was poured into woks, the sting of chilli wafting over. But overpowering all of this, dominating everything else in the room, was a huge flat-screen mounted on the wall above them. It was playing Coldplay, live in concert at Madison Square Garden or wherever, and it was loud and bright and flashing. Fireworks exploded, the camera panned across a sea of fluorescent dots — wristbands held aloft, it turned out — and, as Chris Martin sang one last 'Para, para, paradise', the music dropped out, and the crowd carried the final line by itself, 'wo wo oh wo-oh oh oh oh'. Then Martin, in close-up on huge screens either side of the stage, let his hands drop from the piano keys, raised his head, and closed his eyes, breathing hard into the mic.

Tom tried to ignore the film, but it was impossible — the swooping cameras, the magnitude of the whole thing, the spectacle, all the carefully orchestrated moments of communion and pathos. The audience filling every breakdown, every moment of quiet with a roar. Clara watched, too, and chuckled quietly at it, but Tom was annoyed. He had felt superior to the whingers in the queue, unable to wait for their seat, who were being, like the man had implied, petty in the face of such good fortune — the good fortune of being alive and in such a place and having nothing else to worry about but a table at a restaurant in a town full of restaurants — but now he was losing his cool. It was very hot in Ubud, hotter, it seemed, than in Sanur with its sea breezes and open spaces, and it was especially hot and humid in this cramped space. The close proximity to the kitchen probably wasn't helping, and it was crowded, but he was most annoyed about the video, the noise of it, and the sentimentality. It made him feel embarrassed by the idea of attempting anything like a serious conversation about what had happened to her or about their relationship or whatever . . . Plus, and he hated himself for it, he was becoming increasingly worried about their shuttlebus. It did rounds, the shuttlebus, and would pick them up from the rendezvous spot at eight-thirty pm, the latest of its rounds, which was now only fifty minutes away. What would happen if they missed it? Catch a taxi of some sort, he imagined, but he didn't know, really. And the drive had taken a while — that could be expensive, and they'd been spending much more than they'd expected on the holiday so far. But he was fighting that, telling himself to stop worrying about the fucking shuttlebus, they would be fine, and who gives a shit about the noise, the video, fucking Coldplay.

But then the deeply tanned man reappeared. He had a microphone in his hand now and was turning the film down on the flat-screen.

Hello, my friends! he said. As it is Friday night, I will do what I do every Friday night and thank you all for coming and making it another great week at School Kitchen, serving great food to our customers and saving money for young Balinese people in need.

He waited for applause, which came, weakly. The man was standing very close to Tom. As he spoke and rocked in time with the modulations of his thoughts, his expressions of gratitude and blessedness, his right hip brushed the back of Tom's chair, and, a few times, he lent further in so that his hip rested on Tom's shoulder. Tom lent away, surreptitiously, and spent the rest of the man's speech in an uncomfortable hunch over the right side of his chair, feeling his shirt stick and unstick from the slick of sweat down his chest, while doing his best to appear to be listening as the man's gaze roamed around the room and locked on the eyes of his guests.

The man singled out a few people to ask where they were from, they were good sports, and he wound up his speech with some stats. This much saved over this many years, this many young people now educated as a result of their work. He then proposed a toast to the waitstaff and the kitchen, mostly young men and women, who looked up briefly and nodded or waved as people clapped. Then he turned Coldplay back up, propped his cordless mic on the countertop, and surveyed the room. He began making his way around the tables, chatting to the diners.

By the time he had made it around to Tom and Clara they were finally being served their food, with about half an hour left before pick-up. If it wasn't for this fact, Tom would have fled to the toilets, both to wipe himself down, and to avoid the man's meet-and-greet, but he badly needed to eat, hoping that maybe it would help. His heart was now racing.

The man knelt down between their chairs and, examining their faces, asked them where they were from. Tom gave him quick answers as he shovelled prawns and rice into his mouth. He didn't care about the shuttlebus anymore, he just wanted to get the hell out of the restaurant.

After a moment, the man said: You're a stressed-out little guy, aren't you?

Tom forced a laugh, and, wiping sweat from his temples with the back of his hand, explained about the shuttlebus. The man did not respond to this, but continued to look closely at Tom and nod his head ever so slightly, as if confirming something about him he had already suspected. Then he got up from his crouch, patted Clara on the shoulder, saluted Tom, and left them alone.

Tom returned his attention to his food. He wasn't calming down. And now he felt deeply ashamed, too. He couldn't look at Clara. He was probably only a few minutes away from having a full-blown panic attack if he stayed any longer in this restaurant.

Clara, finishing her food, put down her chopsticks and drank the last of her water. She was not watching him. He wondered if she knew not to, when he was like this — pulsating, sweating. No doubt he was a mess. He knew how he could look when he was anxious. Like he was on drugs. Pupils dilated, the colour gone from his face. Although right now his face did not feel drained, it felt extremely hot. She turned to make the sure the man was no longer nearby and then did look at him.

Well, he's a cunt, she said.

Tom was so taken by surprise he almost choked on his food. He laughed, for real this time. Then he remembered his beer, saw it as if for the first time sitting in front of him on the table, and downed it all in two long gulps.

He marvelled at her.

He had been prepared to accept all this as just another entry in his catalogue of shame, the archive he would revisit endlessly, forever, for the rest of his life. Another moment of exposure, penance, humiliation: being intimidated by an arsehole; dissolving in front of him. But then, Clara. He was so grateful for her. For her tact, as much as anything. That she understood, that she took his side, yes, but also that she didn't need to go into it, that *that* was all she needed to say. She knew all about him, he felt, then, in that moment. She knew everything. About how bad it got for him, about how humiliated he felt. About how close he was to the edge. All the time. And she knew just what to say, what to do. Knew that he didn't need sympathy in that moment, didn't want concern or any kind of attention. He just needed time. But he did need to feel she was on his side. And she gave that to him. It had such an immediate effect. He felt a release of tension through his body like a wave, as if every muscle in his body simultaneously unclenched itself.

Tom, she said now, her voice changed. She was gathering her things, again not looking at him.

Yes?

I'm obviously not actually jealous of you and Emily.

No, he said. I didn't think you were. Really.

I don't know why I said that.

No, neither do I.

I think I was just looking for something to get angry about.

It's okay . . . good to get it out, he said, cheerfully. Too cheerfully. He stood up from his chair and hitched up his shorts. He felt himself grinning at her, stupidly.

She smiled back at him, less fully, and, he

230

thought later, in hindsight, perhaps a touch pityingly — but he never could tell with Clara.

He wondered if he should say more, then. It was another moment slipping by. And she was talking to him. Really talking. Or, almost she was. But he didn't know what he would say if he did, or how he would say it, and he needed so badly to get off that rooftop, so he didn't say anything. Instead, he paid the bill, and together they descended the stairs and rushed through the streets and made it easily in time for the shuttlebus back to the hotel.

And he was feeling profoundly relieved. Even pretty good about things. Like the bad things were behind them now and everything was going to be fine, somehow. He knew it was irrational — it was adrenaline, endorphins — but he always had moments like this, when the panic was over. Moments when this irrational optimism, even euphoria, overwhelmed him, as if everything in the world was fine now, because he was no longer panicking. He thought stupid things, like they were going be okay, like they should have children after all, like he loved her. That he would start talking to her from now on, properly, tell her things, try harder to reach her. And listen to her, too.

Or, at least, that was how he remembered it. Later, when it became important. When it became, for Tom, their last good moment.

Acknowledgements

Like most books, *The Fogging* could not have been written and published without the kindness and hard work of a lot of people.

I am extremely grateful to everyone at Scribe for publishing this book and doing it so brilliantly. Especially during such a difficult time. A special mention goes to Tace Kelly for all her work publicising the book. But extra special thanks go to my editor, Anna Thwaites, who is not only a gifted editor, but an unnervingly patient and kind person, too.

Thanks to *The Fogging*'s first readers, Dom Amerena, Coco McGrath, Nick Tapper, and David Winter, who either read very early versions of the book or read it when it had been highly commended for the Victorian Premier's Award for an Unpublished Manuscript and I was trying to figure out what to do with it next. Their early feedback undoubtedly made it a better book.

The judges of the 2019 Victorian Premier's Award for an Unpublished Manuscript played an important part in getting this book finished and published. I want to thank Jaclyn Crupi, especially, for her advice and her belief in the book. Big thanks also to my agent, Grace Heifetz at Left Bank Literary, for guiding me through the new and strange process of becoming a published author.

To Léa Antigny, Chris Currie, Jennifer Down,

Alaina Gougoulis, Chad Parkhill, Oliver Reeson, Chris Somerville, Laura Stortenbeker, Veronica Sullivan, Alan Vaarwerk, Rebecca Varcoe, and Jack Vening: thank you all for your support and distraction through the hard times and the good.

Thanks also to all the other friends who have helped in one way or another over the last few years — Duncan Blachford deserves special mention here — and to all the writers I have met along the way whose friendship and solidarity has been so invaluable.

In the final stages of writing and revising this book, I was lucky to be offered a residency at Jacky Winter Gardens. It was a beautiful place to work, and I thank Lorelei Vashti and Jeremy Wortsman for the opportunity.

Finally, much love and gratitude to my family for all their support. I owe my love of books and writing to my parents, to their bookshops and their passion. This book serves in part as a dedication to the memory of my mother. Without her, there would be no book. This is true of my father also, so thank you, Dad.

To my sister, Jess, and her partner, Simon: thank you for everything you do. To Antonia: your love and support, and your insight and notes, have been more important to this book than it is possible to say. You have informed and improved it in countless ways, and I could not have done it without you. And, lastly, to my daughter, Albertine: thank you for all the joy you have brought me while I have wrestled with this story. I couldn't have done it without you, either.

Other titles published by Ulverscroft:

HERMIT

S. R. White

After the puzzling death of a shopkeeper in rural Australia, troubled detective Dana Russo has just twelve hours to interrogate the prime suspect — a silent, inscrutable man found at the scene of the crime, who simply vanished fifteen years earlier.

Where has he been? And just how dangerous is he? Without conclusive evidence linking him to the killing, Dana must race against time to persuade him to speak. But over a series of increasingly intense interviews, Dana is forced to confront her own past if she wants him to reveal the shocking truth . . .

THE SILENCE

Susan Allott

1997: In a basement flat in Hackney, Isla
Green is awakened by her father, Joe, phoning
from Sydney. Thirty years ago, the Greens'
next-door neighbour Mandy disappeared. Joe
claims he thought she had gone to start a new
life, but now Mandy's family is trying to
reconnect, and there is no trace of her. Isla's
father was allegedly the last person to see her
alive, and he's under suspicion of murder.
Her search for the truth takes her back to
1967, when two couples lived side by side on
a quiet street by the sea. Could her father be
capable of doing something terrible? How
much does her mother know? And is there
another secret in this community — one that
goes deeper into Australia's colonial past, and
has held them in a conspiracy of silence?

A MADNESS OF SUNSHINE

Nalini Singh

On the rugged West Coast of New Zealand, Golden Cove is more than just a town where people live. The adults are more than neighbors; the children, more than schoolmates.

That is until one fateful summer — and several vanished bodies — shatter the trust holding Golden Cove together. All that's left are whispers behind closed doors, broken friendships, and a silent agreement not to look back. But they can't run from the past forever.

Eight years later, a beautiful young woman disappears without a trace, and the residents of Golden Cove wonder if their home shelters something far more dangerous than an unforgiving landscape.

It's not long before the dark past collides with the haunting present, and deadly secrets come to light . . .

ALL THE COLOURS OF THE TOWN

Liam McIlvanney

When Glasgow journalist Gerry Conway receives a phone call promising unsavoury information about Scottish Justice Minister Peter Lyons, his instinct is that this apparent scoop won't warrant space in *The Tribune*. But as Conway's curiosity grows and his leads proliferate, his investigation takes him from Scotland to Belfast. Shocked by the sectarian violence of the past, and by the prejudice and hatred he encounters even now, Conway soon grows obsessed with the story of Lyons and all he represents. And as he digs deeper, he comes to understand that there is indeed a story to be uncovered — and that there are people who will go to great lengths to ensure that it remains hidden.

This book may be recalled before the above date.